"WHEN CAN WE BE ALONE?"

Bram's voice echoed in the pit of Tally's stomach.

"Soon," she said shakily. "Very soon."

He raised his eyes from a careful examination of her plunging neckline, and she read clearly his desire, intention and rising heat. Under cover of the shadowed table, she brushed her hand across his lap. His hand clenched around hers, and he drew in a sharp breath. She smiled seductively and purred, "Gotcha."

"Indeed you have," he agreed with a chuckle. "And if you don't behave yourself, you're going to show me your hot tub sooner than you expected."

"The sooner the better," challenged Tally.

"I'll remember that," promised Bram. And he was as good as his word that very same night.

ABOUT THE AUTHOR

It's no surprise that Lee Damon's three previous romances, *Again the Magic, Laugh with Me, Love with Me* and *Lady Laughing Eyes,* have won her rave reviews and the Romantic Times Award for best New Romance Author, 1983. With her sense of humor and unique style, Lee has developed quite a following.

Lee Damon
SUMMER SUNRISE

Harlequin Books

TORONTO • NEW YORK • LONDON
AMSTERDAM • PARIS • SYDNEY • HAMBURG
STOCKHOLM • ATHENS • TOKYO • MILAN

Published October 1984

First printing August 1984

ISBN 0-373-70135-7

Printed in Canada

For Larry Moulter and Mark Scheier,
my very own personal A Team.
This is only the beginning, guys!

PROLOGUE

THE LATE-WINTER STORM had been expected—but not in southern England. The weather forecasts for the past two days had warned of dropping temperatures, rising winds and possibly heavy snowfall across Scotland and northern England. However, during Wednesday afternoon there had been a subtle shift in the large low pressure area and the wind direction. By early evening the roads leading into London from the west were coated with almost four inches of snow, and visibility was reduced to a few yards by the whirling mass of falling, blowing snow.

Traffic was light on the motorway. Most motorists had sought refuge when conditions worsened, and only those with a pressing need to reach London attempted to drive in the blinding storm. A sleek low-slung Jaguar sports car moved silently and slowly through the swirling snow, its silver body blending into the whiteness until it seemed to be a creature born of the storm, floating eerily through the wind-whipped clouds of crystal.

The driver leaned forward, peering intently through the patch of glass kept clear by the hard-working wipers. His eyes searched the shifting whiteness in front of the long silver hood, trying to find some point of reference to tell him where the road was. The luminous lane markers were covered with snow, and he was not at all sure whether he was still on the main lanes or in the breakdown lane. For that matter, he could be on an exit ramp. His hands tightened even more on the steering wheel, and beads of sweat stood out on his forehead and upper lip. At that moment he would have given a year of his very generous salary to be sitting safe and comfortable in the coffee shop at that last highway stop. But, then, the storm hadn't seemed so bad an hour ago, and Mr. Ramsdale wanted to make London this evening if possible.

He glanced at the big man slouched in the seat beside him, long legs stretched out under the dashboard. Returning his eyes to what he hoped was the road, he considered asking his employer to take over the driving. After all, he was younger and used to this kind of tension and to taking risks. *His eyes are closed, but I'll wager he's only dozing. He never sleeps in the car. He looks awfully tired, though. No wonder, with the long hours he's put in these past three weeks to get finished on schedule. Maybe I had better—*

"For God's sake, Merton, why didn't you tell me the driving had become so bad?" The deep, expressive voice startled the middle-aged man behind the wheel. He sensed movement as the large figure straightened up, and he heard the click of the seat belt being fastened.

"I've been thinking about waking you for the past few minutes, sir. It really is becoming impossible to see the road. Should we pull over or try to find an exit?''

"Depends on where we are. Do you have— What the hell! Watch it!''

Merton saw the black shape looming up through the snow at the same moment and tapped the brakes gently, repeatedly, easing the already slow-moving car to a crawl. The shape took form as the back of a stopped truck, and Merton eased to the right to go around it. He tapped the brakes again to slow even more and felt the rear of the heavy Jaguar slide to the right just as a brightening glow behind them resolved into headlights that suddenly started swinging from side to side as the driver fought to bring the approaching car out of a skid.

Time seemed to stand still. Merton spun the wheel, trying to turn the Jaguar away from the on-coming car, sensing that it was going to hit them broadside. One of them yelled, "Look out!'' Ramsdale threw his left arm up over his face and twisted away from the side window, leaning toward Merton and reaching out to brace his right hand on the edge of the driver's seat.

There was an earsplitting crash of metal and a ground-jolting thud as some five thousand pounds of Bentley limousine slammed head-on into the left-hand door and fender of the Jaguar. The force of the impact carried the smaller car side-ways into the back of the parked truck, jamming the long silver hood tightly under the truck body. Luck or Fate swung the body of the Jaguar just enough so that the passenger compartment missed hitting the truck.

The echoes of ripping, scraping, crumpling metal slowly died away. The wind and thick snow deadened the lingering sounds of falling glass and a still-running motor. And then, finally, nothing moved except the sparkling crystals whirling and swooping in their endless dance.

CHAPTER ONE

BLINKING AND YAWNING, Tally turned on her back in the big bed and stretched her arms over her head. Two seconds of exposure to the frigid air in the room sent her diving back under the covers, curling up in a warm ball and pulling the quilt up over her ears. She considered for a few minutes the appealing idea of staying right where she was until the early-morning sun, just beginning to touch the side windows, strengthened enough to warm up the room. *Nice thought, but it would take at least two hours,* she mused, *and now I'm wide awake.* "Oh, well, 'Stiff upper lip and charge,' as mother might say," she muttered.

Taking a deep breath and gritting her teeth, Tally threw back the covers, jumped out of bed, scrambled into fleece-lined ankle-high suede slippers and a long quilted-velvet robe and ran for the fireplace. Fumbling a long match from the container, she flicked it alight against a stone and touched it to the papers under the stacked logs. Tongues of flame licked along the crumpled newspaper and caught the kindling, quickly flaring and spreading up the sides of the logs. Tally sat on one hip on the edge of the wide foot-high hearth and held her cold hands out toward the increasing warmth.

She lingered by the fire, knowing that within a few minutes the heat from her carefully designed, energy-efficient fireplace would begin dissipating the chill from the room. Staring into the flames, she let her mind drift, thinking vaguely about her options for the day.

The shrill ringing of the phone made her jump, and she glanced at the digital clock on the nightstand, wondering who could be calling at 7:13 on a Sunday morning. She dropped onto the side of the antique pencil-post canopy bed as she picked up the receiver and chanted, "Tally's Takeout. Our Sunday-morning special today is fresh-from-the-oven peanut-butter croissants with rose-hip butter and genuine native swampberry preserves. How many, please?"

"Oh, yuck! You beastly girl! I think you've turned me off food for the rest of the day." Tally chuckled at her sister-in-law Jean's anguished groan. "Tally, where in the Great Cookbook of Native Flora and Fauna did you ever find such ideas!" Jean's tone became one of interested curiosity as she asked, "Are there really such things as swampberries? I've never heard of them. Of course, you do have some strange things growing in New England."

Tally fell back against the pillows, laughing, picturing Jean's puzzled expression as she tried to decide whether or not Tally was sending her up. "No, you dim British bird, I made them up. We don't have rose-hip butter, either," she teased, "but I might figure out how to manage peanut-butter croissants."

"No!" yelped Jean in alarm. "Don't bother. Really, Tally, there's no need, and you know what happened the last time you tried to cook. Believe me, I can live without peanut-butter croissants."

"Oh, well, if you insist...but I don't know what all the fuss is about," said Tally airily. "After all, anyone could blow up potatoes. I don't understand why it doesn't happen more often."

"Because everyone else," answered Jean dryly, "knows enough to prick them with a fork before putting them in the oven."

"Details, details. You didn't really call at this hour on a Sunday morning to discuss cooking, did you?"

"Never mind trying to make me feel guilty about waking you. I knew you were up; I could see smoke from your chimney," chided Jean. "You were so late getting back last night that I went to bed, and I wanted to catch you this morning before you took off again."

"Took off where? I'm not going anywhere today except perhaps to Rosemary and Dari's."

"Oh...well, that's all right, then. You'll be coming to Family Brunch, won't you." Jean stated it as understood fact.

"Whoa, chum. Not if I can help it. Small doses of Bishops, maybe. But twenty or so all at once is more than I'm willing to cope with first thing in the morning." Or any other time, thought Tally, visualizing the usual Sunday-morning gathering of adult Bishops in the inn dining room for what her grandfather had termed Sunday Family Brunch.

The younger generation ate in the coffee bar, the teenagers looking out for the smallest children.

"But you've got to come," wailed Jean. "I'm counting on you."

"Now what have you got yourself into?" asked Tally with some exasperation. She had vivid memories of coping with the results of Jean's periodic attempts to introduce the niceties of English country life to the independent, blunt-speaking Bishops.

"Nothing! I swear! I haven't had a new idea this spring. No, this is something else. Alicia called me last night and—"

"From England?" interrupted Tally. Alicia, Jean's lifelong best friend, was married to a charming English viscount. In between raising four children and managing their family estates, they endeavored to spend frequent vacations tripping around to odd corners of the world, keeping in touch with their friends and family via occasional phone calls.

"No, from Bermuda. Nothing very exciting. But her news was, and you've got to come to brunch and hear all about it. Oh, Tally, just wait until you hear who's going to be using Alicia's cottage this summer!"

"Charles and Di?" Tally knew this was not outside the realm of possibility, since the royal couple were friends of Alicia and John's, and the "cottage" in question contained some fifteen rooms.

"Don't be soft. Besides, this is even better than a prince."

"What's better than a prince? A king? Ah, the

queen is going to visit the former colonies and wants to meet a typical New England family. Right?''

''Wrong. And there's nothing remotely typical about the Bishops. Stop guessing, Tally. I'm not going to tell you. You've got to come to brunch. Come on, piglet, just this once,'' coaxed Jean.

That ''piglet'' brought a resigned sigh from Tally. It was Jean's ultimate weapon in pushing her stubborn sister-in-law into seeing things her way. For a fleeting but delightful moment, Tally contemplated various nasty retributions to be visited on her male relatives. It had been their loud and frequent characterization of her as being ''independent as a hog on ice,'' which had inspired Jean to adopt ''piglet'' as a loving goad.

Giving in, Tally muttered, ''Oh, hossapples. All right, I'll come. But it had better be something really interesting.''

''It is, it is. And if it makes you feel better, consider this an act of appreciation. After all, I soothed Uncle Alden's savage breast last night when you skipped out on dinner with the Osgoods.''

''Now wait a minute, you traitor. You know very well that I told Uncle A a week ago I wasn't coming to that dinner. The same time I told him to knock off these dumb attempts at matchmaking.''

Tally's exasperation was rapidly deteriorating into basic anger, and she jumped off the bed to pace around the large bedroom, dragging the long telephone cord behind her.

''For God's sake, Jean, Campbell Osgood and

I have about as much in common as a chipmunk and a whale! He's stuffy, dull, conventional, hidebound, fat and forty-five! His idea of a scintillating evening is four hours of television, no matter what's on, and if you suggest getting outdoors for some exercise and fresh air, he heaves himself into the car and goes for a ride. Furthermore, he—"

"Stop, stop," gasped Jean between whoops of laughter. "Tally, be fair, he isn't quite that bad. Almost, maybe, but not quite. Besides, he's nutty about you and always has been."

"Oh, give me air! Can you really see me with a pompous prig who calls me 'cute' and refers to my profession as a 'nice little hobby'? A nice little hobby, my left big toe," snorted Tally. "It took years of bloody hard work to qualify as an architect and then get myself established with a reputation for quality and a distinctive style."

"I know, Tally," interjected Jean soothingly, "but you—"

"Furthermore," Tally continued, ignoring the interruption, "if he had even half a thimbleful of brain, he'd know better than to call a woman of thirty-one 'cute'! And don't tell me it's because I'm so small. You try being five feet one-and-three-quarter-inches tall and see if you think it's cute to go through life ducking elbows! Be—"

"Tally!" yelled Jean.

"Yes?"

"Why, oh why, did I mention Campbell Osgood? No, never mind. Forget him, as if you haven't already. I really don't understand why Uncle Alden persists in trying to throw you two together."

"It's obvious, pet. He wants to get a toehold in the Osgood banks."

"Well, they have got a lot of money and prestige."

"So have the Bishops, you unworldly bird," said Tally dryly. "Way beyond anything the Osgoods can scrape up. Remember the family reunion that grandpa organized the year before he died? Over six hundred Bishops showed up from twenty-three states and six foreign countries. If you lumped together their net worth, they'd have enough to buy their own country. And I wish they would, and then maybe they'd all get out of my hair!"

Scowling ferociously as Jean exploded into laughter, Tally dropped down on the bed and then immediately bounced back onto her feet to stomp over to the bathroom door, and pushing it open she reached around to turn up the control for the electric heaters.

"You've got to admit," Jean choked, "that it's not all that easy to get untangled from your hair."

"Funny," drawled Tally, pulling the thick honey-blond braid over her shoulder and holding it out at arm's length, watching the sunlight bring out glints of pale gold in the heavy silken hair. "Which reminds me," she added, suddenly becoming practical, "I need some more of my special shampoo. Are you going down to Concord in the next couple of days?"

She flipped the heavy braid over her shoulder as she strolled to the window wall at the front of the room and looked out over the long expanse of

Samantha's Lake. The curling tail of the braid brushed across the firm curve of her bottom.

"Tuesday afternoon. Is that soon enough?"

"Fine, thanks. Well, if you won't give me a clue about your big surprise, I guess I'll have to grit my teeth and go to brunch. See you about ten?"

"Sure. Want to ride down with us?"

"Uh-uh. As long as I'm going to be out, I might as well go over to Dari's afterward. I was planning to get together with him today, anyway. See you later."

Tally replaced the phone and then wandered back to the front windows to wait for the bathroom to warm up. While she'd been talking to Jean, the heat from the fire had brought the temperature in the big room up to a comfortable level, and Tally shrugged out of the heavy robe, tossing it over the arm of the small sofa, which was angled to face both the fireplace and the window wall.

Glancing down at her long flannel nightgown, she vowed for the six-hundred-and-something-thousandth time to overcome her intense dislike of shopping long enough to stock her wardrobe with apparel of *her* choice. Flirty lace collars and cuffs over flower-sprigged lavender smocking had more to do with her mother's wishful thinking than with her own plain and practical, no-nonsense, no-frills taste.

Tally grinned ruefully. It was, after all, her own fault. She had long ago refined the hated shopping trips down to a couple of hour-long raids a year on the nearest large mall. Twenty minutes to grab an assortment of jeans and shirts; twenty minutes in the closest designer shop to pick out a couple of dressy outfits; twenty minutes to whip in and out of other shops for various essentials as she headed for the exit. Blessed with an unchanging size seven figure, she never bothered to try on anything; all new purchases were delivered to Martha Riceton, her mother's dressmaker, to be altered as necessary and eventually arrived on her doorstep, ready to wear.

Such a cavalier approach to maintaining a wardrobe was, Tally knew, too much to expect a normal mother to swallow. When said mother possessed both impeccable clothes sense and an unlimited bank account, it was inevitable that she would leap into the vacuum left by Tally's disinterest.

Looking over her shoulder at the long west wall of her bedroom, Tally laughed out loud as she remembered her original plans for that wall. Now, aside from a wide dormer alcove containing a lovely antique cherry dressing table, the wall was an unbroken expanse of russet chestnut paneling, which was actually a series of cleverly fitted doors.

"Wasted space," Tally muttered, visualizing all the drawers, shelves and racks filled with her well-meaning mother's idea of a suitable wardrobe. She hadn't worn a fraction of the clothes there and probably never would, and still her mother bought more.

"Well, Talia, since it's there, might as well make use of it," she announced, turning away from the window and moving toward the closets. "Let's not spoil Jean's big surprise by starting an uproar with your showing up in cords and a sweater. It won't kill you to stroke their feathers for a couple of hours.''

Shortly before ten, Tally stepped out onto the wide porch that ran across the back of the house and angled out from one corner of the building in a twelve-foot-long gallery leading to the garage. From May to October both porch and gallery were screened; the rest of the year they were enclosed with tightly fitting wood-and-glass panels that served both to help insulate the house and to provide protected access to the garage—winters in the White Mountains of New Hampshire tended to be extremely cold, windy, snowy and long. Even now, on this early-April Sunday morning two weeks into spring, the temperature was several degrees below freezing.

Tally paused to scan the porch and then the snow-covered backyard. ''Idiot cat,'' she grumbled, ''you're missing breakfast.'' She opened the outside door a few inches, kicking a small chunk of wood into the opening to hold the door in place, and set down a remarkably large bowl full of hunks of raw liver. Straightening up, she stuck her thumb and middle finger in the corners of her mouth and gave a piercing two-tone whistle.

Shrugging at the continued emptiness of the yard, she flipped up the collar of her mink-lined suede jacket—one of her mother's more extravagant Christmas presents—and headed for the garage. She paused for a few moments midway along the gallery to enjoy the serenity of the view over the twenty-three-hundred acres of Samantha's Lake.

Most of the lake's surface was still covered with ice and windblown snow, the broad expanse of white broken only by the half dozen small granite islands with their dark caps of snow-dusted spruce and fir. The sun was now well above the low eastern ridges of the valley and had transformed the frozen lake into a field of glittering crystals. A mile and a half away, at the southern end of the lake, Tally could see the sunlight sparkling from the elaborate white gingerbread trim that festooned the sprawling pale yellow mass of verandas, gables, towers, turrets, bays, wings, ells and oddly placed porches that made the 147-room Snow Meadows Inn one of the outstanding examples of Carpenter Gothic—popularly called Victorian—architecture in New England.

As she turned to continue toward the garage, Tally cast a quick, assessing look at Mount Aggie Left and Mount Aggie Right, twin mountains that rose to just over three thousand feet and were joined by a high saddle back. Three miles down the western border, the valley angled to the southeast and gradually widened for another two and a half miles. Tally noted that the snow cover on the upper ski trails seemed to be holding. *But not for too much longer,* she thought, and made a mental note to ask Pip to take a couple of runs with her later in the day.

It only took a few minutes to drive to the inn, and her Jeep Wagoneer was just starting to warm up by the time Tally pulled into the side parking lot by the outside entrance to the main dining room. After a quick scan of the dozen or so cars in the lot, she took her time mounting the broad steps to the wide veranda, which was screened in summer for outdoor dining.

"Just my luck," she mumbled, "that I'll get stuck with all the naggers, and Dari and Rosemary will pick today to stay home."

She was halfway across the veranda when a deep-voiced "Wait up, Tally!" brought her around with a smile. Her favorite brother, Darius, and his wife, Rosemary, were striding quickly toward the steps, their nineteen-month-old son, Seth, gurgling gleefully as he rode on his father's shoulder.

"An Ty! An Ty! Look me!" screamed Seth, wildly waving his arms, his attempts to bounce thwarted by the firm grip of his father's large hand around his middle.

"I see you. And hear you," said Tally, laughing and stretching up on tiptoe to tweak Seth's nose as Rosemary and Dari joined her.

Dari dropped his free arm around his sister's shoulders, giving her a quick hug and asking disbelievingly, "Brunch? You?"

Tipping her head back to meet the laughing brown eyes a foot above her own, Tally grimaced and muttered, "Jean twisted my arm." She swung around so that she could look up at both her six-foot-two brother and five-foot-eight sister-in-law.

"You two don't happen to know what the big surprise is, do you?"

"Uh-uh. She was being disgustingly mysterious when she called last night," said Rosemary. "I couldn't even get a cluuuee...my God, what's that?'' Her face was blank with amazement as she stared over Tally's head.

Dari turned to follow her gaze and let out a roar of laughter. "Oh, you never! Tally, you little fiend, Uncle A will have a conniption!"

"I like it." Tally folded her arms across her breasts and rested her weight on one leg while she beamed smugly at her new Wagoneer, its lavender finish gleaming in the sun.

"Here we go again," groaned Rosemary. "I suppose you put that black cat's head on both doors? A little one on the driver's side wouldn't have done?"

Dari narrowed his eyes against the flashes of sunlight, murmuring, "Looks more like purple than black."

"Plum," said Tally succinctly. "It's the logo I designed for my new letterhead. Neat, huh? Splendid loves it. Just look at that profile. You can even see the tufts on his ears."

"You're going to have tufts on your ears when Uncle A gets a look at that paint job," said Dari unsympathetically, "and we're all going to get our tails singed if we don't get inside. It's five past ten."

They started toward the door but paused and looked back at the sounds of a powerful motor and scattering gravel. A sleek dark green Porsche came to a flourishing stop beside the Wagoneer, and they called greetings as a tall, slim man unfolded himself from the low car and leaped up the steps.

Tally grinned appreciatively as her cousin

Steven, with remarkable deftness, managed to sling an arm around her shoulders, kiss Rosemary's cheek, shake Dari's hand and chuck Seth under the chin—all without missing a step on his progress toward the door.

"Hustle, children, I'm starving. You're looking lovely, as usual, Rosy. Where have you two been hiding, Dari? Haven't seen you all week. Terrific color, Tally. Where did you have it done? The manufacturer never offered that."

"Rosemary," said Dari, grinning at his cousin. "She'll have your scalp if you call her 'Rosy,' or have you forgotten what happened the last time?"

"It wasn't sweet Rosemary who pushed me off the dock," Steven said, smiling benignly at the tall, laughing woman as he bowed her through the door. "It was Tally the Terror, here, leaping once again to the defense of the downtrodden, deprived, picked-upon Bishop females. Oof!" he gasped as the Terror dug an elbow into his ribs.

"Talia! Try to restrain yourself, at least on Sunday." The reprimanding voice had more than a touch of long-suffering impatience in it, and Tally bit back the instinctive retort that flashed through her mind.

She turned toward the imposing figure of her Uncle Alden, her tan eyes wary although she forced a smile to her lips. In a determinedly cheerful voice, she caroled, "Good morning, Uncle A. Lovely day, isn't it?"

She could see at a glance that it wasn't going to work. With his usually full lips drawn into a tight line, his bushy gray eyebrows pulled into a solid bar above snapping slate-blue eyes, and his fleshy cheeks flushed with temper, Alden Bishop was obviously primed for battle.

Damn the man! Why can't he just get off it? You'd think, after all these years, he'd have learned that I'm not going to be dictated to. If he's so hot for Campbell Osgood, why doesn't he sic 'im on Ciel? 'Cause he knows his darling daughter would turn green at the thought, that's why. God, I'm getting bored with this argument.

"Never mind the lovely day," snapped Alden, glaring down at his diminutive niece. "Where were you last night? I distinctly remember informing you that the Osgoods were dining with us, and that you were to partner Campbell. It was most embarrassing—"

"Just you hold it right there, Uncle Alden," interrupted Tally, her deceptively delicate chin lifting to an all-too-familiar angle. She shrugged Dari's restraining hand from her shoulder and ignored the despairing groans of "Here we go again!" from the various relatives hovering nearby.

"I distinctly remember informing *you* that I had plans for last night, and that I wouldn't be able to attend your dinner. If you were embarrassed at my absence, then it was your own bullheaded fault. No!" she exclaimed, her rising voice overwhelming Alden's fuming attempts to interrupt. "I don't want to hear it! I'm not some mindless doll to be displayed before the company and told to entertain the likes of Campbell Osgood. I'm perfectly capable of running my own life and picking my own men, thank you. And you can bet your size twelve booties that the last man I'd pick would be old Campbell Wet Fish!''

"Talia!''

Alden's bellow was almost drowned out by the deep roar of laughter from Dari and Steven.

Terrific, Tally! Now why don't you tell him his mother wears combat boots? Really! Thirty seconds with the men in this family, and you regress to all of twelve years old.

"Oh, dear...oh, Tally...now, Alden...not on Sunday...." Edna Bishop waved agitated hands between her incensed brother-in-law and her belligerent elder daughter. "Please...there are hotel guests in the dining room. Whatever are they going to think? Oh, dear, I told you, Alden...."

"Perhaps you'd do better to tell that nasty-tempered overaged tomboy of yours something about good manners and respect for her elders," suggested a cold voice, and Tally turned to meet her Aunt Myra's equally cold blue eyes.

"I'll give respect to—"

"Enough! You all sound like a fifth-grade playground at recess!" The sharp-voiced comments were punctuated by the solid thumps of a sturdy cane.

There were gasps of laughter and yelps of surprise as the dozen or so people in the foyer dodged the quick flicks of Grandma Amy's path-clearing oak cane. Tall, imperious, and still at eighty-five carrying herself with the bearing of an honor-guarding marine, Amy Foster Bishop was the undisputed matriarch of the far-flung Bishop family.

Tally looked up into implacable hazel eyes and

clamped the lid on her temper. She knew that the argument with Alden and Myra was unimportant, and that she'd merely been indulging her aggressions, but none of it was worth getting into a face-off with her formidable grandmother. Tally didn't have to prove anything to anyone about the strength of her will. She well remembered, as did everyone present, that the only major battles Grandma Amy had ever lost had been to Tally. She also remembered how mentally and emotionally exhausting those confrontations had been, and she had no intention of expending that much energy in a hassle over Uncle Alden's little pique.

"Well, girl? What have you to say for yourself?"

You wouldn't want to know! Aloud, Tally said, with her most charming smile, "My, you're looking very regal this morning, Grandma Amy. That royal blue is a lovely color for you."

"Hah! It's a good thing you're wearing boots, girl, if you're going to pile it up that deep." The tip of the cane flipped at the hem of Tally's black wool skirt. "At least you managed not to wear pants for a change, although I'm not sure those knee-high boots are any improvement. How do you expect a man to tell if you've got decent legs when you keep them covered up all the time? No, never mind any of your smart answers, missy. I've heard it all before."

She waved a dismissing hand at Tally as she flicked her cane with unerring aim at Dari's and Steven's shins. "Here, you two, stop that silly giggling," she snapped, ignoring the bass tones of their laughter. "Take this young troublemaker along into the dining room, and I suggest you pick one of the smaller tables, well away from Alden and Myra. Rosemary, you go with them and keep the peace. Yes, yes, Seth, I hear you," she said in a softer voice, turning her attention to the grinning child who was reaching for her and demanding, "Gamma, me hug."

Dari held Seth out so that he could reach his great-grandmother. She calmly accepted his damp kiss and exuberant hug before turning to a young teenager lingering nearby who showed the promise of a lovely smile once her braces were removed.

"Ah, Cindy, have you come to fetch this young man? Good. Don't fuss, Rosemary. He'll have a fine time with the other young ones. Cindy, you make sure he gets something decent to eat. None of those peculiar concoctions of yours."

Dari grinned and winked at his young Adderly cousin as he handed Seth over to her. She smiled back, but waited until she was well out of range of Grandma Amy's cane before calling over her shoulder, "What's peculiar about orange fritters and ice cream with maple syrup?"

"Wait a minute!" blustered Alden. "Mother! Surely you're not going to let her feed that child—"

"Pull the zipper, Alden," said his mother scathingly. "How any son of mine could have reached the age of sixty with absolutely no trace of humor... well, what can't be cured must be endured, I suppose. Come, come, Alden, don't stand there dithering. Move along. We're late enough as it is. Myra!'' she snapped, interrupting her daughter-in-law's low-voiced tirade. "Leave Edna alone. *Your* daughter is not my idea of a piece of perfection, either, and so I shall inform her the next time she shows her face. Well? Well? What are you all waiting for? Move along.''

With resounding thumps of her cane, Amy herded the stragglers toward the dining room. Tally, lingering in the doorway with Dari and Steven to watch the show, choked back laughter and resisted the impulse to applaud her grandmother's performance.

"Come on, let's go before she gets within range," muttered Dari, pushing Tally ahead of him. "That cane should be registered as a lethal weapon.''

"Fastest cane in the Northeast,'' said Steven solemnly. "It's so well-known that I've been thinking about setting up a small company to make copies. Should do well in the local gift shops, or we could use them as a—''

His further plans were lost in rising laughter as the three of them sat down at a round table already occupied by Rosemary and a strikingly handsome couple.

"Morning, Pip, Phil.''

"Hey, you two, where's my darling?''

"Hi, Phil. Pip, is there any skiing left? Pip!'' Tally leaned across the table to tap her sister's hand.

Pip's dark blue eyes were darting rapidly from one face to another, her pale blond hair gleaming in the sunlight as she turned her head back and forth. Her beautiful smile was directed at Tally in response to her attention-getting tap. Before either sister could say anything, their mother's chiding voice brought quiet to the table.

"Hush, all of you. You know better," scolded Edna as she settled gracefully onto the chair that Dari held for her. "Thank you, darling," she said, patting her son's hand as he sat down beside her. She cast an admonishing look around the table. "Pip can't follow you when you all talk at once." Making sure that her younger daughter was looking at her, Edna asked, "How's Lissy this morning? Has her cold cleared up?"

Pip smiled and nodded before saying, in her slightly husky voice, "She's fine. Full of bounce. She's having breakfast with the other kids."

"I hope someone's watching what she eats. After all, she's only three and...."

Tally tuned out both her mother's voice and the muttered conversation between Dari and Phil. For a few minutes she concentrated on her half grape-fruit while she psyched herself into a calm and reasonably cheerful frame of mind. This morning's contretemps with Uncle Alden, she decided firmly, only reinforced her strong belief that she and he should never occupy the same room—or even the same building—at the same time.

She glanced to her right where two of the larger tables had been pushed together to accommodate several Bishops and a smattering of Preston and Adderly cousins and in-laws. *Nothing changes,* she thought, as she noted the same old division of the sexes. The men, most of whom were involved in some way with the family's multimillion-dollar business empire, were grouped around Alden at one end of the table, while Grandma Amy reigned over the women at the other end.

"Tally, what did you want to ask me?"

Pip's question brought Tally's attention back to her own table. She turned her head slightly so that she was directly facing her sister and said softly, "Is there any decent skiing left?" She spoke clearly, slowing down her normally rapid speech just enough so that Pip could easily read her lips.

Pip flipped her gaze from Tally's mouth to her eyes and said blandly, "A couple of the upper runs are still good. We could take a jaunt down Aggie's Revenge later on if you'd like."

At Tally's "heaven help me" expression, Pip lost the struggle to keep a straight face, and her coolly beautiful mask broke as she dissolved into mischievous laughter. There was a brief moment of silence from their tablemates. Tally knew they were picturing, as she was, the sight of her with all her Sunday-skier skill trying to follow Pip, a former world-class competitor, down Snow Meadows' toughest run.

As the group erupted into laughter, Tally slanted a look at her mother and was pleased to see her indulgent smile as she watched her youngest child. Tally knew how long and hard her mother had struggled to overcome her natural instincts to coddle Pip, to protect her from thoughtless people and to shield her from the occasional disasters lying in wait for a deaf person. Pip had refused to permit it. Once she'd learned to cope with what she called her "little problem," she'd proceeded to force first her family and then the rest of the world to accept her on her own terms. Tally caught her mother's eye and winked, smiling to herself as she remembered just what some of those terms had involved—downhill ski racing, water-skiing, basketball, touch football, mountain climbing and white-water boating, to name a few.

"May I have everyone's attention for a few minutes?" Jean's clear English voice and the chiming sound of a knife tapping a water glass brought Tally back to the present. She half turned toward the other table where Jean was now on her feet and sending a smiling look around the group, waiting for them to quiet.

"I'm sorry to interrupt everyone's conversations, but I wanted to tell you the most marvelous news before anyone left." With her eyes sparkling and her fine English skin flushed with excitement, Jean looked all of sixteen, and Tally couldn't suppress her smile as her sister-in-law rushed on, "Alicia called last night, and.... Oh! You'll never guess who's going to be using their cottage for four months! Her brother! Can you imagine it? He'll be here for the whole summer! Isn't it exciting?"

Tally couldn't quite understand why Jean was so overjoyed. Granted Alicia was Jean's best friend, and she undoubtedly knew this brother, but it hardly seemed all *that* impressive. She realized suddenly that the others' puzzled expressions were beginning to give way to varying degrees of interest and to a rising cacophony of questions and exclamations.

"Alicia's brother? You mean that actor?"

"Here? Right here? Troy Castleman is going to stay here all summer?"

"No, no, not Troy Castleman. Bram Ramsdale. Castleman is the character he plays."

"Such a lovely young man. Wasn't he the one who came with Alicia and John a few winters ago for the skiing? Yes, I'm sure he was. So polite. Nothing like one would expect of an actor."

"Oh, Aunt Edna, he's not just an actor. He's a superstar. Those eyes and that utterly sexy voice and that panthery walk. He's just awesome."

"I thought you were watching Seth, Cindy."

"I just had to come and hear about Brawny Bram. Ruthie's got Seth. Is he really going to stay here all summer, Jean? Wait until I tell the kids at school!"

"Why is he coming here, of all places, for four months? Is someone making a movie around here?"

"A movie! Here? Nonsense! Alden, I won't have it. Aside from everything else, this is my home, and—"

"Oh, no, Grandma Amy...oh, dear, I didn't mean to interrupt, but...it's nothing like that. Please, everybody, wait a minute. Let me finish telling you—"

"Quiet! What's gotten into all of you? All this fuss over an actor, for God's sake. All right, Jean, go ahead."

"Right, Uncle Alden. Perhaps some of you remember my telling you about a year ago that Bram had been in a terrible auto crash. His left leg was badly crushed, and for a while the doctors weren't sure they could save it. He's had several operations, and they've done all they can, but he'll always have some impairment in the knee and something of a limp. The problem at the moment is that he's exhausted from almost a year in and out of hospital and one operation after another. Alicia says the doctors have advised several months of complete rest and quiet, and this is the only place anyone can think of where he won't get mobbed by fans and will have access to the facilities he needs."

"What facilities?"

"All the things we have here, Uncle Alden. Bram's going to be following a physiotherapy program, and he needs a heated pool, whirlpool, sauna, gym equipment and so forth."

"I thought he had a house on the Riviera or one of those places. Didn't you visit there once?"

"He does, Aunt Myra, but that's the problem, you see. Everyone knows about it, and if he goes there, the press and all those silly groupies will be hounding him, and he won't have the privacy he needs. The same is true for just about anywhere else over there. He's so well-known that it would be almost impossible for him to avoid being recognized. But here, you see, it's a different story. Since he's never made a film or any public appearances in the States, the press won't look for him here, and the public probably wouldn't recognize him even if they have seen his films. Actors rarely look the same in person as they do on the screen, you know. Besides, Alicia says he's very thin and doesn't look at all himself right now.''

''Furthermore, young lady, very few of the people who visit Snow Meadows would be particularly impressed by an actor. You know very well that many of our guests and those who own cottages and condominiums come here for the privacy as much as for the excellence of our facilities.''

''Of course, Grandma Amy. That's what Alicia and Bram are counting on.''

Tally leaned back in her chair and looked around at the varying expressions ranging from Uncle Alden's slight scowl to Cindy's ecstatic glow. She let the ongoing discussion wash over her, no longer hearing individual words, as she prodded her memory for past knowledge of Bram Ramsdale. All she could come up with were disjointed fragments of half-heard comments about Alicia's actor brother.

Wrinkling her brow in concentration, Tally vaguely recalled something about his having inherited a title and an ancient estate but very little money. Jean, she remembered, had been relieved that the estate had some unique historical significance, so the National Trust had agreed to take it over. But it had all been years ago, and Tally had had too many problems of her own at the time to pay much attention to those of an impoverished English lord whom she had never even met.

What did mother say about his coming with Alicia and John for the skiing? Must have been more than three years ago, before I came back to stay. Mother and Jean wouldn't have been able to resist throwing me at his head if I'd been here. Superstar actor or not, they'd have thought first of that title. You can take the English out of their country, but you can't take class awareness out of the English! No, that's not really fair. Mother and Jean have adapted very well.

I wonder... with luck maybe he's married... but, no, Jean once referred to him as a bachelor playboy. Oh, fine, just what we need. If Cindy's reaction is anything to go by, he's probably one of those superstud types who has women flinging themselves across puddles for him to walk on. God forbid he should get his Guccis damp. Thank heavens I'm loaded with work for the next few months. I won't even be around most of the time. If mother and Jean are plotting to snare a title, they'll have to toss him to Ciel. She's probably more in his line anyhow. So much for that. Now, let's see if I can get Dari and Rosemary out of here so we can go do something more interesting.

CHAPTER TWO

BRAM SHIFTED RESTLESSLY and eased his left leg to a less strained position. His knee ached abominably from the dampness of the drizzly May morning. After all of Alicia's paeans to the glories of spring in New England, he'd expected a lot more than this unceasing rain and chill temperature. For this he could have stayed in England.

"What's wrong? Leg playing up?"

Bram turned his head against the plush seat back and gave Sid a slight smile. "A bit. About what you'd expect in this weather. Where's all that sun Alicia was raving about? Haven't seen a glimmer since we landed in Boston yesterday."

His resonant baritone voice carried easily to the front of the big car, and the driver glanced into the rearview mirror, commenting, "I heard a weather report earlier, sir, that said it's due to clear tomorrow and become much warmer. Chap at the garage said this was nothing unusual for early May."

"Let's hope so, Merton. I'm looking forward to spending the next few months lying in the sun. Any problems with the car?"

"Oh, no, sir. Somewhat larger than our usual, but it handles beautifully."

"This *is* rather excessive," Bram murmured to Sid, as he gestured at the luxurious dark blue interior of the elegant gunmetal gray Cadillac limousine. "Whose idea was it? I thought we agreed to keep a low profile over here."

"My secretary's." Sid gave Bram a rueful smile. "She revels in American films and thinks all American millionaires speed around in huge cars or travel in their own planes. She evidently got a bit carried away in playing one-up with the Bishops. Sorry, but I didn't realize what she'd done until I saw the car."

"No matter. We can exchange it for something else later. For now we can just say that I needed the room because of my leg." Bram glanced out the window at the rolling green meadows and clumps of woodland that bordered Interstate 93. "Pretty country. One can understand why the first colonists called it New England."

"Yes, it does remind one of home," Sid agreed. "Strange, though, to see so much open land so close to a major city like Boston."

"New England has a remarkable amount of undeveloped land. Wait until you see the White Mountain region. Miles and miles of nothing but forests and some quite rugged country. Very reminiscent of parts of Scotland in some places."

"That's right. You've been here before, haven't you? How long a drive is this?"

"I'm not sure. The last time, we flew into New York, and the Bishops sent one of their Lear jets to meet us. There's a small airdrome just outside Bishops Falls, a few miles from the Snow Meadows complex. Jean offered to send one to pick us up in Boston, but we'd already arranged for the car, and so.... Merton, do those directions indicate how long the drive will take?''

''About two and a half hours all told, sir. We should be coming up on the New Hampshire border shortly, and the notes say it's approximately two hours from there.''

''That will bring us in around noontime,'' said Sid. ''You did mention a first-class dining room, didn't you?''

''Three of them, actually, and an excellent head chef. When I spoke with Jean last night, she said luncheon with the family is all laid on for one o'clock.''

''Red carpet?''

''Hmm...not exactly. They were very hospitable when I was here with Alicia and John, but most of that was on Alicia's account, and the rest was, I believe, their natural Yankee hospitality. You must remember, Sid, that this place caters to a clientele ranging from the well-to-do to the superrich. Not the jet set, but the conservative, quiet, old-money types who probably wouldn't bat an eye if the Queen Mum joined them for lunch, never mind an actor—although one or two might 'ohh' a bit if Sir Laurence sauntered in.''

''The title?''

''The talent. They understand and appreciate quality.''

''Hmm.'' Sid gave Bram a considering look. ''I was going to mention that you have a rather dusty and neglected title of your own.''

"And let's leave it that way, if you please. I've been managing very nicely without it for some years now. Furthermore, if you once saw the way they treat John, you'd know how unimpressed they'd be. During our visit, there was a heavy snowfall. Next thing we knew, Darius was showing John how to operate a snowplow and then sending him off to clear car parks. Before you ask, John loved it!"

Bram shifted position again and flexed his leg to relieve the stiffness. Intercepting a commiserating glance from Sid, he grimaced.

"Yes, it aches like the very devil, but at least it's still there to ache. And if we're counting blessings, the operations are all done with."

"True, but you really do look like...ah, well, let's just say you're much too thin. Those jeans are practically falling off."

Bram chuckled and pinched a large fold of navy blue cord between his fingers. "I would have sworn I didn't have any excess weight to lose. I think a lot of this is due to flaccid muscles. Do you realize how long it's been since I've been able to do anything really physical? Both my appetite and energy level are next to nil."

"Mmm, but that's what this jaunt is all about, isn't it?"

"Right. Don't look so worried, Sid. A couple of days' rest, and I'll be ready to start that swimming-and-exercise program. With that, fresh mountain air and Merton's cooking, I should get back to normal...well, almost normal...within a few weeks."

"Four months, Bram. Not a day less. Have you thought about what comes next?"

"Not yet." Bram sighed and shrugged. He couldn't blame Sid for worrying. It was part of his job to worry and plan ahead.

Bram turned to study the man lounging beside him. Despite his silver-flecked dark hair, Sidney Cater looked much younger than his fifty-six years. He'd kept himself in good shape, and his dark gray suit had been tailored to complement his trim physique. The suit together with the pale blue shirt and regimental tie might, at first glance, indicate a conservative nature. However Bram knew better, and he examined Sid carefully, looking for his aberration of the day.

It only took a few seconds for him to spot the gold tie tack in the form of a meticulously detailed lion's head—a lion with a lascivious grin and an audacious wink. He met Sid's laughing blue eyes and chuckled, then dropped his gaze when the older man ostentatiously shot out his cuff. Bram burst into a deep laugh when he identified the oddly shaped gold cufflink as a lioness lying on her back with all four feet dangling limply in the air.

"Lovely!" Bram shook his head in disbelief. "Where did you ever find those?"

"A gift from a . . . friend," Sid replied with unmistakable emphasis.

Bram laughed again. Sid had been happily divorced for many years from a very nasty-tempered actress, who had been one of his first clients when he set up as a theatrical agent twenty-odd years ago. That one brief taste of marriage had been more than enough. Tall, distinguished looking and sophisticated, he had had no difficulty for over fifteen years in conducting a series of mutually enjoyable relationships with several equally sophisticated women. During the eleven years that Sid had been his agent-business manager, Bram had marveled at the man's uncanny knack for recognizing the moment that a woman was about to become serious—before she was aware of it herself. With great charm and finesse, Sid would ease out of the liaison, managing to leave the lady believing it was all her own doing. Bram had learned a great deal more from him than how to read a contract.

"Do I take it you and Helen have come to a parting of the ways?"

"Mmm."

"A farewell token," Bram suggested, flicking a finger toward Sid's wrist.

"More of a friendship token," Sid corrected. "An exchange, actually. I gave her a rather pretty gold chain with a rabbit's-foot charm carved from moonstone."

"Best wishes and lots of luck," intoned Bram with a suppressed grin. "Style, Sid. You're positively overflowing with style."

"Take notes, my lad. *I've* never been given the push in a public dust-up—on live telly, yet."

"Please," groaned Bram, "don't remind me. God, what a bitch it was."

"Indeed. We aren't, I trust, going to be having problems of that nature here," said Sid, a slight questioning inflection in his voice.

"I shouldn't think so."

"No available birds?" Sid exuded skepticism.

"I didn't say that," commented Bram, smiling faintly. "As I recall, there are several quite attractive women fluttering about the place, but they all know how to behave properly in public."

"If your memory's that good, how about filling me in on some of these people we'll be meeting? The only one I know is Jean."

"My memory's *not* that good," Bram contradicted, "which is why I asked Alicia for brief descriptions of the immediate family. Remember, I was only there for a week, and that was over four years ago in the middle of skiing season. There were cousins, aunts and uncles flying in and out from all over the lot, plus the resort's regular clientele. Very confusing.

"Can you reach my jacket?" Bram gestured to his white leather jacket, which had been tossed over a jump seat. "There's a letter in one of the pockets. Ah, that's it. Alicia, the sloth, dumped it in Jean's lap. It's Hobson's choice which one is dottier."

Bram pushed up the sleeves of his Fair Isle sweater, baring bony wrists, and sorted through the several typewritten pages of Jean's letter. Checking the thin gold watch that slid loosely on his wrist, he murmured, "About another ninety minutes. It'll take almost that long to get through this tome of Jean's."

Flipping rapidly through the pages, Bram pulled out three. "Jean tends to get rather flowery, so I'll just hit the high points. You'll probably hear frequent mention of Carleton Bishop. He was still alive when I was there. In his early eighties then, and unquestionably the final voice in how the Bishop millions were managed. His wife, Amy—*everyone* calls her Grandma Amy—was, and still is, according to Jean, something of a Tartar, but she can also be exceedingly charming. Sharp tongue, dry wit. Watch out for her walking stick. She whacks you on the shin when she wants your attention!"

"Charming, did you say?"

"Delightful. Now, four years ago, the two eldest sons, Otis and Alden, were sharing the second-in-command spot under their father, and grooming several of the next generation to step into key positions. Just after Christmas the following year, Carleton and Otis were killed in a motorcar accident. Since then, Alden has been head of both the family and the business and investment interests. Odd duck. Absolutely no humor, very proper, dictatorial, but brilliant in analyzing investment potentials."

"He's coping with the whole lot by himself?"

"No, not at all. Remember there are innumerable relatives all over the States, and many of them are involved in one or another of the family enterprises. However, the ones who will take the top spots are his two sons and Otis's eldest son."

"Who are. . .?"

Bram turned a page of notes. "Hmm, let's take them by family. Otis married Edna Carrington in England in 1945. County family, public school—

Madden Dane—a classics scholar. That's why their four children have such odd names."

"Such as?"

"Cyrus. Born in England shortly before Otis was demobbed and sent home. He's...let me see...thirty-five now and the heir apparent. Met Jean during a visit to his grandmother, married in 1969, two children.

"Darius—Dare—is thirty-three and something of a rebel. He didn't like the family businesses, so he started one of his own—a construction company. Does both buildings and heavy equipment stuff like roads. Terrific chap. I had a marvelous time with him. Great sense of humor, knocked the birds for six. Married a smashing girl, Rosemary Bishop, three years ago. I remember her very well. Beautiful, tall, lovely legs, great figure."

"Bishop? A relative?"

"Ah...here it is. Third cousin. I'm not sure what that means over here, but it must be safe. Let's see, the next one is Talia, called Tally, thirty-one, unmarried. Wonder what's wrong with her? There was something...I didn't meet her...come on, Jean...got it!

"Jean says...family's official problem child...insisted on going to the Massachusetts Institute of Technology against everyone's wishes...degree in civil engineering...worked her way through with some help from great-grandmother when her father and Carleton cut off her trust income...went on to Harvard School of Design for degree in architecture...worked for major firm in Boston to qualify for certification...returned to Snow Meadows a few months before accident...built her own house at north end of lake on land left to her by said great-grandmother and lives alone...stubborn, feisty.... Feisty? Brilliant, wild sense of humor, wicked temper, the most incredible hair in New England...."

Sid burst into laughter, gasping, "Good God! A Tartar-in-training!"

"Quite," Bram grunted. "Sounds like the ultimate feminist. No wonder she lives alone. There's more here. Jean rather goes on...growing reputation for restoring old buildings...much in demand for vacation homes, et cetera, et cetera...developed distinctive style she calls 'Queen Vic the Second'...Jean can't wait to introduce us. I can believe that! She'd just love to lumber me with some hairy female militant who probably stomps around in old Wellies and has an incipient mustache."

"With some careful planning, perhaps we can avoid her," Sid commiserated. "She wouldn't seem to have much time left over for pursuing her victims. Who else do you have there?"

"Phedra. Everyone calls her Pip, and she's the most incredible lady you've ever met."

"Oh?"

"No, not that kind of 'oh.' Try an 'ohh' of admiration or amazement. She's married and... where is it...here...twenty-seven. Husband's Phil Stanton, a former professional golfer, who manages the very fine course at Snow Meadows."

"That doesn't sound all that unusual," said Sid, puzzled.

"Pip is—definitely. She's deaf, you see. Has been since she was ten. They were visiting some of Edna's relatives who had a summer place on one of those tiny islands in the Outer Hebrides. When Pip came down sick, they all thought it was a type of flu. By the time they realized it was more serious and got her to hospital, she was dangerously ill with spinal meningitis."

"Poor scrap. What a tragedy."

"Don't let Pip hear you say that. She considers it a minor annoyance. It's never seemed to slow her down an inch. A few years back, she was one of America's top women skiers. She made the '72 Olympic Team but missed the games when she broke her arm in a bad fall. She and Phil manage the whole skiing operation at Snow Meadows."

"An impressive lady. Something of an Amazon?"

"Not really. Tall, of course, like all the family, slimly athletic, but very graceful, very feminine and very attractive. In fact, the whole family is remarkably good-looking. Even Alden's wife, Myra, has a certain handsomeness, despite her prune mouth and frigid glares."

"Sounds a treat," said Sid dryly.

"An unhappy woman, I'd say. Don't imagine Alden is any joy to live with, and Jean thinks... mmm...here it is...that she's always been jealous of Edna, but doesn't say why."

Bram turned to the next page and read silently for a few moments. "Now, Alden and Myra have three children. The oldest is Preston, thirty-four, married to one of his Adderly cousins, Janet, three children. He's a financial wizard and has taken over most of their banking interests. Spends most of his time in Boston and New York. Don't believe I met him.

"The second son is Steven, thirty-two, single, something of a conservative playboy. Haven't a clue what Jean means by that. A corporation lawyer, a specialist in taxation, has office in Concord—that's the state capital—and another in Boston. Travels frequently. I think I remember him. Great fun. He and Dare were thick as thieves."

"Nice to know you'll have some kindred spirits around and about. Who's the third one?"

"Believe it or not, you know her. Ciel Valmont. Jean says she's twenty-five and—"

"Wait up. Valmont? That French pouf who brewed up a thumping great scandal a year or so past? It was...something really vile involving his wife and his boyfriend, wasn't it?"

"Worse. She evidently didn't know about his little aberration when she married him, and it was some time before she discovered just what was going on in the garden house. She was in the process of packing to leave him when Valmont and some of his *dolce vita* friends, including his current chum, decided to make her the star turn in one of their wilder parties. She managed to get away from them, and headed straight for the gendarmes, the press and the family lawyers. Created an incredible brouhaha. She filed assault charges and had the bruises to back them up, wreaked havoc with some rather prominent reputations and generally gave the press a field day."

"I did meet her earlier this year," said Sid thoughtfully. "At some charity thing, I believe. She was with Alicia and John."

"That was just before she returned to the States. She'd been staying at Slaytner Park for several weeks after the divorce. Last place the press would look for her."

"She's going to be here?"

"Jean says she'll be home for the summer. Take that look off your face, Sid. She's not my style. Too brittle, too highly strung, incessantly searching for diversion. She needs help, but not from me."

They exchanged a look of mutual understanding, and Sid gestured at the papers in Bram's hand, asking, "Is that the lot?"

Bram riffled the sheets and chuckled. "Unless you want to hear all about everyone's darling tots, the latest family gossip and a detailed description of all the facilities."

"Spare me," Sid groaned. He waved toward the window, commenting, "Seems to be clearing."

They spent the next half hour watching the passing scenery and remarking occasionally on the differences between this nearly unpopulated wilderness and the tamer environment of England. Bram's spirits lifted as the car outran the storm clouds, and brightening sunlight gave new life to the brilliant green of spring meadows. The miles of forest that softened the rugged contours of the land provided a fascinating contrast between the dark greens of spruce and pine and the pale green buds on the bare branches of the many varieties of hardwood trees.

Periodically they passed a sign indicating that the next exit led to one or more towns, but they rarely saw more than a few widely scattered houses and a gas station or two. Ahead and on either side, they could now see the hazy blue silhouettes of mountain peaks. As the highway began a slow but steady climb, more and more of the distant mountains became visible. Finally the car topped a long rise, and they could clearly see for the first time the massiveness of the White Mountains spread before them in undulating waves of blue, gray and purple. The colors changed with distance from the greenish blue of the foothills and near ridges to the dark blues and purples of the towering peaks of the Presidential Range, still capped with the last of their winter snow cover.

"My word," gasped Sid. "I had no idea...."

"I know. Amazing, isn't it? For some reason, we never seem to hear about the mountains of New England. I vaguely recall my geography lessons mentioning the Rockies in western Canada and the U.S., which are very rugged and rise to a quite respectable height, and also another range in the eastern U.S. of older, smaller mountains called the Appa-something. I believe these New England mountains are the northern end of that range."

"You keep saying New England mountains as if there were more."

"There are. Dare told me that from the top of Mount Washington—that's the tallest peak in the Northeast, but we can't quite see it from here—you can see range after range of mountains spreading across Vermont and the northern half of New Hampshire and Maine."

"Too bad I'm not up to mountain climbing," sighed Sid. "That would be a sight to behold."

Bram opened his mouth and then closed it without speaking. He slanted a sly grin in Sid's direction and decided to save a few surprises for a later time.

"Excuse me, sir. The turning for Bishops Falls is coming up directly."

Merton eased the big car to the right, slowing and angling onto the exit ramp. At the foot of the ramp, they turned right onto a three-lane road, which passed under Interstate 93 and then followed a winding route through densely wooded low hills. After some four miles, the road forked, and they followed the Bishops Falls-Snow Meadows signs to the right, rounded the base of another small hill and broke out of the woods into an area of rolling pastureland and fields, stretching for acres on both sides of the road. Cattle and horses were grazing in several of the pastures, and the rich brown of recently plowed earth made a pleasant contrast to the vibrant green of the meadows bordering a narrow, swiftly flowing river on their left.

"Beautiful," breathed Sid. "Is this Snow Meadows?"

"Oh, no," said Bram. "This is only the beginning of the lower valley. Bishops Falls is just over that rise, and then it's another few miles to the upper valley where Snow Meadows and Samantha's Lake are located."

There was little traffic on the valley road this late on a weekday morning, and Merton slowed the car to let them get a close look at the several complexes of farm buildings that were widely spaced along the road and set back at the ends of long driveways. In a few minutes, the road went up a slight incline and through a stand of white birches before leveling off. There were more houses now, some with a few acres of plowed field around them, and here and there a narrow road led off toward the far ridges bordering the valley. Between the houses, they could catch an occasional glimpse of the river, rushing on its way down the valley, its banks barely containing the spring freshets from the melting snow on the mountains.

"This is Bishops Falls," said Bram, as the road became the main street of a small town. They swung around one side of a large green, passed through an area of shops and old mill houses and then paralleled a series of two- and three-story granite and brick buildings that bordered the river. "That's the old Bishop Mill. Ran on water power controlled by the dam," Bram explained, gesturing to the structure stretching across the river above the mill. "I don't believe it's in operation at all now."

Traveling past the outskirts of the town into a lightly wooded area and then again through a rolling landscape of farms, meadows, and patches of woodland, Bram dredged up half-forgotten information and answered Sid's questions as best he could.

"That's the Snow Meadows Ski Area," Bram said, pointing toward the twin peaks of the Aggies rising majestically above the high ridges and foothills sheltering the left side of the valley. "There's a summit lodge on Mount Aggie Right, and a base lodge complex, which you can't see from here."

The road swung in a wide curve, following the

dogleg turn of the valley, and Bram indicated the ski-area sign pointing to a side road on the left. "The less affluent skiers stay at the base lodge, which has dormitory-style accommodations. There's another road along the base of those ridges that leads directly from the inn."

They were going through an area of wild meadows that undulated gently away from both sides of the road, to be lost in the gradual thickening of the forest of mixed hardwoods, spruce and pine that covered the high, rough land defining the valley's limits.

"In the winter," murmured Bram, "these really are meadows of snow."

"What are those houses?" asked Sid, motioning to the right. "I thought we were on the resort property."

"We are. Those are vacation homes of avid golfers," explained Bram with a hint of facetiousness. "Look to your left and you'll see part of the golf course. It was covered with three feet of snow when I was here, but I was told that it's a very fine course. Professional quality. There's a major tournament held here in, I think, August. That's enough to lure some fanatics into building a summer home within easy walking distance."

"The river seems to cut right down the center of it. Aren't those bridges?"

"Mmm. . . I'm trying to remember the name. . . something odd. Ah, yes. Goodwives Run. Named for the long-suffering wives of the first settlers. It flows out of Samantha's Lake. You should be able to see it in a minute. There, through the trees a bit to the left, you can see the sun flashing on the water.''

The upper end of the golf course was bordered by a long, low rise that was topped by a thick growth of shrubs and cedars. As the road rounded the rise and swung slightly to the left, a wide vista of lawns dotted with gardens and ornamental shrubs and trees opened up, leading the eye unerringly to the sprawling, but somehow fairy-tale, splendor of the Snow Meadows Inn. It gleamed yellow and white in the sunlight, looking like a fantasy against the darkness of the high, wild ridges rising behind it, with the deep blue waters of the lake spreading out mysteriously into the distance on the right.

''Lovely. Simply lovely,'' sighed Sid. ''I never expected anything like this.''

He kept his eyes fixed on the incredible structure, picking out details and amusing Bram with his unexpected reactions. They turned into the wide entrance drive, crossed a bridge over the river and moved slowly up the gentle slope of the curving drive, stopping finally at the broad, shallow steps leading up to a deep veranda.

''They must have been watching for us,'' remarked Bram as the double-width paneled oak doors opened and Jean came running across the veranda and down the steps.

Merton opened the car door and assisted Bram to come stiffly to his feet. Sid handed him a sturdy but elegant silver-handled ebony cane, and Bram had just time enough to brace himself before Jean threw her arms around him, crying, ''It's so good to see you! Did you have a lovely trip? You must be worn out. Come in, come in. Everyone's so anxious to see you again, and lunch will be in a few minutes, but you have time to wash up and have a drink first. Oh, I'm so pleased you're here!''

She finally took a breath and held out a hand to Sid. "How lovely you could come with him, Sid. We can't wait to show you around. You play golf, don't you? You'll—''

"Jean, Jean, slow down.'' Bram laughed at her bubbling spirits. "That drink sounds marvelous. My word, what a welcoming committee!''

With an encouraging hand on her arm, Bram urged Jean toward the steps and the group of people waiting on the veranda. Laughing, chatting, acknowledging introductions, they all moved inside, while one of the younger Adderly boys joined Merton to show him the way to Alicia's cottage.

Twenty minutes later, everyone was settled at a long table next to the lakeside windows in the main dining room. Talk flowed easily around the table, and Bram divided his attention between the conversation and the peaceful view of the lake.

"Preston and Janet were so sorry they couldn't be here to greet you,'' said Jean, leaning across the table toward him. "They had to be in New York today, but they'll be back sometime tomorrow. Grandma Amy should be here in a few minutes. She likes to make an entrance. And Dare's out checking the gondola pylons, but he and—''

She broke off at the unmistakable sound of a motorcycle and turned to look out at the parking lot. Bram followed her gaze and saw a large red-

and-gold Yamaha with a wraparound windscreen sheltering two riders come to a gravel-scattering stop next to the steps to the side veranda.

Odd-looking helmets. Bram peered more closely. *No, they're hard hats. The big one riding pillion looks like Dare, but who's the boy wearing a lavender hat? Lavender? By God, it is lavender!*

He watched as the pair leaped up the steps, Darius laughing uproariously at something his small companion said. Bram couldn't get a good look at the boy, since Darius partially blocked his view. He glanced questioningly at Jean as they passed from sight.

"I recognize Dare, but who's the little one?" asked Bram. "One of your young cousins? He doesn't look big enough to be climbing pylons or driving a motorbike."

Jean choked on a sip of wine, and before she could recover enough to speak, the pair in question strode into the dining room. Bram had only a moment to note that, unlike the others who were dressed rather formally for luncheon, Dare and his companion were wearing work boots, heavy denim jeans, flannel shirts and down vests. They had obviously come straight from their morning's project and were even now, as they crossed the dining room, pulling off leather gloves and stuffing them in their hip pockets.

Bram rested one hand on the table for support as he rose and held out his hand toward Dare, a smile and words of greeting on his lips. Before he could speak, Edna's voice rang out in a distressed cry.

"Oh, Tally, how could you! I asked you just this

morning to please, please take time to change before.... Oh, dear, isn't it just like you to.... What
will Bram and Mr. Cater think with you coming to
lunch looking like a...a lumberjack!''

Bram didn't hear anything else. He stared,
stunned, as the small "boy" pulled off the lavender hard hat and released a thick braid of hair
the color of honey in sunlight. He watched in
fascination as the braid uncoiled down her back,
the curly end coming to rest against the lower
curve of her trim bottom. Automatically his eyes
made a quick, but thorough tour of her slim,
beautifully proportioned figure. He had to guess
at the size of her breasts, since they were effectively concealed by the puffy vest, but her narrow,
slightly curving hips looked as if they were made
for a man's hands to grasp.

Bram's wide mouth was beginning to curl into a
pleased, sensuous smile when he met a pair of
scornful beige eyes sparkling with gold flecks of
anger. *Tally! Did Edna call her Tally? This is the
Tartar-in-training? This little bit of a thing that
would blow away in a high wind? How could such
a delectable little bird be a raging feminist? On the
other hand, she looks mad enough to spit bullets.
What could have gotten her back up, unless it's
Edna's scolding? Embarrassment, that's it. Jean
said she's thirty-one, and that is a bit old to be
having your mother tear a strip off you in public.
God! She looks about eighteen. I'll have to put her
at ease and then—*

"Bram! Hey, man, snap out of it!"

Dare's laughing voice brought Bram back to

alertness, and he realized how intent his stare had been. He flushed with unaccustomed self-consciousness as he got his wandering thoughts under control and turned his attention to the big man waiting to greet him.

"It's great to see you," said Dare, grasping Bram's hand in a firm shake and slapping him on the shoulder. "You're looking kind of peaked, but we'll have you back in shape in no time."

"Oh, no, you won't! Merton will get me back in shape." Bram laughed as he gave Dare's 210 pounds of solid bone and muscle a jaundiced look. "Your methods of body building would probably finish me off. Swimming and controlled exercises are my limit for now. But you haven't met Sid yet."

While he was performing introductions and bantering with Dare, Bram was intensely aware of the intriguing woman hovering impatiently a few steps behind her brother. One of the quick glances he gave her coincided with her removal of the thick vest, which had hidden part of her figure. Unable to stop himself, he stared for a long moment at the unexpected flatness of her chest.

No, not exactly flat. There's a slight fullness, but not what one would expect. I would have said she'd have small breasts, but firm and high with a nice shape. Too bad, but perhaps. . . .

"All right, Bram, I'll be a good guy and introduce you before your eyes fall all the way out." Darius stretched out a long arm and grasped Tally's braid, pulling her forward to stand beside him. "Tally, this skinny hunk is Bram Ramsdale, who, in better days, is the heartthrob of millions of swooning women." Dare chuckled at Bram's disgusted groan. "True, too true. Get some color back in your face and pile on about twenty pounds, and we'll have to hire you a bodyguard. My young cousins are going to drive you bats."

"Ignore him," said Bram, extending his thin hand. "I'm delighted to meet you."

The irrepressible Darius continued blandly, "Don't count on it. This is my infamous sister, Tally the Terror, and one breath of discrimination due to her size or sex will bring showers of voracious locusts down on your head." He winked at Bram and whispered loudly, "She's a witch, you see."

Tally directed a killing glare at her once-favorite brother as she took Bram's hand in a brief, firm clasp, pulling back immediately when she switched her gaze to his face and saw the unmistakable gleam of male interest in his light green eyes.

Oh, no. No way, chum. I'm not up for playmate of the week. Or day. And you can forget the charming, sexy smiles, and stop looking me over like a—

Dari gave her braid a sharp tug. "Snap to, sis. Stop glaring at the poor man. He's only trying to say hello, not put the make on you. I'd say it'll be another two or three weeks before he's up to that."

"Belt up, Dare," pleaded Bram. "You're going to give Tally entirely the wrong impression."

"Oh, I don't know," Tally said thoughtfully, a warning gleam in her eyes. "Your advance publicity has been more than impressive. One might say it's been downright astonishing. Almost unbelievable," she purred, twitching her braid out of Dari's hand and sliding into a seat well removed from Bram's.

Smug, egotistical, blatant tomcat! Looking me over like that. Maybe it knocks over the women you're used to, but it won't work on me, buster. You'd do better to try it out on Ciel. Too bad he's such a Casanova. He's really quite handsome. That dark auburn hair and those light green eyes are kind of nice. Too thin, but he's probably Cindy's Brawny Bram when he's in shape. Stop it, Tally. That's not on your summer schedule. The last thing you need in your life is an oversexed, self-centered actor.

Across the table, Bram was drawing some conclusions of his own. *Witch! What a little bundle of antagonism it is. No wonder she's still single. Disposition like a shaved cat. Tally the Terror is just about right. Well, it shouldn't be too difficult to avoid her in a place this size. But... too bad... I'll bet she's something with that incredible hair loose... astride a man with that mass of honeygold silk draping around you like a tent. Mmm. Wonder if she makes love as passionately as she glares daggers at one. Oh, hell, man. The last thing you need in your life is a temperamental, militant feminist, no matter how adorable she is.*

CHAPTER THREE

TALLY LINGERED ON THE FRONT VERANDA of the inn for a few moments, her gaze drifting dreamily over the colorful grounds, her head lifted as she breathed deeply of the intoxicating air. A week and a half of warm May sun had brought many of the flowering shrubs and trees into early bloom. The soft morning breeze now carried the sweetness of lilac as a counterpoint to the strong, pervasive scent of pine and balsam.

A smile quirked the corners of Tally's mouth as she remembered the Yankee entrepreneur who, many years ago, had marketed cans of "fresh Maine air" and had amazingly found thousands of people who were willing to pay good money for a clever label stuck on an empty can. She wondered fleetingly why none of the equally sharp Bishops had thought of bottling White Mountain spring air. Still smiling, she reluctantly turned her feet toward the front entrance.

Absently distributing smiles and morning greetings to the several people in the lobby, Tally headed for the reception desk, trying to shift the two large dress boxes she was carrying into a more secure position.

"Hi, Beth," she muttered to the pretty blonde

behind the desk. "Drat these things! Do you know where my mother is at the moment?"

"She was headed for the Gazebo a few minutes ago, Tally. Do you want some help with those?"

"No, thanks. I think I've got 'em now."

"Don't tell me *you've* been shopping," Beth teased, well aware of Tally's aversion to her mother's favorite hobby.

"You know better," Tally chided with a tolerant grin. "These are mother's. I'm just the delivery service. See you later."

Her progress was hampered several times by the necessity of exchanging pleasantries with some of the permanent guests, many of whom had known her since she was a child. The warm, relaxed atmosphere of the inn, coupled with its attentive, first-class service, had over the years induced many annual vacationers to make the inn their permanent home when they retired or lost their husbands or wives in their later years and did not wish to live entirely alone.

Finally Tally made it to the entrance to the Gazebo Garden, which the family had dubbed "Edna's Folly." It had been her first project, at her mother's request, when Tally had returned to the valley three years ago, and she still felt a glow of satisfaction every time she walked into the intriguing structure. Borrowing the design of the lovely hexagonal Victorian gazebo in her great-grandmother's rose garden, Tally had built a large hexagonal room off the northeast corner of the main dining room. One wall, of course, was the entrance from the dining room, while the other five walls were of triple thermal glass so the room could be used year-round. The fancifully carved corner posts and the lacy gingerbreading that bordered the eaves of the pagoda roof were all painted white and, together with the thick moss-green carpeting and plethora of floor and hanging plants, gave the room a summery aura even on the coldest, stormiest winter day. The happy "good morning" mood was enhanced by the furnishings of slate-topped, white wrought-iron tables and white wicker chairs with gay daffodil-patterned cushions.

Spotting her mother on the far side of the room, Tally awkwardly shifted the dress boxes so she wouldn't hit any of the diners and began wending her way between the tables. It wasn't until she'd stepped around a lush schefflera that she saw the two men sharing the round table with her mother.

The presence of Sidney Cater came as no surprise; even Tally, who was the first to admit she didn't always pay much attention to what was going on around her, had noticed the charming Englishman's marked preference for her mother's company over the past two weeks. Tally was, however, rather startled to find Bram Ramsdale sharing breakfast with the older couple. She hadn't seen him since the day of his arrival. According to Jean's periodic bulletins, he'd been staying very close to the cottage except for a daily swim in the inn's indoor pool.

"Darling!" Edna exclaimed as she caught sight of her daughter. "I thought you'd be long gone by now. It's nearly nine."

"Morning, ma." Tally dropped a kiss near Edna's right eyebrow as she dumped the dress boxes on the floor next to her chair. "Morning, Sid, Bram," she said, sharing a smile impartially between the two men as she slid into the nearest empty seat.

"Please, not 'ma,'" sighed Edna. She turned to Sid with a rueful grimace, explaining, "It's this North Country upbringing. No matter how I pleaded, I could never get the children to call me 'mummy' as any proper English child would do. They claimed their friends would laugh at them."

Tally grinned unrepentantly at her mother. "I'd certainly sound like a *proper* fool to be calling you 'mummy' at my advanced age. You might as well give it up, ma. The closest you're going to come is having your grandkids call you 'grandmum.'"

"I understand you designed this intriguing structure." The rich baritone voice startled Tally. At the luncheon two weeks earlier she had spoken with him only briefly, and his voice had been husky and strained with fatigue and probably pain. Jean had mentioned at the time that the trip had played havoc with his leg. Now, Tally stared at him, listening to that sensual voice with its elegant accent echo in her head.

"Yes, she did," said Edna into the silence, and Tally snapped out of her trance. She felt like a perfect ninny, sitting there goggling at Bram like a star-struck teenager. So he had a beautiful voice; so what? She suddenly remembered that the most impressive tenor voice she'd ever heard belonged to a short, round, forty-year-old baker who sang with the White Mountaineers, a choral group in North Conway.

She met his amused gaze and bit back a tart comment, taking a deep breath instead to enforce her self-control. However, she had second thoughts as she saw his eyes drop to the thrust of her breasts against her long-sleeved yellow T-shirt.

"It's delightful," he murmured. He smiled knowingly as he raised his eyes to her flushed cheeks and indignant look. Before she could open her mouth, he added, "The view is spectacular," and gestured at the panorama of lake, forest, mountains, gardens and golf course that was visible from the Gazebo.

Tally sizzled. She was sure if her hair hadn't been securely pinned in a knot, it would be standing on end in a three-foot-high ruff. Outrageous man! What did he think he was playing at, flirting with her? He must be getting bored already, if she was looking good to him. Lord knew she wasn't anything close to his regular type of playmate if Jean's reports could be believed.

"Tally, what is the matter with you? I've spoken to you twice."

"Sorry, ma. I was...thinking. What is it?"

"One, have you had breakfast? Two, why are you late? Three, why did you bring these in here?" Edna concluded, gesturing to the dress boxes beside her.

"No to number one. Thanks, Ellie," she murmured to the waitress who was setting a cup of coffee in front of her. "Could you ask Bill to make me a peanut-butter-and-bacon sandwich on rye toast? Oh, and I'll have a large glass of cranberry juice, please." Tally redirected her attention to her mother. "Two, I changed my schedule this morning. I have to swing by Loon Lake to get some more photos of the McLaughlins' lot, and I wanted to give the sun time to dry up some of the mud. The access road to the site was a quagmire the other day. Then I'm heading for North Conway."

"Oh, lovely," Edna said happily. "You can drop by the Eastern Slope Weavers and see if they've finished the new spreads and drapes."

Tally gave her mother a wry smile. "Who did your errands before I showed up? Never mind, I'll check. Now, about those boxes. Dari's going to Concord this noon, and I'm stopping by his place on my way out. If you'll check your goodies over, I can drop off anything that has to be returned, and Dari will take it along with him."

"What a *good* idea!" Edna enthused—and then seemed to be struck by an even better one. Her blue eyes sparkled gleefully as she looked from Tally to Bram and back again.

"Darling, I've just had the most marvelous thought!" she bubbled, carefully avoiding direct eye contact with her unpredictable daughter. "Loon Lake is so lovely, and then you'll be going through some very pretty country to get back to the interstate, and of course the Kancamagus Highway is just spectacular." Edna turned to Bram, explaining, "It's a beautiful drive, about thirty-six miles of wilderness road right through the mountains. It's all part of the White Mountain National Forest so there aren't any houses or com-

mercial buildings. Just forest and mountains, and
the most beautiful view from the top of the Kancamagus Pass. I know you'll enjoy it, and it will do
you the world of good to get out into all this lovely
mountain air."

"Ma! Now, wait a minute," Tally sputtered, realizing where her mother's travelogue was leading.

"You'll love North Conway," Edna continued
quickly. "Lots of interesting shops, and on a lovely, clear day like this, you'll have a marvelous view
of Mount Washington right from the middle of the
main street."

"Ma!"

"And the Eastern Slope Inn does a very nice
lunch," Edna soldiered on. "Lovely view from the
dining room. Be sure to make them give you a good
table, Tally. Tell them who you are. After all, there
is professional courtesy, you know."

"Oh, ma," Tally groaned, dropping her head
into her hands. She caught a fleeting glimpse of
Sid's bemused smile and a gleam of unholy enjoyment lighting Bram's peridot eyes.

Tally was only minimally aware of the conversation during the next half hour. She concentrated on
stewing and fretting, trying to find a way around the
trap her loving mother had set. But other than an
outright rude refusal to take Bram with her, there
seemed to be little that she could do. Although he
was staying in Alicia's cottage, he was still something of a family friend, and she had no concrete
reason for denying her mother's plans for his "entertainment." She could only hope that his ideas
weren't along the lines of Edna's wishful thinking.

After one futile attempt to convince Bram that he'd be bored waiting around for her to complete her various errands, she gave in with as much grace as she could muster and led him out to the Wagoneer.

"I take it that lavender is your favorite color," Bram commented after his first look at her car, remembering her hard hat. "Interesting decoration," he added, examining the large cat's-head silhouette on the door panel.

"That's Splendid," said Tally over her shoulder as she moved to open the rear of the car to deposit a rejected dress box on the carpeted loadbed.

"Er. . . yes, most unusual," said Bram doubtfully, eyeing the odd shape of the cat's head and wondering just what breed it was.

He was still wondering as he opened the car door, bent to slide his cane behind the seat, and came face-to-face with an enormous cat who was fully occupying the passenger seat. The beast was sitting proudly erect, only its head turned toward the intruder to examine him with curious yellow eyes.

"Good God," Bram breathed, not daring to move a muscle. The animal didn't look like any domestic cat he'd ever seen. It had to be almost three feet long, and he'd bet that it weighed something over two stone.

"That's Splendid," said Tally, opening the far door and sliding into the driver's seat.

"Splendid?"

"My cat."

"Your *cat*?"

"Don't worry. He's perfectly tame," Tally

assured him, scratching the huge feline behind one tufted ear. "Come on, you monster, get in the back."

Splendid pressed his head back against her hand and began a deep rumbling purr. He showed no inclination to move from his chosen perch.

Feeling slightly discomposed at being upstaged by a cat, of all things, Bram dryly suggested, "Perhaps I should get in the back."

"Nonsense," Tally said briskly, looping a finger under Splendid's collar and tugging gently. "Over you go, cat. Look on the bright side; you've got more room to stretch out back there."

Bram watched in considerable awe as Tally encouraged the reluctant beast to wriggle between the front bucket seats and climb onto the wider back seat. He noticed that one of the cat's huge back paws was neatly bandaged and that he was definitely favoring it.

"What happened to his paw?" Bram asked as he slid into the passenger seat and adjusted his left leg to a comfortable position.

"He cut it a couple of days ago, but it doesn't seem to be healing right. I want the vet to look at it. There may be something embedded in the cut that I couldn't get out when I cleaned it."

"Where's the vet? I didn't hear you mention that to Edna."

"North Conway. There's one closer, but Splendid doesn't like him and won't let the poor man near him."

"And I don't imagine that one argues with Splendid," Bram murmured, glancing back at the cat just in time to get an enlightening view of his formidable teeth as Splendid yawned.

"Too true," Tally agreed. "However, he really has a sweet disposition and wouldn't think of biting or clawing a human. Except in extreme circumstances, a snarl and a show of teeth is usually enough to encourage anyone to back off."

Bram cast a doubtful look at the cat and thought that "sweet" was the last word he'd choose to describe what surely must be a wild animal. That doubt was still in his eyes as he shifted his gaze to look questioningly at Tally.

She braked at the end of the driveway and, feeling his eyes on her, turned toward him, one eyebrow lifted inquiringly. "Something?" she asked.

"That's a, ah, unusual pet," he muttered. Bram mentally kicked himself. He couldn't remember the last time a woman had thrown him off balance, but then he'd never met one who had eyes that matched her cat's. Fascinated, he stared at Tally's gold-shot tan eyes, slowly deciding that it wasn't the color so much as the expression of intense curiosity that reminded him of Splendid's first examination of him.

"Lots of people have cats," said Tally lightly as she swung onto the main road. "I thought they were favorite pets in England."

"Well, yes, I suppose they are, but I've never seen one that size. He's at least half as big as you are, and he certainly doesn't look like any domestic pussycat I've ever run across."

Tally flashed him a mischievous grin. Bram's loss of composure had softened her attitude, at least temporarily. For now, she was prepared to be friendly, particularly since he seemed to be interested in one of her favorite subjects.

"Nobody mentioned the Bishops Bobs when you were here before?" She caught the negative shake of his head from the corner of her eye and continued, "Well, to begin with, they're a cross-breed between the wild bobcat, which is part of the lynx family, and a very large strain of domestic shorthairs. My Great-Great-Aunt Sarah Preston was fascinated with zoology, particularly as it pertained to the wildlife of New England. When she had a chance to obtain a couple of orphaned litters of bobcat kittens, she grabbed them with both hands, determined to prove that wildcats could be tamed with proper handling. From there it was just a short step to finding the largest domestic cats she could, mating them with the smallest bobcats, and hoping for the best."

"Your great-great-aunt? How long ago was this?" asked Bram.

"Around the turn of the century. Sarah was a bit ahead of her time. According to Great-Aunt Ellen, her daughter, she was also stubborn, outspoken and considered a first-class eccentric. But, to give her credit, before she was through, she'd developed a new breed of cat. Not that you'll find Bishops Bobs listed in any of the official breed books except as a footnote."

"Good heavens, why not? That's quite an achievement. I should think—"

"No, no. You have to understand the North Country mind. Just because *we* have it, that doesn't mean we want all of *you* to have it, too. Just think of the cachet of having your personal breed of cat! No Bishop worth the name would think of sharing such a phenomenon with the world."

"I thought you said Sarah was a Preston."

"Same difference. Bishops, Prestons and Adderlys have been marrying back and forth for years—with, of course, due consideration given to not mixing the bloodlines too closely. Nothing less than third or fourth cousins, and we make sure we bring in lots of fresh blood each generation."

"My word," said Bram faintly, wondering if Great-Great-Aunt Sarah had infected the whole family with her passion for controlled breeding.

"Don't worry," said Tally, gurgling with laughter. "It's been going on for over two hundred years and doesn't seem to have hurt us any. Now, about these cats. You can't take Splendid as typical. He's actually something of a throwback to his wild forebears. The majority of the Bishops Bobs run about eighteen to twenty-four pounds and stand between fifteen to eighteen inches at the shoulder—about the size of a medium-small dog. Their tails vary from full-length to the four or five inches that you'll find on wild bobcats. Splendid, on the other hand, weighs close to thirty pounds, stands twenty-one inches tall, and is thirty-four inches from the base of his spine to the tip of his nose."

"Not exactly a lap cat."

"No, but unfortunately he thinks he is. It's one of our major differences of opinion."

"How old is he? He is fully grown, isn't he?"

"Oh, yes. He's two and a half. I'd wanted one for years, but Aunt Ellen won't let them go to anyone living in densely populated areas. They need room to roam, so I had to wait until I moved back here. As it was, I only got Splendid because he was so big. Ellen couldn't use him for breeding, even though he's beautifully marked and has nice conformation, since he was obviously going to be too large to mate with her breeders. She finally said I could have him as long as I agreed to have him neutered so he wouldn't go chasing after the wild bobs and get himself chewed up."

Bram glanced around as Tally stopped the car and turned off the ignition. He'd been so caught up in listening to her and observing Splendid that he hadn't even noticed the passing scene. The Bishop Construction sign on the building in front of them indicated that they'd arrived at Dare's office, and he opened his door to follow Tally.

"Does that animal go everywhere with you?" he asked, watching Splendid scramble out through the rear door when Tally opened it to get the dress box.

"Most of the time. Right now, he's going to visit Dari's watchdogs. They get along just fine as long as there's a high fence between Splendid and the shepherds. I hope you won't mind if we keep this visit short," she continued, leading the way toward the office door. "We're pushing the time a bit as it is."

"No problem. I'm having dinner with Rosemary and Dare this evening so we can save our chat until then."

Tally continued to be pleasantly surprised during the following hours with the friendly accord that she and Bram seemed to have reached through their mutual interest in Splendid and his history. Although she was at first alert for signs of the hunting male that she'd seen at their initial meeting, Bram's relaxed casualness and obvious fascination with the White Mountain area and its history gradually lulled her into letting down her guard.

He waited uncomplainingly in the car with Splendid while she slogged through mud and clambered over rocks and deadfalls at the McLaughlins' lakeside building lot to take her site photos. When they reached the top of the Kancamagus Pass, he agreed without hesitation to her suggestion that they wait and stop on the way back to admire the view. By the time they were pulling into the parking lot at the Eastern Slope Inn, after dropping Splendid off at the vet's, Tally was feeling very charitable toward him and had decided that the coming summer might be more fun than she had expected. Bram seemed to like Dari and Rosemary, and they were the people she spent the most time with. If her relationship with Bram continued to be this friendly and relaxed, Tally decided, then perhaps the four of them could really enjoy teaming up for the summer.

It would be such a lovely change. No strain, no fighting off passes, no arguments with the family about their attempts to matchmake. Just a nice, relaxing fun time with congenial people.

"Aren't we rather casual for this place?" asked Bram as Tally stopped the car. He gestured at the beautiful old white-painted hotel, its graceful four-story main building with its attendant wings set in carefully landscaped grounds.

Tally flicked a quick glance over his tieless brown silk shirt and the obviously tailor-made long vest and slacks of fine loden-green wool. His mahogany leather shoes, she noted in passing, were polished to a positively glittering sheen.

"You're fine," she said. "In fact you're dressier than I am." She grinned as she kicked out one small foot clad in a short gray suede boot. "It's a good thing I had a change of boots. They probably would object to my mudhoppers. Come on. There's no problem. Most of the places in the mountains are pretty casual about dress, at least in the daytime."

"I'll take your word for it. Do you mind if we walk about a bit? I'm rather stiff from sitting for so long."

She watched him move around the front of the car toward her and noticed that he was leaning heavily on his cane, his limp more pronounced than it had been earlier.

"Sure. Let's stroll over there," she suggested, nodding toward the far side of the parking lot where a path led to the tennis courts and their surrounding flower gardens. The velvety green lawns were dotted with a variety of ornamental trees and shrubs in full blossom, spilling a rainbow of color against the distant mass of evergreens.

Although Tally slowed her normally brisk stride to Bram's pace, he managed to lag behind her by a step or two. His motives were strictly ulterior.

This was one of the few opportunities he'd been afforded during the morning to watch her unobserved. Despite the fact that she was totally alien to the type of woman who normally attracted him, he'd found himself becoming more fascinated by this odd Yankee female as the hours in her company passed.

His first shock had come that morning as she stood by the breakfast table, giving him a flick of her eye and an impersonal greeting. Her lack of interest might have annoyed him if he hadn't been so busy adjusting his initial impression of her figure. Far from being flat-chested as he'd thought, she had beautifully formed firm breasts. True, they were a bit small, but far from negligible. He realized that she must have had some sort of binding around them before, perhaps as protection when she worked with Dare. He also noticed that her navy cords revealed a slimmer figure than he'd seen before and decided that she must have been wearing what the Yanks called long johns under her heavy jeans.

Somehow, today, she looked far more feminine, he decided, despite the casual T-shirt and cords. Perhaps it was the softer hairstyle, with its deep waves around her face and the silky mass of the French twist at the back of her head. All the way across that wilderness highway as she chatted about cats, hiking trails, and conservation, he'd had the strongest urge to reach over and bury his fingers in her hair, pulling the pins out and watching the silken skeins tumble around her. He'd have done it, too, if he hadn't been reasonably sure that her friendly chatter and occasional smiles would have been immediately replaced by cold hostility.

No, not yet. This is beginning to get interesting. A woman of temper, volatile moods, a creative woman, which all adds up to a woman of passion. Oh, yes, under that cool facade, I'll be willing to bet there is a core of blazing passion. I wonder if any man has ever discovered it. I wonder.... She's wary of me. Even the friendliness today is impersonal, cool, very controlled. It would be an interesting challenge to see if I could bring her around.

Why not? Not my type, but rather attractive in an offbeat way when she's not scowling at me. But slowly, man, slowly. Let's not spook the quarry. Gain her confidence first. If that wariness is any indication, she's already attracted but fighting it. All it's going to take is the right moment. Oh, yes, this may be a far more interesting summer than I expected.

"OH, GOOD. HARDLY ANYBODY'S HERE," sighed Tally with relief as she swung the Wagoneer into the parking lot at the Kancamagus Pass Overlook. She pulled into a parking space at the far end, well away from the other two cars in the lot.

"Splendid tends to startle people," she explained when Bram gave her an inquiring look. "I usually avoid taking him around crowds of strangers."

"Do you think he's steady enough to walk on his own?" asked Bram, glancing in the back at the drowsy cat. "I'm afraid I can't help you much if you have to lift him."

"He should be okay by now. Doc Vener said he only had to knock him out for about ten minutes, and he's been sleeping for the past three hours. It's time he stretched his legs, and I'd rather stop here than along the road."

Tally slid out of the car and opened the back door, reaching in to attach a long inch-wide woven nylon lead to Splendid's collar. With gentle tugs and a coaxing voice, she cajoled him out of the car. The big cat blinked sleepily up at her as he braced his legs against a slight lingering weakness.

"Is he all right?" asked Bram, coming around the back of the car.

"Oh, yes. I'm going to take him over into the woods a way. We'll go slowly, and he'll be fine. Why don't you enjoy the view for a few minutes. There's a map on the display over there that tells you what all the peaks are that you can see from here."

Bram welcomed the opportunity to work the kinks out of his leg, and he slowly circled the parking lot before stopping in front of the large map. He'd only been glancing now and then at the spectacular view, most of his attention directed toward easing the cramps in his leg. Now, though, he forgot about his discomfort as he slowly looked at the surrounding mountains. There was a deep valley, narrow where it began just below the ridge he was standing on and then gradually widening out to the east until it turned out of sight around a distant foothill. Far below in the shadows cast by the late-afternoon sun, which was partially blocked by the high peaks behind him, he could see the silver thread of a river weaving in and out of the thick forest and around rock ledges, spreading now and then into a small pond and then continuing on its inevitable course.

Examining the detailed map in its weatherproof frame, Bram discovered that he was presently standing 2860 feet above sea level, that the silver thread below was the beginning of the Swift River, and that most of the mountains around him were over 3500 feet high. Impressive, he thought, but the numbers don't really tell you much about the overwhelming power of those masses of solid rock thrusting up into the sky, dwarfing every living thing as much by their timelessness as by their size. No Alps, certainly, but rather nice nonetheless.

"Beautiful, isn't it? This is one of my favorite views."

Bram turned at the sound of Tally's voice to find her standing beside him, most of Splendid's twelve-foot lead looped in her hand to hold the now wide-awake cat close to her leg. He suddenly became aware of children's squeals and the excited exclamations of mature voices. He'd been so absorbed in the view that he'd forgotten about the people at the other end of the lot. Looking over his shoulder, he saw several adults and two children staring at Splendid, half fascinated, half afraid.

"It's all right," Tally called to the children, a girl about nine and a boy probably two years older. "He's very tame and friendly. You can come pat him if you're quiet and don't jump around."

Bram leaned back against the sturdy map table and watched Tally introduce the children to Splendid. Any thought of being merely a spectator, however, vanished as the adults came up to him and began questioning him about the huge cat.

A bit stiffly at first, Bram answered their questions, but as it dawned on him that none of them knew who he was, he relaxed and began to chat quite naturally. Of course they recognized his British accent, and within a few minutes he found himself discussing his impressions of New England, New Hampshire, British-American relations, and half a dozen other subjects.

"Amazing," Bram murmured a short time later as he climbed into the car and leaned back, staring unseeingly at the panorama in front of him.

"What is?" asked Tally, pausing with her hand on the ignition switch. She eyed his bemused expression and wondered if he'd heard her question.

He was looking a lot healthier she noted, as she waited for his response. She wondered if he'd been using the small sunning deck adjoining the master bedroom at Alicia's to acquire that tan. He also seemed to be gaining some weight and putting a layer of much needed padding over his previously too-prominent bones. At least now his cheekbones didn't look as if they were about to break through the skin. She let her eyes drift down over his face and wondered what was amusing him as she saw the slight quirk at the corner of his mouth.

Bram blinked a couple of times and turned his head to meet her puzzled gaze. His abstract expression faded as amusement extended the quirk into a smile and brought a dancing light to his eyes. Tally did some blinking herself when his beautifully modulated voice practically purred his belated answer to her question.

"The day, those people, your pussycat, all this." He gestured toward the surrounding mountains, then held her with his intent green stare as his voice deepened and he added, "And you."

"Er. . .yes," muttered Tally in a rare state of confusion. Groping for firm ground, she glanced at the digital clock on the dashboard and said quickly, "Oh, my, it is getting on, isn't it? We'd better be on our way or you'll be late for dinner at Dari's."

Watching her maneuver the car out of the parking lot onto the road, Bram smiled to himself, well pleased with her flustered reaction. Even though she'd made a fast recovery, he'd thrown her off balance for a few moments. It augered well for his plans. He settled back, unbothered by her retreat into silence, since it gave him ample time to plot his next approach.

CHAPTER FOUR

"TALLY! WAIT! Thank heavens you're here. I don't care what you're doing, dear, I need your help for about fifteen minutes."

Tally halted her progress across the lobby and turned to see her mother rapidly descending the wide main stairway. Continuing to munch on a cheese danish, she strolled back a few feet to wait at the foot of the stairs.

"Really, darling, I do wish you'd eat a proper breakfast instead of filling up on sweets in the middle of the morning. Now, I suppose, you'll skip lunch, and goodness only knows what you'll have for supper," Edna scolded in a familiar litany.

Tally listened, nodded agreeably, and waited for her mother to wend her way to the point.

"Come along, dear," said Edna as she reached the bottom of the stairs and dropped a guiding arm around her petite daughter's shoulders. "It must be fate, don't you think, since you're actually wearing something decent, and so early in the day, too."

She skimmed an assessing eye over Tally's gold silk shirt and her waist-length jacket and tailored pants of a silk-wool blend in tobacco brown. "Is this some sort of occasion, dear? Shoes instead of those dreadful boots—I do like that lizard—and jewelry and your hair up? Well, never mind, it's just so fortunate, isn't it?"

"Mother, hold up a minute," Tally said firmly. She planted her feet just inside the dining room entrance, effectively bringing her mother's rapid pace to a halt. "Before we go any farther, would you mind telling me what sticky stew you're about to dump me into? And I really have got just about fifteen minutes. I've got to be in Steven's office at eleven-thirty with a client. In simple sentences, ma, what is it you need me to do?"

"I was telling you, Tally, before you interrupted. A garden club from Newton, Massachusetts—thirty-two women—arrived half an hour ago on one of those day trips, and everything's totally confused. I was supposed to hostess a brunch for them, then give a little talk on the history of Snow Meadows, and then MacDevitt was to take them on a tour of the grounds. They came up particularly to see our azaleas and the rhododendron and, of course, the Alpine gardens."

"Ma!"

"Yes, well, first poor dear Mrs. Hawthorne *insisted* on seeing me immediately, so Sidney— he's such a lovely man, isn't he—volunteered to host the brunch. Wasn't that thoughtful of him? Bram even offered to help. We're praying none of them will recognize him, but they seem to be older ladies and.... Yes, yes, dear, I'm coming to the point. The painters have just arrived to start on the Verrazzos' condo, and I simply must see them and verify the colors, and the ladies are almost ready for my little talk and... well, if you could just fill in for me this once.''

''Oh, ma,'' groaned Tally, ''you know how I hate playing a Bishop of *the* Bishops. Isn't there anyone else who—''

''No, there isn't. Now, Tally, I know how you feel, but it's an emergency, and I do think you could manage just this once. After all, you do know all the history, and you look so nice today, and if you just smile, well, I know everything will be simply splendid, and I'm sure they'll like you. So run along, dear. They're in the Gazebo Garden.''

Edna rattled through her peroration at twice her normal speed without so much as a second's pause. Tally was left with her mouth open, watching her mother rush out the side door, her final words drifting back on the breeze of her passage.

''Oh, hossapples,'' Tally muttered, knowing she was trapped. From spring through fall Snow Meadows received a steady stream of tour groups. It had become a tradition for a member of the family to welcome them with a brief talk on the history of the resort. In recent years this chore had fallen to Edna, Pip or Jean, who were the Bishops most involved in the day-to-day operation of the complex.

Still muttering under her breath, Tally headed for the Gazebo. Fully involved with her own work, she usually managed to avoid these command performances. However, she knew that Jean and Pip were unavailable at the moment, and since her mother had fled. . . .

Calling on years of early training, Tally summoned up a friendly smile as she entered the Gazebo Garden. She paused fractionally to take a quick look around the room. For once something was going right, she decided. The ladies were relaxing over their second cup of coffee or tea, and she wouldn't have to wait at all.

She began moving unhurriedly across the room toward Sidney Cater's table, using the few seconds to assess the group with a practiced eye. Spring suits prevailed, obviously from designer shops, with discreet touches of gold and silver jewelry. A preponderance of traditional diamonds on the ring fingers, although the sunlight pouring in the windows sparked flashes of red, green and blue from several other gem stones. Professionally styled hair, some beautiful touch-up jobs, a few heads of lovely silvery white.

"Good morning, Sid," she said as she reached his side. "Mother's sent me to the rescue. If you'll introduce me, I'll try to keep them diverted until she can get here."

"But, my dear Tally, I've been having a delightful time with all these lovely ladies," murmured Sid, distributing a charming smile around the room. "I do believe even Bram has been enjoying himself."

Tally turned to follow the direction of Sid's nod and found Bram watching her with a rueful smile on his handsome face. She couldn't help grinning back at him; she could just imagine his reaction at finding himself entertaining a ladies' garden club, of all things.

Not his usual scene, she mused, and who would have believed he'd go along with it? He really was much nicer than she'd ever expected him to be. In fact, they'd been on surprisingly good terms since their trip to North Conway a week ago.

"Are you ready, Tally?" Sid's low-voiced question brought her attention back to the matter at hand.

"Sure. Fire away."

With considerable amusement Tally listened to the sophisticated Briton as he effortlessly wrapped thirty-two savvy ladies from Newton around his thumb. Momentarily distracted by the thought that her mother, who was not always as featherheaded as she seemed, also appeared to be falling under his spell, Tally almost missed her cue.

"It's a pleasure to present Miss Talia Bishop."

Bram leaned back in his seat fully prepared to enjoy watching Tally's performance. There was no doubt in his mind that it was a performance. No one could be around the Bishops for long without becoming aware of Tally's fierce insistence on retaining her individuality and independence. A public appearance as a representative of the New Hampshire Bishops simply wasn't her scene. Although, Bram admitted as he tuned in on what she was saying, she did it very well.

"The valley was discovered in 1783 by Alden and Otis Bishop and a cousin, Carleton Preston. They returned in 1784 with their families and a group of relatives and friends to establish a settlement. Eventually they acquired title to the valley and most of the surrounding high country, using methods that probably wouldn't bear close examination in terms of our present laws. However, in those days...."

Bram smiled as a ripple of laughter spread around the room. He wondered if she'd missed her calling. That was a neat piece of staging: a shrug, a raised eyebrow and a rueful "what can I say" smile. He had to applaud Tally's clever ploy in nipping any uncomfortable questions in the bud. After all, who could argue with the implied statement that "I am not my ancestors' keeper?"

Only vaguely aware of Tally's description of the inn's architecture, Bram let his mind drift back to the previous weekend, most of which he'd spent as part of a foursome with Tally, Rosemary, and Dare. It had all started Saturday morning when Dare and Rosemary had invited him to an auction at an old farm. Tally joined them at the last minute when she discovered that the contents of the barn included a significant amount of board feet of tiger maple, black walnut, cherry and oak burl. They'd enjoyed themselves so much that it seemed natural to stay together for dinner at the inn, followed by an impromptu and hilarious Scrabble tournament at Dare and Rosemary's house. On Sunday they all met for lunch, and in the course of a rambling discussion they discovered a mutual interest in Impressionist art and Chinese jade. A heated debate on jade-carving techniques had resulted in the four of them spending much of Sunday afternoon in the museum wing of Bishop House.

Bram tuned in to Tally's ongoing description of

the development of Snow Meadows and then let
her voice fade into a pleasant background murmur
as he concentrated his attention on watching the
sunlight shimmer in gold and silver streaks over
the soft mass of her hair, which was again loosely
coiled into a French twist. He remembered how
enticing it had looked Sunday when she'd left it
down, merely restraining it at her nape with a gold
clasp, and how much he'd wanted to run his fingers through its silken length. It was a rare woman, he knew, who was willing to take the time
these days to care for such hair. Unbraided, Tally's hair was long enough for her to sit on, and he
couldn't help wondering at the apparent contra-
diction between her aggressively independent life-
style with its feminist overtones and her insistence
on retaining that most feminine possession: an extraordinary, shining mass of uncut hair, referred
to appropriately in Victorian times as "woman's
crowning glory."

The temptation of that hair had distracted his attention from a full appreciation of the various col-
lections displayed in the museum wing of Bishop
House. Built by the first Otis in 1809, the original
fourteen-room main house was still used as a
residence, currently by Alden and Myra. However,
since Tally and Dare knew the security code for the
museum's separate entrance, they'd all avoided
another in the long series of confrontations between Tally and her uncle. Bram wondered why the
man had never developed any finesse in handling
volatile women. Surely being raised by Grandma
Amy should have taught him. . . .

"And we do hope that you'll enjoy your tour of the inn and the gardens. Now, if you have any questions, I'll be pleased to...ah, I take it back. Here's my mother at last, and, believe me, she's much better at all this than I am."

Bram brought his wandering thoughts back to the moment as he saw Tally switch places with her mother and, with great alacrity and numerous charming nods and smiles, take herself swiftly toward the door. With equal swiftness and charm he excused himself from his table companions and followed in Tally's wake.

"Tally! Wait up," he called from the top of the front steps.

The sound of her name halted Tally's quick pace, and she turned to grin up at Bram from her position halfway down the walk. "Are you escaping?" she asked, taking a few steps back toward the porch.

"That rather depends on you," he answered as he carefully descended the stairs.

"You seem to be moving more easily," she commented when he joined her on the walk.

"I should think so, considering that swimming-whirlpool-exercise-rest routine that Merton insists on maintaining. Not that I'm complaining, mind you," he added hastily. "He's worked wonders. Even your Dr. Markham agrees. When I went in for my weekly checkup yesterday, he was amazed at how much stronger the leg was after just three weeks."

"How much longer will you have to use a cane?" asked Tally as they began strolling toward the parking lot.

"A few more weeks perhaps. Until I can be sure the knee won't give out under normal stress. Where are you headed?" he asked with an admiring look at her coordinated outfit. On a weekday morning she was usually garbed in a shirt or sweater, jeans and work boots.

"Concord. I'm meeting a client in Steven's office to sort out a problem about contractors," she said absently. Her mind was busy assimilating that admiring look she'd noted out of the corner of her eye. It wasn't the first time she'd caught the unmistakable gleam of male appreciation in his regard.

Tally inwardly heaved a sigh. She hoped he wasn't going to start living up to his reputation. She'd really enjoyed his company this past weekend when they'd made up a foursome with Rosemary and Dari on both Saturday and Sunday. The conversations had been stimulating, the laughter frequent, and she'd relaxed far more than she usually did with a new man, secure in her belief that she didn't have to worry about Bram's motivations.

Perhaps she'd been too secure, she thought regretfully, or too quick to believe that his motive was purely a desire for friendly company. On the other hand, he hadn't made anything remotely like a pass or even hinted at a suggestive comment. Maybe that fleeting gleam was nothing more than normal male appreciation for a reasonably attractive woman. After all, even if she was no raving beauty, she wasn't exactly Hannah Horrible, either.

Bram's voice finally impinged on her mental debate, and she belatedly realized that he'd been asking the same question several times.

"Sorry. I was...sidetracked for a minute with ah, a problem I'm having on one of my designs. What did you ask me?"

"I wondered if you'd like to have some company. There are a few errands I could do while you have your meeting, and then perhaps we could find someplace interesting for lunch." Noting the hint of wariness in her eyes, Bram added, "Do you think Steven might be able to join us? I haven't really had an opportunity to get to know him at all well."

They'd halted beside the Wagoneer, and now Tally looked up at him assessingly, but she could see nothing in his expression except friendly inquiry. Awareness of her own motives hit her with a sickening suddenness.

My God, woman, what's gotten into you? Have you become so paranoid about men that even a simple invitation to lunch is cause for suspicion? So what if he should be interested in your potential as a playmate? It certainly won't be because of your money or your name. According to Jean he's got plenty of money of his own, enough so he doesn't need yours. Why don't you just relax, Talia, and stop picking apart every word and look. Enjoy the man's company. He's intelligent, witty and definitely easy on the eyes. In fact, if you were smart....

"Tally?"

To compensate for her brief, uncharitable

thoughts, she gave him a class-one smile. "Of course you can come along. I don't know Steven's schedule, but I'm sure he'll join us for lunch if it's at all possible."

Between Bram's confusion over Tally's distracted mood and her vague guilt feelings about leaping to unjustified conclusions, there was an awkward silence for a few minutes. In fact they were through Bishops Falls and almost to Interstate 93 when Bram finally broke the impasse.

"You do that very well, don't you?"

"What—drive?"

"No. Oh, well, yes. That, too, of course, but I was actually referring to your talk to the garden-club ladies. It was very smoothly done with some nice touches here and there."

"I wonder why you sound surprised," she mocked, flashing him a smile as she began picking up speed on the interstate.

"I thought you only acted in the privacy of the family," he mocked back.

Tally licked her forefinger and made a checkmark in the air. "Caught again. Can't get anything past that Ramsdale eagle eye, can I?"

She tossed him a quick grin and discovered that he was half turned in his seat, watching her with a curious intentness.

"No, you can't," he said slowly. "Not now, not after all the time I spent with you this weekend. It's a defense, isn't it? The wisecracks, the clever comebacks, the cool repartee. You do it whenever anyone gets too close, too personal, too hurtful. Oh, yes," he said quickly as she started to protest. "I've seen you with your Uncle Alden and Aunt Myra, remember. Some of the things they said to you Saturday evening when they stopped at our table would have had any other woman in tears, but you—"

"All right," said Tally with a resigned sigh. "You're far too observant, you know. You weren't supposed to pick up on all that. Nobody else does." She gave him another quick glance and found that he was still watching her, *willing* her to answer him honestly. "You're right. It is a form of defense," she admitted reluctantly. "I've learned not to let too many people get too close. It's also a way of hiding my feelings. Between mother's early training in the British stiff upper lip and the New England Yankee habit of keeping deep personal emotions under rigid control, it was necessary to build defenses and devise ways of ensuring privacy. We all have our own methods, although Dari and I have probably carried it further than the others, since we've long been the family rebels."

"So I've noticed," said Bram dryly.

"I didn't think we were that obvious."

"Face it, luv, some of those routines you and Dare go through do have a flavor of...conspiracy?"

"Conspiracy? Mmm, okay, I'll buy that," she agreed. "Dari and I often do conspire to send certain people up or to distract unwelcome attention from our personal affairs."

"Affairs?"

Tally gave him a quick look, noted his too bland

expression, and laughed. "A figure of speech, as you very well know. Stop fishing. Mine can't possibly be of the least interest...."

That's what you think, luv.

"And Dari's not only not interested, but he knows very well that Rosemary would skin him and roast the remains over a slow fire if she ever caught him messing around with another woman."

"Rosemary? Sweet, charming Rosemary?" Bram gave Tally a hard look. "Are we talking about the same person?"

"You bet," she assured him. "You're forgetting that for all her warmth, delightful personality and quick wit, Rosemary's a born Bishop. Underneath all that charm and laughter, she's tough as old boots and has a wicked temper."

"I find that difficult to believe," he scoffed. "She's got one of the calmest dispositions I've ever seen. She seems to—"

"Tut-tut, now," Tally chided with a sly grin. "You know what they say about leaping to conclusions. I'll grant you that Rosemary's normally the most even-tempered person in town. In fact, it takes a hell of a lot to ruffle her feathers, but it can be done. For instance, you should have been here during the Week of the Dragon Lady."

"What," asked Bram carefully, "was the Week of the Dragon Lady?" He didn't trust the twitching at the corner of Tally's lips and her obvious effort to maintain a straight face.

"It was actually the last week in July, a month before Dari and Rosemary were married. It had been a wild summer," she explained with a reminiscent smile. "As you've probably heard from Jean, the Bishops have always kept a pretty low profile. The bulk of the family fortune was already firmly established long before the Internal Revenue Service and tax returns existed, and we've always felt that it was nobody's business but our own what we owned or how much it was worth."

"Understandable," Bram murmured. "The English have a well-developed penchant for privacy."

Tally flicked him a questioning glance. "Pertinent to?"

"The first Bishops did arrive on these shores from England, didn't they?" he asked, assuming an expression of casual interest.

Tally laughed and lifted one hand in acknowledgment. "Checkmate. In any event, despite the IRS and other curious people, most of the family—with one or two notable exceptions—had managed to avoid personal publicity through the years, and our private business remained private. Until, that is, earlier in that year when Grandpa Carleton and my father were killed in that accident."

"What happened then?"

"Obituaries."

"Obituaries?" Bram echoed in confusion.

"Exactly. No one who runs a business empire the size of ours can possibly remain anonymous, no matter how much they avoid publicity. Every major newspaper and news magazine maintains an obituary file on prominent people, and—"

"Oh, yes, I see. We do it, too. When someone dies suddenly, all that needs doing is to add the last date."

"And send out reporters to interview other prominent people to get reaction quotes. Well, when dad and grandpa died, one sharp reporter got more than he expected from one of our New Hampshire congressmen. He quickly added two and four and came up cherries. By the next morning, every major paper in the country had a front-page story that detailed almost two-thirds of the family's holdings and included a list of the estimated personal fortunes of more than two hundred family members."

"My word. Your Uncle Alden must have done a fair imitation of Vesuvius in full eruption."

"Believe me, he wasn't alone. Until then very few people knew anything about our personal finances. Or about the extent of the family. You'd be amazed how many of us in my generation had managed to develop careers and satisfying lifestyles without anyone knowing exactly who we were or how much money we really had."

"And this interesting tidbit was made public? It must have brought out the fortune hunters in droves," Bram said thoughtfully. Remembering the odd flashes of wariness he'd occasionally seen in her eyes, he turned to give her a long speculative look. He wondered how many men had approached her with an eye to the main chance.

"Oh, yes. Also in herds, flights and flocks. Believe me, we all ran for cover. And if that wasn't bad enough, a few months later in June an enterprising lady in New York published a book about the hundred most eligible bachelors in the U.S. Would you believe six of my cousins made the list along with Dari and Steven?"

Bram couldn't contain a burst of laughter. "Oh, Lord," he gasped, "they must have gone spare."

"To put it mildly. Steven, of course, took the whole thing as a great joke and simply found some new hangouts. He also moved his living quarters and the legal offices to a new location and expanded his security staff."

"Wasn't that a bit drastic?"

"Not really. The author had evidently gotten to somebody who knew the family well. She published home addresses, private phone numbers, favorite restaurants and recreation spots, vacation homes and every other bit of private information you could think of. Even with Steven's fast footwork, a number of women managed to fling themselves in his path for months afterward."

"How did he handle it? Those women can be bloody persistent," Bram said, obviously recalling his own experiences.

"Steven has an interesting sense of humor. Brian McKay, his chief bodyguard, took to carrying an attaché case full of T-shirts and—"

"*T-shirts?*"

"Whenever a strange woman accosted Steven, he'd give her his most charming smile, kiss her cheek and pass her along to Brian while he made his escape. Brian would also smile charmingly, hand her a T-shirt, and take off after Steven while the woman was still staring at her new purple shirt with the bright pink writing on the front that said, I've Been Kissed By Steven Bishop."

Bram laughed until he choked. Finally he managed to gasp, "Should I ask what Dare did?"

"He literally ran for the hills. For once his sense of humor took a vacation, and he was so mad he was just about frothing. He and Rosemary had announced their engagement a week before the book came out, and they'd planned to spend the summer celebrating with all the relatives who vacation at Snow Meadows. Well, the relatives started arriving—and so did a steady stream of women who were all just dying to meet 'darling Darius.' By Fourth of July weekend Rosemary was muttering to herself and practicing karate kicks every morning in the gym, and Dari had found a strange female lurking in his room for the third time in a week."

"I've had *that* experience," Bram growled. "Bloody cheek some of these women have."

"Don't they, though," Tally agreed. "Dari decided that the best defense was retreat. A group of us took off at dawn the next morning and back-packed up to the saddleback between the Aggies. There's a lovely little lake up there, and we had a great few days camping out. No strange women, no reporters, no photographers. Did I mention that we'd also been inundated by those? Eventually we decided to get back to work, and we returned to civilization at the end of the week. Except for Dari. He insisted he wasn't coming down off that mountain until the valley had been cleared of bar-racudas."

"Barracudas?"

Tally flipped a dismissing hand. "Whatever. With the combined efforts of the family, our security people, the inn staff and most of the population of the Falls, we finally managed to get rid of the fortune hunters and the media people. Probably our methods wouldn't bear too close a scrutiny, but they worked, and Dari agreed to come down. By now, of course, Rosemary was ready to slice and dice the next Dari-hunting woman who crossed her path.''

"Need I ask if one did?''

"As luck would have it, the afternoon that Dari arrived back at the inn one got by us.''

"The Dragon Lady," Bram said wryly.

"The same. Actually she slipped through quite easily. She was a very well-known actress, you see—no, I won't tell you who—and a couple of my California cousins knew her. Dari had, in fact, met her several months before when he was visiting them. She was perfectly charming to everyone for the first two or three days, and we even agreed to let her secretary take some photos for her personal scrapbook.''

"The plot thickens?''

"Did it ever! Rosemary got a look at some of the pictures one day and called Steven. Seems all of them showed the Dragon Lady and Dari apparently alone and apparently having a lovely private vacation. For a secretary, that gal was an exceptionally clever photographer. Steven agreed that it all looked rather suspicious—you must realize that by then the whole bunch of us were slightly paranoid—and he arrived that evening just in time to prevent Rosemary from committing murder.''

"The mind boggles," Bram commented, starting to chuckle. "What set her off?''

"Dari had gone upstairs to change for dinner—he was still living at the inn then—and Rosemary decided to join him so they could have a few minutes alone. She'd just turned the corner into his hallway when she saw Miss Secretary fling open his door and start shooting pictures. I was coming along behind Rosemary on my way to my own room, and the next thing I knew she was yelling fit to wake the dead and charging into Dari's room. Then Dari started bellowing, someone began screaming, and the secretary was busily snapping away. She hadn't seen me, so I didn't have much trouble grabbing the camera on my way into the room."

"A setup, I take it."

"Lord, yes. There was Dari soaking wet and wearing nothing but a towel, obviously just coming out of the bathroom, and there was the Dragon Lady bare as an egg and screaming like she'd just been cracked. Rosemary was hauling her off the bed by her hair and swearing a blue streak. You couldn't blame the Dragon Lady for being terrified. She wasn't much bigger than I am, and here was this Amazon threatening to throw her out the window and looking mad enough to do it."

"What did happen?" Bram asked weakly between bouts of laughter.

"Dari and I managed to convince Rosemary that she couldn't toss her out the window, so she shoved the dear thing out into the hall, still naked, and told her to scat. Unfortunately, she didn't know when to leave well enough alone. As soon as she saw her secretary, she started screeching about having a witness and selling her story to the papers. Rosemary went through the roof. She got a fierce grip on the Dragon Lady's wrist and began tearing down the hall, dragging her along behind. Dari was still dressed in a towel, so he shoved me out the door, roaring 'Stop her before she kills the bitch!' I don't know what he thought I could do, but I raced after them and caught up in time to see Rosemary hauling the Dragon Lady down the main stairs into a lobby full of guests and transients who were coming in to dine."

"She never dragged this naked actress through that crowd!"

"Oh, yes, she did. Muttering all the time about the best way to get rid of cats is to drown them. By then I was hanging onto Rosemary's free arm and trying to at least slow her down until Dari could catch up."

Tally shook her head and grinned at the memory. "You should have seen it. Pure chaos. Half the crowd was trying to get out of the way, while the other half was pushing forward to get a better look. Grandma Amy was whacking every shin in reach to clear a path through the mob, and Uncle Alden was bellowing like a wounded moose at everyone in general. And Rosemary just kept plowing ahead, hauling the Dragon Lady and me in her wake."

"Where does Steven come into all this?" Bram was making an effort to restrain his mirth so he could concentrate on Tally's narrative and her laughing face.

"He and Brian arrived just in time to block Rosemary's charge out the front door. I managed to give him the gist of what was happening, and he started sweet-talking Rosemary to calm her down while Brian tried to pry the Dragon Lady loose. They might have made it except that Steven made the mistake of pointing out that the Dragon Lady's hand was turning blue from loss of circulation. Rosemary got this really weird expression, like she'd seen a vision, and then suddenly whipped around and headed for the dining room. Everyone raced after her as she made a beeline for a display of old hand-blown bottles filled with colored liquids. Rosemary had arranged the display, and she knew that the darker colors were inks rather than vegetable-dyed water."

"She didn't!"

"Want to bet? She yanked the stopper out of a beautiful swan-neck decanter that must have held at least two quarts, and began slowly pouring blue *indelible* ink over the Dragon Lady's head. Did I mention that she was blond? I think she went into shock. She just stood there staring at the rivulets of blue ink trickling down across her breasts and stomach. After a minute Rosemary let go of her and began rubbing the ink into her hair and then guiding the flow over her shoulders and across her back. It was incredible. Rosemary had this expression of total concentration, as if she were creating a work of art, and everyone just stood there watching her turn this famous actress into a Blue Meenie. You could have heard a leaf curl. Finally Rosemary stood back, nodded once and marched over to the buffet table. She scooped a huge bouquet of long-stemmed red roses out of a vase, marched back to the Dragon Lady, shoved them into her arms, and literally snarled, 'Red roses for a truly blue lady. Sell *that* to the papers!' Before anyone could move, Steven muttered in my ear, 'Quick! Get a picture!' I realized I still had the camera so I started snapping away and managed to get half a dozen clear shots before Brian wrapped a tablecloth around her and led her out.''

They were pulling into a wide driveway beside a large brick colonial house before Bram managed to get himself under control again. ''Rosemary, of all people. Lord, but I wish I'd been there.'' He leaned back and gave Tally a sardonic look. ''Am I right in assuming that the lady decided that a lawsuit wouldn't be worth having those pictures see print?''

''You know it. However, one good thing did come out of it all. With a crowd that size it was impossible to keep the incident quiet, and word spread like poison ivy. Would you believe we weren't bothered by the press or Dari-hunters for months? Even the media people who covered Dari and Rosemary's wedding asked permission first.''

''Oh, I believe it,'' Bram said absently, his attention focused on her relaxed, laughing expression. As she switched off the engine, he reached out to capture her chin between thumb and forefinger and gently turned her face toward him. ''I also believe that you're extremely talented at evasive tactics.''

Tally caught her bottom lip between her teeth and looked at him with a mixture of wariness, guilt and amusement. He smiled at her encouragingly, but she could see an unmistakable sense of purpose behind the wry humor in his eyes.

"Hossapples," she muttered finally, dropping her eyes from his too knowing gaze and letting her breath out in a gusty sigh. "You definitely see too much, Ramsdale. Are you going to leave me with any secrets?"

"I'm not sure yet," he murmured, sliding his hand up to cup the side of her face. He lightly brushed his thumb across her lips and grinned as her startled eyes snapped wide open. *Slowly, man, slowly. This isn't the time to push it.*

With practiced skill he subtly relaxed the tension of the moment, lightening his expression with a teasing grin and gently tweaking her nose as he withdrew his hand from her face. "Perhaps we could work a trade-off," he purred with an exaggerated leer. "You tell me your secrets, and I'll tell you mine."

For just a moment, force of habit brought her chin up and her eyes flashed gold sparks, but then she chuckled and gave him a wide-eyed ingenuous look and gasped in a little-girl voice, "You mean you'll tell me how you make all those women fall in a heap at your feet!"

"Vixen," he said with an appreciative grin. "That can't be explained. I'll have to show you. In fact—"

"Never mind," Tally said hastily, reaching for the door handle. "We'd better get a move on or I'll be late."

Bram looked around for the first time, noting

the handsome house set in carefully maintained lawns and gardens and shaded by huge maple and beech trees. "This is a lovely place, but what are we doing here?"

"This is Steven's office," Tally explained, laughing at his surprised expression. "It's also the legal heart of the Bishop empire, complete with computers, vaults, and a security system that has the CIA green with envy. Steven lives in the barn."

"In the *barn*?"

"Former barn. It's now a very plush bachelor's pad. Hot tub, fur rugs, waterbed—you name it, he's got it. Come on. We'll see about lunch and then I'll borrow one of Steven's bright young things to chauffeur you around."

As Bram followed her along the walk to the front door, lunch and shopping were the furthest things from his mind. He was far more occupied with speculations as to just how and when he could find some time alone with her when they weren't in a moving vehicle.

CHAPTER FIVE

BRAM CAUGHT STEVEN'S EYE and lifted an inquiring eyebrow, tilting his head slightly toward Tally. She hadn't said a word since she and Steven had joined him in the restaurant a few minutes earlier. From the tight, mutinous line of her mouth and the golden sizzle of her tan eyes, he concluded that she was laboring under strong emotion.

"Ignore her," Steven said breezily. "She's just having a fuming fit, but it'll pass off as soon as she gets a couple of ounces of alcohol in her system."

"Would you like something from the bar before ordering?" asked a waitress who seemed to have materialized at Steven's elbow.

"Good thinking, Karen. I'll have a Beefeaters, please. Bram?"

"A very dry martini, please."

"And the Ugly Duckling, there, will have a Seabreeze," Steven added, laughing at the scowl his cousin directed at him.

With an incoherent mumble, Tally abruptly left the table and headed for the foyer and the ladies' lounge.

"What brought on the fuming fit, or shouldn't one ask?"

"Our Tally has never learned to suffer fools gracefully," said Steven somewhat cryptically. At Bram's snort of amusement, he chuckled and added, "Sorry. It's not a secret. Tally's client wants to give the building contract for his house to Jaketon Brothers Construction, and she's adamantly opposed."

"And Tally doesn't often lose a battle?"

"Not often, and she hasn't lost this one. We make sure her contracts include a clause giving her right of approval of the general contractor. After all, if she designs a beautiful structure, she doesn't want it thrown together by some cut-rate builder."

"The Jaketon Brothers?"

"The same, but don't quote me. Nothing's ever been proved, but it's general knowledge that they've cut more than a few corners on building specifications to make an extra buck."

"Why in heaven's name would anyone hire them, then?" asked Bram in some confusion.

"Low bids," Steven explained succinctly. "If it's anything to do with state or federally funded construction, they have to take the low bid. There's also a number of individuals who'll go first for price and count on being able to keep an eye on the job to ensure quality. However, if a contractor's clever—and the Jaketons are—it's almost impossible to catch him cheating unless you want to sit on the job every minute or start tearing up finished work to find out what's underneath."

"So if Tally blocked the Jaketons from getting the contract...." Bram left the question unspoken as the waitress delivered their drinks.

"Mr. Hitchley, her client, doesn't like opposition, either. Things got a bit heated, and he accused her of trying to throw the contract to Darius, implying that her brother gave her kickbacks for steering lucrative jobs his way."

"What!" Bram was torn between laughter and sympathetic umbrage. "Doesn't he know...?"

"Who we are? Evidently not." Steven shook his head in mock amazement. "The man must have been living in a cave for the past few years. He doesn't seem to have a clue."

"Don't keep me in suspense, man. Tell me how you solved it," urged Bram as Tally slipped back into her seat.

"I didn't have to," said Steven. "The Terror, here, leaped on her high horse and announced that she'd only accept Pete Morelli—he was the third bidder—and that if Hitchley was too strapped to pay the extra two thousand, she'd be more than happy to cover it herself."

Steven lifted his glass toward Tally and asked teasingly, "Did you learn that in Client Handling 210, or does it just come naturally?"

"Funny," Tally growled, but there was finally a hint of laughter in her eyes, Bram noted. "Come on, Steven, you know perfectly well the man's a pompous...clod. I used up all my tact trying to overcome his and dear Muriel's appalling taste in architecture to design them a reasonably attractive house."

She leaned toward Bram and smiled wryly. "Would you believe she wanted a waterfall in one corner of the living room—just a small one, mind you, nothing ostentatious—with a lucite-covered stream wending its graceful way across to the greenhouse where it would empty into a rock pool full of goldfish? That's right, laugh, you two. It took me three weeks to talk her out of that one. Then she decided she wanted a sun porch on the roof. No problem, you say? Ah, but she wanted *her* porch to turn 'just like that lovely restaurant on the Seattle Space Needle, you know.'" Tally did a creditable imitation of Muriel Hitchley's high gushing tones.

"How did you talk her out of that?" asked a fascinated Bram.

"I didn't even try. I just gave old Skinflint Hitchley a detailed estimate of the engineering and maintenance costs for it. He did the rest—after he turned back to his normal color."

As the men's chuckles died away, Steven turned to Tally and asked, "Did you have a chance to look over the prospectus on that condo development in the Thousand Islands? Do you want in?"

"I haven't decided yet," she answered. "I've only had time to glance over the specs, but it does look interesting. Good design, and they've been careful not to damage the ecology of the island. If, that is, the developer follows through on his stated intentions."

"If we back it," said Steven, "we'll put a watchdog on the project."

"Are you looking for investors?" asked Bram with obviously serious interest.

The cousins turned to him with chagrined expressions.

"Sorry," Tally apologized. "That was rude of us."

Bram waved the apology aside. "Not at all. But if you are looking for investors in a condo development, I might be interested—especially if the Bishops are backing it."

"Not as a family holding," Steven explained, looking at Bram speculatively. "Some of us think it looks good as a personal investment. The development is on one of the Thousand Islands in the St. Lawrence River which, as you probably know, forms part of the border between the U.S. and Canada. It's a beautiful area, and a well-planned condo community should do well as a vacation retreat."

"Sounds interesting," Bram said. "I don't have many holdings on this side of the Atlantic. Just bits and pieces in Canada. Interest in some wheat land, a couple of speculative things to do with oil and gas leases."

He glanced at Tally as she made an inarticulate sound. Her expression of surprised curiosity brought a gleam of mischief to his eyes. "Did you think I was just another pretty face?" he teased, enjoying the flush of color that rose in her face. "It's shocking the way actors get stereotyped." He sighed, winking at Steven. "Brawny, brainless, and bent on blowing all their money on life's more extravagant pleasures."

"Blame your press agent," said Tally, finally rallying her forces. "You have to admit that you're usually touted as the playboy of the Western world. I've never heard a word, not even from Jean, about your being an investment pro. In fact, I was under the impression that Sid handled your business affairs."

"He does, for the most part," Bram agreed. "He's very good at it, too, and has a nice touch with speculative investments. That's the part I got interested in a few years ago. Sid taught me everything he could and encouraged me to take some courses. Finally, he decided I was ready to solo and turned over a certain sum of money, telling me to have at it."

"How have you done?" asked Steven with unfeigned interest.

"Not too badly, actually," said Bram, clearly amused by the cousins' reactions. "I've managed to build my little lot into a reasonably tidy fortune in the past five years. Of course," he acknowledged, "I could afford to take some rather high risks since I knew that the bulk of my money was safe in Sid's capable hands."

"Don't downgrade your achievements," chided Tally. "It takes a fine instinct to make money on high-risk investments."

During lunch they discussed investment potentials in a number of areas, and Bram easily held his own with the savvy Bishops. By the time they finished eating, he'd sensed a subtle shifting in Tally's and Steven's attitude toward him. A new element of respect had been added, and he couldn't help but wonder how this would affect his growing involvement with Tally.

"Bram?"

"Mmm? Oh, sorry. A sudden thought."

"Did you want anything else?" Steven asked, glancing at his watch. "More coffee? I've got an appointment in fifteen minutes, but if you two would like to linger, I'll send the car back for you."

"No, no, I'm fine. Tally?"

"I'm full. We'll go back with you, Steven. We ought to be getting on our way anyhow. I want to catch up with Dari before he goes home."

Over Bram's protests Steven signed the check, with the bland explanation that he could use it for a tax deduction since he and Tally had more or less discussed business. Tally's teasing recounting of her cousin's creative approach to tax deductions kept them laughing during the short drive back to Steven's, and Bram had to wait until they were standing beside the Wagoneer to extend a reciprocal invitation.

"The next time you're at the inn you must come over to the cottage for dinner. Merton does marvelous things with steak-and-kidney pie. You'll come, too, won't you, Tally? And perhaps Rosemary and Dare would like to join us."

"Sounds good to me," Steven said agreeably. "Tally?" At her nod of acceptance, he flicked an enigmatic look between his unusually acquiescent cousin and the handsome, charming Englishman at her side, and added, "Will it be all right if I even out the odds?"

"By all means," Bram said. "Shall we set a date?"

"That's easy enough," Tally chimed in. "This next weekend is the long Memorial Day holiday, and you'll be up then, won't you, Steven?"

"Wouldn't miss it."

"Uncle A would have your head if you did," Tally muttered.

Steven ignored the interruption and explained to Bram, "Saturday night is the first dinner-dance of the summer season, and it's one of our rare command performances. The inn is probably booked full with relatives and our regulars. Even the seasonal guests who won't be coming to stay for another few weeks try to make it for this weekend."

"Sounds like quite a party. Perhaps we should wait—"

"We don't have to," Tally interrupted. "Saturday night is the only unalterable commitment we have. How about Sunday? Steven?"

"Fine by me. Let's see. Who'd be a good one to add to this group? What about Merrylegs? Is she going to be there?"

Tally groaned. "Steven, you've got to stop calling her that. Her name is really Meredith," she explained to Bram, "and she's one of the Phoenix Prestons. I think mother said they were all coming, Steven. At least she's got one of the Lears scheduled to meet a Phoenix flight in New York on Friday."

"Terrific. If you see her before I do, nail her down for Sunday. You'll like her, Bram. Strange sense of humor. Comes of living with all that hot southwestern sun."

Bram chuckled as he slid into the car beside Tally. "That explains your Phoenix cousin," he goaded Steven. "What's the excuse for you two?"

"New Hampshire mountain high!" chorused Tally and Steven, laughing.

"Too right," Bram agreed. "Thanks for lunch, Steven. See you this weekend," he called as Tally began moving down the driveway.

The drive back to Snow Meadows was quiet. When Tally noticed Bram rubbing his leg, he admitted that it was aching. "Probably from walking so much on pavement. I haven't gotten used to that, yet. Not to worry. A session in the whirlpool when I get back should set it right again."

She gave him a quick, assessing look. "You've done too much in too short a time. See? You can't even hold back a yawn. Take a nap," she ordered succinctly.

To ensure his compliance, she slotted a Mozart tape into the stereo deck and retreated into her own thoughts. That those thoughts were centered on the man dozing beside her was a fact that she didn't consciously acknowledge. His surprising financial expertise had added a new element to a situation that she was finding more disconcerting at each of their encounters. His growing understanding of her was also rather unnerving. She wasn't at all sure that she wanted Bram, or any other man, to be so tuned in to the inner workings of her mind. Perhaps, she decided finally, it would be just as well to cool things for a few days.

Much to his chagrin, Bram did fall asleep and didn't wake until Tally nudged him. "All out, Bram. Sorry to drop you and run, but I still want to catch Dari. I'll be in touch about the arrangements for Sunday. Bye."

He barely had time to close the car door before she was whipping around the circle in front of the cottage and heading back for the road. He stared after her, shaking his head in ongoing disbelief. The woman was unreal. She obviously didn't have a dissembling bone in that enticing little body. Anyone else would have waited at least long enough for him to ask for another date if he wished.

Although "date," he thought a few minutes later as he relaxed in the soothing warmth of the whirlpool, was something of a misnomer for their encounters. So far they'd all been spur-of-the-moment engagements initiated by either Edna or himself. Even the hours spent as a foursome with Rosemary and Dare had been at their invitation, not Tally's.

He acknowledged that she intrigued him more and more after each meeting. On the surface they were very compatible, each having a broad general background in the arts, world affairs, history and current events, and they were both articulate and witty conversationalists. He enjoyed her rather cynical, offbeat sense of humor, and she clearly appreciated his understated English style of wit.

So why did she keep him at arm's length? Bram stretched restlessly in the churning water while the question nagged at the edges of his understanding. She was neither frigid nor a man-hater, he was sure. Once or twice, from the corner of his eye, he'd caught her looking at him with an unmistakable awareness and a definite hint of interest. Also, no woman with such a volatile temperament could be indifferent to man's—and woman's—

strongest basic drive. Nor did he believe for a moment that she was anything so antediluvian as a thirty-one-year-old virgin.

He thought about that for a moment and then shook his head decisively. No, not when one considered the way she moved with that graceful freedom and complete lack of self-consciousness. There was also that knowing gleam in her eye, he remembered, when she teased Dare and Rosemary or, as today, Steven. No question about it, even if she was soloing now, she'd gained some degree of experience in the past.

Well, then, he fumed in frustration, what was her problem? She was at least mildly interested, but she wasn't sending out even a faint try-me signal. She had to know he was intrigued, but she wasn't giving him as much as half an inch to approach her on any but the most casually friendly basis.

He climbed awkwardly out of the hot tub and began toweling himself dry, still provoked by the question of Tally's coolness.

By the time the holiday weekend and its accompanying influx of visitors had arrived, Bram's provocation had turned into irritation. He didn't know whether she was deliberately playing least-in-sight, but the fact remained that he'd had no more than fleeting glimpses of Tally since their trip to Concord.

Brooding over breakfast Saturday morning, he mentally berated himself. Boredom, he decided, that's what it is. *Now that I'm gaining strength and mobility, I don't have enough to do. Why else would I be sitting around in what could only be termed a sulk because that little witch is ignoring me? This is ridiculous. What am I doing here alone when I could be breakfasting with Steven and his clutch of mad cousins? And if that half-size Tartar doesn't want to give me an opportunity to invite her to be my partner at that dinner-dance tonight, I'll damn well find someone else who will!*

"Merton!"

"Yes, Mr. Ramsdale? Did you decide on eggs or—"

"Nothing more, Merton. I'll be finishing breakfast at the inn. Oh, and don't expect me for lunch," he called back on his way toward the front door.

Bram's pique, which he freely admitted was an accurate description of his mood, lasted all the way to the entrance to the Gazebo. It died a sudden death when his searching gaze found, instead of Steven, Tally's laughing face turned toward him.

"Bram! Over here," she called, motioning for him to join the dozen or so people grouped around a long table. "Can you move down a bit, Phil? Thanks. Grab that empty chair, Bram. You should be able to squeeze in between Caro and me."

To Bram's amazement, Tally leaned even closer, smiled happily at him and murmured under cover of the laughter and talk, "I wondered where you were. Steven said he'd asked you last night to join us for breakfast, but as you can see we've already started." She reached for a huge bowl still half full of fresh fruit salad. "Would you like some of this? It'll be a few more minutes before the hot dishes come out."

"I, er, yes, that's fine," stammered Bram, groping to make some rapid mental readjustments. "Sorry I was late. I don't recall Steven specifying a particular time."

"He probably didn't. These gatherings tend to be on the casual side. Come as you are when you're ready," said Tally before turning her attention briefly to the rest of the group.

With a deep but well-hidden protective instinct, she looked first for Pip and found her holding court from a strategic position at the end of the long table. Tally smiled to herself, knowing that Pip had cleverly chosen her spot so that she had the clearest view possible of the majority of the people at the table and was thus able to follow at least the gist of the several conversations.

Pip caught her eye, and her flashing fingers signed a pithy comment about gabbling geese and pâté de fois gras. Tally laughed and signed back an utterly scatological pun that sent her sister into whoops.

"What was that all about?" Bram's warm breath feathered across her ear, and she knew that if she turned her head, his lips would brush her cheek. It was undeniably tempting.

Reluctantly opting for discretion, she shifted two inches to her left and turned just far enough to meet his quizzical gaze. "It's sign language. Oh, all right," she capitulated when he merely quirked a well-defined eyebrow. "We were exchanging some raunchy repartee. A commentary on the passing scene, one might say."

"I'm not even going to pretend to understand that," said Bram with an exaggerated sigh. "But it hardly seems fair to leave a visitor—a guest, so to speak—in ignorance of the most interesting conversations. Yes, you ought to look ashamed," he said blandly, ignoring her gurgle of laughter. "I think you owe it to me to offer compensation."

"Such as?"

"Such as attending this dinner-dance with me tonight," said Bram, quickly grasping opportunity with both hands. "Not that I can do much dancing, but I'm sure I'll enjoy watching you. You're not going with anyone else, are you?"

Tally turned to look at him more fully, and Bram was surprised to see a shadow of uncertainty cloud her eyes. It only lasted for a second, and then she was smiling and murmuring, "No, I'm not going with anyone in particular, and, yes, I'd like to attend with you. We usually form tables of six or eight. Okay?"

"Fine. Dare and Rosemary? Who else— Steven?"

"And Merrylegs. Oh, drat, he's got me doing it now."

"Why Merrylegs?"

"Wait until you see her dance! That's six. Shall I ask Pip and Phil to join us?"

"I'd like that, but will it bother Pip that I don't know sign language? You all seem to."

"I don't think Merrylegs does, but Pip won't mind anyhow. Just make sure that she's looking at you and has a clear view of your mouth when you speak to her. She's a whiz at reading lips. Hardly ever misses a word, and she'll let you know if she does! Hang in a minute while I check with Phil.''

Tally swung around and put her hand on her brother-in-law's shoulder. He turned at her touch, his tanned, handsome face breaking into a warm smile. "What's up, Mighty Mouse?"

Tally groaned in mock agony. "I *was* going to ask if you and Pip would like to make up an eight for dinner tonight, but if that's the way you're planning on carrying on, perhaps I'd do better to ask Uncle Alden and Aunt Myra," she threatened.

Phil let out a bark of laughter. "When the Aggies melt to anthills, that's when you'll voluntarily sit at the same table with Myra and Alden. An eight sounds fine, although we've made tentative plans with Dare and Rosemary."

"That's okay. We want them, too."

"We?" Phil's knowing blue eyes widened in interested inquiry.

"Bram and I," Tally muttered, trying to scowl him down.

Blue eyes met green over Tally's head. After a few seconds Bram winked, and Phil uttered a satisfied, "Ah."

"I wish you two would stop that," Tally complained, looking from one smug masculine face to the other. "I don't like the feeling that I'm missing something."

"If you are, it would be the first time in recorded history," Phil assured her. "Who else is making up this eight?"

"We thought Steven and Merrylegs. She seems to be his partner for the weekend." Tally chose to ignore Phil's smirk at that second 'we' and simply smiled sweetly at him, enjoying his look of mild alarm. Sweetness, as he very well knew, was not one of her character traits.

"Sounds like a winning combo. Everyone meet in the lobby at seven-thirty? That should give us time for a drink before dinner."

Tally and Bram nodded their agreement, and the conversation turned to plans for the rest of the day.

TALLY STRETCHED AND THEN RELAXED in boneless contentment on the blanket, her head pillowed on Seth's diaper bag. She could hear Seth and the other young children shouting and laughing in the fenced playground beyond the tennis courts. One good thing about having such a huge family, she thought idly, was the availability of ready-made babysitters. Another was that there was always someone to entertain guests if one should wish, as she did right now, to lie peacefully in the sun and meditate.

She wriggled her bare toes and hoped that everyone would take the hint of her closed eyes and leave her alone for a while. From the noise level of the chatter coming from the broad patio overlooking the tennis courts, it sounded as if both players and spectators were managing to amuse themselves quite happily.

Under the mildly enervating force of the sun, she let her mind drift. *Beautiful day... didn't do too badly for the first tennis game of the year . . . wonder where mother found this outfit . . . skimpy doesn't begin to describe it . . . at least it's lavender, but did she have to get lace-edged panties? Too much. . . . Wonder what's bugging Dari and Steven . . . something is . . . did they think I wouldn't notice those looks they keep exchanging? . . . something recent . . . Rosemary doesn't seem to know . . . I wonder . . . those accidents at the motel complex . . . Hardy Jaketon really wanted that job . . . would he dare? Probably, and Sonny definitely would . . . Steven can be bloody stubborn, but I might be able to worm it out of Dari. . . .*

Tally felt as much as heard the thud beside her, but didn't open her eyes until a heavy, warm weight settled on her stomach. She looked down into Splendid's unblinking yellow gaze.

"Silly cat. What are you doing down here with all these people?" she crooned, running her fingers through his cheek ruff, then tracing the finely drawn black markings on his head, and finally sinking her agile fingers into the thick fur behind his left ear.

The big cat stretched luxuriously before settling back down with his eyes closed ecstatically and his muscular body vibrating with his deep, rumbling purr. Tally briefly considered and then discarded the idea of moving Splendid's heavy head off her stomach. It was really too hot in the sun to have all that warm fur spread over her. Splendid, she decided ruefully, was in one of his cuddly moods, and he could be incredibly persistent when he wanted to play lap cat. Oh, well, she could stand another half hour, and then she'd take him for a swim. The lake was still too cold, but the sun should have warmed the Olympic-size pool to a comfortable temperature.

What was she going to do about Bram? The question floated across the surface of her mind, spun around and returned to hover insistently. Maybe she should be asking what she wanted to do with him. Of course there was the obvious. He was undoubtedly one of the most sensual men she'd ever met, and there was no denying that he appealed to her physically. The attraction had been getting stronger over the weeks as he gained back lost weight and muscle tone. She'd always liked that broad-shouldered, lean-hipped athletic look, and when it came packaged with a ruggedly handsome face and those enticing green eyes and all that lovely thick red hair. . .it was well nigh irresistible. The fact that he was intelligent, witty and fun to be with was simply too much frosting on an already rich cake.

And we're back to the obvious, she thought with a mental groan. *So what's the problem? If that periodic gleam in his eye is anything to go by, he's more than willing.* She paused to consider that. Perhaps she should be wondering *why* he was interested. From everything she'd heard, she was definitely not the type of woman he usually dated. Novelty? That was a possibility. His usual companions, according to Jean, were tall, elegantly thin, very stylish and either models, actresses or socialites.

Well, thought Tally with wry amusement, that lets me out. The top of her head barely cleared his shoulder; she was slim but not thin and more athletic than elegant; although she recognized high fashion, she wasn't particularly interested in it; and despite the fact that she had the entree to capital-S Society in Boston, New York, London and a few other places, she'd long ago found the whole scene boring and decided that there were far more interesting and satisfying things she wanted to do with her life.

Next question. Did she want to be Bram's American novelty? She choked back a giggle. That made her sound like something fished out of a Crackerjack box. Was it important? Did it really matter how he thought of her? We aren't talking about the love affair of the century, she admitted, with her usual devastating honesty. We're looking at two healthy, reasonably well-adjusted adults who have a strong physical attraction for each other and who enjoy each other's company. The stars aren't falling out of the sky, and the Aggies aren't splitting asunder.

No, they weren't—but perhaps they should be. She tried to consider the matter logically. Was she being too dispassionate about this? An intellectual decision to have a summer affair was one thing; actually doing it was another. Or perhaps it was her libido making the decision. After all, despite everyone's belief that she'd been living it up when she was out of the family's sight, she'd never really been all that free with her favors. Two affairs in thirty-one years wouldn't win her even a small Miss Promiscuity button.

Her drowsy train of thought was once more interrupted by the sound of a body coming to rest beside her, followed by a deep, masculine "Ah" of relief. She opened one eye and looked to her left. Her other eye flew open at the sight of Bram stretched out on his side next to her, leaning on one elbow as he smiled smugly down at her.

"I had a bet with myself that you weren't really asleep. Your toes are twitching."

"If it weren't for this cuddly cat, you'd have lost. I was almost asleep when he decided to use my stomach for a pillow."

"Smart cat," murmured Bram.

"Forget it," Tally said, correctly reading the gleam in his eye. "I have a feeling that being a pillow for you would be a lot more—" She stopped abruptly and gave him a chagrined look.

"Yes?" he drawled encouragingly. "A lot more what?"

"Never mind. Forget I said that. Where have you been all afternoon?" she asked with a hopeful change of subject. "I haven't seen you—"

She stopped again and rolled her eyes up with a grimace of self-disgust. It was perfectly obvious where he'd been, she thought, as she belatedly took in his bare torso and legs, their virile sweep of sinewy muscle broken only by an exceptionally brief maroon swimsuit. She also noted in passing his damp hair, rapidly drying in the sun, and the towel he'd spread out to lie on.

"Oh, Lord," she muttered, closing her eyes against his amused expression. "The sun must be frying my brains."

"Don't go," he said quickly as he sensed her gathering herself to rise. "Do you know how difficult it is to ever find you alone?"

She lifted her head and looked around pointedly at the children in the distance, the tennis players on the courts below and to their right, and the milling group on the patio. She turned a laughing face toward him and asked, "Alone?"

"Close enough," he said with a shrug. "I doubt that anyone will interrupt us."

His quirked eyebrow acknowledged his awareness of her family's matchmaking tendencies, and she sighed an agreement. "You're probably right. However, the term 'alone' is a bit relative in this case. We may be out of earshot, but we're certainly in full view. Just what did you have in mind?"

He held her gaze for a beat before murmuring, "Conversation?"

"About?"

She wasn't really paying much attention to their verbal exchange. Her senses were overloading on her all too intense awareness of his size, strength and near nakedness. His handsome face was much too close, his green eyes much too bright, his soft thick hair much too tempting to her fingers, his sensuous mouth much too enticing. . . .

She closed her eyes and quickly turned her head away. The silence between them lengthened. She could feel him watching her, smell the chlorine from his swim in the pool, and hear the deepening rhythm of his breathing.

She cleared her throat, but her voice was still

husky as she asked, "What did you want to talk about?"

For a moment she didn't think he was going to answer, and then she sensed as much as heard him shift his position. His one-word answer, "You," came from at least two feet farther away.

Squinting against the bright sunlight, she turned her head back toward him and, much to her amazement, heard herself ask, "What do you want to know?"

I don't believe I said that. This man is dangerous. How could I have given him an opening like that?

Bram had turned onto his stomach and was propped up on his elbows watching her changing expressions. Knowing how closely she guarded her privacy, he was almost as surprised as she that she'd given him such a lead, but he wasted no time in taking advantage of the opportunity.

"Will you tell me why you're so wary, so defensive?"

"I thought I had."

"Not really. You know I'm not a fortune hunter, nor am I trying to chalk up a conquest of a Bishop heiress, nor am I a reporter. Yet, despite our obvious attraction for each other, you keep holding me at arm's distance. Time and again I've seen that cautious, measuring look, as if you're trying to figure out what I'm *really* after. If I didn't know better, I'd almost think you were afraid of me. Or are you? Do you think I'm going to hurt you somehow?"

"Of course not," she said quickly and then continued more slowly, "It's not you personally. It's—"

She broke off in confusion, unsure how much to tell him. Meeting his waiting gaze, she saw something deeper and more intense than mere casual interest and felt a response, a reaching out to him from her most private self.

"All right. I'll tell you," she said, reaching down to shift Splendid's head off her stomach. She turned on her side to face Bram, propping her head up on one hand. "You're quite right. I am wary of involvements with men, even with someone I'm attracted to. Even with someone I'm sure isn't trying to take advantage of me. I learned the hard way, long ago, to be cautious, and I guess it's now become such a habit that I do it automatically."

"You had a bad experience with a user," Bram said, making it more of a statement than a question.

She looked beyond him, staring unseeingly at the granite outcroppings of the high ridges. "True. And not once, but twice. And to complicate matters, the first time was all tangled up with a bitter battle with my family."

Bram rolled onto his side to face her again and caught her free hand, which was nervously plucking blades of grass. He wrapped his hand around hers in a warm clasp and said, "Tell me."

With her gaze fixed on the distant ridges, she began to talk about experiences she'd never discussed with anyone.

"As you've discovered by now from Dari, Steven and some of the others, I've always had a strong, independent streak and a mind of my own. It didn't matter too much when I was very young, although there were occasional arguments when I balked at fitting into the expected mold. However, when I was eighteen and ready for college, everything blew up into a major battle between me and my father and Grandpa Carleton. I was determined to study engineering at MIT, and they were determined that I should go to a 'regular' college and study something 'proper.'

"Finally, after months of arguing, they tried to force me into going their way by threatening to cut off my trust income. Dad and Grandpa Carleton were the trustees for the trust funds that belonged to Cyrus, Dari, Pip and me."

She glanced at Bram and, noting his quizzical expression, explained, "The basic trusts were established early in the century. I couldn't begin to explain the complexities of the legal end of it. It's incredibly intricate, but the end result is that every Bishop descendant acquires a trust fund when he or she is born. The principal is controlled by trustees until boys reach twenty-one and girls reach twenty-five, and then control is turned over to us. The income from the trusts is used for allowances, education, extraordinary expenses, and reinvestment—all at the discretion of the trustees."

"I wish my ancestors had planned as carefully," said Bram. "Between gambling and a rotten business sense, they threw away a sizable fortune in the last century. By the time Alicia and I came along, there was nothing left but a meaningless title and a useless estate that didn't have enough land left to pay for itself.''

"How did you manage?'' asked Tally. "I'd assumed from things Jean said that you'd always had money. Didn't she and Alicia meet at a private girls' school?''

"My father was a career army officer. He was killed in the Far East when I was ten. My mother's family helped to supplement the benefits from the government, and paid for Alicia's and my schooling. Enough of me. What happened between you and your father and grandfather?''

"They refused to pay tuition and expenses for MIT, and I was ready to work my way through when my Great-Grandma Letty came to the rescue. She was in her eighties then, but still sharp as a tack and handled all her own business affairs. I was her favorite, probably because we were so much alike. She was small, too, and I look very much as she did when she was young. In any event, she gave me enough money to get all the way through graduate school as long as I was careful and reasonably thrifty.

"One of my schemes for supplementing income was to work summers as a waitress at a popular restaurant in Rockport, Massachusetts, which is a mecca for artists and tourists. That's where I met Neil the summer after I graduated from MIT. I was twenty-two and had been accepted at the Harvard School of Design.''

Tally stopped abruptly, unsure how to continue. Bram waited for a minute or two and then prompted, "Who was Neil?''

"He was an artist. Unknown but working hard. Handsome, intense, good sense of humor, intelligent—all the things that are guaranteed to capture the interest of a relatively inexperienced young woman who was overdue for a first love. I hadn't really had time, you see, to get involved with anyone before then. I'd been concentrating for four years on studying and working. Too much of both, probably, but I was determined to show dad and grandpa that they'd been wrong."

"And then Neil came along at the right moment," Bram murmured. "What happened?"

"We fell in love, became lovers and lived together for almost two years," said Tally. "The details aren't important now, only the way it ended. Neil had no idea, you see, that I was potentially rich. We were so involved with our relationship, his painting and my academic work at Harvard that we'd never spent much time discussing the past. I knew he came from Ohio and his parents were dead, and he knew that I came from New Hampshire and was at odds with my family."

Tally sighed and shrugged. "I probably should have seen it coming. Things were getting tense that last spring. I was buried in my studies and projects in the last push to complete my degree from Harvard, and Neil was becoming increasingly frustrated because he wasn't gaining the recognition he expected. It all came to a head the night we attended the opening of a touring Picasso show at the Museum of Fine Arts in Boston. We'd been arguing for days over his decision to move to New York where he thought he'd do better. I had no desire to live in New York, and things were very tense that night at the museum. The last thing I needed at that moment was to run smack into half a dozen Boston Adderlys.''

"More cousins?" asked Bram with a grin.

"What else?" Tally grimaced. "It was a mess. Oh, not at that point. I introduced Neil, and everyone chatted politely. They even invited us to have a late supper with them. It wasn't until Neil and I got home that I discovered he'd been doing a lot of questioning of my younger cousins while I was talking with Winton and Helene. He'd found out about the Bishops, my trust funds, my fight with the family and the fact that Helene Adderly was a power in the Boston art world. We had a fight to end all fights, and he finally packed his gear and walked out in a rage. Stupid, really. He'd made it clear that my money and influence were of prime importance, and then he went tearing off, ending everything, just four months before I got control of my three-and-a-half-million-dollar trust fund. It took a while, but I finally saw the humor of it all and could laugh about it.''

"But not at the time it happened," said Bram.

"No, not then. At the time I was rather devastated that I apparently meant no more to him, in the final analysis, than a meal ticket and an entree to the art world. I'd believed him, you see, when he kept telling me that he wanted to make it on his own, and I'd deliberately *not* called Helene Adderly on his behalf. Oh, well, I got over it in—"

"Did you?" asked Bram. "Hasn't that disillusionment stayed with you to some degree?"

"You're right. It has. It taught me not to trust too quickly and to look for motives when men start coming on to me. Even two years later when I had a brief affair, I never thought of opening up completely, and I wasn't all that surprised when I found out that Ian was as interested in my future plans to start my own practice as he was in me. He was also an architect and apparently decided that latching on to my talent, money and family contacts was a quick road to success."

Bram wasn't fooled by her light tone of voice. He could see the shadows of old hurts and disillusionments in her eyes. Just remembering had created a tension in her that he could feel through the tight grip of her hand in his.

"It's bloody hot out here," he said, wanting to give her time to unwind. "Why don't I go find us a cool drink of something."

"Sounds good. Make mine iced tea, please." She gave him a slightly wavery smile as he rose to his feet and walked toward the patio.

Feeling the sting of unexpected and unwelcome tears behind her eyes, she rolled onto her back, closing her eyes against the sun, and dropping one hand down to rest on Splendid's head. She willed back the tears, wondering why she should be letting long-healed wounds bother her so, wondering why she'd told Bram—

"Tally! I know you're awake; your toes are wiggling."

Tally blinked and squinted up at Jean, who was kneeling beside Splendid. "Hi. Where have you been all afternoon?"

"Running errands and chatting up the older generation," said Jean, wiping a trickle of perspiration from her flushed face. She shrugged out of her beach jacket, revealing a modest one-piece bathing suit. "Why don't you come swimming with me. The water in the pool's just right."

"Good thinking. As a matter of fact I'd already planned to take Splendid for a dip, but I'm waiting for Bram." Tally sat up and glanced over at the patio. "Looks like Grandma Amy's caught him, which means we've got time for a quickie before he gets back. Up, cat," she commanded as she rose to her feet in one fluid motion.

"But...but you can't take Splendid in the pool," Jean wailed.

"Why not? He loves to swim."

"Wait! Wait for me. And you've forgotten your tennis shoes," Jean called after her sister-in-law's strolling figure, which was accompanied by the majestically pacing feline.

Tally paused to let Jean catch up. "I don't need shoes. What do you suppose this outfit is made of?" she asked idly as she looked down at the narrow straps and low neck of her tennis dress. She fingered the hem of the very abbreviated skirt. "Polyester, isn't it? I do hope it doesn't shrink."

"Shrink? Why should it shrink?" Jean asked in a failing voice. "Oh, Tally, you're never going to—"

"Don't bet on it! Let's go, cat. Last one in's a shaggy dog!"

Tally broke into a run with the big cat galloping beside her. She angled toward the deep end of the pool, which was momentarily free of swimmers, and with hardly a break in her stride dove from the edge in a clean, deep dive, while Splendid leaped in after her with a tremendous splash.

"Cor!" exclaimed Bram inelegantly, coming up beside Jean and panting slightly after his quick walk from the patio. "Never say that beast swims!"

Jean waved an ineffectual hand and asked in heartfelt tones, "Which one?"

Bram merely chuckled, his attention fixed on the small woman and the huge cat pacing each other down the middle of the pool to a chorus of laughter and cheers from the other swimmers who were scrambling out of their way.

Oh, yes, indeed. I do believe it might be worth all the trouble.

CHAPTER SIX

"I SEE WHAT YOU MEAN about Merrylegs," Bram said, his gaze on the dancers' gyrations as everyone jitterbugged to "Chattanooga Choo-Choo," the last number in a medley of Glenn Miller favorites.

"Ma and Sid aren't doing too badly, either." Tally motioned to the far end of the dance floor where her mother and Sidney, elegant in evening clothes, were executing a restrained but nonetheless energetic lindy.

"You didn't have to sit this out with me, you know. I don't mind watching."

"Since you know perfectly well that I rarely do things I don't wish to do...." Tally let the sentence trail off as Bram gave a rueful grimace.

"Point to you. I shall protest no longer, but simply enjoy your company." Bram favored her with the grin that had sent theaters full of women into palpitations.

Tally blinked, looked into peridot eyes that were rapidly heating from "simmer" to "medium high," and managed a shaky laugh. "Stop that. If you make me blush, it will cause no end of gossip." She made a fast recovery although she had to call on all her reserves of self-possession to do so. On the theory that if you can't stand the heat, stay away from the stove, she deliberately gave him a look that should have sizzled his eyebrows and purred, "Want to try for the sprinkler system, or shall we quit when the smoke detectors go off?"

Bram stared at her for a long disbelieving moment and then burst into laughter. Propping her chin on her hands, she watched him with a smug smile.

"Whew," he sighed at last, wiping tears from his eyes. "No wonder Jean says you scare the wits out of most men. That's certainly an original method of damping the ardor."

"Mmm, yes, I've found it to be quite effective," she said blandly. "It's been my experience that when a man's bent on seduction, he has difficulty coping with the interjection of humor. If he gets mad, he's considered a poor sport, but if he laughs, he destroys the romantic aura of the moment."

"Damned if he does, and damned if he doesn't?"

"Exactly."

"Are you two going to share the joke or just sit there chortling to yourselves?" Steven's voice brought their attention back to their surroundings and the realization that the music had stopped and the rest of their group had returned to the table.

Tally flipped a dismissing hand. "You had to be here."

"I wish they'd play some disco," Merrylegs said wistfully.

"Not with this crowd," Dari explained.

Merrylegs looked around the room again. "Shades of Jimmy Dean, we're surrounded by the older generation. Where did Caro and Mugs and the others disappear to?"

"They've probably gone down to the Thunder Hole," said Steven. He glanced around the table and asked, "You guys up for some real dancing?"

Under cover of the ensuing discussion, Bram leaned closer to Tally and murmured, "What, or do I dare ask, is the Thunder Hole?"

"It's the disco lounge. Probably no one's mentioned it because it's been closed for a face-lift since the end of ski season."

"I thought I'd been all over the inn. Where is it?"

"In the basement under the gym. We put it as far from the guest rooms as possible. Even with the soundproofing, the vibrations can be a nuisance." She looked at him questioningly. "We don't have to go if you—"

"No, no, I wouldn't miss it."

"Okay, as long as you're sure."

"I'm sure," he said emphatically. In actual fact, he wouldn't have missed this for the world. Tonight she'd shown a completely different side of her personality. He was still trying to figure out if it was due to the three glasses of wine she'd had or if it was a party persona she donned along with her dress.

That dress had been his first surprise of the evening. He could still remember the feeling he'd had of being punched in the stomach when she'd walked into the lobby at seven-thirty, wearing several yards of deep russet brown chiffon. It was fastened at one shoulder with an intricate gold-and-topaz clasp and draped across her breasts in clinging folds to her waist, where the thin silk layers were cinched by an exquisite belt of gold links set with topazes. The chiffon was so fine that the several yards of material in the skirt seemed to glide over her hips and thighs before blossoming into a froth of tiny pleats at knee level. It wasn't until he'd seen Dari spin her out at arm's length in a showy step during a fast waltz that he'd realized just how full her skirt was. The multiple layers of silk had swirled up and out in a perfect circle, revealing not only the full length of her shapely bare legs but also the panties that matched the dress and had obviously been designed for just such dancing.

He'd been almost as surprised by her shoes. Heretofore he'd only seen her wear boots or low-heeled walking shoes. Her frivolous concoction of gold-lace ankle boots on narrow three-inch heels had kept him staring until she finally asked if he'd like her to get him a pair in his size.

Bram glanced at her as they followed Pip and Phil down the stairs to the Thunder Hole. He wondered if he was developing a fetish about her hair. Almost from the first time he'd seen her when she'd removed her hard hat to let the long silken braid slither down her back, he'd been fascinated. There was something incredibly erotic about imagining that soft, thick mass of hair spilling across his bare body.

Tonight he'd found it increasingly difficult to keep from staring at the intricate style she'd devised and wondering how long it had taken her to arrange and how long it would take him to pull it all down. On the other hand, it would be a shame to mess up anything so attractive. He had no idea what the style was called, but it looked vaguely Grecian with the hair around her face pulled loosely up and back, then wound into an intricate coil from the center of which the rest of her hair fell in a thick golden "tail" to just below her hips.

Dare's facetious inquiry, "Did everyone bring earplugs?" recaptured Bram's wandering attention. He turned to look back up at Dare who was two steps above him and asked, "Do we need them? I can't hear anything."

"Put your hand on the wall and feel the vibrations. If that much is coming through the soundproofing we packed in there, you can bet they've got the amplifiers jacked up to max."

Before Bram could comment, they'd reached the foot of the stairs, and Phil was pushing aside an oak-paneled sliding door. Bram followed Tally through the opening and found himself inside a robin's egg.

"Amazing," he breathed, as he took two steps and then turned in a slow circle to take in the full effect of the room. It was definitely egg-shaped except for the flat expanse of the floor, and the entire enclosure—floor and curved walls and ceiling—was made of a pale blue translucent material that glowed with an eerie light, the only source of light in the room. There were only four disruptions in the sweeping curves of the walls: the door by which they had entered at one end of the egg, an oval opening at the other end giving access to the rest rooms, and a wide door on each of the long walls. The doors were curved to conform to the walls and were marked, To the Inn, To the Parking Lot, Welcome to the Thunder Hole.

"How do you like it?"

Bram looked down at Tally and then glanced around at the other expectant faces. "It's marvelous, but how did you do it?"

"Trade secret," said Tally and Dare in unison.

"Did you two design this?" asked Bram looking from Tally to Dare.

"And built it," said Dare.

"With a little help from a certain manufacturer and some spin-offs from the space program," Tally added.

"Are you saying that this thing could blast off?" teased Bram.

"Only when the door to the Thunder Hole is open," Phil assured him.

"Speaking of the Thunder Hole," said Steven, leading Merrylegs toward the door, "let's go." He looked back at Bram and grinned. "Besides, this is tame compared to what they did inside."

"Kinky, isn't it?" asked Steven a few minutes later as he dropped a casual arm across Bram's shoulders. "Makes one wonder what kind of dark secrets Tally and Dare are harboring in the subterranean depths of their minds."

Bram smiled but continued to examine his surroundings. "It's a weird sensation," he said slowly. "You could really believe that this was a huge cave hewed out of a black glass mountain."

The band had taken a break, and Bram and Steven stood at the end of the dance floor, empty now, while Bram looked around the Thunder Hole in fascination. The large central cavern contained, besides the dance floor and a tumble of glistening black rocks that was actually the bandstand, a black glass service bar and a number of strange shapes that seemed to be growing out of the mirror-finish black floor. Since people were sitting on and around them, Bram realized they were a wild version of tables and chairs. Both of the long sides of the cavern were broken by a series of wide, arched openings that revealed deep grottoes and more of the futuristic tables and chairs.

"Come on, Steven, have a heart. Tell me how they did this," Bram coaxed as he walked over to a section of wall and ran his hand over the irregular surface. "No sharp edges, but you'd swear it was carved from black glass with some kind of blade. And how did they get that effect of tiny red flames flickering deep in the glass?"

"I swear I don't know," Steven vowed, raising his right hand. "Tally and Dare kept this place locked up like a vault while they were working on it. Absolutely no one was allowed in except for a few of Dare's most trusted workmen. In fact he and Tally did a lot of the work themselves."

"Surely some of the workmen have talked. The temptation—"

"Wrong. You have to understand the North Country mind," Steven explained. "Those guys just love to have someone ask them about the Thunder Hole. They give you a perfectly blank look and say something like, 'Ain't got a notion whatcher talkin' 'bout. Mebbe you been seein' too many them space movies.' I'm convinced Tally also threatened them with plagues and unnatural disasters if they talked.''

"Would that really stop them?" Bram asked in some surprise.

"You better believe it," said Steven in dire tones. "Why do you think we call her Tally the Terror? Things have been pretty quiet lately, so you'll have to take my word for it, that woman has an absolutely fiendish mind when it comes to thinking up methods of retribution.''

"Is that the voice of experience?"

"You know it. Well, if you've seen enough for the moment, why don't we join the others? The band will be back in a few minutes, and you won't be able to hear yourself think out here."

Bram followed Steven as he cut across the dance floor toward a grotto on the far side of the room. Intrigued by the strange quality of illumination that filled the cavern with what could only be described as "dark light," Bram slowed his pace to examine the chamber more carefully. There was no single source or type of light, he discovered, and nothing that resembled a bulb or lamp. The dim incandescence that seemed to fill the air was, rather, from a combination of things. A small portion of it came from the cumulative effect of the tiny flames in the walls while a larger source was the deep red glow that pulsed under the black surface of the dance floor, but the most interesting point of origin was the geometrically shaped crystals that jutted from the irregularly curving ceiling at random angles. Looking up at them, Bram had the sense of being in someone's fantasy of a gemstone mine. Of various sizes, the crystals glowed with the dark-fire colors of rubies, emeralds, sapphires, amethysts and garnets.

"I know it's fascinating, Bram," said an amused Steven, "but the band's coming back, and if we don't get out of the way...."

"Oh, quite. Sorry. I was trying to figure out how they managed that effect."

They reached the grotto just as the youthful audience around the dance floor began applauding the returning band. Bram dropped down beside Tally on a surprisingly comfortable padded bench that seemed to have been carved out of the wall.

He half turned toward Tally and waved a hand in an arc. "I simply don't believe this place. What are you doing buried in these mountains? Do you realize you could make a fortune as a set designer for films?"

She laughed up at him, her eyes sparkling even in the diffused light from the crystals in the ceiling. "I'm delighted that you're impressed. However, I don't really need another fortune, and I doubt if I'd like working in the film world. Besides, this isn't all me. The Thunder Hole was actually conceived one evening when Dari and I were playing 'what if.' We began trying to top each other's wild ideas, and finally Rosemary told us to put our calipers where our mouths were and see if we could really do any of those things."

"So you did."

"And had a ball in the doing," she added happily. "Oh, good, they're starting again."

Bram looked up as the opening bars of a fast disco number burst forth. He saw Merrylegs and Steven weaving between the tables toward the dance floor, closely followed by Pip and Phil.

"The music doesn't seem to be as loud as I expected," Bram remarked, turning back to Tally. He noticed her tapping foot and that the shoulder left bare by the cut of her dress was twitching in time to the strong beat.

"We designed the grottos to cut down the noise level so people could talk. That's why all the kids sit in the main room. Come on over to the entrance," she urged, tugging him to his feet. "You can get the full effect of the music there, and you'll have a better view of the dance floor. You've really got to see Pip do her stuff. She's even better than Merrylegs."

Bram leaned a shoulder against the side of the arch and pulled Tally to stand in front of him where he could easily see over her head. He leaned down to speak in her ear so she could hear him without his shouting. "How does she manage without hearing the music?"

She turned her head to answer him and found her mouth a breath away from his. She froze as a sudden prickle of awareness raced up her spine from tailbone to nape. Her startled gaze met the green heat of his, and she felt the warmth of his hands close around her waist. *I didn't realize his hands were so large,* she thought dazedly.

Someone bumped against them, and it broke the spell. Tally moved her head back a few inches, and Bram tilted his so that her mouth was next to his ear.

It was another moment before she remembered his question and answered, "Pip's got great natural rhythm, and she picks up the beat from the lights. Both the floor and the crystals are programmed to pulse with the beat of the music. She also feels the sound vibrations. Watch her. She's terrific."

Bram straightened, took a deep calming breath and redirected his gaze to the rapidly moving dancers. But he didn't remove his hands from Tally's waist.

It didn't take him long to agree with Tally's judgment. Merrylegs was very good. A few inches taller than Tally, her lovely legs looked even longer than they were due to her very short miniskirt, and they flashed in quick rhythm as she followed Steven's intricate steps. Pip, however, was something else again.

Since first meeting her, Bram had thought of Pip as one of those fabled tall, blond, athletic American women. He could hardly equate the woman who was performing the most sensuous and exciting disco dance he'd ever seen with the practical, down-to-earth Pip he thought he knew. She and Phil were beautifully matched, both in looks and in dancing ability. They were both tall, tanned and handsome, and Phil's dark brown hair, burgundy silk dinner jacket and black trousers provided a perfect foil for Pip's cap of pale blond waves and the strapless white satin jumpsuit that lovingly molded every curve of her supple figure. The severity of their dark-light contrast was relieved by the gay whimsy of their matching hot pink cummerbunds.

Tally looked up at Bram and laughed at his incredulous expression. She motioned for him to bend down. "What do you think?"

He gave her a speaking look. "Do you really want to know?"

She grinned and said lightly, "That's okay. Phil won't mind if you look as long as you don't try to touch. If you do, you just might get a five iron wrapped around your neck."

He shifted his gaze back to Pip, then shook his head ruefully. "It does make one wish one's dancing days weren't over."

"Are they?" Tally frowned slightly as she looked up at him questioningly. "I thought you were only going to have some permanent stiffness in the knee. That shouldn't stop you entirely from dancing."

"Time will tell," he said with a shrug, "but I doubt that I'll be able to dance like that again."

The number ended, and as they moved back to their seats, Tally slanted a curious look up at Bram, wondering if he was as reconciled to his limitations as he sounded, or if this was an example of the British stiff upper lip.

The laughing dancers swirled back into the grotto and dropped onto their seats, gasping for breath and trying to talk at the same time. Pip accepted Bram's compliments with a knowing grin and a decided twinkle in her dark blue eyes.

"Unreal, isn't it?" she said, laughing. "I just seem to turn into another person on a dance floor."

Phil sent her a smoky look that told Bram plainer than words could that the dance floor wasn't the only place she turned into an exciting, sensuous woman.

Bram leaned back, sipping on his wine and wondering if Tally, like her sister, turned into a creature of passion in the bedroom. He rather thought she did. He'd felt her reaction and seen the flickers of gold in her eyes when they'd almost kissed.

His speculations were cut short as the music began again and, simultaneously, a tall, brawny young man materialized beside him. Bram vaguely recognized him as one of the California Bishops and seemed to remember that he did something involving a lot of running on his college football team.

"Hey, Bram, you don't mind if I borrow Cousin Tally, do you?" asked the young giant with a winning grin.

Tally smiled at him with deadly sweetness and purred, "If you want me to dance with you, Mugs, you're asking the wrong person."

"Huh?" Mugs responded with less than his usual insouciance. "Oh, yeah, gotcha. So will you dance with me, Tally?" He flashed an apologetic grin at Bram and then laughed at the older man's surprised expression. "Didn't you know she's a whiz at this? We don't call her Tally the Terrific Terpsichorean for nothing."

"Mugs, your mouth runs faster than you do," sighed his long-suffering cousin. "Come on, let's get with it before the number ends."

Bram choked back a laugh as Tally jumped up and swiftly led her large relative toward the dance floor. He hadn't realized just how big Mugs was until he saw the two of them standing. The top of Tally's head barely reached the middle of Mugs's chest. Bram wondered how they managed to dance together.

"Hurry up, Bram." Dare punched him lightly on the shoulder to get his attention. "You won't believe this unless you see it."

Grabbing his cane, Bram followed the others as they worked their way to the edge of the dance floor. He gradually became aware that apparently everyone in the Thunder Hole was crowding around the open area, clapping to the driving beat of the music, which seemed to be predominantly brasses, and shouting "Go, Tally, go!" and "Let'er fly, Mugs!"

Darius shifted to one side and motioned for Bram to squeeze in between him and Phil. It was Bram's first clear view of the dance floor, and he could feel his jaw dropping as he took in the scene before him. *Although why I should be surprised at this point at anything that strange bird does is beyond me. God, I don't believe this!*

The pounding, brassy rhythm of the music seemed to be a cross between jazz and disco, and

the fast, whirling, hip-swinging, strutting, acro-
batic routine that Tally and Mugs were performing combined the flashiest elements of both. He
caught his breath as Mugs spun her out, then
grasped her outstretched hand just as she ended
her series of quick turns with a high kick. Her foot
came down as he gave a hard pull, and she leaped
through the air toward him to be caught in midair
by his big hands around her waist. With his feet
still moving in an intricate step, Mugs threw her
up in the air over his head with a quick twist of his
wrists that sent her spinning in a complete turn
before she dropped back into his waiting hands. In
a smooth move, he flipped her into the cradle of
his left arm as her right hand slid up behind his
shoulder and tightened. He whirled down the
floor in a series of fast back-turns that created
enough centrifugal force to lift Tally's small body
horizontally. Her long hair bannered out behind
them as did her full skirts, and she flung out her
left arm and curved her legs back in a graceful line
with one foot drawn up almost to the opposite
knee.

Stunned, Bram watched as the two of them,
never missing a step, went through a routine that
was as energetic, clever and professional as anything he'd ever seen in a hit musical. Tally spent
more time in the air than on her feet as Mugs used
the advantage of his size and strength to fling her
up, over, out and around. By the time they were
halfway through the dance, all her hair had tumbled down, and thereafter it whipped around like
a golden curtain through all her whirling turns and

flying spins. The dance came to a spectacular end when Mugs swung Tally high over his head, balancing her on one huge hand spread across her stomach with his arm at full stretch. With her back arched, arms flung wide and her skirts and extraordinary hair floating in the breeze of their passage, she posed like an exotic bird as Mugs did a series of quick turns around the center of the floor before sinking to one knee still holding Tally poised over his head.

The audience exploded into applause, cheers and whistles as a grinning Mugs set a laughing, panting Tally on her feet and then stood up, taking her hand as they bowed and threw kisses to the excited crowd. To the cries of "More, more," Tally laughed and shook her head, then flung out her arms and let herself fall backward toward Mugs. He caught her around the waist, swung her up to sit on his shoulder, and did an exaggerated jazz strut across the floor, stopping in front of Bram and Dare.

"Here she is," said Mugs happily, setting Tally on her feet in front of them. "Now that I've worn her out some, do you think you guys can handle her?"

Tally tipped her head back to look up at him, narrowing her eyes speculatively. She could see the faint beading of sweat on his forehead, felt a similar dampness on her own skin, and wondered if his legs were as rubbery as hers. Cousin or no cousin, she decided, she wasn't about to let any twenty-one-year-old jock get the best of her.

"Dear boy," she crooned with a challenging

gleam in her eyes, "anything you can do I can do longer. Would you like to go round again?"

"Uh, no, no!" Mugs backed away hastily. "I've, uh, promised, er, Cindy the next dance."

"I almost wish he'd called your bluff," said Dari as the group moved toward the grotto. "One of these days you're going to challenge the wrong person and end up with mud on your nose."

Tally gave him the most innocent look she could summon up. "You mean you've never caught on that I never dare anyone who isn't a cream puff."

"Mugs?"

"He's soft as a grape when it comes to women. On the other hand, I wouldn't get within miles of a football field when he's on it."

Tally dropped down on the bench beside Bram and eyed a large interesting-looking pitcher which Phil had just picked up. "Is that sangría?" she asked wistfully, batting her thick lashes at her brother-in-law.

"Sure is. Here you go, and now you can stop with the eyelashes. How come you never do these seductive things when we're alone?" He grinned and batted his longer, curlier lashes back at her.

"Because Pip's bigger than I am," said Tally succinctly, winking at her sister as the others laughed.

She leaned back and drank half the rather large glass of sangría in slow, steady swallows, letting her muscles relax in the pleasant euphoria that comes after strenuous physical exercise.

"Where did you learn to do that?" Bram's voice

came from just above her ear as he spoke under cover of the others' chatter.

"Dari and Steven, although it was actually beer that they taught me to chugalug." She slanted an amused glance at him.

"You know perfectly well I meant that incredible dance. You two are well nigh professional. Why on earth are you burying all these talents in this backwater?" he demanded, waving an expressive hand toward their surroundings.

Tally began to do a slow burn. She knew that his reference to "talents" included what he believed to be her film-set-designing abilities. Much as she might appreciate his admiration of her accomplishments, however, she most definitely did *not* like his use of the term "backwater." Furthermore, where she chose to live and work, and how she decided to use her talents, were none of his damn business.

She twisted around angrily to face him but was hampered by her unbound hair, which she was sitting on. With a muttered oath she stood and swept the shining mass forward over one shoulder. Sitting back down she automatically began braiding her hair into a single plait while fixing Bram with a smoldering look. Her voice had a decided bite to it as she attempted to correct his thinking.

"I appreciate the compliment, if not the unsolicited opinion. Whether it's with Dari, Mugs, Steven or any of my other cousins, I dance only for the fun of it and only here or at a private gathering. I'd no more think of dancing like that in a public place than I would of running down the street in my skivvies."

Bram tried to interrupt, disconcerted by the anger that had flared so quickly, but she didn't give him a chance to get out the first word.

"No. I don't want to hear anymore," she snapped. "Just keep in mind for the future that I'm an architect, not an entertainer. Nor a set designer. There are a number of things I enjoy doing for amusement, but that doesn't necessarily mean I want to make a lifetime career of them. Nor do I want to live in a noisy, dirty city crawling with muggers and other weird people. You may consider this a backwater, but there are many of us who think it's a beautiful, healthy, enjoyable place to live. Have you got a string?"

Bram blinked in utter confusion as her tone abruptly switched from scathing to one of polite inquiry. It was a moment before he collected his wits enough to notice that she was holding up the end of her braid.

"Never mind," she said, flicking a glance at his dark gold silk dinner jacket. "Of course you haven't."

"Here, Tally." She turned at the sound of Pip's husky voice and reached for the bright blue rubber band that her sister was offering. Pip chuckled at her surprised look and gestured with her pink satin clutch. "Every bag I own has a supply of elastics. Lissy's always losing hers."

Within moments, once more smiling and composed, Tally had drawn Bram into a general discussion of everyone's favorite restaurants. With laughing ease and a quick change of topic, she evaded all his attempts to return to the subject of their disagreement. He finally gave up the effort and waited for the evening to end, when he was determined to have at least a few minutes alone with her.

Tally was aware of his intentions. She'd noted a gleam of purpose behind the laughter every time he looked at her. By the end of the evening she'd devised and discarded several plans for evading a private confrontation with him. She knew she wasn't ready for any more probing; their true-confessions episode that afternoon had left her feeling unbelievably vulnerable, and she'd been berating herself ever since for revealing so much of herself to him.

She admitted only to herself that that was why she'd overreacted to his remark about her talents and choice of life-style. Reluctantly she also admitted that she owed him an apology for flaring up at him, but she'd much rather wait until tomorrow when she'd had time to get her defenses back in place. However, she could tell from the determined set of his mouth as he escorted her from the Thunder Hole at the end of the evening that he wasn't going to wait any longer for a confrontation.

Bram managed to contain his impatience until they were crossing the parking lot toward her car, but finally he asked, with barely suppressed ire, "What was that all about, Tally? I asked an innocent question, perhaps a bit strongly worded but certainly not insulting, and you went off like a rocket. The rest of the group must have wondered what the hell I'd said to you to set you off so."

Tally turned as they reached the car, leaning back against the door with her arms crossed defensively in front of her. "Look, I'm sorry about that. I didn't intend to embarrass you. It's just...I guess I don't always take criticism well when it comes to my work or the way I choose to live."

"You didn't embarrass me," said Bram impatiently. "I'm more concerned with this penchant you have for downplaying your talents."

"Bram, please. You've latched on to a fun thing that Dari and I did, and you've built it all out of proportion. I know you're oriented toward show-business thinking, but, believe me, I have no desire to become involved in that world. I know what my talents are, and they're all centered on designing buildings. That so-called set designing is just a game."

"It's not, you know," Bram insisted. "It takes a remarkable creative imagination and a flair for practical considerations to turn out something like the Thunder Hole. You could easily become a top-notch set designer."

"I don't *want* to be a set designer. Can't you understand that? Read my lips, dammit." Tally looked up at him, seeing the frustration in his expression. "Bram, Bram, what are we arguing about? I like my life. I like my work. I don't want to change either."

"Stubborn," Bram muttered, relieving some of his frustration and anger by banging a fist on the fender of the Wagoneer. "You have got to be the most stubborn woman I've ever met. Did it ever occur to you that you could broaden your horizons and expand your interests without losing anything? It would be a matter of adding—"

"Stop right there," Tally snapped, becoming riled all over again. "It's late and we're both tired. I think this discussion is pointless right now. I can't even figure out what you're so aggravated about."

"Well, if you don't know, lady, I'm not going to explain it, but you can think about this while you're puzzling it out," he snarled, grabbing her and pulling her into his arms none too gently.

She had time for no more than a startled "Oh!" before his mouth locked on her parted lips and his tongue thrust deeply. Before she could catch her balance or react, he pulled away, stared at her for a moment, muttered "Oh, hell!" and strode off with only the barest hint of a limp.

"Oh, indeed, I do have something to think about—but not tonight, thank you," Tally murmured, stifling a yawn as she slid into the car. "Too much, too fast, too damn confusing. I'll think about it when I'm awake. Lordy, but that is one nerve-racking, fascinating man. And this whole thing is getting completely out of hand."

CHAPTER SEVEN

UNDER THE INSISTENT BURSTS of harsh sound, Tally's dream swirled, fragmented and drifted away like morning fog beneath a rising sun. Coming partially awake she groggily identified the unceasing clamor as the telephone. Without opening her eyes she rolled over, stretched one bare arm out from under the covers and groped across the night table for the receiver. The cool morning air raised goose bumps on her sleep-flushed skin, and as soon as her fingers closed over the phone, she snaked it back under the warm cocoon of bedclothes.

"Mmmpff."

"Tally? Tally! Wake up, dammit!"

Her eyes flew open as she came fully awake in one mind-snapping jolt, recognizing Dari's voice in one instant and reacting to the extraordinary sound of anger and impatience in the next moment. Something was wrong, she realized, for Dari to blow his cool, especially at—she peered at the clock in the dim light—five-thirty in the morning.

"Okay. I'm awake, wide awake," she assured him, sitting up and swinging her legs over the edge of the mattress. "What's happened?"

"Too much. For starters, I'm at the motel complex. Someone cut through the fence in the night, vandalized the place and stole everything they could carry out. Dammit, we'd have had construction completed in another two weeks."

"Oh, hell. What do you want me to do, come down...?"

"No, not here. I need you to help out with my other problem."

"You mean there's more?"

"Someone evidently decided to wind up their holiday weekend with a bit of Bishop-baiting. Besides this mess the equipment yard at Twin Mountain was hit. Sam Toomey's in the hospital, and at least half the vehicles are out of commission. I'm going to be stuck here for a few hours, assessing damages and talking to the cops and insurance people."

"So what do you want me to do? And what happened to Sam, and what do you mean 'out of commission'?"

"Remember I told you a few weeks ago that we seemed to be having too many minor accidents at the motel site?"

"Yeah. And now you're going to tell me there's been more that you didn't mention, and that Steven's got some of his security people on it."

"I didn't think we were getting past you. Sam's been acting as a night guard at the Twin Mountain depot since the state police surprised a prowler a couple of weeks ago. Sometime around three o'clock this morning, at least three men apparently came over the back fence, surprised Sam and beat the hell out of him. Rosemary got the call from the police after I'd left to come down here. She got O'Neil out of bed and sent him to check out the depot, while she headed for the hospital. He just called me. There's sand in all the gas tanks that don't have locks, batteries and rotors were removed and apparently taken away since he can't find them anywhere, and it looks like they attacked the truck tires with a machete. That's just the major stuff. O'Neil's calling in all the men he can reach, but it's going to take the best part of two days to get those machines back in operation. Meantime, we've got to keep working on the project."

"Rebuilding some ten miles of road and replacing a bridge, isn't it?"

"Right, but you don't need to worry about that part. You've still got a valid trucker's license, haven't you?"

"Sure." Tally, with great effort, restrained her impulse to say something pithy.

Much to the consternation of the Bishop men, she'd qualified for a Class One license three years before, when a friend of Dari's who owned an interstate trucking firm had imbibed one swallow too much at a New Year's Eve party. In a lamentable display of chauvinism, he'd loudly claimed that a "little bit of a thing" like Tally couldn't possibly handle an eighteen-wheeler. With that "little bit of a thing" ringing in her ears, Tally had immediately bet him a thousand dollars that she could not only handle an eighteen-wheeler but could pass the test for a Class One license. She'd won the bet, driven Uncle A's blood pressure up another notch, and given Dari fits by keeping her skills honed ever since on his big tractor and flat-bed-trailer rigs.

"Good. Now here's what I want you to do. Better take notes so you don't forget anything." Dari paused until Tally gave a grunt of acquiescence. "First, roust out Mugs and Jeff. I know they were going to take the rest of the week before starting their summer jobs, but we need them now. You can pick them up on your way by the inn. Then call Don Ellison and ask if he and one of his boys could get up to Twin Mountain as soon as possible to give O'Neil a hand. He's going to need a couple of good mechanics to help check out those vehicles."

"What about batteries and rotors?"

"Ask Don to take along as many as he can find in a hurry. Once he has a clearer idea of what else is needed, he can have one of his people start rounding it all up. Tell him we'll cover any extra costs. After that call Chris and Johnny Adderly and tell them to meet you at the main yard instead of going straight to Twin Mountain."

"So far you've handed me four football players. What am I doing with all this muscle power?"

"Moving equipment. I need to get some trucks and the big bulldozer up to the site."

"Who knows how to drive the dozer? And are you sure the stuff in the yard is okay?"

"I had the local cops check it out after Rosemary called. Everything looks secure, the alarm system is on, and the dogs are patrolling. Steven's got Brian and a couple of his men on their way up anyhow, and one of them will ride shotgun with you just to be on the safe side. As for the dozer, you know how to drive it. I know you have trouble reaching some of the controls on that one, but all you have to do is get it on the flatbed. O'Neil will have someone unload it. The flatbed's already hooked up to the tractor, but be sure you check out the coupling before you move a foot."

"Right. Which tractor?"

"Number eleven, the big Mack. You've driven it before and shouldn't have any problem with that. What about the flatbed? With that big dozer on it, it's a heavy haul. Are you sure you can handle it?"

"I did before. Remember? Last summer when I took the grader up to Gorham? I should be okay. What do you want the boys to drive?"

"Chris and Johnny are checked out on the dump trucks, the GMCs, twenty-six and thirty-two. Have Mugs drive the oversize blue pickup, and have the guys load it with all the extra batteries, the two red toolboxes, a couple of rolls of cable and anything else that looks useful. Thank God the new tires just came in. Some of them are in the storeroom loft and the rest are in the fourth bay of the garage. They should all fit in the dump trucks. Jeff can drive your Wagoneer, and you'd better pack in half a dozen of the portable CBs. Have you got all that?"

"Yeah, yeah. Do we need the Wagoneer? Shouldn't he drive something—"

"You'll need it to get back. I want to leave the

big rig up there in case we have to haul something down to the main yard for repair. I've made arrangements with the state police to have a patrol car with two officers meet you at the main yard at seven-thirty—you should be loaded up by then—and they'll give you an escort to Twin Mountain. Have—"

"Is that really necessary, Dari? You said one of our security people was going to ride with me."

"He is, but you're going to be quite a parade, and I want the patrol car, too. That security man, by the way, is going to stick with you for a few days, so don't give him a hard time."

"Oh, come on, Dari, I don't need—"

"Indulge me, Tally. Steven and I agree that you're too tempting a target if someone's bent on carrying out a vendetta against the Bishops. That crazy lavender chariot of yours stands out like a beacon, and everyone knows you romp all over the countryside by yourself. Some of your building sites are damn isolated, and so is your house."

"What about ma and...?"

"Don't worry. You're not the only one who's going to have a bodyguard. Brian's already called in extra men. Until we find out what's going on, no one in the family is going anywhere alone. Now it's almost six. You'd better get a move on. And Tally?"

"Yes."

"Be careful."

"I intend to. Wait! Don't hang up. What about Pip? She's the most vulnerable and—"

"All taken care of. Steven's arranging for her

and Lissy to fly back to Maine with Aunt Barbara. She'll be safe enough. That island's as secure as Fort Knox. Stop worrying. Steven and Brian are raising the drawbridge and manning the parapets. By noon they should have the boiling oil ready and all the catapults restrung. Keep in touch. I'll see you later."

"I wonder if they make armor in my size. I'll call you from Twin Mountain. Take care."

Tally had been gathering her clothes with one hand while she finished talking to Dari. Now, she hung up the phone and began scrambling into faded, comfortably worn jeans, a beige T-shirt that announced Architects Do It on a Firm Foundation, and her steel-toed work boots. A quick look in the mirror and she decided not to take time to rebraid her hair.

Ten minutes later she'd completed her calls and was stuffing a large leather shoulder bag with such essentials as a spare shirt, a first-aid kit, her wallet and checkbook, and a large multi-functional Swiss Army knife that did everything but walk by itself. She'd already whistled twice for Splendid and had left the porch and back doors open while she dashed around collecting her gear. Now she heard the clicking of claws on the porch and looked up as the big cat prowled into the kitchen.

"Good boy. Your breakfast's by the refrigerator, and I want you to stay here until I get back. If the alarm goes off and anyone tries to come in who doesn't know your name, you can eat 'em for lunch. Okay?"

He leaned against her leg and blinked sleepy

yellow eyes at her as she gave him a quick rub behind the ears. She wasn't even half joking. Under certain circumstances Splendid could be extremely hostile to strangers.

Slinging her bag over her shoulder, she headed rapidly for the back door, pausing only long enough to reach in to the back of the broom closet to trigger the first stage of the burglar-alarm system. She was on the porch with the back door almost closed when she remembered the electronic locks on the gate and all the doors at Bishop Construction. She hesitated and then decided not to chance it. She so rarely had to open any of those locks, she couldn't be sure of remembering all the codes.

With an oath that would have turned her Uncle Alden to stone, she ran back inside and skidded to a stop in front of what looked like a wall-mounted microwave oven with a totally opaque black glass door. She quickly tapped out the combination and pulled open the door to reveal a sturdy safe. She flipped rapidly through a small loose-leaf notebook, extracted two pages, and replaced the book in the safe.

She had her hand on the door ready to close it when her eye fell on the polished rosewood box. For just a moment she wavered indecisively before reaching back into the safe and flipping up the lid of the box to reveal a .38 Police Special. Dari hadn't mentioned the gun, but perhaps he assumed she'd know enough to take it.

"Damn," she muttered as she picked up the gun, checked that it was loaded, and dropped it into the deep side pocket of her bag. Although she was an excellent shot, she still didn't like carrying a gun around with her.

She closed the safe and ran for the side entrance to the garage. Inside, she flicked a switch that actually triggered the alarm's second stage and then moved a few feet along the wall to press the button that opened the garage door behind the Wagoneer. Once she'd backed clear, she tapped the remote control on the dashboard and waited to make sure that the overhead door dropped into place correctly. When its bottom edge was seated on the metal strip along the floor, the alarm system was fully activated.

During the short drive to the inn, she debated again about taking the gun. Emotionally she loathed the idea of extreme violence—throwing things in a temper was one thing; shooting somebody was another—and loathed even more the thought that someone hated her enough to try to harm her.

The practical side of her nature pointed out that probably no one hated her personally but rather what she represented. The Bishops were no more immune to threats of violence than any other wealthy, powerful and prominent family. She remembered the two men who had been killed when a pipe bomb exploded in the executive washroom at Bishop Electronics' California headquarters in the late sixties. The extremist group who took credit for the blast claimed they'd been after her Uncle Foster, Mugs's father, who was president of the company. And then there were the kidnap attempts that had been made over the years, all of which had fortunately been foiled although a couple had come too close for comfort.

All things considered, Tally decided as she turned into the inn's driveway, she'd better carry the gun, bodyguard or no bodyguard. If Sonny Jaketon was behind this mess, as she suspected, he wouldn't hesitate to try to take out her bodyguard and then come after her. He'd been spoiled rotten by his father, Hardy, and now at twenty-three he was hot-tempered, spiteful and malicious. For almost two years he'd been publicly nursing an increasingly bitter grudge against the Bishops, the cause of which was one of the mysteries of the county since he'd never yet told anyone what was behind it.

Tally ceased her musings as she saw Mugs and Jeff waiting for her at the foot of the front steps. She stopped just long enough for them to climb in and then circled around to head back out to the main road.

"Now tell us what's going on, Tally," demanded Mugs.

"We brought you coffee and a couple of hot croissants from Henri," said Jeff from the back seat, holding up a thermos bottle and a foil-covered box.

"Thanks. I'll have some while you guys are doing all the muscle work. As for what's going on...."

She spent the rest of the fast trip to the Falls filling them in on the night's happenings and passing along Dari's instructions. They arrived at Bishop

Construction five minutes later to find the Adderly boys as well as Brian McKay and two of his men pacing back and forth in front of the gates, while the guard dogs snarled and glowered at them from the other side.

Tally slid out of the car, pulling her notes of the lock codes from her pocket as she walked toward the waiting group. As soon as the dogs saw her, they whined a greeting and began wagging their long tails.

Brian raised a skeptical eyebrow. "Are you sure they'll let you in? They've been going hysterical every time one of us got within five feet of the fence."

"No problem," she said as she tapped out the correct sequence on the lock. "It might be best, though, if you all stay right where you are until I can get them into their pen."

Once she was inside, the dogs vied for her attention, almost knocking her over in their enthusiasm. They gamboled around her as she led them across the dusty expanse of the yard to their large fenced run at the end of the long garage.

It was the beginning of an hour of almost non-stop activity as the four younger men loaded the trucks, while Brian, Williams and Donnelly helped her check out all the vehicles and start up the diesels. Then with Brian and Donnelly monitoring her progress from the ground and Williams guiding her from the far end of the flatbed, she carefully eased the huge bulldozer up the ramp and onto the trailer.

She scrambled down thankfully while the men

secured the machine in place. That dozer, she decided as she rubbed her aching arms, had not been designed for operation by someone of her size and strength. It was fun driving the smaller cats, but she was quite happy to bequeath that monster to the male operators.

"Why don't you take a break while they finish loading," said Brian, coming up beside her. "Jeff says there's coffee and croissants in the office, and this would be a good time for us to have a private talk."

She gave him a sharp look, but could read nothing in his guileless expression. She'd often thought that he could make a fortune if he could patent that expression and sell it to budding poker players. Of course it really needed the rest of the package for full effect: the curly black hair, Irish blue eyes, and lithe six-foot frame. Talk about smoke screens. He looked as innocently charming as an oversize choirboy, but she was one of the small select club who knew that, when necessary, he could be as sharp and lethal as a cobra's fangs.

"More surprises?" she asked as they walked toward the office.

"No, no," he assured her. "More like an exchange of information and perhaps a dash of speculation."

Neither said any more until they were inside with the door closed, facing each other across Dari's desk.

"Okay, McKay, let's have it," Tally said briskly, pouring two cups of coffee from the thermos.

"Do you want to beat around the bush for a while, or shall we jump right into it?"

"Ah, jump into what?" Brian asked cautiously.

"Whys and wherefores," she said as she began nibbling on a buttery croissant. Noting his yearning look, she broke off a piece and handed it to him. "I think it can all be summed up in two words: Sonny Jaketon. What do you think?"

Brian finished his snack while his level blue gaze assessed her steady tan gaze. "I think," he said at last, "that you and Splendid are a matched set. You both go right for the jugular. No playing around. Spot your victim and. . . wham!"

"You see Sonny as a victim?"

"Hmm. You're right. Target would be more accurate." Brian accepted another piece of croissant. "We've suspected Sonny was involved in the accidents at the motel. He's been getting wilder and louder lately about his resentment of the Bishops."

"I've heard about it, but I figured it was beer and braggadocio talking."

"For a long time it was, but now we're reasonably certain that he's taking more direct action. Given his penchant for foul-mouthed belligerence and that gang of young toughs that hang around him, you'd figure that he'd go in for the obvious bullying tactics. You know, like barroom brawls with Dare's men or harassing any of you they found driving alone, that sort of thing. However, I did some checking up on Sonny a few months ago. Just as a routine precaution. Did you know he's got an IQ of 143? Old Hardy spent a fortune on prep schools before he finally got the kid graduated. Took five schools to do it. Seems Sonny had a knack for pulling some pretty foul practical jokes and setting someone else up to take the blame. He also had sticky fingers. Radios, watches, tape recorders, sports equipment, money and anything else not bolted down just seemed to start vanishing within days of his arrival at a new school—and kept on disappearing until he left.''

"Hardy must have spent another fortune covering up. I haven't heard any of that." Tally set her cup down with a small bang. "The IQ does surprise me. Sonny's always come across as a clod just in from the backwoods. I knew Hardy'd bought his way through school, so I just assumed he was slow and it was the only way he could get a diploma. I take it you're telling me that Sonny's really smart enough and sly enough to have engineered all these incidents.''

"You got it. I'm sure he either planted one of his own men on the motel job or he bought one of the temporaries. As for last night, the Hebron police have found a witness who saw a van parked on the motel access road shortly after 3:00 A.M. He thought it was kids parking so he didn't call the cops, but the description he gave of the van is a damn close match for Sonny's.''

"And Twin Mountain? He couldn't have been in two places at once, and the time frame must have been about the same.''

"Some of his good buddies, I imagine." Brian stood up as Tally finished cleaning up the debris of their picnic breakfast. He nodded toward the window. "State cops just arrived. Time to be on our way. I'm riding up with you, and Donnelly can go with one of the others. Williams'll keep an eye on things here."

Tally shot him a questioning look as she headed for the door. "Just what kind of trouble are you expecting?"

"None, really. At least not this morning. I want to ask a few questions in Twin Mountain...and maybe make a couple of suggestions. I'll be coming back with you. Donnelly's going to stick with Rosemary."

It was half an hour before they had a chance to resume their conversation. Once the miniconvoy was on its way, Brian sat back and left Tally to concentrate on maneuvering the big rig along the narrow, curving road between Bishops Falls and Interstate 93.

"You can talk again," said Tally as the half dozen vehicles spaced out in the right lane and settled to a steady speed.

Brian reached toward Tally's shoulder bag lying on the seat between them and patted the bulge of the side pocket. "Is that what I think it is?"

She nodded. "My .38."

"Smart girl. Sorry, woman. I wasn't looking forward to trying to convince you to carry it."

"Are you suggesting that I'm stubborn?" she asked incredulously.

"Does the sun rise in the east?" he asked with equal incredulity.

Tally flashed him a companionable smile. "Don't get overconfident. We may have missed that argument, but I'm sure something else will crop up before the day is done."

A prophetic statement, Tally decided early that afternoon, but the argument was shaping up with her mother rather than with Brian. Although the trip to Twin Mountain had been without incident, she'd been delayed returning to the Falls since O'Neil had decided that the front-end loader was too badly damaged to be repaired on site. She'd had to wait, therefore, for his men to winch it onto the flatbed, and then she'd had to drive the rig back down to the main yard, a much slower trip than it would have been in her Wagoneer.

At least, she thought, Brian had brought her car back, following the rig all the way even though he must have been chafing at the slow speed she had to maintain.

She glanced through the doorway into the dining room where Brian was eating a late lunch and conferring with several of the security people. They were all dressed in casual clothes and looked like any other guests wandering around the inn. She noted in particular the two women in the group. They were unfamiliar to her, and she wondered if they were new additions to Brian's staff or if he'd brought them in from one of the other Bishop facilities.

"What could Darius have been thinking of, sending you off up there in that enormous... *thing*?" asked Edna Bishop for the second time.

Tally turned back to the three people sharing her table and watching her consume a generous helping of fresh fruit salad heaped in a honeydew melon half. Sidney and Bram were subtly opting out of the conversation between mother and daughter, leaning back in their chairs and idly toying with their wineglasses.

For just a moment Tally let her gaze linger on Bram's hair. A beam of sunlight had found its way through the thick, screening foliage of the plants hanging in front of the Gazebo's windows, and had settled like a glowing cap around Bram's head lightening the deep auburn hair with streaks of gold and copper.

"Tally! I want to know—"

"Ma, will you please calm down. I'm perfectly all right. Dari wouldn't have asked me to drive the big rig if he wasn't sure that I could handle it. Nothing happened. I'm fine." Tally strove to subdue her impatience and to keep her tone reassuring. She quickly realized she wasn't entirely successful.

"Don't try to dissemble with me," said Edna in what was, for her, a very sharp tone. "I can tell a bodyguard from a Boston stockbroker just as well as you can." She gave the group in the dining room a telling look. "I've been through these things a few times before if you'll remember. There was the kidnapping attempt on Pip, and those threats we all received from those lunatics with their nasty bombs, and—"

"Ma, this isn't the same thing. We know—"

"No! You don't know at all. That watchman is in the hospital with a fractured skull. Don't try to tell me that this is just someone playing pranks. I didn't believe it from Alden or Steven, and I'm certainly not going to believe it from you. Not when I see Brian's people swarming all over the place, and especially not when I see that bulge in your bag.''

''Ma, you're getting all excited about—''

''Talia,'' Edna snapped, slapping her hand on the table. ''Are you going to tell me that's not a gun? I know perfectly well you only carry it when Darius and Steven twist your arm, and they only do that when—''

''It's just a precaution, ma.'' Tally reached over to pat her mother's hand soothingly. ''Like their insisting that I take it with me when I'm driving alone late at night or in really remote areas.'' *Oh, damn, that was the wrong thing to say.*

''And I've never liked you doing that. I don't see why you can't let one of the security people drive you. Phil never lets Pip go off by herself, and Jean and Janet always have a driver. It's all of a piece with you living alone way out there at the far end of the lake. I've always said it wasn't safe, and now you see what comes of it,'' said Edna in a muddled rush of words.

Tally shook her head and decided not to even attempt to sort *that* all out. She was concerned, though, at how upset her mother seemed, but didn't know what to say to calm her down. So far everything she'd tried had just made matters worse.

She glanced at Bram and Sid, wondering what they were making of all this. They couldn't be totally unfamiliar with such situations. Bram had been in the public eye for years and was a favorite target for the gossip sheets. Anyone in that position had to have learned about the dark side of fame and fortune.

Sidney held her gaze a moment and then, as if sensing her dilemma, cleared his throat and leaned forward, grasping Edna's hand and drawing her attention to himself. His first words confirmed Tally's supposition.

"My dear, I know how unpleasant and upsetting this is for you. I've been through it all with Bram. Threatening letters, obscene calls, a couple of absolutely barmy women who tried to kidnap him, a jealous husband who believed his wife's fantasies and decided to perform a certain surgical removal with a table knife in the middle of Maxim's. Well, I could go on, but why dwell on unhappy memories, hmm?"

Tally met Bram's amused regard and firmly restrained an urge to giggle. She could just picture the scene at Maxim's.

Sid's voice became a background murmur as she exchanged a long searching look with Bram. After their flare-up Saturday evening, they'd been constrained with each other for the rest of the weekend. Even with the lighthearted group that gathered at Bram's Sunday evening, the two of them had managed to direct their talk and laughter to the others. Their manner with each other had been polite and coolly friendly on Tally's part and warily congenial on Bram's.

"I'm sure she'd agree if only to set your mind at rest." Sid's last few words impinged on Tally's distraction, and she sensed that it was time for her to rejoin the conversation.

"You will, won't you, darling?" Edna asked, turning pleading blue eyes on her recalcitrant daughter. "Sid's right. You'd be much safer, and I wouldn't be awake half the night worrying about this nasty Sonny person blowing up your house."

"Wait a minute," Tally protested. "I've apparently missed something here. Neither Sonny Jaketon nor anyone else is going to blow up my house. Where did you get such a harebrained idea?"

"Oh, it really doesn't matter whether they do or not," Edna said impatiently, waving a dismissing hand at the prospect of $150,000 worth of house being reduced to kindling.

Tally's eyebrows shot up and her mouth opened, but she found herself for perhaps the fourth or fifth time in her life without a thing to say.

"The important thing, darling, is that you won't be there," Edna continued, carefully avoiding her darling's fulminating glare. "We can put you in the west tower. You've always liked that lovely view, and it's got two floors so you'll have a place to work, and you can use—"

"Just hold it right there," said Tally ominously. "When did I agree to move out of my house? It's ridiculous, and besides I don't have time for all this. Do you have any idea how busy I am right now? I've got four designs to complete in the next two weeks, plus six projects under construction that I've got to keep an eye on."

"But, Tally dear, Sidney thinks—"

"Ma," Tally chided, sighing in exasperation. She looked across the table at the still-handsome Englishman. "With all due respect, Sid, I have to tell you that it's a lousy idea. I know you're trying to help, but you simply don't understand what would be involved in my trying to set up a working area in the inn."

She saw the pleading look her mother gave him and paused to rein in her rising temper. There seemed to be something developing between him and her mother, and she didn't want to offend him. But still. . . .

"Look, believe me," Tally urged, "this is all unnecessary. I'm perfectly safe at my house. I've got an alarm system that's as sophisticated and effective as the one at Steven's place. No one can get onto the peninsula from either the water or the road, never mind into the house, without setting off sirens, horns and whoopers that can be heard in the Falls. At the same time an alarm is set off in the security office here and in both the state and local police stations. Brian and I gave it a test run, and a guard can make it from the inn to my dooryard in two minutes."

"A lot can happen in two minutes," Edna said gloomily.

Tally literally threw up her hands. "Ma, have a heart. Knock off with the Dora Doomsayer bit. I've got a gun and I know how to use it. I've got Splendid, and only an imbecile would argue with thirty pounds of snarling wildcat. I've got—"

She stopped as she noticed everyone looking

over her head. Turning around, she met Grandma Amy's glinting hazel eyes and groaned. She wondered once again, as she had many times before, just how necessary that famous oak cane was. When she wished, Grandma Amy could move with the stealth of an Indian stalking a deer.

"You've got a sassy tongue in your head, young lady." Amy nodded a regal acknowledgment as Bram rose and offered her his chair. "You'd do better to keep it firmly between your teeth," she continued as she settled herself comfortably.

For the moment Tally had no choice. A young waitress hurried to the table and carefully deposited in front of Grandma Amy a gleaming silver tray complete with a lovely Revere tea service and a single English bone-china cup and saucer.

Terrific, thought Tally, *we're in our Queen Mother mood.* She glanced at Bram, who had pulled another chair up for himself between Sid and Grandma Amy. He had the expectant look of someone about to view a highly recommended play.

Amy took her time pouring a cup of tea, tasting it and returning cup to saucer with a firm click. "This is all nonsense," she announced, directing an intimidating scowl at her granddaughter. "There'll be no shooting of guns. A properly behaved lady wouldn't even think of picking up a gun."

Tally stared at her grandmother in disbelief. Amy stared back with militant purpose. Will you look at her, thought Tally, choking back a bubble of hysterical laughter. Her nose should have grown a foot. Prattling about proper ladies and guns when everyone knows she used to go hunting with grandpa every fall and never came back without her deer.

Tally summoned up a charming smile and bestowed it on her grandmother. "You win, Grandma Amy," she said lightly, raising her hands in surrender. "No guns. But that's all right. I really don't want to shoot a prowler anyhow; I'd much rather watch Splendid tear out his throat."

"Talia," Edna gasped faintly.

"Don't be a fool," snapped Amy. "It would probably make him sick. Besides which, this discussion is unproductive. To return to the matter at hand, the solution is very simple. Brian can assign you a bodyguard to accompany you when you're away from Snow Meadows, and the man can sleep at your house. You've got a perfectly adequate guest room and bath downstairs, and if you're worried about the proprieties, which would be a novelty, you can lock your bedroom door."

"Masterful," Tally said dryly. "Why didn't any of us think of that?"

She mentally admitted defeat. She'd already argued Brian out of the idea when he'd proposed it that morning, but she didn't feel like taking on Grandma Amy and the rest of the family. With her luck Uncle Alden and Aunt Myra would show up next, and that was definitely more than she was willing to cope with at the end of a hard day. As it was, she'd be willing to bet that sly fox, Brian, put Grandma Amy up to this. It was just the sort of end run he'd try to pull off. Stubborn people, the Irish.

"Don't sit there sulking, girl." Amy chortled with restored good humor. "Even you have to lose an argument once in a while. Besides, I expect this is all just a tempest in a teapot," she said decisively as she lifted that item from the tray and poured another cup. "It will probably all be over within a few days, and we can get on with more important matters. Edna, how are the plans coming along for the Midsummer's Eve party?"

"Ah, before you get into that," Tally said, "will you excuse me. It's been a rather strenuous day, and I need a swim to work out the kinks. I'll see you all at dinner."

She distributed a smile around the table as she slid out of her chair. Bram smiled back with an unreadable look in his eye that had her in a puzzle all the way to the indoor pool.

CHAPTER EIGHT

HUMMING SOFTLY, Tally turned slowly around under the warm spray of the shower, luxuriating in the feeling that she was being reenergized as the pounding water rinsed away soap, sweat and dust. The only flaw in her enjoyment was that she couldn't wash her hair. She made a mental note to bring another bottle of her special shampoo to restock her locker. For now, her hair would just have to wait until she got home.

She tugged at the bathing cap to make sure it was secure. The last thing she wanted was to have her head pickled in chlorine, and she intended to go straight from the shower to the pool.

She firmly suppressed a twinge of guilt. It had been a stroke of luck finding the indoor pool empty in the middle of the afternoon, and she'd quickly flipped on the Closed signs and locked both the outside door and the door to the rest of the recreation wing. She loved to swim naked and rarely had the opportunity unless she used the pool late at night or very early in the morning.

Turning off the shower, she stepped out of the enclosure and wrapped a bath sheet around her dripping body. Without bothering to dry off, she padded across the locker room and out to the deep end of the pool.

Feeling as if she was in an enormous goldfish bowl, she hesitated a minute before dropping the towel and scanning the smoked glass dome. There were a couple dozen people in sight outside, lounging on the patio overlooking the tennis courts and strolling around the grounds. She had to remind herself that, although she could observe them, they couldn't detect her. Not only was it difficult to see through the smoked glass from the outside, but the inside perimeter of the dome was lined with large plants, some of them the size of small trees, and several groupings of summer furniture.

"What the hell, if you've got it, flaunt it," she exclaimed aloud and then grinned at the hollow sound of her voice in the empty vastness of the dome.

"In for a penny, in for a pound," she muttered, dropping the towel and vaulting onto the low diving board. *Where are these clichés coming from,* she wondered in disgust, as she stood poised at the end of the board.

Clearing her mind of extraneous thoughts, she let her arms hang limply at her sides, shaking them a little to loosen her shoulder muscles. She bounced lightly twice, then harder the third time and jumped high with the spring, swinging her arms over her head and arching her body at the apex of her leap, then straightening out as she dropped to cut the water cleanly in a deep dive.

Bram stood motionless against the one section of solid wall in the pool room, an eight-foot-high by thirty-foot-long expanse of brick that was the common wall between the natatorium and the main structure of the inn and that contained the entrances to the men's and women's locker rooms and the utility room.

He knew Tally hadn't seen him; he was effectively screened by a benjamina fig tree and an exuberant schefflera, and if she had spotted him, she'd never have dropped that towel. Voyeurism wasn't actually his style, and he felt mildly—very mildly—ashamed of himself for not speaking out as soon as she'd come from the locker room.

He'd only intended to play a harmless practical joke, waiting out of sight until she was in the pool and swimming away from him, then diving in behind her and swimming underwater until he could grab her ankles. A bit sophomoric to be sure, but he'd hoped to startle her into dropping that cool politeness that was driving him wild. He knew he'd been making progress with her until Saturday night when he'd unwittingly put his left foot in his mouth and then rapidly followed it with the right.

Knowing he should reveal himself, he still hesitated. How was he going to explain this? She had locked the door and put the Closed sign on, but he'd assumed she just liked to swim alone whenever possible. He did himself, which was why Edna had given him a key to the natatorium. It was doubtful if Tally even knew about the key, and if she did, she'd have no reason to suppose he'd invade her privacy.

Damn. How was he going to handle this? So far she had no idea he was here. He'd come in just as she'd started her shower, and he'd immediately gone into the men's locker room and changed into his swimming briefs. The shower was still running when he was ready so he'd slung a towel around his neck and, leaving his cane behind, had limped as rapidly as possible out the door and concealed himself behind the nearest large plants. The best laid plans, he decided ruefully, always get knotted up.

Tally had turned at the far end of the pool and was coming back toward him in a steady, rhythmic Australian crawl. The light in the dome was softened by the smoked glass, and if he didn't *know* she was naked, he would have assumed she was wearing a suit for all that he could see through the water in the dim light.

However, he did know—vividly—and his mind kept replaying the sound of her voice and the stunning sight of her nakedness as she dropped that huge towel. He couldn't remember when he'd last been so surprised. Despite the signs he'd seen in her of a deep passion and an untrammeled individuality, he'd never have believed that she'd romp around, happily naked and totally uninhibited, in a public place.

Well, let's admit it, he conceded, she didn't know that she was being observed by one incredulous but fascinated Englishman. He hadn't a doubt that she never would have dropped that towel if she hadn't believed she was secure in her privacy behind those locked doors.

Bram sighed and shifted his feet. It wasn't like him to dither, but he couldn't decide what to do. Should he follow his male instincts, which were clamoring for attention, or should he be a proper gentleman? Reprehensible as his conduct in the last few minutes might be, he refused to regret it. He wouldn't have missed the sight of that perfectly formed, perfectly proportioned body for a week in the harem of his choice. Who would have believed she could hide that lovely little figure under those formfitting jeans and T-shirts?

When he'd mentally stripped her, which had become an increasingly frequent pastime, he'd visualized her as being more obviously muscled and a bit too thin, and he'd suspected that she probably wore a padded bra and that her breasts were really smaller than they looked. Perhaps that's why he'd become so entranced with her hair. He'd known that when it was unbound and draped around her, it would hide any imperfections of her figure. That honey-in-sunlight mane would be the focus of her sensuality.

How could he have been so wrong? Just the thought of how she'd looked poised at the end of that diving board brought a hot, deep ache surging through his loins. It seemed impossible that a man with his extensive experience with women could have been so misled. He must have seen dozens of women over the years clothed, unclothed, partially clothed. Women that he kissed, stroked, made love to, in the bright glare of noon and in the dim glow of nightlights. Many of them had been actresses and models, and he'd seen at first hand all the artifices that women had devised to enhance their best points and hide their flaws. If any man should have been able to perceive what was underneath those jeans and T-shirts, it was he.

His eyes had been following her progress up and down the pool, even while his mind was debating the available choices and trying to come to terms with the shock it had received. She was swimming away from him again, her body riding high in the water, and he could see the pale curve of her bottom flirting with the little waves caused by her kicking feet.

Once again he pictured her standing at the end of the diving board. With her hair tucked into a bathing cap, there'd been nothing to interfere with his view of her naked form. Yes, she was too short for the contemporary definition of the ideal woman, but her slimly curved body was so beautifully proportioned, the ratio of length of leg to torso to head so perfectly balanced, that her lack of height no longer mattered. In an earlier age she would have been called a Pocket Venus, and men would have vied for her smiles and dueled to possess her.

He gave a choked laugh as he carried the scenario one step further. *This* Pocket Venus would probably have scowled at the smile-viers and told them to go do something useful, and she definitely would have discouraged any man's ideas about *possessing* her. For a delightful moment he imagined how she'd go about stopping a duel. Glue in the sword scabbards? Wax pistol balls? A flock of angry geese set loose on the dueling ground? Once her creative sense of humor was turned loose, the possibilities were mind-boggling.

Enough of this vacillation. He had to decide *now* what he was going to do. As a gentleman he should return to the locker room, dress and unobtrusively slip out the door while her back was turned. As a man with a gut ache and whose brief bathing suit was becoming uncomfortably tight, he wanted nothing so much as to join her in that pool and discover if she felt as marvelous as she looked.

He took a couple of steps forward between the plants, then stopped, still not quite in full view. She was coming back, but she was keeping her head down, occasionally turning it to the side to breathe, and she probably wouldn't notice him if he were standing on the pool edge. He took another step and shifted his weight to his right leg. This was it. The next step had to be either forward or to the side. He breathed in deeply and rubbed his hand over the taut bare skin of his abdomen, then slid it lower and tried to adjust himself more comfortably within the brief French-cut suit, which had become decidedly constricting.

Oh, hell. What was that Americanism? Go for it. Right. I'm going, he decided, watching the movement of her arms as she swam away from him again. Favoring his left leg, he walked unhesitatingly to the edge of the pool and slipped quietly into the water.

Tally had reached a pleasant state of mindlessness. The rhythmic reach and pull of her arms and the counterpoint beat of her kicking feet had

become automatic. She wasn't concerned with setting any speed records. A nice easy pace was all
she wanted so she could just enjoy the silky, sensuous glide of the water over her bare skin. The
goal was relaxation, not a race against time, and
she was vaguely aware that she'd achieved it. If
she became any more relaxed, she'd fall asleep.

It was lovely. For this space in time she didn't
have to worry about a thing. All her problems
were on hold. In fact she wasn't even going to list
the things she wasn't worrying about. This was her
private time, her private space, and she was going
to do nothing more than move languidly through
her aquatic world, turning her head now and then
to breathe and opening her eyes once in a while to
check the guidelines on the bottom of the pool. In
every other way she was most definitely tuned out,
turned off and drifting in orbit.

Something touched her right foot, and she
flicked it sideways to push away whatever was
floating in the pool. She'd have to remember to
mention it to the maintenance people. Someone
wasn't doing his job. The pool was supposed to be
checked constantly to make sure it was clean at all
times.

Hands slid around her calves. *Hands?* Definitely hands. Large, strong hands pulling against her
forward momentum, and what was she waiting
for? Oh, hell. No bodyguard. Who...?

She abruptly snapped out of her initial shock.
Kicking, twisting, turning, she exploded into a
struggling bundle of well-honed muscles, sharp
teeth, gouging fingers and lethal knees. She blinked

furiously trying to clear the water from her eyes, but could catch only a glimpse of a tanned shoulder, the lower part of a leg, a dark shadow moving beneath the water, obscured by the turbulence from her flailing arms and legs.

Then the hands were gone, the presence of another was gone, the shadow was gone. Panting, her heart hammering with the surge of adrenaline and fright, Tally propelled her body in a circle with a strong sweep of her arms, turning her head from side to side to scan the unbroken surface of the water and then the rest of the room.

A cold frisson swept down her spine, bringing an awareness of her vulnerability. She was in the deep part of the pool, at about the nine-foot mark, and suddenly she was frantic to have something solid under her feet. How long had it been since her attacker vanished? A minute? Two? He couldn't have gotten out of the pool without her seeing him. Could he? If he was still in here, clinging to the bottom at the deepest part.... She lunged into a fast crawl toward the shallow end with one thought blazing in her mind. *Get out! Get out and find a weapon!*

She rammed into a solid wall that immediately gave under the impact as hands grabbed her arms and a strong voice commanded, "Don't fight! It's me."

Dazed from the collision, she looked up, blinking in confusion, and found herself staring into Bram's rueful green eyes, which were no more than a foot away. It seemed like an hour but was probably only a minute or so that she gaped at him while her pulse rate returned to normal and her brain scurried to adjust to this newest shock.

"Tally?"

"Er, yes, I think so," she said faintly.

"Are you all right?"

"No. I may never be all right again." Her voice was stronger, she was pleased to note. She was recovering fast, and several items were clamoring for attention.

"Did I hurt you?" asked Bram anxiously.

"That depends on your definition. You scared me half out of my wits, almost put me into cardiac arrest, and have probably given me a permanent tic. Just what were you playing at?"

She was only marginally aware of what she was saying. Most of her mind was busily assessing several very unnerving facts. She was naked. He was the next thing to it. As near as she could tell through the distortion of the water, he seemed to have something dark covering his loins, but there didn't appear to be much of it. He still had his hands on her arms, the water only came to just below his shoulders, and he wasn't moving his feet, all of which indicated that he was standing on the bottom. She wasn't, and a glance at the depth markers along the wall told her she couldn't.

Now what? Help!

"Tally?"

"Sorry. I was...thinking." She finned her hands through the water, trying to put more space between them.

"I'm the one who should apologize. I didn't

mean to frighten you blue." He shrugged helplessly. "It was a dumb prank, and I . . . ."

She was suddenly so close to him that he could feel the tips of her breasts brushing against his chest, and the rest of his sentence went right out of his head. He realized that he'd subconsciously compensated for her efforts to move away from him by pulling her closer.

"Bram, please." She was all too aware of her hardened nipples rubbing against the firm contours of his chest. The contact was generating an inordinate amount of heat deep in her loins in proportion to the friction involved.

"Oh, yes," he murmured, sliding his hands across her back and gathering her into his arms as his head bent toward hers.

Somehow she wasn't all that surprised; she'd sensed his intent from the moment she'd looked up into those peridot eyes and seen the desire vying with the apology. There was a feeling of inevitability to it all. The chemistry between them had been growing steadily stronger for weeks, and she'd known that this moment would come sooner or later. Perhaps it was the very strength of that attraction that suddenly scared her, an instinctive knowledge that this man was changing her perception of herself and her life as no one else had ever done.

I'm not ready for this! She started to repeat it aloud, but it was too late.

His lips touched her half-opened mouth and immediately firmed to secure his advantage, allowing free passage for his eager tongue. Her breath caught painfully in her chest as the warm, moist invasion sent a surge of desire burning through her. This was nothing like the angry kiss of Saturday night. For just an instant longer her hands pushed against his ribs, and then they slid around to his back as she gave in to the urging of his arms and her own need and pressed the full length of her naked body against the bare, sinewy strength of his.

Rational thought dissolved in the heat of their searching tongues, kneading hands and the sensuous stroking of their bodies against each other. Tactile sensation was everything. The flexing of the long muscles of his back drew her exploring fingers. Her hips instinctively began a weaving motion, both enticed and controlled by the hand curved under her bottom and the hard ridge of his manhood rubbing rhythmically against the juncture of her thighs. She arched her back, flattening her breasts against his chest, and his hand holding her head still shifted down to spread across her shoulder blades, anchoring her tightly in place.

She was vaguely aware of a sense of weightlessness and a sudden inexplicable fear that without the hard arms holding her, the strong vibrant body to cling to, she'd drift away into a steadily diminishing speck on an unknown horizon. No! Convulsively she wrapped herself around him, her hands scrambling over his back to grip his shoulders, her legs opening and sliding up along his hair-roughened thighs to lock around his hips.

Despite the buoyant help of the water, Bram staggered under the sudden impact of Tally's full weight. Although his stance had been reasonably firm, it had favored his weak knee, which buckled at her unexpected onslaught. He couldn't regain his balance and plunged under the water, taking her with him.

The abrupt transition from vertical passion to horizontal inability to breathe jolted them out of their erotic embrace. In a tangle of flailing arms and legs they managed to struggle to the surface. Choking on a mouthful of water, Tally tried to cough and gulp in much-needed air at the same time. She grasped Bram's shoulder with one hand to stay afloat while she brushed the water from her eyes with the other. Feeling the slither of water over her bare skin, she opened her eyes just enough to see that Bram was half walking half swimming to the side of the pool, the arm wrapped around her waist drawing her along with him.

"Are you all right?" he asked as he finally gripped the rim and got his feet firmly placed.

She nodded, shifting her hand from his warm shoulder to the cool tile. Her immediate thought, aside from getting her breath back, was to put some distance between them. In a rush of appalled awareness, she'd just realized how close they'd come to a total joining right there in the middle of the pool, in full view of anyone with a key who might decide to take a private swim. Since the key holders were almost all family members or employees, she shuddered to think of the uproar that would ensue. What her least favorite uncle would have to say about sin in the swimming pool and loose-living career women didn't bear thinking about, and she squeezed her eyes shut in rejection of the all-too-vivid vision of an avenging Alden chasing her and Bram around the natatorium, waving a giant wedding ring. She groaned.

"Tally, are you sure you're all right? You have a very odd expression."

"I was thinking of Uncle Alden," she said absently as she opened her eyes and looked at him for the first time since he'd pulled her into his arms.

"Why on earth would you be thinking about your uncle when—"

"I was actually thinking about the color he'd turn if he'd walked in here a few minutes ago." She saw the mixture of desire and amusement spark in his eyes and chided, "It could have happened. He has a key, and he only swims when the pool's closed to the guests. I think he's embarrassed by the paunch he's developed, although thumbscrews and hot pincers wouldn't get him to admit it."

Bram watched the ebb and flow of color in her cheeks and the flickering of her lashes as she looked away from him. He could sense her effort to regain her composure, but, although his own arousal had subsided with their sudden dunking, he wasn't ready yet for her to return to fighting trim.

At the moment their only contact was through their clasped hands, and he fleetingly wondered when that had happened. He looked down at the pale, water-distorted shape of her body, and his abdominal muscles tensed as he remembered the excitement of having her in his hands, pressed against him, wound around him.

"Would you accept that I didn't intend things to get so out of control?" he asked.

She pulled her gaze away from an intent examination of the large black 5 on the wall beside her and looked at him warily. She was too aware for comfort of her total nudity and his near-nakedness and tried to subdue the memory of their fervid kiss. His contrite expression didn't help as much as it should have. The banked fire she could see in his eyes and the sensual tension flowing between their linked hands were unmistakable signals that he was not much calmer than she was. *Words,* she thought, *that's what we need, lots of words.*

"You weren't alone out there, you know," she said, nodding toward the middle of the pool. "Let's admit that it was a mutual loss of control, and leave it at that."

"I'm not at all sure that I want to leave it there." Bram tightened his fingers as she tried to free her hand. "I can't remember ever having such a strong response to a woman or a kiss. Tally," he said, with a note of pleading in his voice, "I really think we owe it to ourselves to talk about—"

"A moment of intense physical desire? What's to talk about? It's not that unusual between two healthy people of different genders who probably haven't had a sexual relationship for some time." She cocked a sardonic eyebrow and gave him a level look. "The 'probably' refers to you. I *know* I haven't had that kind of relationship for several years. I'm assuming you haven't been very...active lately what with hospitals, operations, casts and a fair amount of pain."

"Er, yes, too right. Very off-putting, all of it." He wasn't sure why he was so disconcerted. If he'd ever met a woman capable of plain speaking, there she was floating right in front of him. "Is that all you think it is? Hormones or glands or something, clamoring for attention? Even after our discussion Saturday afternoon?" He carefully avoided mentioning their fight Saturday night. This wasn't the time.

Curious. What does he want, a declaration of love? A man of his experience? He must recognize passion, pure and simple, when he's holding it in his arms. So I'll admit it was rather mind-bending, but still, after such a long dry spell and with someone that exciting, it was bound to be strong. Fiery? Unbelievable? Oh, stop.

"I'm cold. Not to change the subject, but could we get out of here and talk about this somewhere more comfortable?"

"How stupid can I get? Of course you're cold. Here."

Before she realized his intention, he'd grasped her around the waist and lifted her from the water to a seat on the pool rim, quickly hoisting himself out to sit beside her.

"Where—" He forgot his question about her towel as his searching glance touched her body and then rapidly returned to become fixed on her breasts.

She was still regaining her balance after the quick shift from tepid water to cold tile when she noticed his stare and read the hungry fascination in his eyes. For the first time she felt a twinge of self-consciousness. Perhaps it had been the illusion that since she was covered to her shoulders in water, he couldn't really see her, or maybe it was her basic lack of prudery and inhibitions, but her nudity hadn't affected her, aside from its erotic implications, until this moment. But right now she felt impelled to remove her very bare self from the intent clearly visible in his heated gaze.

At a slight rising movement from Tally, he circled her shoulders with one arm, pulling her in snugly to his side, while his other hand drifted almost of its own volition to close gently over one firm, pink-tipped breast. Kneading gently, he savored the satiny texture of her resilient flesh and the small pressure of the taut nipple against his palm.

Caught up in his own fantasy, he ignored her pushing hands and subdued her wriggles by squeezing her more tightly to his side. He teased the nipple with his thumb and delighted in its hardening response. *So pink,* he thought, *I've never seen such a pale pink. Not cherries nor even strawberries, more like strawberry ice cream.*

"Bram," she gasped pleadingly.

"God," he breathed.

"I think I prefer Bram. It's more human, don't you think?" she asked with a faint chuckle that turned into a moan as he lightly pinched her nipple.

"Human...indeed...warm, soft, enticing...."

His arm tightened around her, lifting her, as he lowered his head. Despite the hot tide of desire washing over her, she was just rational enough to remember the potential for disaster. She grabbed a handful of his thick, damp hair and tugged hard enough to stop his descent.

"Bram, remember Uncle Alden."

He turned his head slightly to slant her a reproachful, questioning look. He wasn't in any mood to think of anything except the familiar hot tension in his loins.

"I don't want to remember Uncle Alden right now. Or talk about him. Or think about him. I want to make love to you," he explained carefully, hoping that she would take the hint and concentrate on important matters and forget her bloody Uncle Alden.

"Yes, I know you do," she soothed, gently but firmly untangling herself from his arms and putting a few inches of space between them. It was an effort. She loved the feel of him against her. She loved what his clever hands did to her. She knew she'd love his mouth on her.

"Then what are you doing way over there?"

"It's no more than six inches, and I'm trying to bring us both to our senses. Truly, Bram, this isn't the time or place. Anyone's apt to come in here any minute, and I'd really rather not be caught cavorting with you in the altogether."

"But your altogether is so altogether enchanting," he sighed mournfully. "Ah, well, a gentle-

man never embarrasses a lady, even if she is bare
a— Ow! Don't pinch.'' He rose to his feet with
some awkwardness, reaching down for her hand
to help her up. "Come along, luv, we'll get
dressed and go find someplace to undress with
guaranteed privacy.''

As naturally as if they were fully clothed, he
took her hand and started walking toward the
locker rooms beyond the deep end of the pool. She
shivered violently, and he looked down at her,
prepared to tuck her under his arm for warmth,
for himself as well as her. He, too, could feel a
chill from his drying skin.

He stopped dead in his tracks, staring down at
her head in shock. He couldn't have been more
stunned if the dome had collapsed on him. No hair.
Not so much as a wisp of honeyed silk in sight. Just
a white-polka-dotted mint green bathing cap
puffed at the crown where her braid was coiled. All
his fantasies about making love to her had revolved
around that incredible hair. And what happens?
The first time he really has her in his arms she's the
next thing to bald, and he's so consumed by the
wonder of her body he doesn't even notice the absence of her hair. How could he have been so blind?

"Bram? What's wrong? Is it your leg?''

"No, it's your hair.''

"My hair?''

"Lack of hair.''

"Ah. . . where else. . . do you think I should have
hair?''

"Nowhere. If you had it any place else, it would
look a bit odd, don't you think?''

"You're the one who said I didn't have enough hair. Although, considering that I have more than the whole family put together, I don't understand why you think—"

"I think your hair is beautiful. If you had any more, it would be an excess of riches. Tally, could we discuss your problem after we get dressed? Not that I quite understand what it is, but I'll do the best I can to help."

"But I don't have a problem. At least I don't think I do. Well, I do have problems, but not with my hair."

"Are you sure you haven't caught a chill, luv? You don't seem to be thinking with your usual clarity."

"I. . . . You. . . ."

"Oh, good, here's your towel. Looks more like a blanket. Run along now and get some clothes on. No more than five minutes, mind."

She gave him a wide-eyed look over her shoulder and asked a shade too innocently, "What happens after five minutes?"

"I come after you," he answered, and his smile was a promise. "Oh, and Tally? Don't forget to take off that bloody awful cap, hmm?"

She threw him a killing glance as she pushed through the door to the women's locker room, but he had already disappeared into the other room.

"Chauvinist," she muttered, pulling off the cap and flinging it across the room. "Give a man a kiss, one stupid kiss, and—wham! kazap! zowie!—it's the pluperfect macho stud and his helpless little doll!"

She stomped toward the shower, detouring to retrieve her cap and pull it on again. "Did you hear him? 'Run along now, no more than five minutes, take off that bloody awful cap.' Why did I think he was half bright?" She whipped in and out of the shower in less than a minute, just long enough to rinse off the pool chemicals. "It's a classic case of role reversal; kiss the handsome prince, and the next thing you know you've got a lapful of horny toad."

The bathing cap went flying again, swiftly followed by the large now-damp towel, as she crashed her locker door open and snatched the first clothes that came to hand.

"And whose fault is all this?" She pulled on lace-edged blue bikini panties. "Yours, Miss Free-wheeling Free Spirit." With a minor contortion, the matching bra was in place. "You had to go romping around playing water nymph." She slid into lightweight white jeans. "In the middle of the afternoon, yet." Her voice was muffled as she yanked a pale blue sweatshirt over her head. "Ask for trouble and, lo, there it is." She pulled her braid from the neck of her sweatshirt and let it fall free down her back as she reached for a hairbrush. "But, damn, that was some kiss. It's a wonder it didn't vaporize half the pool."

Turning toward the big mirror on the wall to smooth back her hair, she became aware for the first time of just which sweatshirt she'd grabbed. Ron Taylor, one of the Bishop pilots, had given it to her the last time she'd flown with him a few weeks ago. It advised the economy-minded to Save Airfare. Fly United.

She debated changing it, but a quick look in her locker revealed only two other shirts, both with even more suggestive messages. How did all this start, she wondered, then remembered that it had begun last winter when Steven had dared her to wear a shirt that proclaimed Snow Bunnies Like It in the Cold! Since then she'd been inundated with T-shirts and sweatshirts carrying erotic, irreverent or downright blue slogans, each one accompanied by a dare to wear it.

Looking down at the black lettering on the blue shirt, she wrinkled her nose and then shrugged, muttering, "It's better than naked."

Hurrying now, she took a white plastic bag with her name on it from a stack in her locker, stuffed her dirty clothes in it, pulled the drawstring closed and tossed it in a large hamper in the corner. Within a day or two, she knew, the freshly laundered clothes would appear back in her locker.

"Tally!"

"Coming," she yelled, grabbing her shoulder bag and checking to make sure her gun was secure. She was halfway to the door before she realized her feet were still bare and ran back to dig a pair of sandals from the jumble in the bottom of her locker.

Bram's next call broke off in midword as she came through the door, face flushed and eyes snapping.

"Will you knock it off?" she demanded impatiently. "I'm not a dog."

His eyebrows rose halfway to his hairline. "I never supposed you were." He curled his fingers around her upper arm in a proprietary hold, urging her toward the door to the inn. "We won't have much privacy at my place what with Merton and Sid roaming around. Why don't you show me that intriguing house of yours? Your car's out front, isn't it?"

Tally firmly disengaged her arm and said coolly, "Drop it to slow ahead for a while, will you? I've got to touch bases with a few people."

Bram frowned as he watched her step to the control panel beside the door and flick quick fingers over the buttons and switches. He didn't understand her sudden withdrawal. She'd certainly been warm enough, not to say blazing, ten minutes ago. What was she playing at? She was no inexperienced young girl, and he couldn't have been clearer about what he wanted. Was she still angry about Saturday night? Perhaps they had better discuss it after all.

Tally opened the door and looked back at him. "Are you ready? The pool's open to the public again, and we can go now."

She almost regretted dousing his fire. He was the most stimulating, interesting and dynamic man she'd met in a long time. Add to that his extraordinary good looks and the potent combination of virility and sensuality that practically seeped from his pores, and he moved into a category all his own. Too bad, she mourned, that at the first hint of a woman's surrender he turned into the classic macho man. Urdo the Magnificent dragging his prey home by the hair. *No way, baby. I may have the hair for it, but I sure haven't got the helpless-maiden mentality.*

Slow speed it is, he decided as he moved beside her across the recreation room. Something was definitely nagging at her, and he knew it was strategic to retreat a mile in one direction to gain ten in another. He'd simply bide his time for a while until she let down her guard again. *And then, you delectable water sprite, watch out! I'll have you and your hair wrapped around me before your bloody great cat can lick his ear.*

"Marvelous timing, my dear," Bram murmured, glancing at his watch. "They're just starting to serve tea in the Gazebo Garden."

"And if I'm a good little girl, I can have jam on my crumpet," muttered Tally under her breath.

CHAPTER NINE

"How ARE THE PLANS for Midsummer's Eve coming along, mother? I trust you're taking steps to ensure that this year's party won't turn into another rowdy affair like last year's."

Tally looked across the table and met her brother Cyrus's condemning gaze. She controlled the impulse to stick out her tongue and, instead, gave him a charming smile. Prig, she thought, just because she and Steven started a follow-me dance that ended with half the party's performing innovative fertility rites in the parking lot. Was it their fault that some people just don't know when to get off?

Leaning back in her chair and taking an occasional sip of her Seabreeze, she watched the people around the table and only half listened to her mother and Jean as they brought Cyrus up to date on the party plans. The tradition of an annual Midsummer's Eve party had been started by her mother many years ago as one of her more successful attempts to add a seasoning of Old England to the rich stew of New England. Falling on June 23, Midsummer's Eve was not only a convenient time to officially open the inn's summer season, but was also an excellent opportunity to extend hospitality to acquaintances, business contacts, political associates and others who fell into the category of those who should be acknowledged, but aren't close enough or important enough to be invited to more intimate gatherings. The party had gradually evolved into a major event attended by several hundred people and had become almost too much for Edna to handle, when Jean fortuitously arrived on the scene, willing and eager to please her new mother-in-law.

Tally let her gaze linger on Jean's animated face as her sister-in-law described the decorations. Her eyes shifted to her brother, and she fought the impulse to wipe that sickeningly indulgent smile off his face. She knew that he considered Jean the ideal wife and mother, which was his definition of the perfect woman, and was happy as a hog in a wallow to have her run his home, raise his children, pursue her "feminine" hobbies and activities, and of course adore him unreservedly. Tally had no argument with Jean. If that was how she wished to live her life, it was her decision, and Tally respected it—most of the time. It was Cyrus's "pat her on the head for being such a clever child" attitude that sent Tally's temper into overdrive.

"Is something wrong with your drink?"

Bram's voice banished her irate musings, and she turned to him inquiringly. "Pardon?"

"You were scowling menacingly at your drink. I wondered if something was wrong with it."

"No, it's fine. I was just having an unpleasant thought." She flicked a look at Cyrus. "Very unpleasant."

Bram noted the flare of antagonism in her eyes as she glanced at her brother, and although he had the natural instinct of one male to side with another, honesty impelled him to admit that Tally couldn't be blamed for her anger and resentment. Cyrus had been sniping at her all day. The rest of the group—Edna, Jean, Sidney and himself—had been waiting with growing trepidation for Tally to retaliate. He didn't know what the others feared, but he personally had half expected her to shove dear Cyrus off a mountain or dump him from a gondola.

Under the guise of listening to the discussion about the party, he watched Cyrus unobserved. As an actor, Bram was a quick study where people were concerned. He habitually noticed the small mannerisms, the voice inflections and the reactions that gave away a person's true character, personality and feelings, which were often quite different from what that person said and how he presented himself. Where Cyrus was concerned, Bram drew an almost total blank. Granted he hadn't seen much of Cyrus on either this trip or the last one. As one of the crown princes of the Bishop empire, Cyrus traveled a great deal and spent considerable time in Boston, New York and Washington. However, during the limited time Bram had spent with the man, the impression he'd gained had been of a cool, very controlled, exceptionally brilliant mind belonging to a craggily handsome, physically fit man who was beautifully mannered and reserved to the point of remoteness.

The only times Bram had seen that facade of the

sophisticated tycoon crack were those occasions
when Cyrus displayed indulgent affection toward
his wife and his mother, gentleness toward Pip
and, strongest of all, sarcasm or biting anger toward Tally. Bram had, in fact, been quite taken
aback by the degree of animosity between brother
and sister, which he had only heard about before
today.

Bram glanced down at Tally, sitting to his left,
and noted the tight set of her mouth and the distant look in her tan eyes. He wondered, as he had
several times through the day, what had possessed
Edna to throw these particular siblings into such
close proximity for several hours. He would have
expected the family to pursue the same policy with
these two as they did with Tally and her Uncle
Alden: keep them as far apart as possible at all
times.

Tally's thoughts at that moment were following
a similar track. She was getting madder at herself
by the minute for letting her mother talk her into
this ill-conceived and utterly unpleasant expedition. She'd had other plans, much more interesting and satisfying ones at that, which had been
designed to keep her out of Bram's orbit for the
second day in a row after their encounter in the
pool.

She wasn't ready, yet, to be alone with him
again; she wasn't entirely sure that she'd ever be
ready. His dominating-male act had been a disap-
pointment. For a few brief minutes there, she'd
forgotten about the disagreement Saturday night
and had begun to believe that an affair with him

might be an exciting possibility. Their response to each other had been so strong, the chemistry between them so potent...and then he'd had to spoil it all.

As things had turned out, it was just as well they hadn't sustained that urge for privacy because there was none to be had. She took a sip of her drink to hide her smile as she remembered Bram's frustration when he discovered that Brian had assigned her a bodyguard with orders to stick with her at *all* times. Her only relief from constant observation came at night when she shut herself in the privacy of her bedroom while her watchdog slept downstairs.

Bram's frustration, however, was a mere pique compared to what she was feeling at this moment. Why, *why* had she gone along with this travesty of a happy family outing? She was normally very adept at avoiding contact with Cyrus from one month to the next. On the rare occasions that they were within speaking distance, it took him no longer than five minutes to start criticizing her clothes, her car, her work, her house, her cat, her independence, her life-style, her character, and endless other things that displeased him. In fact, everything about her had displeased him from that summer day when she was four and he was eight.

A small movement at his left drew Bram's polite attention from the ongoing conversation to the enigmatic woman beside him. Her head was bent, and she was rubbing her forehead. Leaning toward her, he asked quietly, "Are you all right?"

"I think so," she said softly. "As all right as

anyone could be who's just had a major revelation."

She looked at him with an odd mixture of shock and amusement, touched with pleading. He sensed her need to get away from the others for a few minutes and swiftly looked around the room.

"Cyrus has signaled for another round, so it will be a while before they're ready to order dinner," Bram murmured. "Would you like to stroll outside?"

Following the direction of his gaze, she saw the French doors leading out onto a broad terrace. In her sudden state of confusion she was quite willing to let him make a decision or two, and so she simply said, "Yes, please," and left it up to him to get them out of there.

"If you'll excuse us," Bram said to the others, his resonant baritone easily overriding their discussion, "Tally and I are going out on the terrace for a few minutes. I'd like a closer look at that lovely view. We'll be back by the time you're ready to order."

With practiced skill Bram had Tally out of her chair and accompanying him across the room. They stepped out into the lingering warmth of the early June evening and began strolling slowly along the terrace, occasionally sipping on the drinks that Bram had brought along.

"Why don't we sit for a few minutes," he suggested as they reached a low wall out of sight of the dining room.

"Sure."

He settled beside her, half turned so that he

could see over her head to the small valley spreading out below them and the mountains rising beyond it. It was a peaceful scene, hushed and softly glowing in the last rays of the sun, which was slowly sinking behind the higher mountains to the west.

"This is beautiful country," murmured Bram. Sneaking a look at her, he decided she needed a little more time and continued, "This bit here reminds me of some charming areas in the Pennines. I once considered buying a retreat there, a place very much like this."

Tally turned to face him and said with a small smile, "I'm all right now, thank you."

"Do you want to talk about it? You mentioned a revelation."

"A major revelation. I'd just realized why Cyrus has always been so antagonistic toward me. It's been going on since we were small children, so long in fact that none of us could remember when it started. Cyrus was always the supercritical big brother, and of course I'd fight back. Before you knew it, it was full-scale war."

"And now you've remembered why?"

"The summer I was four, I gave Cyrus a black eye."

Bram choked trying to turn a laugh into a cough. "And that led to this?" he gasped.

Tally shrugged. "You don't know Cyrus. He never forgets a grudge. He may not remember *why* he has it, but he doesn't forget *that* he has it." Her mouth quirked in a wry smile. "To be fair, it's not just Cyrus. This 'do me and I'll do you' philosophy is one of the Bishops' less admirable traits.''

In view of the past two days, Bram decided not to touch that last line, asking instead, "Do you remember why you socked him in the eye?''

"Oh, yes. It all came back to me in a few seconds as if I were watching a film clip. The boys had their own secret swimming hole back up in the woods. Of course it wasn't all that secret, since several generations of boys had used it, but they liked to pretend that none of their mothers or any of us girls knew about it. As you can imagine, by the time I was four I was bored with the girl stuff and wanted to do what my brothers and cousins were doing.''

"And still do,'' said Bram, chuckling.

"Hmm. Well, on this particular day, I was playing on the beach when I saw Cyrus, Dari, Pres, Steven and some of the other boys heading for the path up to the waterfall. It's really quite a small falls with a shallow pool that's safe for even the little kids. I was determined to go with them, having decided that the boys had all the most interesting adventures, so I took off after them. I hadn't gotten into my Indian phase yet, so I made all kinds of noise, finally even yelling at them to wait for me. Cyrus, as the oldest, was the leader, and he ordered me to go home. I wasn't about to miss out on the fun and refused. Everybody got mad and finally Cyrus leaned over and yelled in my face that I couldn't go skinny dipping with the boys because I was just a stupid girl. That 'stupid girl' did it, and I punched him right in the eye and knocked him flat.''

"Ah, now all becomes clear. The fearless leader—eight, did you say?—brought down by a wee bit of a girl. I don't imagine you were much bigger than a minute when you were four. And to make matters even worse, you did it in front of all his cohorts. Shame on you, Talia. No wonder the man's been mad at you for nearly thirty years," Bram declaimed, the deepening tones of his voice echoing over the small valley.

"And he'll probably stay mad for the next thirty," said Tally, starting to laugh.

"Now that you've remembered, are you going to tell Cyrus?"

"Hell, no," she said vehemently. "With Bishops, understanding does not necessarily bring forgiveness. It's just as apt to bring on another fight."

"Then how does one go about discussing a difference of opinion," Bram began carefully, "or apologizing for an offense?"

"As long as the problem has remained private," she said with equal care, "and strictly between the people involved—so that nobody's pride has been dented in front of others, you understand—then matters can usually be resolved with some quiet discussion over a couple of drinks in a congenial atmosphere, free from interruption."

"Sounds good to me. Any suggestions?"

"Let me think about it. Privacy, as you know, is at a premium right now."

She smiled at him and met his warm, intent gaze. She thought for a moment that she could see a hint of vulnerability, but it was gone before she could be sure, as he returned her smile.

They sat for a few more minutes in a companionable silence. Tally relaxed with the lessening of the tension between them, thinking about the empathy and gentleness he'd just exhibited. His understanding and willingness to help her through a difficult few minutes had changed her perception of the man. On the other hand, his skill in handling her and responding to her immediate needs made her very nervous. She'd always resented attempts to manage her, as if she weren't bright enough to make her own decisions. Bram's manipulation had been so subtle that she hadn't even realized he was doing it until it was all over. How frustrating! She couldn't complain because he'd given her exactly what she needed: escape from that table, privacy, a chance to relax and a sympathetic ear. Insidious, that's what he was. The man would definitely bear watching.

"We'd better go back," Bram said finally, "before someone comes looking for us."

She nodded and rose to walk beside him across the terrace.

"Interesting house," he commented, looking up at the large white building with its gables and black shutters softening the rather stark design.

"It was built by a lumber baron around 1850 as a summer home. It stayed in that family until seven years ago when the Prendergasts bought it and opened the restaurant. It's off the beaten path, but the food's so good people don't seem to mind the inconvenience of getting here."

"I was just coming to fetch you," said Sidney, appearing in the doorway as they reached it.

"Cyrus thinks we should order now since it will take some two hours to return to Snow Meadows."

Bram felt Tally stiffen as they followed Sid across the room, and he squeezed her hand, whispering, "Confound him with congeniality."

No matter how adverse she might be to further manipulation, Tally had to admit that it was a clever suggestion. With Bram's unobtrusive connivance, she managed to keep direct exchanges with Cyrus to a minimum and to concentrate on a general discussion of their day's sightseeing.

Tally still wasn't sure how her mother and Jean had finessed her into joining this expedition. She'd stopped at the inn to have breakfast with her mother and had run smack into Cyrus and Jean. If it had been just family involved, she would have beaten a hasty retreat and eaten in the kitchen. However, Bram and Sidney were also at the table, and Tally knew her mother would never forgive her if she was rude to them.

For a while she thought she'd be able to eat and escape while the conversation was still on Cyrus's extended business trip and his unexpected return the previous evening. However, as soon as he discovered that Bram and Sidney had done very little sightseeing so far, he immediately began organizing a day tour through the White Mountains. When Sidney mentioned wistfully that he wished he could see the view from the top of Mount Washington, but that he was a bit beyond climbing the highest mountain in the northeast, Cyrus had quickly explained that an auto road went all the way to the top, and that jaunt was added to the day's itinerary. Before she knew it, Tally had been included in the plans, and her mother and Jean had conspired to block each of her efforts to excuse herself.

And now here I am, she mused, *playing Miss Congeniality to Cyrus's Genghis Khan. Wait until Dari and Steven hear about this. They'll never believe it!*

"Not a bad job, guarding the Bishop bodies," Bram murmured to Tally, indicating the three men walking out of the restaurant ahead of them. "First-class food, first-class travel and some first-class bodies," he added, running an appreciative eye over her slim navy slacks and the ivory cotton blouse with its inserts and edgings of antique lace.

"Don't worry, they earn their keep," she assured him with a sly grin. "Tracking around after us isn't exactly a Sunday stroll in the garden. Dari and I, in particular, cover a lot of ground in a day, and we also tend to take off on the spur of the moment. Then there's Pip. She can be incredibly stubborn about doing things for herself."

"Must run in the family," he said sotto voce as they stopped a few feet from the others to wait for the car.

"In a way, but Pip's independent streak has more to do with a refusal to be mollycoddled, whereas mine is based on a need to make my own decisions and run my own life. Oh, damn," she groaned as a seemingly endless dark brown limousine glided to a stop in front of them. "Why did Cyrus have to insist on bringing the mogul-mobile?"

"The *what*?" choked Bram.

"The mogul-mobile. Steven christened it that. He won't ride in it, neither will Dari, and usually I won't. It's so damn conspicuous, not to mention ostentatious, I always feel like I should be wearing a crown and throwing sixpences to cheering throngs. I don't know why we couldn't have used one of the RVs. They're even more comfortable, and they don't stand out like a peacock in a flock of sparrows."

"They're also not bulletproof," snapped Cyrus, waiting impatiently by the open rear door, "and this is."

"Paranoid," muttered Tally under her breath as she preceded Bram into the back of the car.

Custom built to her grandfather's specifications some fifteen years ago, the enormous Cadillac measured almost five feet from thickly carpeted floor to padded ceiling, and Tally barely had to bend her head as she moved across the oversize passenger compartment to drop onto the wide rear-facing seat. Bram settled beside her. The generous proportions of the two-passenger seat allowed plenty of elbow room while being intimate enough for private conversation.

"It is something of a mogul-mobile, isn't it?" Bram murmured, looking around the luxurious compartment with new eyes.

He was no stranger to opulent cars. For years the major share of his road travel had been done in limousines, and he'd paid no particular attention to this one other than a vague awareness that it was roomier than usual. Now as he examined it

more carefully, he realized that the compartment
was the size of a small room and furnished much
like a miniature den.

Tally watched him curiously, wondering what
he was thinking, and finally asked, "What's
amusing you?"

Bram's smile became a chuckle. "I was wondering if that rear seat could possibly be concealing a
bathtub."

"Not for lack of trying," she said with a wry
smile. "Grandpa Carleton liked his home com-
forts, but the engineers talked him out of that particular one."

"Are you saying he really did ask for a bathtub?"

"Oh, yes. However, the problems of fitting in a
large enough water tank, a hot water heater, and
an adequate waste storage tank, to say nothing of
the tub itself, proved to be insurmountable. The
only way it could be done was by sacrificing the
trunk space, and that was unacceptable to grandpa. Luggage, of course, could have been secured
on the roof, but grandpa refused to travel around
looking, he said, 'like a damn tourist.' Go ahead
and laugh," she said in mock disgust, "but don't
you think it would have been a nice human touch?
Can't you just see him and Grandma Amy being
tooled along the highway in all the splendor of
their mogul-mobile with a dozen pieces of matched pigskin luggage piled on the roof?"

There was an arrested look on Bram's face, and
then his eyes met hers, and they burst out laughing.

"What are you two finding so amusing?" Edna asked with a hopeful gleam.

"By all means," said Cyrus coolly, "share it with the rest of us. I'm sure we'd all enjoy a good laugh."

"I, er, we were just...."

"Tally was describing some of the more unusual features of the car to me," said Bram smoothly. He was sure that Tally's proud uptight brother wouldn't appreciate what they'd actually been discussing. The man obviously had no real sense of humor.

Seizing the opening Bram provided, Tally plunged through. "I was just telling him about the sterling silver chamberpot with the cut crystal lid that matches the light fixtures." She turned a bland face toward Bram and explained, "Grandpa did consider gold but finally decided it would be too nouveau riche. After all this is just a homey little old family car." *Oh, hell, I shouldn't have said that.*

"Your attempts at levity are, as is so often the case, quite tasteless, Talia," Cyrus intoned.

Bram couldn't resist. "You mean there isn't a silver-and-crystal chamberpot?"

"As a matter of fact, there is." Cyrus's look was quelling. "I don't, however, believe it's necessary to dwell on it."

"Who's dwelling?" Tally snapped belligerently. "I simply think it's the most interesting—"

"Oh, dear," Edna wailed. "Is that car following us?"

As a subject-changer, that was a beaut, thought

Bram with amusement. Life with the Bishops certainly has those ghastly soap operas beat all hollow. In fact it was turning into more of a cops-and-robbers extravaganza. Bodyguards, bulletproof cars, and a Venus with a gun in her pocket. What next?

Everyone was turning or craning forward to see out the rear window as Cyrus pressed the intercom button. "Donnelly, how long has that red Firebird been behind us?" he asked the bodyguard-chauffeur. "And where are Fitzhugh and Williams?"

"We picked up the Firebird coming through North Conway, Mr. Bishop," Donnelly reported, sounding alert but unexcited. "It cut in front of Fitz at the traffic lights, and he decided to tag along behind it for a while to see if it's coincidence or otherwise."

"Has he made up his mind yet?" asked Cyrus on a note of impatience. "We're almost through Conway, and the turn for the Kancamagus Highway is just ahead."

Tally twisted around to look into the front of the car. Donnelly was talking into the microphone of a powerful radio transmitter. This was no ordinary CB, she knew, but the same type of radio used by the state police.

"Cyrus, perhaps we should go home the other way. I know it's longer, but it's almost dark and the Kancamagus doesn't have much traffic at this time of the evening," Edna said nervously. "Some of those curves...and the dropoffs...oh, dear. Jean, talk to him. I'm sure—"

"Mr. Bishop," Donnelly's voice interrupted, "Fitz can't be sure about the Firebird. He thinks there are two, possibly three, men in it, but it doesn't answer the description of any of the Jaketon cars, and it has Massachusetts plates. There's a shopping mall up ahead that's still open. We're going to pull in there and see what the Firebird does. Also, Williams is going to phone Brian. The mountains cause too much interference for us to reach him by radio from here."

"Very well, Donnelly. Tell Williams we'll take the Kancamagus, Firebird or no Firebird. The longer route has just as many danger points, and it would take us right through the Jaketons' backyard. If we haven't already got trouble, why ask for it? Have him pass that along to Brian, and also tell him that we'll phone in from the ranger station. We should know positively by then if we're being followed."

Bram bent his head toward Tally and asked softly, "Is your life always this exciting, or are you trying to keep Sid and me from being bored?"

She tore her gaze away from the window long enough to flash him a laughing look. "No to both. This Jaketon thing is—"

She broke off as the big car turned into the entrance to a small shopping mall. Leaning across Bram she craned to see out the side window, then quickly shifted to the other side, exclaiming, "They've gone past! No, wait, they've pulled into the Texaco station on the corner."

"Damn," muttered Cyrus. "We still don't know."

Tally caught his eye, and they exchanged a long, intense look. For the moment the animosity between brother and sister was shelved. She saw him flick a glance at her shoulder bag, and when he looked back at her, she nodded slightly. She knew he couldn't be carrying a gun; it would have been impossible to conceal it with the casual clothes he was wearing. However, they were both aware that at least two handguns were kept in the cabinets and a high-powered rifle was secured in a hidden drawer under the seat she and Bram were occupying.

Noticing Cyrus checking the master door-lock switch, she looked out the windows and found that they had parked at the curb in front of a drugstore, and that the dark blue LeBaron driven by Fitz was stopping behind them. Williams got out and walked up to the curbside window nearest Cyrus, who pressed the button to lower it a few inches.

"They pulled into the Texaco station down the street," said Williams without preamble, "but didn't stop at the pumps. It looks like they're parked by a phone booth, but we couldn't see if anyone had gotten out."

Tally suddenly felt a twitching sensation across her scalp as if her hair were trying to rise. It was a danger signal that she'd come to trust over the years, a form of premonition that even the family had learned not to scoff at. It had never been wrong.

She scrambled across the compartment to kneel beside the window. "Williams," she said quietly, hoping her mother and Jean wouldn't hear, "tell Brian that I said my hair was standing on end and the odds just narrowed."

"Hell," muttered Cyrus, casting a quick look at Jean and Edna. He breathed a relieved, "Good," as he saw Bram and Sidney begin talking quietly to them. Turning back to Tally, he asked, "Are you sure?"

"Very sure. As much as you can be with something like this, but it's never been wrong before." She looked at Williams, who was obviously about to protest, and said firmly, "I know you don't understand it, but Brian will. Make sure you say it the way I did."

"Tally said to tell you her hair was standing on end and the odds just narrowed," he recited rapidly. "Right?"

"Right. Don't forget it. It's important."

Williams straightened up and headed for the drugstore, and Cyrus closed the window. He leaned forward, elbows resting on his knees and his head close to Tally's so they could talk without the others overhearing them. Tally threw a quick glance over her shoulder and met Bram's inquiring gaze. She tipped her head slightly toward the other women; he nodded briefly and resumed talking to Jean.

"We'd better discuss some options, Tally," said Cyrus, drawing her attention back to him.

She shifted a few inches nearer to him and sat back on her heels. "There don't seem to be too many," she said thoughtfully. "We can't call for police protection without an overt threat. So far, we don't *know* that the guys in the Firebird have anything to do with the Jaketons. All they've done is driven behind us in traffic on the main road between North Conway and Conway. So did a number of other cars. Out-of-state plates, doesn't match our descriptions of the Jaketon cars. What do we tell the cops? That my hair's standing on end?''

"Hardly," Cyrus said dryly. "All we'd need is for *that* to get leaked to the press. Well, we do have the choice of staying. Not here. This place will be closing in another ten minutes, and a deserted parking lot doesn't appeal. We could go to Vinings and wait in the lounge there until Brian can send help.''

Tally peered at his face, trying to read his expression. It was now dark outside, the only light in the car coming from the mall and the parking-lot standards.

"That's one possibility," she said slowly, "but it'll take almost two hours for anyone to get here, and mother and Jean will probably be having spasms by then. On the other hand, if we head for home...."

"We'll be there in the same length of time," he finished. "One thing in favor of that choice is that we're probably safer in the car than anywhere else.''

"You do remember, don't you, that this thing isn't quite as bulletproof as we've encouraged everyone to believe," Tally reminded him.

Cyrus frowned and rubbed his forehead slowly with both hands. Finally he dropped his hands and stared at his sister questioningly. "Do you really think Sonny Jaketon is dumb enough to try shooting at us? For some unspecified grudge? He can't be that stupid."

"No, I don't think he is. He's smart enough to know, no matter how mad he is, that he'd never get away with that kind of violence. *He'd* be more inclined to try to catch one of us alone and do a bit of roughing up, claiming of course that we'd started it. However, I don't trust some of those buddies of his farther than I can throw this car. I know positively that four of them have been run in by the game wardens for jacking deer, and at least half of them have spent more than one night in jail after barroom brawls. The ones that are the closest to Sonny right now have their own little motorcycle gang, and there's no question that they're quick to flash knives in a fight."

"How do you know all this?" Cyrus asked in an appalled tone.

"Come on, Cyrus, I work with construction crews all the time. Everyone talks, especially about the Jaketons. The point I was making is that although Sonny might not start shooting, some of those punk friends of his are more than apt to. I'm inclined to think, though, that they'd probably try playing road games. If those guys in the Firebird are Sonny and his cohorts, I'll bet they're going to try to push us off the road or play chicken or something else stupid."

"Harassment," Cyrus said slowly. "Sounds more logical, but it could be damn dangerous on any of these roads. They've all got bad drop-offs.

Well buffered, of course, but this car is heavy enough to crash through anything.''

"And that's our advantage, don't you see?" Tally urged with controlled excitement. "Grandpa decided not to have this monster fully armored because of the excessive weight and loss of maneuverability, but he did get shatterproof glass and a heavier gauge steel in the doors. Not only will those deflect most anything but a high-powered slug, but that solidity makes hitting us with an ordinary car a very risky business. We get paint scratches; they get mashed. There's no way that Firebird can nudge this thing off the road. Let 'em bump away to their hearts' content. All they'll get is mangled fenders.''

"I hope you know what you're talking about. All right, let's—" He looked past her shoulder and began lowering the window. "Here's Williams. Let's find out what Brian thinks.''

Williams and Fitzhugh reached the window together, and Williams began speaking rapidly. "I got Brian at Snow Meadows. He says he'll go with Tally's hair, and he's starting two carloads of security people on their way. He says to take the Kancamagus, definitely, and don't hurry. Stop at the ranger station to check in with him, and try to kill fifteen or twenty minutes there without alarming anyone. He doesn't want them brought into it. Nothing concrete to go on and too much risk of publicity. Otherwise he'd have us wait there.''

"What about the police?" Cyrus asked.

"He says not until someone makes a hostile move. In other words we're on our own.''

Tally could sense the listening silence behind her and wished her mother and Jean weren't hearing all this. "No problem," she said with all the confidence at her command. "I take it Brian has a meeting spot in mind."

"The lower parking lot at the top of the pass," said Williams, adding in a slightly aggrieved tone, "He says for Tally to drive the limo because it maneuvers more like a truck than a car and she's had more experience than the rest of us with trucks."

Cyrus snorted but didn't comment, and Tally quickly smothered a grin.

"He also said," Williams continued, "that if we had to put the Firebird up a tree, she'd hesitate less than anyone else and have the best chance of getting away with it." He started to say something else but stopped.

Tally grinned at him and patted his hand resting on the door. "Never mind, Williams. I'm sure Brian had something pithy to say about my nasty temper and letting it work *for* us for a change. Okay, guys, let's get organized. I doubt if anything will happen before the ranger station. You two stay behind us for now as a buffer. If the Firebird does follow us onto the Kancamagus, we'll make some changes at the station. Lord knows who they've been calling. We may have trouble as well as security people coming at us from the other end."

"One point," said Fitzhugh. "They've got a CB antenna. It might be a good idea for us to switch frequencies. If they've been monitoring us, it should take them a while to find us again."

"Good idea. Name it," said Tally reaching for the door handle. "Unlock it, Cyrus, so I can get out."

"You're not getting out of this car, Tally. Go over the seat." He pressed the control that lowered the partition behind the front seat.

"Okay," she agreed, rising from her cramped position. "One thing that still bothers me about this is that Massachusetts license plate."

"I gave Brian the number," Williams said. "He's calling someone in Concord to get it checked out. Be careful," he added as he started for the other car.

"Don't worry," Tally called after him. "We're the ones with the tank and the white hats."

CHAPTER TEN

TALLY PASTED A WIDE SMILE on her face and waved to the ranger, who was standing at the edge of the porch to see them off. At Cyrus's muttered "Dammit, Tally!" from the depths of the car, she quickly slid into the driver's seat, closing and locking the door.

"Cool it, Cyrus." She turned the ignition key and the powerful engine purred to life. "After all Brian's clever lies about an urgent business deal that you had to keep on top of, let's not blow it now. Everybody was nice and natural. They didn't suspect a thing."

"It was a smart move on Brian's part to call ahead of time and prepare them for our visit. With the floodlights on, the Firebird didn't dare even slow down. Where do you think they are?"

"Somewhere ahead of us." Tally stopped at the end of the drive to let the LeBaron move out in front. She used the pause to fasten her seat belt and pull her braid around in front of her shoulder so it wouldn't catch behind her hips and limit her freedom of movement.

"Radio check, Donnelly," she murmured as she pulled out a reasonable distance behind the LeBaron and began to pick up speed.

She listened to him verify the new frequency with Williams. Brian must have mobilized half the family, she thought, to get this operation moving so fast. He'd been a step ahead of Fitz on the frequency change, and not only did the two cars meeting them have the new channel, but Brian had sent out almost a dozen Adderly and Preston boys in their CB-equipped pickups and vans to set up a relay network linking Brian to the security cars. Spaced out at intervals of several miles, they could pass messages along the chain without worrying about the mountains interfering.

Tally kept most of her attention focused on the road, checking frequently in the side and rearview mirrors. There were several access roads to campgrounds and scenic spots along this stretch of the Kancamagus, and the Firebird could be lurking in any one of them, hidden by darkness and the thick growth of trees and bushes.

Since talking to Brian, there was no longer any question about the Firebird following them intentionally. Brian's contact in Concord must have set the computer terminals singing because he received a reply from the Massachusetts Registry of Motor Vehicles in just under twenty minutes. The Firebird, as it turned out, *was* owned by a Jaketon—Jessica, Sonny's twenty-two-year-old sister who lived and worked in Boston. Tally wondered if Jessica knew where her car was tonight.

As planned Fitzhugh and Williams had moved out ahead by about half a mile. Tally could see their taillights only intermittently as the road wound through a series of shallow curves.

Tally flicked another quick glance at the rear-view mirror and saw nothing but unrelieved blackness. Cyrus, she knew, had turned off every light in the rear compartment, even the tiny ones by the ashtrays. She doubted that a very dim light would show through the smoked glass of the windows, but she could understand her brother's extra cautiousness in his concern for his mother and his wife, not to mention Bram and Sidney. If it were a question of just her and Cyrus, she knew he'd be a lot less tense. Despite their severe differences, when it came to the bottom line, Cyrus knew damn well she could take care of herself even if the odds weren't entirely in her favor.

She smiled a bit grimly to herself. It was those very qualities in her that Cyrus and some of her other relatives so deplored that enabled her to wiggle out of tight spots relatively unscathed. Tally had learned at an early age that few people could keep their wits about them when confronted with a totally unexpected or outrageous act, especially when said act is perpetrated by a small, harmless-looking female. In certain situations it also helped if the female in question could forget everything she'd been taught about good manners, proper behavior for a young lady, and civilized conduct in general. Tally always operated on the advice her first self-defense instructor had given her when she was fourteen and had asked, "How can I tell before it's too late whether someone is truly hostile or is just being obnoxious or pushy?" He'd answered, "Don't waste time wondering. When in doubt, take him out any way you can, the fastest way you can. If you were wrong, you can always apologize later."

Have I turned that into a general mistrust of men and their motives? She didn't know where that thought had come from, but perhaps it would bear examination—later, much later.

She flipped on the high beams and peered ahead. "We should be coming up on Rocky Gorge about now," she said to Donnelly. "Watch for the road on the right that goes into the parking area. It's parallel to this but screened by underbrush. Be an ideal place for them to wait."

She heard the click of a lighter and could tell from the direction of the sound that it was Sidney, who was sitting in the right-side seat. Cyrus was across from him in the left seat, while her mother and Jean occupied the well-protected rear seat. She could hear the light murmur of the women's voices as they tried to distract themselves from the growing tension. Bram was still in the rear-facing seat, but he'd moved over behind Donnelly and half turned toward the front. Tally could feel his eyes on her, and every time she glanced at Donnelly she could see Bram from the corner of her eye, watching her.

"Rocky Gorge," said Donnelly as the headlights picked up a carved wooden sign.

"The entrance drive should be just beyond this next curve," Tally said. "It goes all the way through the parking area and exits farther down the road. I think that's where we might have problems." She raised her voice and turned her head slightly to be heard in the back. "Anyone who isn't buckled in had better do it now."

"Do you see something?" asked Cyrus.

"Not yet." Tally smoothed one hand across her hair. Her scalp was twitching. "But I expect to any minute. There's the entrance. The drive goes along on the other side of those bushes. Watch for the gleam of metal, Donnelly," she said as he ended a low-voiced exchange over the radio.

"Williams says they didn't see anythi— There! Something's moving. I'm sure I saw a flash of glass. No lights."

Tally sat straighter, closing her hands more firmly around the steering wheel. She called up a mental picture of the road ahead.

"Donnelly, keep your eyes on that exit. Bram, watch ahead for the glow of oncoming headlights and warn me. I'm going down the middle."

She was already easing the huge car to the center of the road as she finished speaking. Pressing gently on the accelerator, she began to pick up speed.

"They're pacing us," said Donnelly.

Suddenly she knew what was going to happen and she reached for her big leather bag. "Bram, quick! Hold this beside my face to block—"

"Bloody hell!" he snarled as he read her mind and lunged up on his good right knee, stretching across the two seat backs so his upper torso was to her right and turning his shoulders to provide maximum screening effect.

"Watch your eyes, Donnelly!" she yelled over Bram's voice.

Then everything happened at once. They reached the exit road, and a dark mass shot out of it heading straight for them. Tally rammed down the accelerator just as the eye-aching intensity of high-beam halogen headlights flared into the driver's compartment, whose windows were clear glass for maximum visibility, unlike those in the rest of the car.

Screened from the direct glare by Bram's broad shoulders and the wide leather bag he held as an extra shield for her eyes, Tally merely squinted slightly and concentrated on her driving. Within a second or two they were past the beams from the headlights. She heard Donnelly groan and swear and knew he hadn't turned away quickly enough. Looking directly into halogen headlights was not only painful but caused momentary blindness, as she'd learned the hard way.

"Where's the 'Bird'?" she asked urgently. She could hear curses and shrieks of alarm from the back.

"Coming up on your right," Bram answered, dropping her bag back on the seat and straightening up partway so that he was no longer blocking her view of the offside. "He left it to the last second before swerving off."

"Scare tactics. He'd have loved to send me off the road." She made a derisive sound. "When moose sing madrigals, he'll put me off the road."

She held the limo steady on the center line at an even fifty miles an hour. She glanced quickly to the right and saw the hood of the Firebird inching past the window.

"Donnelly, are you all right?"

"Okay."

"Can you see? Try to get a look at the driver."

In the radiance of two sets of high beams reflecting back from the thick leafy growth along the road, both the cars and the highway ahead were well defined. She knew that they were rapidly coming up on a wide, sweeping curve to the right, and she had plans for that curve.

Timing is everything, she thought, *and if that's Sonny-boy, he's about to pop his mainspring.*

The road was starting to bend to the right, and she eased up a hair on the accelerator. From the corner of her eye she could see the Firebird pulling up even with them. A low murmur impinged on her consciousness, and she realized she'd been hearing it for a couple of minutes. She looked quickly at Donnelly, saw that he had the microphone near his mouth, and deduced that he'd been doing a running commentary for Fitz and Williams. Donnelly's gaze, however, was fixed intently on the driver's window of the Firebird.

"How does longish curly blond hair, a square face, crooked nose and strong chin strike you?" he asked Tally and the microphone. "Early twenties, big hands, a smug grin that shows perfect teeth."

"Sonny," said Tally in a flat voice "Well, well. Okay, little boy, you want to play games with the grownups, let's just see what you're made of."

Her smile was definitely predatory as she pressed ever so slowly on the gas and began inching very gradually to the right, letting the curve of the road work for her.

"Did you say Sonny?" asked Cyrus sharply.

"Yep."

"What are you doing?" he demanded with some

alarm. It was now obvious that Tally was crowding the Firebird steadily closer to the edge of the road, which was bordered by thick brush and sizable trees.

"Playing my version of show-and-tell. I'll show Sonny how it feels to be pushed off the road, and when I get my hands on him, he'll tell me how he liked it."

"You got 'im, you got 'im," Donnelly chanted. "He's gotta stop or go off."

"He's going off," she said grimly.

"No, he's slowing."

"Like hell! Hang on everybody!" Tally yelled.

She stomped on the brake and swung left, throwing the rear of the heavy car into a controlled skid. Those inside felt a jolt and heard the crunch of metal. The next instant Tally had straightened the limo and was again picking up speed as she came out of the broad curve onto a long stretch of rising road.

Bram and Donnelly had lowered two of the side windows and were leaning out to look back.

"Lovely!" Bram shouted exuberantly. "Well done! You smacked him right off into the bushes."

"Damn," said Donnelly. "He missed the trees. He'll be after us again unless he's bottomed out on a rock."

"If he's dumb enough to try that again, he's going to end up with one plucked Firebird," said Tally, and it sounded more like a promise than a statement.

"Oh, dear, Tally, did you have to do that?" cried Edna. "My heart was in my mouth. And what have you done to this lovely car?"

"Don't worry, ma, the car's all right. Probably nothing more than a few scratches and maybe a little dent or two. That crunch you heard was the Firebird. Flimsy things," she said blithely. "They don't make cars like they used to."

She heard a soft chuckle from Bram and turned to give him a quick smile.

"Too bad this isn't one of your movies," she said, turning back to watch the road. "You could duck into the trunk—sorry, boot—do the secret chant and leap out as Troy Castleman. We could probably use him before we're through this."

"I'm almost afraid to ask," said Bram, "but what's the secret chant?"

"Off wif 'er 'ead, 'enery!" Tally cried in fractured Cockney.

Bram and Sidney roared with laughter, and even Cyrus managed a short bark of amusement.

"Am I mistaken or are we starting to climb?" asked Bram after a few moments.

"We've been climbing for some time, but it's so gradual that you don't notice it for a while," Tally explained. "The rate of ascent will start increasing in another couple of miles."

She glanced at Donnelly, who had been leaning close to the crackling radio. "Something?"

"Car coming down. Late model, light colored, probably normal traffic."

"I see the lights." She checked the side mirror. "More lights coming up behind us. Somebody see if you can identify the car."

She watched the oncoming headlights, keeping the limo squarely in the middle of her own lane but easing back to forty. The approaching car seemed to be traveling at about the same rate of speed. Another minute and it was past.

"Nothing," she breathed in relief. "Has anybody figured out what's behind us?"

"I think it's the Firebird," said Cyrus. "I could see red when the lights of that other car hit it."

"It seems to be hanging back there for now," said Bram after a few minutes.

Donnelly murmured into the mike, and Williams's voice could be heard in the silence of the car as he replied, "We've moved out about two miles ahead of you. We're turning around at Sabbaday Falls and coming back to take a look."

"Do you really think Sonny will try it again?" Bram asked quietly.

Tally turned her head just enough to catch a glimpse of him from the corner of her eye. His folded arms were resting on the seat backs a few inches from her right shoulder, and he'd propped his chin on one fist so he could speak almost directly in her ear.

Somehow he was creating the impression that they were in this together, a sense of the two of us against the world that Tally found more than a little unnerving. She took a deep calming breath and then wished she hadn't. The subtle scent of his cologne, evocative of leather and woodsmoke, triggered the memory of his warm hand stroking her naked breast. She felt the same deep heat rising again, and she impatiently shifted her hips within the confines of the seat belt. This was most definitely *not* the time for such reminiscing!

"Tally?"

"Sorry. I was watching Fitz," she prevaricated as the LeBaron swept past them. "I can't even guess what Sonny might do. If it's a matter of pitting the Firebird against the mogul-mobile, he'd have to be totally stupid to try it again. He's got to know now that I won't hesitate to run him up a tree and that he can't do much damage to this tank with that thing."

"He does seem to have learned some caution if the distance he's maintaining is anything to go by."

"That's what's bothering me. If he's going to give it up, why keep tagging us?" She was thinking out loud as much as answering his question. "I wish I knew who he called. I've got this nagging feeling that the danger is ahead of us, not back there. Those bikers he's been hanging out with are real hoody types. Sonny'd stop short of wiping out a carload of Bishops, but—"

"What was he playing at back there then?" Bram interrupted to ask.

"Games. A form of chicken. He wanted to see if I'd panic and go off the road. But I don't think he'd have done it if there'd been a steep drop-off there rather than brush, rocks and trees. He knew that between my hitting the brakes and the weight of this beast, all we'd have gotten would be some scratches and dents on the car and perhaps a bruise or two on the passengers."

Light flashed in her eyes, and she squinted at the side mirror, noting a second set of headlights. The radio hissed, and Williams reported, "It's

Sonny all right, and what's left of his sister's shiny red Firebird. You did a nice job on the left rear fender, Tally, and the right side looks like he had a close encounter with a tree or a large rock. Doesn't look like anyone's hurt. They're all drinking. I'd say it's beer from what I can see."

"Waiting?" murmured Tally half to herself. She motioned to Donnelly to hand her the microphone. "Move out in front again, guys, but be damn sure not to get out of radio contact. We're coming up to the steep winding climb to the pass in about ten minutes. If we're running into trouble, that's where we'll meet it."

"Got any idea what?" asked Williams.

"Noooo," drawled Tally slowly. "But I can't get those bikers out of my mind. Just...expect anything."

Fitz had to wait for the next straight stretch of road before he could pass. As first one and then another car flashed by in the opposite direction, Tally crossed her fingers that nothing else would be coming along for a few minutes. This was the last passing zone before the ascent to the top of the pass. Of course, with no traffic to speak of one could pass on a couple of short straights farther up, but it was risky.

She rounded a curve, and her lights picked up the broken yellow line down the center of the road. From the corner of her eye she saw headlights reflected in the side mirror, moving out to the left lane and coming up fast. She eased the limo to the right to give Fitz plenty of room. Then he was past and swinging back to the right side of the road. She flickered her lights at him, and his taillights blinked an acknowledgement as he increased speed and began pulling away.

Tally could feel herself tensing up and consciously tried to relax. The quiet murmur of voices drifted from the back. She could distinguish those of her mother, Jean, Cyrus and Sidney, but Bram seemed to be content to watch silently over her shoulder. She could smell his enticing cologne with every breath she drew. It was no help to her efforts to relax.

"Now, dammit, do it now before the drop-offs," she muttered as she guided the mogul-mobile through a series of long sweeping curves.

They were climbing steadily now, the angle of ascent becoming increasingly steeper. Bram looked to the right but saw only a black nothingness beyond a sturdy post-and-cable guardrail and a thin line of brush. He brought his gaze back to Tally's profile, and in the dim glow of the dash lights he could discern the deepening tension in her face and in the tightening of her hands around the wheel.

Williams's voice crackled over the radio. "Station wagon coming down. We're just going into the first bad curve. Thought I saw lights way up at the pass."

Tally's scalp twitched. "Tell him to try to raise the backup cars."

Donnelly repeated the instruction, and they listened to Williams's attempts to contact the relief cars.

"No use, Tally," Williams finally reported. "The mountain's in the— Heads up, Fitz! Lights right across the road. Four bikes spaced out abreast. Coming like bats. We're going... meet...worst place...." The transmission was breaking up, and everyone strained to hear as Donnelly increased the volume. "Hold...middle!...it, Fitz...ing in his hand...out! Look ou...n't see. What...ue paint!"

"Paint!" Tally yelled. "Those bloody damn bastards threw paint across their windshield! And they're at that bitch of a curve with a straight drop-off. Gimme that!" she snapped, lunging to her right to grab the mike from Donnelly while one-handedly whipping the huge car into the first of a tight series of right-angle turns.

"Fitz! Get onto the turnout and wait for us," she shouted into the microphone. "Williams! Are you all right? Answer!"

She tossed the mike to Donnelly, grasped the wheel with both hands and tapped the headlight dimmer switch as a station wagon rounded the acute curve ahead, approaching at a conservative speed. Far too conservative for Tally's temper.

"Dammit, get out of the way, you clod," she snarled just as Williams's voice came over the receiver.

"Blue paint all over the windshield. Made it onto turnout. Both okay. Watch out, Tally."

The station wagon went by, and now Tally could see lights flickering through the thin brush edging the road above and to her right. That road and the section she was on formed a V, meeting in an extremely sharp turn dead ahead. The V was in the last and steepest part of the climb to the Kancamagus Pass. On the right was a precipitous slope, covered with brush and rocks, which disappeared into blackness several hundred feet below. On the left, just a few feet from the road, the granite bastion of Mount Kancamagus rose almost perpendicularly, lightly wooded with birch and spruce.

Tally let the car slow slightly as she watched the bobbing lights above, judging distance and speed.

"Tally, what are you going to do?" asked Cyrus, clearly recognizing her anger and fearing her retaliatory steps.

"Get even. Brace yourselves, everyone. Here we go!" she whooped as she saw the four headlights come out of the turn and spread across the road a hundred yards ahead.

She simultaneously slammed down the accelerator with her right foot and hit the high-beam switch with her left foot. Blessing every gas-guzzling cylinder of the superpowerful engine, she whipped the surging behemoth to the middle of the road and began weaving rapidly from side to side, while she pressed her thumbs down on the ring around the inside of the steering wheel to activate the Klaxon.

Bram braced himself across the seat backs and stared unbelievingly at the rapidly unfolding scene. He felt as if he were in a Troy Castleman film. He expected to hear an amplified voice yell "Cut!" at any moment. But it didn't, and the action continued second by second.

With the raucous blaring of the Klaxon bouncing off the mountains in deafening soundwaves,

Tally roared erratically up the road to meet the oncoming bikers whom she'd half blinded in the sudden blaze of the halogen high beams.

They panicked. Unable to see clearly through tearing eyes, heads ringing from the ear-shattering blasts of the Klaxon, terrified of the huge black mass that seemed to be charging at them from six angles at once, they tried frantically to get out of the path of the oncoming monster.

Tally saw them begin to swerve and try to scatter. Fury and adrenaline surged through her. With a full-throated scream of, "Chaaarge!" she yanked the wheel in a short arc from side to side, throwing the long car halfway across the right lane and then immediately back across the left lane. She felt a scraping bump against the left front fender and had a brief glimpse of an irregularly shaped dark mass flying through the air out of range of her peripheral vision. There was another thump at the right rear, and then she was past them all.

"Are any of them coming back?" she called as she began applying the brakes and moving to the right side of the road. She was almost to the sharply angled turn.

She silenced the Klaxon just as someone lowered a window, and they heard the crashing and screeching of tortured metal, the tinkle of broken glass and the groans and curses of the fallen enemy.

After a few seconds Cyrus said, "I don't think any of them can." There was a note of awe in his voice.

"Good heavens, Talia," said her mother faintly.

"You scuppered the lot!" Bram exulted. "Even got the Firebird."

Tally barely heard the rest of the jumble of exclamations. With intense concentration she was jockeying the mogul-mobile to a relatively safe spot at the side of the road. She stopped, shifted to Park, and firmly set the emergency brake. Leaving the headlights on high, she turned on the flashers and then pressed the trunk-lid release.

"Cyrus, we'd better set some flares back there before someone comes along behind us and smashes right into all that."

She'd taken one quick look in the side mirror when she stopped. In the reflected light from the high beams, she'd seen the tumbled motorcycles and sprawled bodies and the Firebird slewed sideways across the road.

"Slide over here, Donnelly, and stop this thing if the emergency lets go," she said, opening the door and getting out of the car. "Has Williams been able to reach anybody?"

"Not yet. He's still trying. Fitz is on his way down."

"I thought the car—"

"On foot. It's less than half a mile."

Tally started for the rear of the limousine intending to help Cyrus, but her attention was caught by the argument going on between Sidney and her mother. He and Bram had gotten out of the car and were standing at the open rear door. Sidney was leaning back inside, involved in a heated discussion with Edna, while Bram leaned on his cane, surveying the scene along the road.

"What's going on?" Tally asked softly as she stopped beside Bram.

"Your mother and Jean want to get out and help. Sidney wants them to stay safely in the car, just in case," he explained succinctly.

He looked down into her upturned face and promptly slid a comforting arm around her shoulders. She looked so tired, he thought, and her eyes were shadowed with a bitter acceptance. He knew what she was feeling: the letdown in the aftermath of an overdose of fear and adrenaline, and the despair of knowing what her protective actions may have caused.

Tally stared back at him, reading the understanding and encouragement he was trying to give her. *He's doing it again,* she thought, *sensing my needs even before I recognize them and then answering them whether I want him to or not. Oh, hell, I don't want this on top of everything else right now.*

But she did, and despite her efforts to deny his gift, she could feel the hard knot of tension in her chest begin to unravel. His arm tightened imperceptibly, and for just a minute she let herself relax in his firm hold and lean against his warm, solid strength.

"You're trembling," he said, bending his head so that only she could hear him. "It would be surprising if you weren't suffering from some degree of shock. Why don't you wait in the car with Edna and Jean? Maybe they'll stay put if you—"

"No. No, I can't," she muttered, straightening away from him. "I've got to help Cyrus, and I should see if...I managed to kill anybody." Her voice choked on the last words.

"Bloody hell," Bram growled. "It wasn't your fault if you did. What were they trying to do to us? It's a miracle Fitzhugh and Williams didn't go over the damn cliff, and those bastards would have pulled the same stunt on us. Didn't you see the paint splashed on the road? They were carrying more bags of it, ready to throw at us."

Tally turned to look down the road. There was just enough light for her to see the streaks of light blue paint splattered in three places. She closed her eyes momentarily at the thought of that blinding mess spreading over the windshield as she went into that sharp turn with the rock wall on one side and the sheer drop on the other.

"God," she breathed. "What if—"

"It didn't happen," he said compellingly. "Because of you. Because you had the courage and the quick wits to prevent it. Tally, you only did what you had to. There's nothing—"

He broke off at the sound of running feet, and they turned in time to see Fitz pound around the curve into the glare of the headlights. He'd left his jacket somewhere, and even in the cool night air his light blue cotton shirt was damp with the sweat that was running down his face and neck.

"Are you all right?" he panted as he grasped the top of the open door and tried to catch his breath. "Is anyone hurt? What happened?"

Bram waved a hand at the carnage spread across the road and announced, "This time the Charge of the Light Brigade carried the day."

Tally managed a wobbly grin as she added, "Because this time they were led by a Yankee—the real kind from New England—and you know what a determined breed we are."

"I know what a terror you are when you lose your temper," Fitz said to Tally. His approval, in this instance at least, was clear in his voice. "Well, I'd better give them a hand with the mopping up."

Taking another look down the road, Tally noted that at some point Sidney had joined Cyrus, and he was helping one of the bikers to stand up. "I should—"

The inimicable look in Fitz's eye stopped her. "You should stay right here," he said firmly. "You've had more than enough for one night. There's no need for you to try to cope with that mess. The others will be here soon enough."

His words were prophetic. They heard the radio crackle to life and Donnelly's low voice reply. Seconds later he leaned out the window to report, "Williams is in contact with the backup units. They're just topping the pass and will be here in a few minutes. They've sent word back along the network, and Brian's alerting the cops, and then he and Steven are heading out here."

Tally groaned. "What are they doing that for? Cyrus is here, and I'm perfectly capable of. . . ."

Her voice trailed off as she realized she was talking to empty air. Fitz had moved down to join Sidney and Cyrus, and Bram was leaning into the car to talk to her mother and Jean, who were still protesting their enforced idleness. She shifted from foot to foot indecisively, watching the activity around the Firebird, then began walking in that direction.

She hadn't taken two full steps before a strong hand clamped around her left wrist and pulled her to a halt. She swung around and found herself facing Bram's admonishing look. His attempt at sternness was diluted by the amusement glinting in his eyes.

"Will you for once do as you're told?"

"Will you let me go?"

"Will you stop being so bloody stubborn?"

"Will you stop being so damn bossy?"

"I will if you will."

"Will what?"

"Will discuss the terms later in private, you little Tartar."

"Who are you calling a Tartar, you big British bully?"

Bram's reply was lost in the honking of horns. They looked up to see two station wagons and a pickup truck speeding down the road above, then slowing to negotiate the turn and finally coming to a stop along the edge of the pavement opposite the limousine. Doors flew open and a dozen men swarmed out of the vehicles.

Two tall familiar figures separated from the group and began strolling across to the mogul-mobile. They paused at the center line to stare down the road at the scene of confusion, their hands stuck in the back pockets of their jeans and their heads nodding judiciously in unison.

"Yep, it has all the earmarks of a Tally the Terror epic extravaganza," said Dari loudly. "We could call it *Carnage on the Kancamagus*."

"Not bad," said Phil, equally loudly, "but I rather like *Mayhem on the Mountain*."

"Or how about *Bashing the Bikers*?" suggested Dari as they continued strolling.

"You're forgetting the Firebird," chided Phil. "What do you think of *Junking the Jaketons*?"

They stopped and gazed in polite inquiry at Bram, who was doubled over laughing.

"Sorry," he gasped finally, "but...does it run...in the family?"

"What?" asked Dari.

"He's been in the starlight too long," said Tally. "What are you two doing here?"

"I'm only an in-law," Phil reminded them.

"Alliteration," Bram explained.

"Oh, that," Dari said, chuckling. "It's a game Grandma Amy's always played with the kids. Says it sharpens the wits, improves the vocabulary and encourages a sense of humor."

"And it's catching," added Phil.

"It didn't do much for Uncle A or even pa," muttered Tally.

"Win some, lose some," Dari said blithely.

Despite his laughter, Bram was momentarily disconcerted by everyone's lighthearted raillery. Then he remembered Tally's explanation about stiff upper lips and Yankee stoicism. He took a closer look at Dare and Phil and finally saw the concern underlying their laughter and teasing. With his increased perception he turned to Tally and noted once again the unmistakable signs of strain and shock in her face and the slight trembling of her hands. When she caught him watching her, she quickly stuffed her hands in her pockets, squared her shoulders and gave him a challenging look.

Before Bram could react, the rear door of the limousine opened, and Jean stepped out followed by Edna, who held out her hands to the newcomers, exclaiming, "Darius! And Phil! What are you doing here?"

"That's what I asked," said Tally.

"Where did you think we'd be?" Dare hugged his mother and gave her a quick once-over. "Did you think we'd just sit around the inn waiting to hear whether you'd all gone tumbling ass over teakettle down a mountain? Brian had to stay to coordinate everything and to wait for Steven. *He* borrowed the governor's helicopter and should be at the Falls by now. In fact, both of them are probably on their way here."

"Oh, for God's sake," Tally all but snarled, "Cyrus and I—"

"To borrow one of Grandma Amy's favorite expressions, sis, 'pull the zipper!'" Dari placed a callused finger under Tally's chin and pushed up, firmly closing her mouth and tilting her face up to his. He gave her a no-nonsense look and said decisively, "No arguments, no discussion. This is what you're going to do. Hear me? You, mother, Jean, Bram and Sidney are going to get in that station wagon over there, and one of the men is going to drive you all back to the inn. No arguments, I said. This place is going to be crawling with cops very shortly, and we want all of you out of it."

He waved his free hand at the busy scene below them. "Donnelly will take the rap for that. We don't want it known that you were driving. It's a clear case of self-defense, and we've got the paint-smeared LeBaron to prove their lethal intentions."

"But—" One word was all Tally managed, but her eyes sparked gold defiance.

"Cool it, sis, dammit. Think. The press is going to get hold of this, if they aren't already on the way. This isn't just for your sake or mother's or Jean's. It's also to protect Bram and Sidney. God knows what the gossip columnists would make of it if they got hold of this story and discovered Bram was involved. He doesn't need that kind of publicity, and besides, it would blow his cover."

As reasonable as she knew his arguments were, Tally still seethed, and for another minute stood, fists on hips, staring mutinously up at her sometimes-favorite brother.

"You could have asked," she grumbled finally. "I'm not some wimp who has to have her decisions made for her."

Bram winked at Dare and slung an arm across Tally's shoulders, starting her reluctant footsteps on the way to the station wagon. Step by step he could feel the tension draining out of her. He sensed that this last argument had been a matter of principle rather than conviction. She'd had all she could take, and he was sure that deep down she knew it. He didn't say anything, just guided her to the rear seat of the large wagon and settled her beside him.

"Don't forget this," said Dare, handing Bram Tally's lethal leather bag before he escorted Jean around to the front passenger seat.

Sidney helped Edna into the middle seat, and

within moments their driver had turned the car around, and they were on their way home.

Bram pulled his tired Tartar closer and said softly, "You've done a hell of a job of work. Now why don't you sleep for a while? I'll wake you up before we reach the inn, so no one will know you went all wonky."

She was suddenly exhausted, but she managed to look up at him through half-closed eyes and mutter, "Bully!" before she shifted onto one hip, wrapped her arms around his taut waist, and snuggled her head into the hollow of his shoulder. She was asleep before they topped the pass.

CHAPTER ELEVEN

BRAM LEANED FORWARD, staring intently through the windshield as he tried to see through the thin belt of trees between the lake and the road to Tally's house. He could catch a tempting glimpse here and there of the intriguing structure perched on the end of her two-and-a-half-acre peninsula, which angled out into Samantha's Lake from the northeast shore.

"It looks like natural wood," he said to Dare, who was driving the station wagon.

"It's cedar," Dare replied, "which weathers beautifully. Mostly clapboards, but she's got some vertical silo-type siding on the bay and the tower. Look through the trees at the next bend. You'll see she's also used lots of glass on the south-facing areas, which overlook the lake and the most spectacular view."

Dare slowed the wagon to a stop when they reached the bend, and Bram got his first clear sight of the house. Since it was still some distance away, he had difficulty picking out all the details, but he could see at least three gables, deep porches around the first floor and an odd structure, which looked like an attached gazebo off the front corner of one porch. Perhaps the most interesting feature was an angled expanse of glass resembling half of a greenhouse that seemed to connect the main house to a sizable two-story tower with wraparound windows on each floor. The roofs were steeply pitched, and those on the tower, gazebo and two-story bayed porch were conical.

"My word but it's large. How many rooms are there?" Bram asked.

"Who knows?" Steven said from the seat behind Bram. "She's always fooling around with the thing. Some of the inside walls slide back into other walls. One day you come out and find two huge guest bedrooms in the east wing, and the next day they've become four."

"Her latest kick," Dare added as he continued along the road, "is to put a small indoor pool behind the greenhouse so she can swim at night in the winter without having to go down to the inn."

"I thought she was going to put it in the basement," said Brian, who was sharing the middle seat with Steven.

"She decided she didn't like swimming underground," Dare said dryly. "Besides, she's already got the spa in the greenhouse so most of the basic piping is available."

"Spa, pool, guest rooms—what is she running, a mini-inn?" asked Bram.

The other three chuckled knowingly, and Steven explained, "She claims, one, that she likes elbowroom; two, that you never know when a spare bedroom will come in handy; three, that her friends have odd tastes in entertainment and she likes to offer a full range of facilities—"

"What does that mean?" Bram asked.

"You gotta see for yourself," drawled Brian. "Words just aren't adequate."

"We wouldn't want to spoil the surprise," added Steven.

"Heaven forbid," said Dare. "After all, a certain amount of shock is good for you. Jolts the circulation, you know."

Bram eyed them all with a wry grin. "I just remembered why it took four years to recover from my last visit."

Dare turned onto a wide paved drive and stopped in front of a pair of heavy steel-mesh gates. Bram saw that they were set into a high fence of the same material that stretched off into the trees on both sides of the drive. Dare picked up what looked like a pocket calculator from the seat beside him and tapped out a series of numbers. A few seconds later the gates slid open, and he drove through, continuing along the winding road, which wound through two acres of neatly kept woods.

"Does Tally garden?" Bram asked in some surprise as they stopped on the turnaround by the garage, and he noticed the flowering shrubs and the gardens bordering the lawns.

"Just designs them," explained Steven. "She sets this up as a 4-H project for some of the kids."

"Always thinking, that's our Tally," said Dare as he and Steven unloaded two stainless-steel boxes from the rear of the wagon.

They were almost at the porch when Splendid came bounding across the lawn, rumbling a greeting as he nudged the men's legs. Bram reached down to rub him behind the ears while Dare crossed the porch and began opening the security lock on the back door.

"Hold on a minute until I get the system shut off," he called, striding quickly inside.

Within a few minutes the men and Splendid were milling about in the long galley-style kitchen. Bram wandered toward the front of the room while the other three argued over who was going to wake Tally. He glanced at his watch, noted that it was not quite seven-thirty and decided to let someone else rouse the sleeping lioness. It had been a long tough night; perhaps the most tiring part for her had come after they'd reached the inn and she'd found herself pitched in battle with her Uncle Alden.

Bram muttered an expletive under his breath. He simply didn't understand that man. Tally had been in no shape for even a quiet discussion of the evening's events, never mind the tirade Alden Bishop had unleashed, in which he'd blamed her for all the trouble with the Jaketons as well as every other unpleasant event that had befallen the family in the past ten years. He'd been abetted in his attack by that cold fish of a wife, and Bram wished he'd had the right to tell them both to belt up.

Darius or Steven, Bram knew, would have put a stop to it, and Phil Stanton did try his best. However, as an in-law, he did not have as strong a position as the other two, and despite his best efforts, Alden and Myra seemed set for a night-long donnybrook until Tally had finally lost her temper and stalked out the door. And of all times for his knee to decide to give out, it had to be then. Before he could catch up to her, Phil had her in his car and was driving her home.

"Hey, Bram," Dare called, "if you want your choice for breakfast, you'd better get it before these vultures scoff the lot. Looks like I've been elected to wake up the Terror. With luck I'll be back in a few minutes."

Bram turned back into the room, noticing for the first time that he'd walked through what was apparently the dining room, although it was open to the kitchen. Then he looked more carefully and discovered the tracks for a sliding wall. His eyes skimmed over the walnut burl table with its eight walnut chairs upholstered in antique gold velvet, the lovely old sideboard with its rosewood panels, and hanging above it a painting that looked suspiciously like an original Monet. On his right beyond the sideboard, the room opened into a hall. On his left the entire wall was glass, and through it he could see the lush plants in the greenhouse, which was two steps down from the dining room. In the midst of the garden area was a small round table and two chairs. He wondered if Tally used it as an informal place to dine when she was alone.

He walked over to the glass wall, found the release lever and slid the wall back, watching it disappear into its slot in the kitchen wall. With a quick glance at Brian and Steven busy in the kitchen unpacking covered dishes from the steel warming boxes, Bram stepped down into the greenhouse's moist air, still cool from the night.

He stopped a few feet into the room and looked around with a delighted grin. Along the south wall the plants, some of them the size of small trees, were set out in random-sized brick-walled gardens. He heard the trickle of water and, searching for the source, discovered a small bronze dolphin fountain in the midst of the gardens. At the far end of the slate-floored room a very solid-looking door with another of those security locks led to what he assumed was that intriguing tower.

The north-facing ceiling and wall were of wood rather than glass, and that half of the room was raised. Except for the two wide, shallow steps leading up from the garden area, it was partially screened from outside view by an intricate wrought-iron fence backed by long narrow planters full of lush ferns.

"Bram, are you coming?" This time it was Steven's voice, and Bram called back, "Just a minute."

Unable to resist, he mounted the two steps, took one comprehensive look and laughed. If he'd had any doubts left about her sensuality, he thought, this sybaritic playroom would have put them to rest. In the far corner was the unmistakable enclosure for a sauna, and a sunken hot tub large enough to hold half the Bishops took up most of the floor space on the left. The rest of the area was furnished with natural wicker loungers cushioned in lavender and white, and several low, two-drawer wicker chests, which also functioned as tables.

"Makes you want to jump right in, doesn't it?" asked Steven from the foot of the steps.

"Mmm," murmured Bram, "but not alone. Why does she want a swimming pool? That thing's almost big enough to do laps in."

"Ours not to reason why," Steven intoned as he led the way back to the kitchen. "You'll have to ask Tally why she gets these bees in her hard hat. In fact, you can ask her now. I think that's her disgruntled grumble I hear coming down the stairs."

"Why are you miserable marplots dragging me out of bed at this ridiculous hour? Do you realize what time I got to sleep?"

Tally's voice and Splendid preceded her into the kitchen with a grinning Dari bringing up the rear. Tally distributed a ferocious scowl impartially among the four tall men.

Bram took one look at her and bit his lip. He didn't think she was ready yet for humor. Besides the scowl she was wearing a ragged pair of denim cutoffs and a sleeveless navy sweat shirt, which informed anyone interested that Small Persons Think Big. Don't Ask If You're Under Six Feet. With some effort Bram controlled the impulse to remind her that he was six-two.

"At least you brought your own breakfast," Tally muttered as she examined the array of food on the counter.

"We wouldn't dream of asking you to cook," said Steven with a shudder.

"Ha! What would she cook?" Dari said dryly. "The only things in the refrigerator are raw liver for Splendid and grapefruit and cranberry juice for Seabreezes."

Catching sight of Bram's puzzled look, Brian explained, "Our Tally is many marvelous and unique things, but a cook she's not."

"She burns water," Dari finished succinctly.

"There are those who cook and those who serve," Tally said insouciantly, perching on the chair at the head of the dining table and flipping her rather frazzled braid over her shoulder. "I, on the other hand, enjoy the results of both. Where's my breakfast?"

With a wink at the other three men, Bram filled two plates from the tempting array of food prepared by the inn's chef and carried them to the table. Setting one plate in front of her, he slid into the seat to her right with the other one. Someone, he noted, had set the table with placemats, silverware and glasses of juice.

"Good morning," he murmured to Tally as the others settled around the table.

She sent him a smoldering look. "Do you know why my darling brother dropped thirty pounds of cat on my stomach at this ungodly hour?"

"Umm," he said around a mouthful of waffle and maple syrup. "Council of war."

One graceful eyebrow shot up. "I thought we ended the war last night."

"New war," he explained. "Win one, along comes another."

She paused in her dissection of a golden fried-in-cornmeal brook trout that had been caught at five o'clock that morning. "Obfuscation, Ramsdale."

"Good word," he said, nodding judiciously. "I like it."

"Want to hear another?" she asked ominously.

They stared at each other for a long moment and then both laughed.

"I don't know what you two find so amusing about all this," Steven complained.

"All what? So far, no one's explained why I'm being blessed with all this company at the crack of dawn."

"Dawn was three hours ago, sis," Dari muttered. "Dawn is when the cock crows, the world awakens and the newspaper trucks begin to roll."

Suddenly alert, Tally looked around the table. "Newspapers?"

"And TV cameras," said Steven disgustedly. "God knows how they found out, but someone said the wrong word at the wrong time, and before we got that mess out there cleaned up last night, we had reporters and minicams swarming all over us."

"We did *not* confirm the rumors that Tally Bishop was driving the mogul-mobile," Dari continued, "or that Bram Ramsdale, the English superstar of films and bedrooms who has been mysteriously missing for the past several weeks, was a passenger in said vehicle. We did, however, assure everyone that Mr. Ramsdale was not a guest at Snow Meadows Inn."

"There's no question but what the valley will be inundated with reporters today," said Steven. "In fact there are two or three of them having breakfast at the inn right now. They may pick up rumors from some of the guests, but we've passed the word to our people, and they'll get no confirmation from any of the family or employees. However, it would be a good idea if Bram were among the absent today."

"And I thought it might be pleasant," Bram

said with considerable understatement, "if we took ourselves off for a picnic to someplace quiet, scenic and a goodly number of miles from here." His gaze was fixed on Tally, but in case she didn't get the point, he explained, " 'We' is you and I."

"Umm," she replied absently, her attention focused on the silent message he was sending with those bright green eyes.

She forgot about the interested observers at the table as she and Bram concentrated on each other. It actually took no more than a minute or so for her to decide that work could wait until tomorrow. She remembered their conversation of the evening before on the terrace at the restaurant and Bram's support and encouragement during that wild ride over the Kancamagus. Mostly she remembered his tender concern and understanding at the end of it when he'd sensed the confused, exhausted state she was in, despite her denials, and had provided the silent, undemanding comfort she needed. They deserved some quiet time together, she concluded, and a picnic sounded like an excellent idea. She knew the perfect place, too.

"Are you up to a short walk over a good path?" she asked him. "No climbing and no rough footing."

Bram nodded. "Sounds fine. I shouldn't have any problem."

"Okay," said Tally, refocusing her attention to her trout. "Let me finish this and get myself put together, and we'll be on our way." She glanced at the others, who were making a great show of ignoring the exchange between her and Bram. "I don't suppose anyone thought of providing a picnic basket?''

"They're getting it ready now," said Steven smugly.

"Sure of yourself, weren't you?" Tally murmured, making a face at him.

Steven ignored it and continued, "You can pick it up at the kitchen door, then go out by the back road. Those reporters won't be able to see you from where they're sitting.''

"What if they're wandering around?" asked Bram.

"They won't be," Brian assured him. "Service is very slow this morning in the dining room, and when they've finished eating, a couple of my men are going to want to know who they are and what they're doing there.''

"Well, you seem to have covered all contingencies," said Tally, pushing back her chair and rising to her feet. "While you guys clean up the kitchen, I'll just run up and get ready.''

"Hey, wait a minute," Dari cried, grabbing for her as she passed him. "We brought the breakfast. You should clean up.''

She laughed and dodged away from him. "Oh, no. Those who conceive great ideas must be willing to follow through to the bitter end.'' Ignoring her relatives' outrageous suggestions for her bitter end, she skipped down the hall toward the stairs.

IT WAS ONE OF THOSE BEAUTIFULLY PERFECT June days with an eye-achingly blue sky providing a fitting background for the towering majesty of the mountains. Not a cloud nor a hint of haze marred the dramatic views, and a gentle breeze relieved the heat of the blazing sun. At midweek this early in June traffic was light along the popular tourist route that Tally was following, and she had time to point out the famous scenic attractions in the area.

"We're heading for Bretton Woods," she told Bram as they started the long, gradual climb through Franconia Notch. "There's a longer but more fascinating way to get there through Bear Notch on a beautiful wilderness road that winds right through the heart of the mountains from the other side of the Kancamagus Pass to Bartlett. However, I thought that we'd had enough of the Kancamagus for a while."

"Too right," Bram murmured. "Perhaps we can go that way another time. What's in Bretton Woods?"

"Not too much aside from the Mount Washington Hotel, one of the last of the famous old mountain hotels. But we're not really going there. We're going to a lovely spot I discovered just beyond the back end of their property."

Bram stretched his jeans-clad legs out under the dash and reached up to scratch Splendid behind the ears when the big cat rested his chin on Bram's shoulder. "I think this cat is warming up to me."

"It would seem so," agreed Tally. "I must admit, though, that I was surprised when you suggested bringing him along."

"He's beginning to fascinate me." Bram gave her an amused look and didn't bother mentioning that making friends with her monster cat was another step in his game plan.

"I was still half asleep during breakfast and then Dari distracted me when he mentioned reporters," said Tally, changing the subject, "and I never discovered whether anyone had found out what Sonny Jaketon's vendetta was all about."

"Oh, yes, but I'm not surprised that no one mentioned it. Steven is livid, and he announced that he didn't want to hear another word about it. Seems young Jaketon's pique had to do with Steven breaking his sister's heart."

"What!" exclaimed Tally. "Steven doesn't even know her, does he? What's her name? Jessica?"

"I believe that's it. And, no, Steven doesn't really know her. Seems she attended your Midsummer's Eve party a couple of years ago, and someone introduced her to Steven. She's evidently a pretty girl, and he vaguely remembers dancing with her several times during the evening."

"And probably flirted a bit, as he does with every reasonably attractive woman," said Tally. "Don't tell me that she took him seriously and built a big romance out of air and wishful thinking."

"Apparently that's exactly what happened, but she seems to have led Sonny to believe that Steven showed definite interest and said that he'd be in touch, but then he never called, et cetera, et cetera. When she decided to move to Massachusetts, Sonny was convinced that wicked Steven had trifled with her affections and broken her heart. Add that to the long-standing enmity between the Jaketons and Bishops, and you'll understand why an unstable young lout like Sonny took it into his head to 'even the score,' so to speak. That was his main excuse for all the vandalism and that little episode last night."

"It's all so stupid," Tally grumbled. "At least we know now what his problem was, and I trust someone's going to straighten out his thinking—preferably with a two-by-four."

In an effort to lighten her mood, Bram began asking questions about her house, and the rest of the drive passed quickly in a lively discussion of architectural innovations. They stopped only briefly at the beautiful old Mount Washington Hotel while Tally ran in to request formal permission from the manager to use their access road to reach her chosen picnic spot. Having known him for years, she neither expected nor received any objection.

"All set," she said, sliding back into the car and heading for a narrow road that circled the formal grounds. "It's just as well you didn't go in with me. There's a bankers' convention going on, and I spotted at least two reporters I know."

"Did they see you?"

"I'm not sure, but they probably wouldn't pay much attention if they did. It's not unusual for me to be in this area. In fact I've got two projects going not far from here. All right. This is where we leave the car and walk. It's not far."

Bram looked around the small clearing as he got out of the car, but could see no break in the thick growth of trees and shrubs around them. Tally and Splendid came around the car to join him, and she handed him the picnic basket.

"If you'll take this, I'll carry the blanket and cope with the beast," she said, snapping the long leash to Splendid's collar.

Bram followed her as she walked straight toward what looked like an impenetrable wall of dense bushes. After his previous experiences with her, he wasn't at all surprised when she pushed aside a thick branch and revealed a distinct path. He trailed her silently through the sun-dappled woods, enjoying the coolness and the mingled sounds of the wind rustling through the trees and the gurgle of tumbling water. Within a few minutes they stepped out of the shade into another small clearing beneath a high ledge.

He stopped and caught his breath at the beauty of the scene. The ground was thick with pine needles and dotted with large moss- and lichen-covered rocks. A small waterfall rippled down from the ledge into a rock-rimmed pool, which overflowed in a narrow, burbling stream that disappeared into the trees to his right. Clusters of alpine flowers grew among the rocks near the pool.

"We could be a hundred miles from civilization," he said in a hushed tone. "What a lovely place."

"It is, isn't it? And hardly anyone knows it's here, so it's never littered with beer cans and film wrappers."

Tally dropped the blanket on a handy rock and unhooked Splendid's leash. "Stay here," she commanded, indicating the small circle of the clearing. The big cat merely twitched his ears and paced to the edge of the pool for a drink.

"Is that safe for him?" asked Bram, setting the basket beside the blanket.

"Sure. That's pure water coming right down off the mountains. Too cold for swimming, but great for dangling your hot feet in," Tally said, kicking off her moccasins and bending to roll up the legs of her jeans, which had replaced the ragged cut-offs. "Come on," she urged him as she sat on a wide, flat rock and lowered her feet into the chilly water.

He crouched and dipped his hand in the water, withdrawing it hastily as his fingers instantly went numb. "I'll forgo the pleasure, thank you," he said with a wry smile. "Do you know what that would do to my poor knee?"

"Sorry. I forgot," she said contritely. "Ah, a little of that goes a long way," she gasped, pulling her feet out of the water and standing up. "Let's sit in the sun and—"

Bram had risen to his feet as she moved to the edge of the low, flat rock, and now they were almost at eye level. He closed his hands around her small waist and drew her closer. "Not quite nose to nose, but a definite improvement over that foot difference in height," he murmured.

"Bram..." she faintly protested, torn between the desire to be in his arms and the need to discuss their recent disagreements.

"I know. We were going to have a private discussion and try to reach an accord, but I can't wait any longer to...."

The rest was lost as he gathered her into his arms, pulling gently on her braid to tip her face up to his, and claimed her parted lips. The eager play of their tongues had the familiarity of a constant memory, and Tally barely hesitated before she gave in to the desire flaring between them and went up on her toes, winding her arms tightly around his neck and leaning her small body against his sinewy length.

She made a deep growling sound at the hot eager thrust of his tongue and nipped it teasingly, then immediately drew it deeper into her mouth, stroking it soothingly with her own tongue. It was too much for Bram, and he cupped her small, firm bottom with one hand, pressing her urgently against his aching loins. His other hand slid under her sweat shirt, seeking and finding one perfectly formed breast.

His clever fingers teased her taut nipple, and she squirmed against him, her hips beginning a tiny thrusting rhythm as she felt his burgeoning arousal pressing against her pelvis. He drew his mouth slowly from hers and trailed licking kisses down her neck.

Splendid's deep warning growl had changed to an angry snarl before they became aware of his agitation. They quickly untangled their arms from around each other as they turned to see what had disturbed the huge cat. They were just in time to see Splendid crouch, his tail twitching ominously, as a flushed, sweating, eager-eyed man trotted into the clearing.

He skidded to an abrupt halt at the sight of the large, spitting cat. Tally leaped from the rock and grabbed Splendid's collar before he could take any aggressive action.

"Pritchard!" she snarled, sounding remarkably

like her pet. She'd immediately recognized the man as a reporter for the state's major newspaper. "What the hell are you doing here?"

"A reporter?" Bram questioned sotto voce as he moved up beside her.

"Yes, dammit," she said, watching the man's speculative, triumphant gaze dart between her and Bram.

"Who'd have thought a bankers' convention could have such an interesting sidelight?" Pritchard moved a few steps forward, glancing now and then at Splendid. "I was sure I recognized you in the lobby, Tally, and in view of all the rumors that have been flying around in the last few hours, I thought it might be interesting to see what you were up to. And it certainly is. Very interesting. So, Bram Ramsdale really is at Snow Meadows and having trysts in the woods with Miss Talia Bishop, of all people. Thought you didn't like men, Tally," he goaded in a voice dripping with innuendo.

"Did I ever say that? You've simply never been in the right place at the right time, Pritchard," Tally replied with commendable cool, considering that she was almost angry enough to let Splendid have him for lunch. "And now that you've intruded on our privacy, we'll leave you to phone in your tacky little scoop."

"Don't be in such a hurry, folks. I'd like to ask Bram a few questions."

"Forget it," Bram snapped. "I have nothing to say to the press."

Ignoring Pritchard's insistent questions, Tally and Bram rapidly gathered their things and returned to the car. Splendid's vocal displeasure with the reporter's presence and his angry prowling around Tally and Bram effectively kept Pritchard at a wary distance behind them and prevented him from trying to block their retreat.

Tally had a sudden fiendish thought when they were halfway back to the car, and she handed Splendid's leash to Bram, nodding back toward the reporter and whispering, "Slow down for a couple of minutes," before she raced ahead along the path.

By the time Pritchard reached the clearing where both cars were parked, Bram was just closing the rear door of the Wagoneer behind Splendid. Pritchard ran for his car as Bram quickly climbed in beside Tally, slamming his door shut as she whipped the car around and tore down the road in a cloud of dust. Bram had time for only one hilarious glimpse of the reporter pounding the roof of his car in frustration, unable to follow them because of two extremely flat tires.

"So much for secluded picnics and private discussions," said Tally after a few minutes.

"Among other things," Bram murmured suggestively.

"That, too," she agreed. "But one of these days...."

"Or nights."

"Mmm. Well, right now, we'd better hustle back for a conference with the others and decide our best course to discourage the media."

"I'd rather scamper off with you to a deserted island surrounded by reporter-eating sharks."

"Don't knock it," said Tally, laughing. "I have

an idea that you, at least, just may end up on an island."

"OH, DEAR, I do hope everything goes well tonight. Did you know we've got reservations for every seat in all three dining rooms up to nine o'clock? All of them for guests at the party. Perhaps we should have planned a dinner as well as a midnight buffet. What do you think, darling? I do hope all of those nasty reporters have really given up and gone for good. So unpleasant. How have you borne it these past two weeks? Poor Bram didn't dare leave the island once all those stories came out. Dear Sidney, he was so gallant about squiring me around. Not that I don't love the island, but it does become confining after several days. Nothing against dear Barbara, you understand. She's quite my favorite sister-in-law and—"

"She's your only sister-in-law, ma," said Tally, finally managing to get in a word when her mother drew breath. "I'm not too sure about this dress. Who designed it—Frederick's of Hollywood? There's no back and no front to speak of."

"I doubt if Frederick secures a gown in quite that manner," Edna said with a distinct sniff.

"I should think not," Tally muttered, eyeing her reflection in the triple mirror in her mother's dressing room.

For once, she thought, she came close to looking beautiful. Her hair, colored a dozen tones of gold by the sun, had been swirled, looped and coiled into a gleaming coiffure by one of the inn's hairstylists. What little there was of the supple silk

gown was in her favorite lilac shade. The left side
of the full-length straight skirt was slit to midthigh. The gown had been cut to fit in a smooth
unbroken line over her hips and waist. It ended at
the waist in back but curved upward around the
sides to just cover her breasts. In front the bodice
plunged in a deep V, and the scraps of material
cupping her breasts were held up by a quarter-
inch-wide silver chain set at inch intervals with
deep purple amethysts. The chain looped around
her neck like a halter, its ends fastened to each side
of the bodice.

"I've seen halter tops, but this is unreal," Tally
sighed.

"Actually it's quite practical," said Edna absently, studying her daughter's reflection. "The
chain unhooks, and you can snap the ends together to make a necklace. Two pieces of jewelry
for the price of one, don't you see. Hmm, it needs
something more. Yes. Definitely, you must wear
the earrings."

Tally examined the amethyst-and-silver concoctions her mother handed her, turning them this
way and that. "I'll bite. How do you wear them?"

"There's a left and a right. Clip the amethyst to
your lobe so the twist of silver follows the curve of
the rim of your ear. Yes, like that. There, now,
you look lovely. Those silver sandals are just
right. I know you don't like heels that high, but do
try to keep them on for the duration of the evening, darling. Oh, no, that watch is all wrong.
Take it off. Let me see what I have. Bother! I've
got to get a second jewel box or a larger one. I

never can find— Ah, here we are. I knew I had an amethyst bracelet. Oh, dear, I forgot they were all set in those diamond circles, but they're such tiny diamonds I doubt if anyone will even notice them, don't you? It's platinum, of course, but it looks so much like silver I'm sure no one will know the difference."

Tally held out her left wrist, laughing as her mother fastened the bracelet. "Only you, ma, would rejoice that people might mistake platinum for silver."

"Pooh! It's the color that counts. Now let's sit down and have a quiet glass of wine before we join the throng. I believe Jean's reserved tables in the Rendezvous Room for the family for six-thirty."

"Are you sure I'm not going to come out of this dress?" Tally asked as she followed her mother through the bedroom into the comfortable sitting room. "Frankly, I'd feel a lot better in something not quite so. . . so airy."

"Nonsense, darling. You look perfectly lovely, and I promise you that bodice has been carefully fitted to stay in place. I'm sure Bram will be impressed," Edna lilted happily, opening an inlaid wall panel to reveal a small bar. "He's never seen you in anything half as glamorous. White wine, dear? I've some nice Chablis."

"Anything," said Tally impatiently, more interested in her mother's apparent matchmaking than in wine. "What's this about Bram? If you've rigged me out in this decidedly tarty outfit—"

"Please," her mother protested. "One could not possibly call a twenty-five-hundred-dollar

original 'tarty.' I simply don't understand where you get your strange ideas, darling.''

''Ma, about Bram—''

''Of course I can't guarantee the security of that bodice if you indulge in any of that wild dancing. Surely for one evening you can manage with a less strenuous style. In fact I'm sure Bram's leg is strong enough for a slow waltz or fox-trot, and you—''

''Ma, have you set me up? Is there something going on this evening I don't know about? When I spoke to Bram earlier—''

''Lovely! He did call you. He said he would as soon as he got back. He did ask you to partner him tonight, didn't he?''

Tally sipped her wine and tried to decipher her mother's enigmatic expression. There was a trace of smugness, more than a hint of excitement, and...she couldn't be sure. There was no question, however, that Edna and Bram had been discussing her during their two-week sojourn on Aunt Barbara's Maine island.

She rapidly reviewed the four brief phone conversations she'd had with Bram. Each time he'd caught her at the inn where there was limited privacy, and they'd talked mostly commonplaces and discussed last-minute changes in plans. He and Sid had originally thought to return to Snow Meadows with Edna this past Thursday, two days before the Midsummer's Eve party. Most of the reporters had given up after ten days of meeting nothing but blank stares when they asked about Bram Ramsdale. However, the persistence of one

London gossip columnist, Pat Drayton, had forced a revision of plans, and her mother had returned alone on Thursday.

Pesky Pat must have a sixth sense, Tally thought sourly, remembering the woman's abrasive insistence on poking into every corner of the inn. They'd had to put a special security patrol on Alicia's cottage when the Drayton woman had been caught peering in the windows and trying all the doors. It was a good thing that Merton had decided to spend his unexpected vacation visiting a cousin in Maryland. If old sharpy Drayton had spotted him, she'd never have left. As it was, she hadn't given up until Friday afternoon when Grandma Amy, at the end of her limited patience, had informed her that if she didn't leave the valley within the hour, she'd find herself accidently stranded on one of the tiny islands in the middle of the lake and that it would probably take a week or so before anyone would discover her whereabouts.

Tally giggled, and Edna asked, "What's so amusing about dear Bram asking you—"

"Not that. I was remembering Dreadful Drayton's face when Grandma Amy described the amenities of the island. She practically turned puce at the idea of living in a tent and whipping up freeze-dried dinners over an open fire. The boys had to rerake the parking lot, she peeled out of here so fast."

"A thoroughly unpleasant woman, but at least she left, and Bram and Sidney were able to return for the party." Edna fixed her slippery daughter with an inimical eye and asked, "Did he or didn't he invite you to be his partner?"

"He?"

"Talia! Stop evading the question."

"Oh, all right," Tally sighed. "If you insist on every little detail, yes, he did ask me. Last week during one of his calls. And when he called me this morning just after he and Sid got back, we agreed to meet in the lobby at six. We're having a drink in the Starshine Lounge before dinner. Now, is there anything else you need to know?"

"Oh, dear, now I've upset you," said Edna unhappily, gazing at Tally with wounded eyes.

"Please, ma, not the poor-puppy look," Tally pleaded in laughing exasperation. "I apologize for being snippy, but, really, I wish you'd remember that I'm almost thirty-two and perfectly capable of handling my own affairs."

"Speaking of affairs, have you seen Ciel yet?" asked Edna.

"Ciel? Is she really here? When did she get in?"

"She arrived in Boston from London late yesterday, and Alden sent a plane down for her early this morning. She's terribly thin and wears much too much makeup. I don't think she's at all happy, poor dear. Such a nasty mess."

With long experience in interpreting her mother's erratic dissertations and talent for understatement, Tally easily read between the lines and concluded that Ciel was in one of her life-of-the-jet-set moods.

Now that, thought Tally cynically, could make for a very uncomfortable evening all around. Alden and Myra had spoiled their only daughter to an appalling degree, and yet on the two occasions in her twenty-five years when she'd really needed them, they'd carried on with abysmal stupidity and callousness. Neither Alden nor Myra would ever admit, probably not even to themselves, that they had been largely to blame for the disastrous endings of both Ciel's marriages, in the first case by interfering and in the second by not interfering. *Ma's quite right,* acknowledged Tally, *that it was all a nasty mess, but even if I do feel sorry for her, she'd better not pull anything tonight and spoil mother's party.*

Edna glanced at the ormolu clock on the mantel and quickly finished her wine. "Come along, darling—it's almost six, and Bram will be waiting for you. I think I'll go down with you and look over the buffet arrangement again. I'm still not sure...."

Tally knew very well why her mother wanted to accompany her, and it had nothing to do with buffets. There was a glint of calculation in the assessing look she gave her parent as Edna stood and shook out the long skirts of her mauve silk georgette gown. Although she'd added a few pounds with her years, Tally decided, her mother's height enabled her to carry them with little diminution of her natural elegance. The simply styled gown with its high neckline and long flowing sleeves was not only flattering, but it provided a subtle background for her mother's favorite diamond chain and eardrops. *Very nice,* Tally mused, *and we know who's going to get the benefit of all this class, don't we?*

"You look lovely, ma," Tally paused and then added, "Sid won't know what hit him."

She watched with interest as a light flush spread over her mother's cheeks and wondered, as she scooped up her silver evening purse on the way to the door, just what had happened during all those cozy excursions along the Maine coast.

"Darling, you won't do anything... wild tonight, will you? I know Darius and Steven egg you on, but you're going to be with Bram and—"

"Don't worry, ma, I wouldn't dare get wild in this dress." Tally tried to lengthen her stride to keep up with Edna as they walked along the second-floor corridor from the family wing of the inn. "Which, I'm sure, is only one of the reasons you bought it. Should I guess why I never got to see it until it was too late to change into something warmer?"

"Warmer!" exclaimed Edna with an elegant snort. "And you claim you haven't been living alone too long. A beautiful summer evening, a handsome, delightful escort, an exciting party, and you worry about being warm. Really, Talia, the older and odder you get, the more I wonder if someone changed babies on me in that hospital."

"Forget it, ma," said Tally, laughing. "You know very well I'm the spitting image of Great-Grandma Letty. Would you slow down, please. I'd rather not be dripping with sweat when I meet Bram."

"Oh, dear, of course you mustn't. So off-putting, don't you think? There, is this better?"

"Better late than never," said Tally. They had reached the head of the main staircase.

Her eyes searching the milling crowd below her,

Tally hesitated on the top step, her fingers rubbing restlessly over the carved bannister. It wasn't that she didn't know most of the people filling the lobby that made her pause. She did. Well over half of them were related in some way. And that, she admitted, was a good part of the problem.

"Tally? Why are you dithering about up here? I'm sure Bram's waiting for— Oh, dear. I do believe that's Ciel with him. Really, it's too bad of her to try—"

Tally followed the direction of her mother's stare and saw, first, the gold-glinting dark auburn of Bram's hair and immediately afterward a frizzy mass of platinum curls in intimate proximity to his cheek. Although the Streisand hairdo was new since Tally had last seen her some eighteen months ago, she had no difficulty recognizing her cousin Ciel.

Before she had time to even hop to a conclusion, Bram lifted his head and saw her poised at the top of the stairs. Ciel Valmont's voice and the crowd around him faded away as he stared up at the small, delectable, unexpectedly stunning woman hesitating above him. Then he noticed her hand clenched around the railing and suddenly remembered a comment Dare had once made about Tally and crowds. With a few absently murmured "Pardons," he rapidly wound his way to the foot of the stairs. He had to allow for the stiffness in his knee as he climbed the steps, and his pace was slower, but his gaze never wavered from his personal Pocket Venus.

Edna smiled serenely as she passed him on her

way down, but he barely acknowledged her, so intent was he on reaching Tally. He stopped two steps below her. They were almost at eye level, and he held her gaze as he slid his hand along the bannister until he could cover her tense fingers in a warm, gentle grip.

"You look so beautiful," he said just above a whisper.

"Thank you. So do you," she said inanely, only marginally aware of the words.

She stared at him with a sense of wonder and an odd feeling of discovery. She'd watched him on his single-minded course, his lean athleticism transformed into slim sophistication by his hunter-green velvet evening ensemble with its ivory-on-ivory embroidered silk shirt. For a few seconds he'd seemed like an impossibly elegant stranger, someone seen on opening night at the Met or at a state dinner in the White House. Then she'd looked more closely at the expression on his face and recognized eagerness, surprised delight and an inexplicable tenderness. Her eyes locked with his, and something deep inside her expanded and dissolved.

Bram slowly held out his free hand, and she slipped her much smaller one into it. Her grip on the railing loosened, and she turned that hand, too, into his warm clasp. Oblivious to the chattering throng below them and the occasional curious glances cast their way, they stood at the top of the stairs holding hands and staring at each other with an odd mixture of welcome, desire and an uncertain recognition of what both feared might be a shattering truth.

"You don't really want to go down there and talk to all those people, do you?" asked Bram. "Can't we get to the lounge from up here?"

"Mmm," Tally mumbled, most of her attention directed toward *not* stepping down into his arms. "Down that hall."

He came up beside her and let go of her right hand so they could turn away from the stairs and walk along the corridor together. For this brief, magical time they were aware only of each other. Neither noticed Ciel watching them from the foot of the stairs, her gaunt face tight with resentment, her heavily made-up blue eyes snapping with anger.

CHAPTER TWELVE

THE STARSHINE LOUNGE was filled with the subtle glow of the westering sun, which was about to sink behind the high ridges bordering the valley. At these high elevations and only one day after the summer solstice, however, the reflected sunlight would brighten the sky long into the evening.

Bram seated Tally and then settled into the one empty chair at the table. *At least I'm sitting beside her,* he thought, with a strong twinge of regret that they hadn't been able to get a table to themselves. If it hadn't been for Dare's determination, in fact, they wouldn't be sitting at all.

Perched like an oversize glass cupola atop the intersecting roofs of the main building and the recreation wing, the small lounge with its panoramic view of lake, mountains and golf course was a favorite meeting place, and on this festive evening it was particularly crowded.

Darius raised his glass to his sister and remarked, "I'd comment on your looking like a dog's dinner, but Splendid would probably take a bite out of me. Let me just say: that is soooome dress. Ma been shopping again? *You* never bought that."

"Ignore him, Tally," said Rosemary. "It's a scrumptious dress. I love the halter."

"A Seabreeze?" Bram asked Tally, nodding to the waitress who had materialized beside her.

"Yes, please." She smiled at Bram before returning her attention to her sister-in-law. "Let's just pray that it's as functional as it is pretty. Frankly, I think ma got a wee bit carried away on this one."

Dari's grin was pure provocation as he teased, "I think she's trying to up your image from Tally the Terror to Tally the Temptress." He reached across the table and flicked a finger at her bracelet. "She's even decking you out in diamonds."

"Shhh. Don't mention that word," Tally whispered loudly.

"What word?" asked Bram.

"D-i-a-m-o-n-d-s," Tally spelled in hushed tones, leaning forward and giving the three of them a significant look. "Ma guaranteed me that they were so small, no one would notice them. So please, all of you, don't even whisper that word. Go ahead, laugh, you clowns. It's not funny. Ma promised. She also assured me that platinum looks just like silver, and I shouldn't worry about anyone spotting this little aberration in my accessories."

"So this is where you all disappeared to, and having such a fun time, too. Mind if I join you?"

The slightly raspy voice with its exaggerated drawl drew their attention to the too-slender woman in a slinky silver-lamé sheath who had squeezed in beside Bram and was now leaning her hip against his shoulder. Tally managed to resist the impulse to reach around his back and pinch her pushy cousin on her skinny butt.

"Hi, Ciel." "How chic you look. Paris?" "Evening, Ciel."

While the others exchanged greetings, Tally examined her cousin's painfully thin figure and haggard face. Slowly shaking her head, she asked bluntly, "What are you on—the 'starve till you drop' diet? You look like hell."

"Dear Tally, always so amusing," said Ciel, giving her most outspoken relative next to Grandma Amy a venomous glare. "Such an odd gown for you to be wearing, isn't it, darling? Just a shade on the tacky side, don't you think?"

"Personally, I thought it was more tarty than tacky," responded Tally with a challenging gleam in her eye, "but ma assured me it was the epitome of high fashion. Perhaps you'd like to explain to her why she's wrong," she suggested silkily.

"Oh, no," Ciel protested hastily. "I wouldn't dream of questioning Aunt Edna's taste."

"Excuse me, please." The waitress leaned past Ciel to set down Tally's and Bram's drinks.

"That's really not a good place to stand," said Rosemary. She gave the room a cursory look and added, with just a hint of relish, "What a shame. There don't seem to be any empty seats."

"No problem," said Ciel, her burgundy-glossed mouth widening in a flirtatious smile as she looked down at Bram. "If Bram doesn't mind my borrowing his lap, I'll be perfectly comfortable," she assured them, suiting action to words and sitting down on his left thigh, giving a little wriggle to settle herself.

He immediately grasped her around the waist and set her back on her feet. "Sorry," he said firmly, "but that's my bad leg."

Ciel's mouth compressed, and she tossed her head, setting the frizzy mass to bouncing. "Oh, well, one lap's much like another," she said with a strained attempt at cordiality. "I'm sure Dare—"

She stared, mouth open, at the decidedly feral gleam in Rosemary's eyes.

"Try it," Rosemary said ominously. For an instant the ghost of a very blue Dragon Lady seemed to hover over the miniscule table.

Ciel bit her lip and tore her eyes away from that implacable smoky look. She hastily scanned the merry crowd, then smiled and waved at someone across the room.

"Excuse me," she said perfunctorily. "I see a friend."

"Treasure him," muttered Tally as they watched Ciel disappear in the throng. "He may be the only one you have."

She sensed Bram's eyes on her and looked up at him. "Don't give me that beady eye." She frowned and shook her head. "I feel sorry for her, especially since most of what's happened to her wasn't her fault at all, but she doesn't make it easy to be understanding and sympathetic."

The others murmured agreement, and then Darius said briskly, "There's nothing we can do about it now, and this is supposed to be a party.

Drink up, gang. We'll just make our call for dinner.''

It was an unusually balmy June evening—generally the temperature cooled rapidly once the sun was behind the mountains—but Bram knew that he'd be enjoying it far more if only he could have Tally to himself. For two weeks he'd spent countless idle hours lying in the sun and dreaming up innovative ways of making love to a delightfully agile woman who was a foot shorter than he was. His visions of being wrapped in sunlight silk and stroked by small, slim hands had short-circuited his normal thought processes to the point where he had trouble concentrating on ordinary conversations.

He sighed, wondering how soon they could politely escape from the party. Damn, and it hadn't even started yet. First they had to get through this interminable dinner. Oh, hell, that was hardly fair, he thought contritely. Rosemary and Dare had become two of his favorite people, and at any other time he'd have thoroughly enjoyed their company. But for tonight he wished that Tally had managed to reserve a table for two. Preferably someplace private. Preferably with a bed nearby. Say, for instance, that charming little dining area in her greenhouse.

Tally caught herself for the umpteenth time glancing at Bram from the corner of her eye. This was becoming ludicrous! She was acting like some lovesick teenager—and at her age.

· She looked around the dining veranda at the elegantly dressed patrons, checking to see how many of the family were in sight. Dari and Rosemary wouldn't say boo if she and Bram were to slip away, but there were others.... No, they couldn't do that. Her mother would have a bird if they didn't at least put in an appearance at the party. But she could think of some other places she'd rather party with this contradictory, confusing Englishman.

She glanced at him again and remembered the various faces he'd shown her in the nearly two months he'd been here. Huntsman scenting his quarry, interested tourist, family friend, man on the make, sensuous lover, macho male, amusing companion, understanding partner, intelligent sophisticate, talented professional...and now? Potential mate? Damn this party! When could they be alone?

"Why do I get the feeling you two aren't quite with us this evening?" asked Darius with a knowing grin.

"Because they're replying to comments two minutes after we've gone on to the next subject?" Rosemary queried innocently.

"There was that," Dare agreed, "but I think it was more clearly indicated when Tally sugared her peas and stirred duck sauce into her coffee."

"And when Bram tried to cut his steak with his butter knife," added Rosemary.

"A momentary distraction," said Bram lightly. "It could happen to anyone."

"It's not polite to stare at other people while they're eating," said Tally, her air of self-righteousness belied by the amused gleam in her eye. She ignored the light flush of pink that stained her cheeks and gave them all a disdainful sniff worthy of her mother's best. "And speaking of staring, Jean's trying to get our attention. I think it's time for us to go do our 'greet 'n' meet' act."

As they rose and began moving toward the doorway to the main dining room, Bram caught Tally's hand and held her back, letting the others walk ahead.

"If you don't mind, I'll play least-in-sight for a while. After all the speculation in the papers, I'd rather not—"

"It's all right," said Tally, stilling his protest. "Believe me, you don't want to join us. Ma insists on a reception line, and you couldn't get much more conspicuous than that. I was going to suggest that you and Sid find a quiet spot on the patio, and I'll catch up with you as soon as I can escape ma's eagle eye."

"Edna must have had the same idea. Sid's waiting by the service entrance. All right, luv, you go do the polite, and I'll have a Seabreeze ready for you." He squeezed her hand before reluctantly releasing it. "Try not to be too long?"

Tally gave him a look of sly mischief. "In about fifteen minutes my feet are going to be killing me. There's just nothing like a Seabreeze for sore feet."

Bram's deep laughter followed her as she walked swiftly across the dining room to where the others waited at the entrance to the lobby. His laughter faded quickly, however, when he noticed how many masculine eyes were fixed on the long slit in her skirt and the enticing shape of her small derriere, to say nothing of the smooth, tanned expanse of her bare back. He resisted the impulse to catch up with her and drape his jacket around her shoulders, effectively concealing her to midthigh, and instead went to join Sid.

Despite her best efforts, it was about forty minutes before Tally managed to slip away from the welcoming committee in the lobby and rejoin Bram. She found him sitting at a shadowed table in a corner of the patio. It was fully dark now, and the decorative lanterns had been lit, adding a festive touch of rainbow colors to the grounds and verandas.

"I don't believe some of the people mother invited to this shindig," exclaimed Tally, although she carefully kept her voice down. "From her surprised expression once or twice, I gathered she wasn't at all sure she did invite them."

She settled into the chair that Bram had moved close to his own and accepted the drink he handed her.

"How long?" asked Bram, taking her hand and raising it to his mouth to nibble quick kisses across her knuckles.

"Soon," Tally said shakily. "Very soon."

He raised his eyes from a careful examination of her plunging neckline, and she read clearly his desire, intention and rising heat. An answering heat coiled and flexed in her loins, and she wriggled in her chair. She saw the flare of green fire in his eyes and knew he was fully aware of what he was doing to her. She leaned against his arm and, under cover of the shadowed table, brushed her free hand lightly across his lap. His hand clenched around hers, and he drew in a sharp breath. She smiled seductively into his eyes and purred, "Gotcha."

"Indeed you have," he agreed with a raspy chuckle. He reached for her drink, thrusting it into her adventuring hand, and with assumed casualness crossed his legs. "And if you don't behave yourself, you're going to have more of me than you bargained for much sooner than you expected."

"We could always—"

"Here they are! Didn't I tell you Bram Ramsdale was at the party?"

The shrill voice with its vituperative tone and slightly slurred speech was as unpleasant as it was unwelcome. Tally and Bram jerked around to find a triumphant Ciel swaying above them. Hovering at her shoulder was the stocky figure of Pat Drayton, her face hidden behind a 35mm camera. Before either Tally or Bram could move, bright light flared, and the grinning columnist lowered her camera.

"Well, well, if it isn't the slippery Mr. Ramsdale. And after everyone swore you weren't within five hundred miles of this place." Elbowing Ciel aside, their uninvited visitor stepped closer to Tally and Bram, leaning forward to ask avidly, "What's going on here? Is she your latest playmate? How long have you been here? Where were you hiding—at that crazy house of hers? How long have you known each other? Is this just a vacation fling or is it serious?"

"Put a sock in it, Pat," said Bram wearily. "There's no news for you here. The Bishops are family friends, and naturally, as long as I'm using Alicia's place, they're going to invite me to their social functions. With certain exceptions," he continued with a meaningful look at Ciel, "they're very hospitable and considerate people. Knowing that I didn't wish to be harassed by the minions of Fleet Street, they've very kindly—and at considerable inconvenience to themselves—run interference for me."

"Lied, you mean," said Pat Drayton belligerently. Her close-cropped brown hair wasn't particularly flattering to her strong-boned face with its determined jaw and searing dark eyes. Her mouth tightened as she gave Tally an insolent once-over. "Sexy little thing, but not your usual style, Bram. That long dry spell in hospital change your tastes in women? Or maybe you think a woman half your size is all you can handle."

"That does it!" snarled Tally, leaping to her feet.

Bram was half a second slower in standing, but managed to grab her before she could get close enough to Pat Drayton to do any damage.

"No, no, luv. Not in that dress." He gave Ciel, who had been giggling inanely for the past five minutes, a quelling look. The effect was somewhat spoiled by another flash of light as the unquenchable Ms Drayton brought her camera into action again.

"Damn! Let go!" Tally squirmed in Bram's hold, but she abruptly relaxed at the sight of Donnelly and Brian closing in on the small group from opposite directions.

"Problems?" asked Brian with deceptive mildness, stopping beside Pat and eyeing her camera speculatively.

"You remember Drayton, don't you?" Tally asked rhetorically. "Incipient lock-picker and general all-round pest? She's now added gate-crashing to the list. Will you—"

"Go to hell!" Pat snapped, an expression of self-righteous indignation forming on her plain features. "I was invited."

"By whom?" asked Brian.

"By me, Brian sweetie," answered Ciel sarcastically. "I do believe I'm still a member of the family, McKay, and as such I can invite anyone I please to a family party. Poor Pat felt so badly when I met her in Boston last night. You were all horribly rude to her, and for what? Bram can take care of himself, can't you, sweetie? You've certainly had enough practice."

"Drop it, Ciel," said Tally disgustedly. "You're three sheets to the wind and even when you're stone sober, you're not strumming all your strings. However, now that you've brought Dreadful Drayton back here, we can't very well toss her out in the middle of the party. It's lousy public relations. Sooo, if you'll just keep her here for ten minutes or so, Brian, Bram and I will take ourselves off."

"Where are you going?" demanded the irrepressible gossip.

"None of your bloomin' business, ducks,"

snapped Tally in an impeccable English accent. "But if I see you again, *you* may be going somewhere you'd rather not."

At Bram's urging, Tally began moving around the group, flashing a thank-you smile at Donnelly and Brian and scowling gruesomely at Ciel and Pat. After a few steps she turned to bestow one of her best evil smiles on Pat, purring sweetly, "If you insist on being considered a guest, then you must do the polite thing. Do take her along to Grandma Amy, Brian, so she can pay her respects to the poor old dear."

The three men laughed; Ciel stared at her cousin in drunken disbelief; and Pat Drayton blanched and gaped like a guppy.

"Ta, ta, all," lilted Tally and, ignoring Bram's sporadic chuckles, took his arm and strolled away with a sassy hip-swinging stride.

Since Tally knew every obscure way in and out of the inn, it was only a matter of minutes before they escaped undetected and were on their way to Tally's house, with Bram driving the Wagoneer.

"Why do I feel that I should be puffing out my manly chest with pride that you've allowed me to drive this chariot?" he asked in amusement when he caught her watching him.

"Because I'm picky about who drives my cars," she said promptly. "Unfortunately, this dress isn't exactly made for driving. . . ."

She let her voice trail off suggestively and watched Bram's sensuous mouth widen in a very tomcatty smile.

"Fortunately, all problems have solutions," he

said dulcetly, "and this one is particularly simple. How did you say that unfastened?"

"Uh-uh. Would I spoil such an enticing adventure? Such a challenge to your ingenuity? Whoa! You have to stop so I can open the gate."

She reached across to a small keyboard set into the driver's side of the dash and punched out a series of numbers. As soon as Bram drove through the opened gates, she tapped two more numbers and turned around to check that the gates closed behind them.

"To get back to that dress," said Bram encouragingly.

"It doesn't have a back," she reminded him. "Just park in front of the garage."

He handed her the keys as she came around the car, and they began walking slowly toward the back porch. "It's a beautiful night," he murmured, sliding an arm around her shoulders.

She looked up to find his gaze fixed on her and a small smile tugging at the corners of his mouth. "Yes, it is," she answered absently, her attention captured by the messages his eyes were sending and the patterns his fingers were tracing on her bare shoulder.

Without volition their feet stopped moving, and she lifted her face to his descending mouth. She slid her arms around his waist and relaxed into his kiss, shivering with pleasure as his warm hands stroked her naked back.

"What the deuce—"

"Splendid! Knock it off, you idiot cat."

His golden eyes glowing in the moonlight and

his tufted ears twitching at the sound of their voices, Splendid wriggled the rest of his solid body between them and sat down on their feet, immediately breaking into a deep rumbling purr of satisfaction.

"I've heard of togetherness, but this!"

Tally giggled and rubbed the big cat behind the ears. "You should feel honored. He's very selective about his close friends."

"Does it have to be this close? I'd be perfectly content if he expressed his friendship from a distance of, say, three feet or so."

Tally pulled her feet from under Splendid's haunch and resumed walking toward the house. "Come on, you two. I can think of more comfortable places to practice togetherness."

In moments she had unlocked the door and shut down the alarm system. Bram, with Splendid at his heels, followed her into the kitchen, and two pairs of eyes watched with interest, albeit for different reasons, as she opened the refrigerator.

"Would you like some wine?"

"Sounds good."

"White or rosé?"

"White's fine."

"The glasses are in the cupboard to your right, second shelf."

"Lavender wineglasses?"

"Why not?"

"Indeed. Would you like me to— Ah, I see you've got it open. Now where, luv?"

"Would you like to sit in the greenhouse?"

"Mmm, that depends. Which part did you have in mind?"

For the first time in several minutes, Tally looked directly at his face, acknowledging the silent, secondary conversation they'd been conducting. Without saying a word, she took his free hand and began leading him toward the greenhouse, carrying the wine in her other hand while he brought the glasses. Splendid, busy with his raw-liver snack, merely cocked an ear in their direction as they left.

In the dim glow of the one small light she'd left on in the kitchen, Tally led the way through the dining room and down the steps to the garden room.

"Pick your spot," she invited, as she released his hand and stepped over to a panel of switches and knobs.

Bram watched as she flipped here and turned there, and then he swung around to assess the effect. The bronze dolphin glowed gently through the thin streams of sparkling water as a faint light began to shine from the depths of the fountain. Pale green lights blinked into life among the plants, their soft glow reflecting from the darker green leaves to impart an eerie underwater feeling to the room. This was enhanced by the rippling reflection from the dim lights placed under the inner rim of the spa.

Bram looked at the petite, quicksilver woman who'd fascinated and challenged him for so many weeks that he hadn't even thought about his leg, his career, or his future—and he knew he was bewitched, happily and forever.

Tally turned slowly to face him and was caught in the simmering green heat of his intense stare.

Bemused, she reached to take his outstretched hand and forgot to breathe as her body tingled and throbbed with sensory awareness. For the first time in her life her quick, clever mind went blank. She wasn't even conscious of moving until the sound of bubbling water drew her eyes briefly to the huge hot tub at her feet.

Her gaze shifted back to Bram, and she dreamily watched him set the glasses on the broad rim of the spa, then take the wine bottle from her loose grasp and place it next to them. He straightened up and, holding her eyes with the rising fire in his, began to undress. Piece by piece his clothes were tossed onto a low set of wicker shelves, which held thick velour towels. The fascinated eagerness with which she watched his lean, tanned body emerge from his formal clothes was foreign to her nature, and she felt increasingly disoriented with every item of clothing he removed.

He was stripped to his dark green French-designed briefs—actually nothing more than an overworked scrap of cloth that was rapidly becoming nonfunctional—before she regained enough control to kick off her shoes and reach for the fastener of her halter. Then he was moving closer, and his hands brushed hers aside. She let him finish undressing her, her attention wandering to a curious exploration of his smooth chest and the light dusting of red-gold hair across his flat abdomen.

Her hands followed the path her eyes had blazed, and she heard his sharply indrawn breath as she trailed her busy fingers over the hard con-

tours of the dark green knit. The arousing feeling
of his large warm hands cupping and kneading her
buttocks impinged on her dazed state and brought
the first awareness that she was naked. With a
vague thought about ganders, geese and sauces,
she slipped her fingers under the band of his briefs
and tugged them down until he could kick them
off. Her hands went automatically to his manhood, stroking and exploring him as he was doing
now with her breasts.

He groaned and caught her hands, muttering
hoarsely, "Not yet, sweetheart."

Drawing her after him, he took the few steps to
the edge of the spa and lowered himself into the
warm water, wrapping one long arm around her
waist to bring her down with him. The water
frothed around his waist, and he lifted Tally until
she could wrap her arms around his neck, her hot,
eager body held tightly against his by the pressure
of his hands clasping her bottom. Hanging onto
the tag ends of his control, he moved to his right
where he could see a raised shelf a few inches below the surface.

She murmured incoherently against his ear and
instinctively wrapped her legs around his waist as
he removed one hand from her to grab the edge of
the tub for balance while he slowly sat down, his
other arm sliding under her hips. As naturally as
breathing, when she felt the searching pressure of
his arousal between her spread legs, she flexed her
hips, wriggled in a small convolution, and filled
herself with him.

A keening sound came from deep in her throat,

and she dug her fingers into his shoulders at the sensation of delicious aching fullness that spread through her. His hands clenched around her buttocks, pulling her even more fully onto him, and he began guiding her hips in a rocking, circling pattern. Their passion had been kindled weeks ago, the tiny flames fed with each sensual encounter, and now their fire blazed rapidly out of control, flaming within seconds into multicolored incandescence.

They were still rocking in each other's arms, totally lost in the power and exultation of their joining, when there was a tremendous splash and they were hit with a spray of water from above and inundated by surging waves from below.

"Bloody hell!" shouted Bram as Tally screamed at the shocking jolt from dream to reality.

She knew immediately what had happened. "You stupid misbegotten cat!" She twisted around in time to see Splendid surface in the middle of the huge tub.

"I don't believe this," Bram said, staring incredulously at the drenched feline happily paddling in circles.

"Dammit, Splendid," muttered Tally as she disentangled herself from Bram and began wading toward her eccentric cat. "He loves the water," she explained apologetically, "and he usually jumps in here with me." She grabbed for Splendid's collar and started urging him toward the steps. "That's one reason I want a pool, so he has his own place to swim laps and maybe I can enjoy my spa once in a while without getting my hair soaked. Come on, you miserable beast, out!"

Unconscious of both her nudity and Bram's enjoyment of her alluring movements, she grabbed a thick bath sheet and gave a disappointed Splendid a quick rubdown.

"Let's go, beast. You can finish drying off in the nice warm night air." With a finger hooked through his collar, she led the big cat around the spa to a door disguised as part of the paneling, pushed a hidden release and shoved him outside.

Bram was out of the water and drying himself off when she turned back to him. The door automatically closed and locked behind her as she walked toward him, enjoying the look on his face as he watched her progress.

"Tally the Temptress," he murmured, dropping the damp towel and shaking open a dry one to wrap around her as she stopped in front of him.

"Some temptress," she complained, tipping her head back to look up at him with a pout. "Do you realize you haven't even kissed me yet?"

He grinned a very smug grin and growled, "You didn't give me time, but we can start all over and include all the steps I neglected before. You have to promise, though, not to rush me this time."

She smiled a very promising smile and shrugged off the towel. Holding his eyes with hers, she slowly slid her hands from his hips up along his waist and across the broad, muscled expanse of his chest to his shoulders. She walked her fingers up his neck and buried them in his soft, thick hair as she went up on her toes and tugged his head down.

Bram gathered her more closely into his arms and lowered his head just that much more to brush his lips softly across hers. Their eyes started to close as he began bringing their open mouths together, and then they were blinded by a sudden intense flash of light.

An unearthly yowl reverberated through the air, stunning them into immobility for a long moment. And then they were grabbing for clothes, Tally racing for the dining room while she scrambled into Bram's shirt and he following more slowly after yanking on his trousers. She pulled the security bar away from the sliding glass doors that led out onto the front porch and thrust them open with one hand as she hit the switch for the outside lights with the other.

The floodlights came on, throwing the entire yard into bright relief and even lighting the lake for a couple of hundred feet out from shore. Bram caught up with Tally as she came to an abrupt halt at the edge of the veranda. Slowly they moved to the end of the porch nearest the greenhouse and descended the three steps to the lawn where they stopped and stared at the tableau before them.

Ciel and Pat Drayton, clutching her camera before her in a death grip, huddled in frozen terror against the glass wall of the greenhouse, while Splendid crouched six feet in front of them, his ears laid flat, his back hair standing on end, a menacing growl issuing from deep in his throat and his short tail twitching in agitation.

Bram looked down at Tally and murmured, "Peace, quiet and privacy. That's what you said, isn't it? So far we've had monster cats in the hot tub and nosy reporters snapping pictures in the shrubbery. What are you planning for the rest of the evening?''

''Don't ask. This,'' said Tally, waving a weary hand at the petrified trio, ''has really, to coin a phrase, set the cat among the pigeons.''

CHAPTER THIRTEEN

"YOU OKAY?" ASKED TALLY, glancing over at the long figure slouched in the seat beside her. "You're awfully quiet."

Bram chuckled and then broke into laughter.

"Whenever you're through, perhaps you'd let me in on it," she suggested.

"Sorry. I was just thinking that I didn't believe the past twelve hours really happened, and then I realized that it's all been quite typical of the crazy things that have happened ever since I met you, and of course I believe it."

"Bram, last night wasn't my fault," she said firmly.

"Mmm. I can think of one delightful episode that was at least half your fault."

"Yes, well, that was...different. I meant the rest of the night, from that point on."

She took a quick look over her shoulder to check on Splendid. He was sitting regally in the middle of the back seat, watching the passing scenery.

"We really didn't have a choice about this, you know," she continued. "Once old Drayton got back to the inn and started screaming about being attacked by a wildcat, the rest of the story was bound to come out. It was just lousy luck that those other reporters had sneaked into the party. If it had been only one or two, we might have been able to put a lid on the story and scare Drayton into keeping her mouth shut.''

''She doesn't scare easily, at least not when it comes to a juicy story. Believe me, I know.''

''I'll bet you do.''

''What are you muttering about?''

''Nothing. Nothing at all. Look, I know you're not exactly overjoyed about this, but there was no way we could stay anywhere near Snow Meadows.''

''With your gate locked and *the alarm system on*, we'd be safe enough at your place. And comfortable. Spa, sauna and whatever else you've got tucked away that I haven't seen.''

''Now listen, Ramsdale, I've apologized once for turning off the alarms. I just never leave them on when I'm at the house. The gate and fence stop strangers, and only members of the family know how to get in on foot with the system off. I knew Drayton couldn't follow us, but I never counted on Ciel showing her the way in. As for staying there now, sure I can keep the reporters out, but they'll just camp at the gates until we show. After all, we can't stay immured in there endlessly.''

''Might be rather interesting, don't you think?''

''You'd have Grandma Amy after you with her trusty cane. She doesn't recognize live-in relationships.''

''Perhaps we should turn her loose on the reporters.''

"Please. Don't even think it. It was all Cyrus and Uncle A could do last night to keep her away from them. As it was, she heard just enough to peel a strip off me for indulging my hormones in public. Wouldn't listen to a word I said about it being inside my own house. She informed me that if *anyone* could see me, I was in public. And where, by the way, were you when I was getting my derriere in a sling?"

"I was trying to explain the situation tactfully to your mother and Sid. Not that tact was necessary with Sid, but I'm years from having to explain my activities to anyone's mother. Dare and Steven wandered by in the middle of everything and found it no end amusing."

"I'll bet they did. Terrific. Another weird Tally story that I'll never live down."

"You certainly won't if those scandal sheet scavengers have their way. It won't take much digging for them to find out all about Ms Talia Bishop, architect extraordinaire and owner of a genuine attack cat."

"Oh, come on, you know he wouldn't harm even a bird."

"That's because you keep him stuffed with raw liver. In all the hasty planning for this expedition, luv, did you consider what the Drayton types are going to make of our dawn escape chaperoned by a monster cat?"

"They won't know—we hope."

"You'll have to brief me on Idaho, in case anyone asks questions. Now, once again, tell me exactly where we're really going. I haven't seen anything but mountains and forest for the past hour."

"And that's about all you'll see for most of the way except for a few small towns and a couple of larger ones. We should hit Colebrook around noon. That's the largest town, which isn't saying much, and the main shopping area in the northern end of the state."

"And that's where we're going?"

"Colebrook? No. We're going farther north to Pittsburg. Actually several miles beyond Pittsburg. The camping area we're heading for is on one of the inlets of First Connecticut Lake."

"Camping. Yes, I do believe I heard that mentioned. You realize, luv, that I've never been camping in my life."

"Don't worry about it. Didn't you hear anything we discussed last night? I'm not going to stick you in a tent in the deep woods, you know. Mugs and a couple of the other boys are bringing up the big RV."

"Which is?"

"A recreation vehicle. Something like a caravan in England. Your caravan is our trailer, and if you put a cab and an engine on it, it's a motor home or an RV. It looks rather like a small bus or van, except it's fancier."

"And better than a tent?"

"Definitely. Ramsdale, I thought you were the rugged, outdoor type. Oh, well, you'll find everything in an RV that you will in a house, except on a smaller scale and with less head room. You may have to duck occasionally. The one we'll be using is the largest of the three we keep at Snow Meadows. It's thirty-four feet long, and has a living room, dining alcove, fully equipped kitchen, bathroom complete with tub and shower, bedroom with king-sized bed, and hot water, electricity, heat, air conditioning and gas. There's some other stuff, but you can discover the rest for yourself.''

"Sounds cozy. Just one bed?''

"One large comfortable bed. There's a smaller one, a double, that makes up out of the sofa.''

"Maybe Splendid would enjoy it. I don't think you'll need it, luv. How long did you say we were staying? A week? How does all this luxury function for a week in the wilderness?''

"We're going to a private camping area run by one of the Prestons who fancies himself as Paul Bunyan. No, I'm not going to explain that now. Anyhow, this place is used mostly by family. Each site has hookups for water, waste disposal and electricity. Once you're hooked up, you can stay for as long as you like.''

"What about Splendid? Won't he bother the wildlife?''

"Not really. I keep him well fed, so all he actually does is chase things around to see them run. It's alien territory to him, even though he's been there several times, and he usually sticks close to camp. There are some wild bobs up there, and they don't exactly welcome him.''

"Hmm. Sounds like a wilderness paradise. Didn't I hear someone mention that Mugs was driving this car back? What if we want to go somewhere? Do we have to unhook everything to drive the RV?''

"Uh-uh. Too much trouble. We'll borrow a car from Bill Preston. He keeps two or three extras for just that reason. You look tired, Bram, and you've been fighting back yawns for the past twenty minutes. Why don't you try to get some sleep?"

"You've got to be more tired than me. Did you get any sleep at all?"

"A couple of hours. We finally got everything arranged about two-thirty, and I flaked out on mother's couch until Dari woke me at four-thirty."

"An ungodly hour to be getting up. Was it really necessary?"

"If we wanted to be on our way before the snoops were up. We'd have left last night and slept at the Camerons, but we never fly over the mountains in the dark unless it's a true emergency. That's why we waited until after dawn. The important thing is that, if anyone asks, we took off in a plane headed for Boston. They have no way of knowing that we swung around and landed in North Conway."

"I liked Cameron. Droll sense of humor. Known him long?"

"A few years. We met in the architectural firm I worked for in Boston. He left a few months after I started and opened his own practice in North Conway. We kept in touch, and when I moved back up here, it seemed logical to pool some resources. We have a sort of loose association. Among other things, we cover for each other if either of us has to be away for any length of time. I'll be overseeing several of his jobs for a week or so in July while he's at a conference in Italy."

"Nice of him to lend us his car. You do realize, don't you, that this elaborate bit of misdirection is worthy of a Troy Castleman film? Between this and high-speed chases over mountain roads and gun-toting bodyguards, I'm beginning to think my days of derring-do aren't quite finished after all."

"Brawny Bram bites the dust? When did you decide that?"

"Come on, luv, what kind of a hero limps up to the villain and bashes him with a walking stick? If you'll remember, I acquired a large measure of that superstud superhero image by doing all sorts of very athletic stunts—in and out of bedrooms."

"Er, I don't want to dent your ego, Bram, but I only ever saw about fifteen minutes of one of your movies. Jean and Cyrus have a small projection room in their basement, and I dropped in one night when they were showing that one where you fall off an Alp. At least that was the part I saw."

"That's *all* you've seen?"

"Don't get bent out of shape, now. You did it very well. I expected poor Castleman to crawl away with half his bones in bits and pieces. Are you going to brood because I don't happen to go to the movies very often? Well, to be honest, I don't go at all."

"What have you got against films?"

"Nothing. I just seem to do other things. Back up a bit in this conversation. What did you mean about your derring-do days being over? Your limp's hardly noticeable now."

"Not when I'm walking, true. However, there's not only a pin in there, but there's a residual weakness that won't allow for unusual stress or strain. I can't even jog slowly, never mind jump from moving vehicles or tumble down mountainsides. As for sweeping sexy birds off their feet and carrying them to the nearest flat surface, if you'll notice, I haven't even tried it with a little bit of a thing like you.''

"Thing?''

"Sorry, luv. Let me change that to little woman.''

"I think I prefer petite person, chappie.''

"Ouch. Please. Point taken. I wonder if you'd approve of the way I really think of you.''

"Which is?''

"A Pocket Venus. A rather old-fashioned term, but it does suit you.''

"Hmm. Not bad. I rather like it in fact. Ah, Ramsdale, you do have your moments.''

"I just wish I could have a few without all the mood-shattering interruptions.''

"I'm doing the best I can. Although, with our luck, we'll probably end up with a moose for a houseguest.''

"Moose? Tally, is this another one of your send-ups?''

"No, no. A moose is— Oh, boy, how do you describe a moose? It's a member of the deer family, but huge. The males weigh almost fifteen hundred pounds. They look like...moose. You have to see them. There's a swampy area not far from the camp grounds where they feed. I'll take you one morning. The trail's well worn, so you shouldn't have any trouble.''

"Excuse me, but I can't seem to stop yawning."

"Go ahead and take a nap. It'll be a while longer before we get to Colebrook, and that's where I planned to stop for lunch."

BRAM DRAPED HIS ARM over Tally's shoulders, holding her close to his side as they walked slowly across the sandy strip of beach and stopped at the water's edge. He gazed for long moments at the incredibly peaceful scene. The water was still and silvery in the late twilight, the thick growth of spruce and fir ringing the inlet cast deep shadows in the dimming light. It was almost completely silent. Only the distant call of a bird and the faint sound of a voice broke the quiet.

"This has to be one of the most beautiful places I've seen," Bram whispered. He looked from side to side along the shore. "If I didn't know there were other campsites along here, I'd think we were all alone."

"Bill planned this very carefully for maximum privacy," Tally murmured, linking her arms around his waist and leaning lightly against his side. "It's my favorite spot for roughing it."

She grinned up at him, remembering his astonished reaction to the luxurious interior of the big RV. "Hot showers inside and all this outside—not bad, huh?"

"Not bad at all. I could get used to this." He bent his head and brushed a light kiss across her lips. "Oh, yes," he whispered and began to kiss her more thoroughly.

A rustling in the brush nearby distracted them,

and they turned toward the sound, Bram with curiosity and Tally, who had left a few things out of her description of the wildlife, with a certain degree of wariness. There was a brief agitation of the leafy cover, and finally Splendid's head emerged. He looked cautiously around, but once he spotted them, he crawled from under the low-growing bush and bounded happily across the sand to wind around their legs, purring happily.

"Foolish animal. Look at you, all muddy paws and burrs in your cheek ruffs," Tally scolded, rubbing him behind the ears.

Bram watched woman and cat resignedly. Obviously he was going to have to wait his turn. Paw-washing and ruff-deburring were apparently matters of some importance. *Oh, well,* he decided, *if I want one, I'm going to have to cope with the other.* With a patience he was far from feeling at that moment, he pitched in to help groom thirty pounds of bobcat.

"And here I always thought cats took care of themselves," he complained some time later, dropping onto the sofa in the lounge area of the RV. "Isn't that why so many people keep them as pets?"

Tally settled down beside him, leaning into the curve of the arm he folded around her. "I don't know about other people, but I like cats because they're such a marvelous mixture of independence and affection. When they want to do their own thing, nothing you can say or do will dissuade them, but when they're ready to be cuddled, you're positively inundated with purring attention."

Bram looked down at her with a gleam of amusement. "Sounds like someone else I know. If you're through with exercising your independence for the moment, I could do with some of that purring attention. It seems to me we were right about here," he murmured, tipping her face up with his free hand and lowering his head, "when we were interrupted." He paused an inch from her lips. "Is that beast settled for a while?"

"Umm," she moaned, her half-closed eyes fixed on his descending mouth.

She was waiting for the quick invasion of his tongue as he finally brought his head down the rest of the way and molded his open mouth to hers. She drew him deeper into her mouth, nibbling and stroking his sweet roughness. The urgency of his thrusts and the eagerness of her acceptance rapidly built their passions to a point where the barriers of clothes and contorted positions were almost painful.

"What are we doing here when there's a lovely huge bed back there?" he groaned against her neck, his mouth tracing a path down to her collarbone. His nimble fingers pushed aside the neck of the loose shirt she'd thrown on over her brief halter and unsnapped the strap at her nape.

"I.... You.... Ohh...." Tally surrendered all attempts at coherency as his large hot hand closed over her bare breast, his palm rubbing in gentle friction against the nipple.

Suddenly the heat and strength of his hands and body were removed, and she opened her eyes to find him rising awkwardly to his feet. He caught her hand and pulled her up beside him. In a matter of moments he'd discarded her shirt and halter, and she stood before him clad only in very short denim cutoffs, her sandals long since having been kicked off.

"Come along, luv," he said, looking her over with an appreciative grin. "For once we're going to take the time to do this in comfort and complete privacy." He took her hand and began leading her toward the rear of the RV. "Does that sleeping area have a door?"

"Folding doors. You've got more clothes on than I have. Unfair."

"Anything to accommodate my lady." He stopped beside the dinette just long enough to yank his navy polo shirt off and drop it onto the bench, then grabbed her hand again and towed her behind him toward that commodious bed that was just waiting to welcome. . . .

"That cat! I don't believe this!"

Tally had been concentrating on the sinuous play of muscles across Bram's wide naked shoulders. His sudden stop caught her by surprise, and she bumped into him before she could halt. It took a moment to shift her mind from tanned supple skin to his outraged exclamation, but when she did, she leaned her forehead against his back and began to laugh.

She didn't need to peer around him to know what he was looking at. However, he turned and hauled her in front of him, giving her a little shake and an exasperated glare.

"It's not funny, Tally. *We are not sharing that*

bed with your crazy cat! I don't know why I say I don't believe these things. Of course I do. I'm even beginning to look around corners and up into trees expecting God knows what to leap at me or fall on me, and while I'm busy doing that, I'll probably tumble into a hole you forgot to tell me you dug!''

"Bram, dear Bram, calm down." She gestured toward Splendid who was sprawled in ultimate feline comfort across the wide bed. "He loves to sleep on beds, but, Scout's honor, I don't let him share mine. He takes up too much room, and he's too hot."

Bram raised an eyebrow and gave her a wicked look. "If you think for one moment I'm going to be a cool bedmate...."

"If you think for one moment that I want you to be...."

"You'll never find out if you don't remove His Royal Highness to a less cozy locale."

"Consider him removed," she said briskly, urging the big cat off the bed.

Bram leaned against the dresser, watching the unequal struggle. When thirty pounds of stubborn beast doesn't want to leave his comfortable nest, it takes more than brute strength from someone Tally's size to budge him. She muttered an expletive that Bram knew she'd never learned at her mother's knee, and headed for the refrigerator with its inducement of liver chunks.

Grinning appreciatively at the sight of his nearly naked darling coaxing Splendid to the lounge, Bram reached for the folding doors. He began closing them as Tally scampered the length of the RV and snapped them shut and locked as soon as she was through.

"Any other potential distractions or surprises we need to take care of before we get on with the evening?" he asked, sitting on the edge of the bed and drawing her between his legs.

"Uh-uh. What are you doing?"

"Unbraiding your hair. . . among other things," he said huskily as he leaned forward to kiss her right breast, his fingers busy with the fastening on the end of her braid.

"Bram, are you sure you want to do that? From our past, limited, experience, I'd say it's a safe bet that things are apt to become a bit wild. There's going to be an awful lot of hair flying around."

"Exactly," he said in a mixture of satisfaction and anticipation. "For once, I'm going to realize my pet fantasy."

"What fantasy?" She turned at the pressure of his hand on her hip until her back was toward him. "What are you doing now?"

"Hand me your brush, luv. I've been having this fantastic vision for two months, in fact ever since the first time I saw you. You took off that ridiculous lavender hard hat, and this incredible plait slowly unwound and kind of slithered down your back. I couldn't believe it was real or how long it was, and almost all I've been able to think about from that day to this is seeing you clothed only in your hair and feeling the silk of it wrapped around my naked body while I made love to you."

"Oh. But—"

"So far, my contrary darling, we've had a passionate interval in the swimming pool when you had every hair tucked in a bathing cap, several very heated kisses when it was braided, and an explosive encounter in your spa when every strand was pinned firmly to the top of your head."

He swept the brush in long sensuous strokes from her head to the tips of her hair, which touched the bottom edge of her cutoffs. "This time I'm going to have it my way."

Tally's eyes were almost closed, and a sound very much like Splendid's purr came from her throat, which arched as she tipped her head back into his rhythmic strokes. She'd never realized before how sexy having her hair brushed could be. The steady gentle pulling at her scalp seemed to draw spirals of heat from deep inside her to spread upward through her body, making her stomach flutter, her breasts tauten, and her nipples harden.

She was so caught up in her own response that she was only marginally aware that Bram had stopped brushing until she felt his hands close around her small waist and his fingers deal quickly with snap and zipper. Her cutoffs and bikini panties hit the floor together, and she drew in a sharp breath as his hands wrapped around the front of her thighs and urged her a couple of tiny steps backward until he could bury his face in the silken mass flowing down her back. She could feel his hot breath against her bare skin even through the thickness of her hair, and she squirmed with unconscious enticement. As he pulled her onto his lap, she whispered a breathy "Oh!" when she felt the hardness of his manhood under her bottom. Arching her back, she slowly flexed the muscles of her buttocks, pressing down against him and moving her hips in a small circular pattern. His mouth was buried in the hair at her neck, and she could both feel and hear his harsh breathing. She reached behind her with both hands, fumbling for the snap of his jeans.

"Let me, luv," he groaned. "It's faster."

With obvious reluctance he lifted her to her feet and stood up to shed the rest of his clothes. He watched her watching him, deriving considerable enjoyment from the flush of pink in her cheeks and the gleam in her eyes as he straightened up, naked and fully aroused, in front of her.

"Oh, no, lovebird, not this time," he admonished with a soft, deep laugh, catching her eager hands. "This time we're playing my fantasy."

He dropped onto the wide bed and rolled to the middle, tugging her along after him, grasping her bottom and lifting her above him, then bringing her down to rest against his hips. She didn't have time to think about what he wanted; it was instinct that made her bend her legs just in time to land on her knees with her hands braced against his shoulders. It was also instinct that made her hips surge forward, but he didn't let her take him by surprise a second time. His hands were firm on her hips, controlling her movements and preventing her from completing their union.

"Bram..." she moaned, making two syllables of it.

"Wait, Venus. First spread your hair around us."

She stared at him from dazed molten eyes. "I'm ready to explode and you want to play with my hair?"

"Please? Next time we'll do your favorite fantasy," he promised, stroking his large warm hands from her buttocks to her breasts, tracing teasing patterns around her hard nipples, then sliding up to cup her head and bring her mouth down to his.

He played with her lips, flicking tiny licks until she responded with flicks of her tongue, finally following his lead and exploring the slick hollows of his mouth. She dug her fingers into the thick softness of his hair and opened her mouth wide to meld with his. Her mind was occupied with the growing ache in her loins and the hot need to have him inside her, and she was only vaguely aware of the movement of his hands in her hair.

With an incoherent mutter he broke the kiss and pushed her up until there were several inches between their chests. Eyes hazy with passion she looked down at him in bewilderment until she realized that he'd spread her hair to make a golden tent around them. Strands of honey-gold spilled across his chest and stomach, and he smiled slowly up into her eyes.

"Now, my love," he whispered hoarsely, his control finally at an end.

His hands closed around her hips, and they became joined. That keening sound he'd heard before seemed forced from the taut length of her throat as her head fell back in an arch of pleasure when she felt the marvelous pressure of him filling her. Following the guiding movement of his hands, she rocked against him, weaving increasingly urgent designs with her swiveling hips. His hands smoothed up the length of her flexing back, then down her arms to finally bury themselves in her hair, taking handfuls of the gleaming silk and spreading it over his shoulders and chest, watching the golden shimmer of it in the dim light of the small lamp on the dresser.

He looked up at the small perfect body, which was sharing so much pleasure with him, and then his glazed eyes moved to Tally's ecstatic face, her own eyes closed in concentration as she answered the urging movement of his hips. He could feel the tautness in his loins growing, readying, and with a last effort at tenderness before passion took over completely, he brushed his hands gently over her face, flushed with heat and damp with the perspiration of full arousal.

"Ohh...Bram...love...." She arched back, her fingers clenching around his waist as the glory burst through her. His hands closed tightly on her buttocks as he joined her with a hoarse shout. For long unbelievable moments they were suspended on an intense plateau of exquisite pleasure that was almost painful. At last, with long gasping moans of pent-up breath, Tally collapsed onto his chest, her magnificent hair spilling over them like a cloak.

It was some time before Tally managed a faint, "Bram?"

He closed his arms more securely around her

and said, in an almost normal voice, "I know, I did promise. Give me a few more minutes and—"

Without moving her head from its comfortable position on his shoulder, she asked, "What are you talking about? I was just going to say thank you."

"Ah. For what?"

"That. This. The whole thing. It was beautiful."

She could feel the rumble of his chuckle under her ear and pinched the tender skin under his arm. "What's so funny?"

"Nothing, love. I'm delighted, delirious with delight, that you're so delighted."

She shook with silent laughter, her breasts rubbing pleasurably against his muscled chest. "Who's delirious? You're not making much more sense than I am, my pet."

"Hmm. If I'm in the pet category, do I get raw liver to recover my strength? Remember, we still have your fantasy to deal with."

"Is that the promise you were talking about?"

"Of course. Turnabout is fair play, or so I was taught on those famous English playing fields. I just hope your fantasy turns out as splendidly as mine."

"Shh. He'll hear you and be yowling to get in here. Was it really s-p-l-e-n-d-i-d?"

He laughed and rolled over with her, leaning on his elbows to keep from crushing her under his weight as he nudged his legs between hers. "I refuse to believe that beast can understand everything you say. Spelling is too much. And yes, it was. Magnificent, in fact, and don't tell me he understands *that*."

Her retaliation was silent. She stroked her hands down the sinewy length of his back until she could sink her fingers into the tautness of his slim buttocks. He laughed softly and surged against her, spreading his legs to open her wide and let her feel the rekindling of his passion.

"You haven't told me your fantasy yet, luv," he whispered against her mouth as one hand closed over a thrusting breast.

"I. . .I've been wondering just what Troy Castleman used to do to have all those beautiful villainesses panting at his heels," she gasped.

"No problem, luv. It starts like this."

She could feel the words vibrating against her neck as his mouth descended toward her breast. His warm lips closed over her nipple, and his wet tongue worked his own brand of magic that had her legs moving up to wrap around his gently thrusting hips.

"That's. . .lovely," she panted, trying to match his control. "What. . .what comes. . .next?"

"Patience, my little cat, I'll show you in my own good time."

And he did, until the sky began to lighten and they fell into an exhausted but fulfilled sleep.

CHAPTER FOURTEEN

"Bram. Come on, lazybones, wake up."

Tally knelt on the edge of the bed and leaned over him with one hand braced on his shoulder. She saw his lashes flutter and then still again.

"Bram, will you wake up. I've got something to show you."

"If I haven't seen it by now...." His voice trailed off into a throaty chuckle, and he opened one eye far enough to see her hovering above him. "What time is it? It's not even daylight yet."

"Yes, it is, and you've got to get up or you'll miss this."

"Miss what? Why are you dressed? Come back to bed, luv, and I'll see that you don't miss a thing."

"Promises, promises. Up, Ramsdale. This is the first time this week you've had such an opportunity. Don't let it get away."

"You're what I'm not going to let get away," he said huskily, snaking his arms around her and pulling her down on top of him.

"Again? Have you been scoffing vitamin E on the sly? Do you realize what will happen to you if you keep on at the pace we've been setting for the past three days?"

"And nights, luv. Don't forget the nights."

"Definitely, we must *not* forget the nights. But right now I want you to see something just as beautiful but in a different way. Please, pet, get up."

"Much against my better judgment— Wait a minute. You're not going to introduce me to a bear, or something equally weird, are you?"

"Why do I feel that you don't entirely trust me?"

"Because you know I know that you have a distinctly warped sense of humor at times. Ah, if you want me to get up, you'll have to move off my chest...unless you particularly fancy another kind of early-morning recreation."

"I'm off, I'm off," said Tally hastily, bouncing from the bed and scooping up his jeans and a sweater. "Here. Hurry up before they leave."

"Who?"

"You'll see. Come on. Don't let Splendid get by you. He'll scare them away in a second. They can't know that he's tame."

"Some tame. He growled at me last night when I tried to get him off the bed."

"You forgot the liver." She closed the outside door softly behind them. "Be very quiet now. Watch where you're walking and try not to crack any twigs."

Moving slowly and almost silently, she led him along the path to the beach. She stopped just inside the edge of the woods and motioned for him to move up beside her. Reaching up she placed a finger against his lips. At his nod of understanding, she took a careful step forward and very gently parted a few leaves of the high bush in front of them and signaled that he was to look through the opening.

Eyeing her with lingering suspicion, he bent beside her and followed her line of vision. He swallowed a gasp of delight, suddenly realizing why she was so insistent on silence. A hundred yards along the shore to their left were three full-grown deer and two small spotted fawns, wading in the shallows and taking an occasional drink of water.

With a light pressure of his hand, Bram signaled Tally to move in front of him. When she had, he put his arms around her, resting his cheek against hers, and together they watched the deer at their dawn play. Every few minutes the adults would lift their graceful heads to sniff the air currents and look around them. Finally, with no perceptible signal, the three grown animals turned, nudging the fawns along, and ambled up the beach, disappearing silently into the thick cover of the trees.

Tally and Bram waited for a minute or two before stepping back onto the path and continuing down to the beach. The sky was a pearly translucent color that was reflected in the still water of the inlet as silver. It was an achingly lovely moment, the dark mass of the towering trees silhouetted against the slowly brightening sky, the air barely moving with the slightest of dawn breezes, the only sound the waking cry of a bird from first one direction and then another.

"Thank you," whispered Bram, stopping at the edge of the water and drawing Tally into his arms.

"Why are you whispering?" she asked, looking up at him fondly and whispering herself as she linked her arms around his waist.

"It seems the thing to do. It's so peaceful, so much like being in a church, that it would be... sort of sacrilegious, I guess, to disturb the tranquillity. How did you know the deer would be here?"

"They always come down to the water around dawn to drink. I've often seen them when I've been here before. This is also one of the best times to catch the moose feeding, but we'd have to start out earlier than this to get there in time."

"But I thought you said—"

"Don't worry. I'm going to take you, but it would be better to go at dusk. There'll be light enough on the way for you to see where you're going, and coming back we can use flashlights."

"It's a deal. Remind me not to start making love to you too early in the evening. Oof! No punching, please. I'm fragile and fall over easily."

"You're only as fragile as you feel," she taunted. "Whyever should you feel delicate and tippy after three days of bed rest?"

"That depends what you call bed rest." Despite her heavy sweater and Bram's warm arms, Tally shivered a little as a light breeze ruffled across the water. He held her closer and then led her back to a dry, soft patch of sand, sitting down and pulling her between his legs until her back rested against his chest.

"Better?" he asked softly as they gazed over the inlet, once again mirror smooth.

"Umm. Lovely. Oh, look, the sun's rising. Over there," she said, pointing to the far shore and a bit to the left. "Watch the tops of the trees."

The cloudless sky had turned a delicate yellowy pink, and now everything hushed. Not a hint of breeze stirred, and the birds had stilled their morning clamor. Bram found himself holding his breath as a line of flame red appeared behind the spiky tops of the dark spruce and fir, their shades of green and blue lost in sharp contrasts of the sunrise.

Barely breathing, they watched the line widen into an arc and then a quarter circle. Minute by minute the brilliant red orb grew more complete, its symmetry broken only by the black cutout pattern of the treetops. The inlet's water reflected the blazing ball and transformed it into a path of flame.

"I almost want to try to walk along it," murmured Tally, pressing back against Bram's supporting chest with a tiny shiver, this time because of the beauty of the moment.

He brought one hand up to cradle her face and tip it up to him so he could look deeply into her eyes. "I'd like to walk it with you," he said, his voice husky with an emotion he'd only just acknowledged.

"Bram?" She stared up at him, seeing something serious in his eyes and recognizing the same feeling in herself. Still, she dared not say the word aloud. *It's been so long coming, I almost missed it and called it a pleasant summer affair, when of course it's so much more.*

His face was taut, his tan coppery in the red tint of the rising sun, his hair almost flame colored.

These were only impressions that Tally would sort out later. Now, all she could see were peridot eyes glowing with a green fire that was tempered by tenderness and. . . .

"For the last time, Talia Bishop, I'm going to say it: I don't believe it. Of all the things I never expected to happen, this had to head the list. After so many years of casual relationships with casual women and casual feelings, I'd given up believing in love. And here you are."

She couldn't help it; she had to giggle. At his bewildered expression, she chuckled but wrapped her arms tightly around his waist to reassure him until she could speak.

"What's so funny?" he growled.

"I'm sorry. Truly. But if that's a declaration of some kind, it has a lot to say for your expertise in the British art of understatement."

He stared at her for a long moment and then kissed her thoroughly with an unmistakable air of possession. Tally's enthusiastic participation contained more than a little possessiveness of her own.

"You are an impossible bird, and I don't know why I bother with you," he said with loving exasperation. "Here I am, trying to tell you I love you, and you laugh in my face. Any other man would get up and walk away."

"Yes, but you've got that gimpy leg," she said, with a gleam of laughter lingering in her eyes, "and you know I'd knock you down again before you were halfway up and sit on you. If I couldn't hold you down by myself, I could always call Splendid to help."

Bram had learned a great deal about this contradictory woman in the past two months, and even more in the past three days of almost total togetherness. He waited her out.

She looked up at the "forever" expression on his handsome, famous, beloved face and decided to worry later about all the problems her following words would cause.

"I love you, too," she said simply.

"Thank God for that," he sighed in obvious relief. "I was trying to figure out how I could keep you here and fend off all your very large, very belligerent male relatives until I could convince you that we belong together."

"You could always swallow the RV keys and whack my rescuers with your walking stick," she suggested helpfully. "But then you'd have to figure out how to ride into the sunset, or sunrise as the case may be, with me."

Laughing, he hugged her tightly, then held her away so he could watch her face. "You're a wicked woman, and now that I've got you, I'm not at all sure what to do with you. And if I had to swallow the RV keys, I could always sling you over a moose and gallop off into the depths of the nearest swamp."

"Ramsdale, you're becoming positively giddy. But I'd like to see you try it. Man, would that be one surprised moose!"

"I feel giddy!" exclaimed Bram, falling back on the sand and looking up at his love leaning over him. He took hold of the end of her braid and pulled her closer. Holding her eyes with his, he wrapped the long plait around his neck and then back around hers, forcing her mouth to within a breath of his. "I feel I've just discovered a new world," he whispered, kissing her softly. "I feel like starting life again right from this moment."

She cradled his face between her small hands and kissed him gently but thoroughly. He was like no one she'd ever thought of as the right man for her, but she knew that he was. Everyone she'd met in her thirty-one years paled to insignificance beside him. "A new world, yes, and we're the only ones in it. We should do something spectacular to celebrate the new dawn."

"Both new dawns," he said, glancing over his shoulder. "My word, look at that. It's the color of your eyes when you're in the throes of passion."

She turned her head to look at the inlet. The sun's initial red had incandesced to fiery orange that reflected as molten gold in the water of the inlet. It was a lake of liquid sun.

"Come on. I know what we'll do to celebrate a new life."

He urged her up, and she scrambled to her feet, reaching down a helping hand in a natural reflex as he started to struggle up. He looked at her hand and then at her face, reading the love and eagerness stamped there.

"You really don't care about this stupid leg, do you?" he asked in considerable wonder.

"Of course I care, darling idiot, but let's not make a federal case out of a minor inconvenience. I thought you wanted to do something."

"I do," he said absently, absorbing the import

of what she'd said. He took her hand, and it was all the leverage he needed to rise to his feet.

Tally looked at him expectantly and finally prompted, "So what is it?"

"What is what, luv?"

"What you wanted to do, you noodle."

"Oh, yes, that. We're going to go for a swim in liquid gold," he said, whipping her sweater over her head before she knew what he was doing.

"You're crazy! It's freezing in there this early. Bram," she protested as he rapidly stripped the rest of her clothes away, "it only looks warm because of the sun's reflection. Bram!"

He kicked aside his jeans, which was all he'd put on besides his sweater. With loving determination he spun her around, then scooped her up into his arms and began walking into the cold, invigorating water.

"Bram! Your knee. You'll hurt yourself," she scolded, but nevertheless she was secretly enchanted with this particular macho act.

At least she was until the frigid water of the lake lapped against her bottom. She let out a shriek that silenced every bird within ten miles and probably woke up most of their invisible neighbors in the other camps.

Bram laughed and slid forward into the water, taking her with him but releasing her legs so she could float beside him.

"Hang on to me until you get used to it," he said cheerfully. "In a minute or so you'll turn numb and won't feel the cold at all."

"Oh, marvelous," she said through chattering teeth. "Is this your idea of romance?"

"Can you think of anything more romantic than a swim in the summer sunrise in a lake of liquid gold? Stiff upper lip, luv. You mustn't let a little discomfort spoil your pleasure."

"A *little* discomfort! I hope you don't have any wild ideas about making love out here. I think all my essential parts just shriveled up."

His shout of laughter echoed around the inlet, and he glanced sheepishly at the shore. "Who's that, Tally?" he asked in a whisper.

Tally looked over her shoulder and waved. "One of the Adderlys, I think. He's probably wondering what two damn fools are doing out here freezing their backsides off."

"Never mind your backside. I'll warm it up later. Come on, sweetheart," he coaxed, "and swim with me."

She looked at him and then around the golden expanse of the inlet. "All right, my pet, we'll swim in gold."

Stroking slowly across the inlet, facing each other and smiling a loving message back and forth, they seemed to float in a magic world created for them alone. The lone figure on the shore had disappeared, and they were alone in their enchantment.

Finally, Bram murmured, "I really would like to make love to you out here."

She smiled and gestured with one hand at their surroundings. "In theory I agree, but in practice I'd rather spend a magnificent number of years with you than the few, but probably glorious, minutes it would take us to drown in all this golden splendor. I do love you, you mad Englishman, but we are not ducks."

"All right, if you insist. It's the thought that counts anyway, and we can save our watery experiments for your spa or the pool. Come on, luv. You're turning a most attractive shade of blue, but I do believe I prefer your natural golden tan."

They turned together and swam at a leisurely pace toward shore, chilled but unwilling to end the fantasy they'd created. They were reluctant, also, to return to the real world and begin resolving what both realized would be some aggravating problems.

"BRAM, WILL YOU BE REASONABLE? How can we tell anyone anything when we haven't been able to agree on a single thing except that we love each other. We've been going over and over all this for five days, and so far all we've decided on are the areas of disagreement."

"I'm perfectly willing to compromise. *You're* the one who's being bloody stubborn."

"Me? I'm not— No, we aren't going through this again now. We have got to agree on this one thing. And we've only got. about twenty more miles to do it in."

"I don't see any good reason to hide how we feel about each other. Your mother will be ecstatic, and my family will undoubtedly faint from shock."

"And the press will get hold of it, and we'll have another three-ring circus, which is what we just spent all this time in the wilderness to avoid. I'm not that anxious to have all those nosy reporters delving around in my life. You may be used to living in a public fishbowl, but I live in a very private greenhouse.''

"Have you got something dire to hide, luv?''

"No, and you can get that gleam right out of your eye. I don't call a couple of discreet, conventional affairs in my distant past *dire*. But if you want to dig around in the past, we could discuss some of your more innovative exploits.''

"My most innovative exploits have been with you, you witchy bird. You've led me into some strange but fascinating adventures in this last week. Are you getting tired? Do you want me to drive? I shouldn't have any problem with an automatic shift.''

"Thanks, but I'm fine. It's not all that far now, and I'm going to take a couple of back roads. Why make a big announcement that we've just spent a week in splendid isolation? No, you stupid cat, I'm not calling you. See, I told you, you doubting Englishman, that you had to spell it.''

"So you did, and since you're so good at it, how do you spell *marriage*?''

"D-i-s-a-s-t-e-r. Bram, I love you, but—''

"But you don't want to live in England, and I can't live here.''

"Why not? You still haven't explained what the difficulty is. You said you weren't attached to your house, and it can't be work because you don't even know what you're going to do. I don't see why you can't do it here as well as there. When you do decide, that is.''

"For a brilliant woman, you sometimes make absolutely no sense.''

"I think I make excellent sense. Since you've decided to give up acting, it should be no problem to come up with something interesting to do that will allow you to be based here. It's not that you need a pot of money and can only get it in England. You've already got several pots of the stuff, and I've got a whole bunch more so—"

"So what am I supposed to do, let the press blazon the news that Bram Ramsdale is through as Troy Castleman but has found a cushy new career as husband to one of the Bishop heiresses? I don't exactly publicize my income, you know. How are they to believe that I'm not trading—"

"Will you knock it off? No one's going to think anything of it. Especially if you decide on something interesting to do and announce it in a blaze of publicity, with of course a slip of the tongue to let them know that you don't really need the money, but you can't stand being idle. Then we can—"

"We can what? Settle down in your enchanted castle in the mountains of New Hampshire? And what is this interesting something that I'm going to do here? All my friends and contacts are in England, mainly in London."

"I hate cities."

"So you've been saying for days. All right, we don't have to live in the city. We can certainly afford anything you want from a Tudor manor to a highland castle."

"Too drafty. If I wanted to live in a castle, it would be one of those cozy Elizabethan jobs."

"With two-hundred-odd rooms?"

"I did say 'if.' And when we're not chasing each other around the turrets, what am I supposed to be doing with my time, pray tell? As you know, housework is not precisely my forte, and if we leave the cooking to me, we'll starve. Look what happened at the lake. If it hadn't been for Abby Preston, we'd have lived on sandwiches."

"Please. I haven't recovered yet from watching you try to boil an egg."

"So? What would I do in England?"

"Design houses or something?"

"Bram, dear heart, it's not all that simple. I'd have to qualify over there to begin with, and then there's the fact that my style doesn't exactly blend in with English architecture of the moment. I've got a marvelous career here, doing precisely the kinds of things I want to do. It's—"

"We're at an impasse obviously. If you'd just go along with telling your family and Sid and Alicia, perhaps they can come up with some suggestions."

"I don't understand why you're being so stubborn. It's so simple. I've got a career tied to this area, while you can design your new career to fit in anywhere. Unless, of course, you're thinking of working in the Bank of England or something equally ludicrous."

"I don't know what I want to do, but it won't be anything on that order. This was one of the primary reasons for my peaceful sojourn in your lovely mountains this summer, to decide what I was going to do with my life. That's before I met you, you understand, and got all my plans, ideas, and thought processes scuppered right and proper."

"Yes, but look what you gained."

"A passionate woman, a wildcat who thinks he's human and a massive headache."

"Take two aspirin and call me at bedtime. If they haven't worked by then, I'll think of something else to soothe your frazzled nerves."

"I didn't have frazzled nerves until I met you, luv. Come on, Tally, concentrate, do. We have to decide what to tell everyone. They're going to take one look at us and figure it out anyhow. You have that smug look that Sple— Sorry, S-p-l-e-n-d-i-d gets when he's sneaked an extra helping of liver."

"Speaking of satisfied tomcats, that permanent gleam in your eye is a dead giveaway. Oh, hossapples, I don't know what to do. And, believe me, that's almost a first. If we tell them, everyone's going to start planning a wedding."

"So let them plan. With luck, by the time the day arrives, we'll have worked something out."

"Fine. Sidestep the issue, you slippery eel."

"I don't think eels can step, sideways or other ways, unless your American eels have feet. Over here, anything seems possible."

"Do you realize that this is deteriorating into another of our nonsense conversations and that we still haven't settled anything. We're going to be in Bishops Falls in five minutes. Where do you want me to drop you, the inn or Alicia's?"

"Neither. Your place will do nicely."

"You can't come home with me!"

"Your eyes are fizzing with little gold sparks."

"Never mind my fizzy eyes! You should feel my sizzling temper. Stop that!"

"Sorry, but you did say I should feel—"

"My temper's not *there*. Oh, you're impossible. You can't come home with me."

"I can and I am. I've waited thirty-four years to find you, woman, and I'm not letting you out of my sight. I'm also not spending any more nights in a cold bed thinking about you. You, my sweet termagant, are staying right under this tomcat's paw."

"Grandma Amy will whack you with her cane."

"If that's the best threat you can come up with, forget it. I'll turn Grandma Amy up sweet in two minutes once I've explained that it's not me who doesn't want to get married. I guess we know who'll get whacked then, don't we?"

"Dari and Steven—"

"Forget it. They're on my side. I think they knew how I felt about you before I did. In fact, I just might enlist them along with Grandma Amy to help me convince you of the error of your wayward ways. You do realize what you've been implying, don't you? You'd rather live in sin than in lawful wedlock. My word, Talia Bishop, with Uncle Alden and Aunt Myra as shining examples, how could you have fallen so low?"

"Oh, shut up. Bram, be reasonable. I'll drop you—"

"I'm not getting out anywhere except at your house."

"That's it?"

"That's it."

"Oh, damn."

Bram sat back in the comfortable passenger seat in the RV and watched his darling fume. He wondered what form her retaliation would take. There was no doubt at all in his mind that she would retaliate. He'd quite deliberately backed her into a corner, and he was going to keep her there until she gave in and agreed to marry him. After all these years, he wasn't about to lose the one woman he'd ever really wanted to keep.

However, he acknowledged to himself, she had raised a basic question that he'd been ignoring in his fascination with her. What was he going to do with his life? He didn't really have to give up acting if that's what he wanted to do. He could still handle most normal parts as a romantic lead. But did he want to act? He'd never actually made that choice.

He remembered suddenly that first audition. He'd gone along to it with a friend who was an aspiring actor to lend him moral support. When someone had mistakenly motioned him on stage, it had been his friend's dare that had led him to that first part. A film producer with an idea but no suitable hero had seen him, and the next thing he knew he had an alter ego named Troy Castleman and fame and money poured down around him. It had been fun, and since he had had nothing more interesting to do, he'd stuck with it. But was it because he liked acting, or just because it was fun and he was too lazy to figure out alternatives?

"You're sure about this?"

Bram looked up, startled out of his self-absorption, to find that they were parked in front of her garage. "Couldn't be surer," he said blithely, sliding out of his seat and heading for the side door. "Come on, Splendid. Home territory again. These birds won't chase you around."

Tally stalked morosely toward the back door, wondering with a certain amount of relish whether she could get inside and reset the alarm system before Bram reached the door.

"If you're planning on locking me out, don't." Bram caught her around the waist and spun her into his arms, kissing her lightly and moving his head back before she could make up her mind whether to kiss him back.

"Oh, come in then, but I don't know how you intend to eat," said Tally, opening the door.

"Same way you do, at the inn."

"Oh, great! I'm supposed to stroll casually in there first thing in the morning with you?"

"What difference will it make? Everyone's going to know I'm living here in any event. Of course, we could move Merton into one of your guest suites, and he can take care of both of us. He's an excellent cook."

Tally let out a scream of frustration and flung a potholder at him before stomping down the kitchen and turning into the short hall to the living room.

Grinning, Bram followed slowly, stretching his leg to work out the kinks from the long ride. He hadn't been in this part of the house and was more than a little curious to see if she'd managed to top her design of the greenhouse. Stepping through the archway into the living room, he stopped to gaze around.

"Ah, Tally, you are a wonder. I love this room almost as much as I love you." He slung an arm around her shoulders and began walking her down the long room. "Talk to me about all this."

She watched the delighted expression on his face and felt a warm glow that this room, which she'd designed solely for herself, pleased him so much. Perhaps. . . .

Bram missed her speculative look as he walked the few feet beyond the lounge area around the fireplace at the front of the room and stopped to stare at the massive structure taking up a good portion of the rear half.

"How did you manage this? Did you build the house around it?" he asked in an awed tone.

"Well, actually we did. I've always wanted it, and when I decided to build my house here, I bribed Uncle A into letting me have it. Isn't it fabulous?"

Tally flipped the protective cover back, and Bram ran his hand lightly over the green felt of the top of the billiard table. It was actually a regulation size, he realized, but looked huge because of the sides, which were elaborately carved and inlaid with intricate patterns and pictures of sterling silver and ivory.

Enjoying his fascination with the unique table, she paused. "Er, do you play?" she asked with a mischievous glint in her eye.

"Occasionally," he answered noncommittally, not trusting that glint for a moment.

He looked around the enormous room again.

Oh, yes, he could move into this room and leave only for meals and bed. Well, perhaps a session now and then in the hot tub, and he hadn't yet seen what that intriguing tower had to offer, and of course he hadn't been upstairs.... Perhaps....

CHAPTER FIFTEEN

"TALLY?"

"Yo! What is it?"

"Rob's on the phone."

Tally continued to shade the foundation on the rendering she was doing for a client. "What phone? Mine hasn't rung."

Bram leaned against the railing at the foot of the spiral stairs leading to the second floor of the tower, which was Tally's office. He looked quickly around the first-floor workroom and spotted the phone receiver lying on the floor.

"He's been trying to get you on this line for an hour, but it's been busy," he called up the stairs. "I just found out why. I think Splendid's been playing with the extension down here. Anyhow, Rob's on the inn line."

"Okay. I'll be there in a minute."

Tally dropped her pencil into the tray with a sigh of frustration. Between Bram and Merton's taking over management of her home life and the long Fourth of July weekend fouling up her work schedule, she was days behind in getting this job done and into her client's hands.

Bram was leaning against the counter in the kitchen talking with Merton when Tally arrived and picked up the receiver. While she discussed the construction sites she was going to oversee for Rob, she watched the source of much of her mental frustration. He was looking as relaxed and happy as Splendid would after a vigorous swim and a bowl of beef chunks. And why shouldn't he, she thought in exasperation. He had it made. He loved her house—and so did Merton, a fact not to be taken lightly—and he had her right under his thumb as far as being a constant presence in her life. It was Chinese water torture, a constant wearing her down by a combination of gestures, hints and reasoned arguments as to why they should marry and live mainly in England. Of course, all of this was punctuated by explosive, delightful, ecstatic bouts of lovemaking. He had a talent for picking the damnedest times and places, and Merton had made a comfortable apartment for himself out of the east wing's first floor where he could discreetly retire in peace and privacy at strategic moments.

"Okay, Rob, I've got it all, and I'll be sure to keep a close eye on your shopping center. I don't trust Vester Jaketon any more than you do. There's also the matter of my nailing his darling nephew. Sonny's his favorite, and when he finds out I'm going to be overseeing that job for a few days, he just might try to get cute. Yeah, you, too. Have a good trip, and don't worry about a thing. Bye."

Tally turned away from the phone, glanced at the clock, and eyed the empty counter-top burners and the bare counters. "No lunch today, Merton?

Is the lord and master planning on starving me into submission now?''

The reserved, middle-aged Englishman had taken to Tally's forthright manner and speech with an unprecedented warmth. He looked at her now with a glimmer of amusement and reminded her, ''You're having luncheon with your mother and Mr. Cater. Didn't Mr. Bram mention it?''

Tally's groan of ''Oh, no!'' was tangled with Bram's laughing admonition to Merton of, ''Don't be subtle. Drive the point home with a meat cleaver.''

''Oh, no you don't!'' Bram exclaimed, catching Tally around the waist just as she began sidling toward the door to the greenhouse, thence to escape in the tower. ''I promised your mother you'd be there. Now run along and get changed. You can't get into the Gazebo in cutoffs and a bikini top.''

''Will you kindly stop organizing me? I know— No, dammit, I'm not going to get into another argument with you.''

''Good, because we haven't time for one. We're supposed to be there in fifteen minutes, so hustle your bustle, lady.''

In a reversion to her childhood, she turned at the hall doorway and stuck her tongue out at him. Feeling slightly better, she marched up the stairs to the sound of Bram's deep laughter and Merton's restrained chuckle.

Forty minutes later she wished she could have made the same gesture of defiance to her well-meaning parent. Tally picked at her lobster salad and wished fervently that she was somewhere, anywhere, else as she listened to Edna, Sid and Bram discuss her contrary nature, her lack of common sense, her stubbornness and several negative points that she'd never known she had. She still didn't think she had them, but she was reasonably sure that a large portion of the conversation was aimed at getting a rise out of her. They knew they couldn't argue her into changing her mind if she wouldn't discuss the subject.

"Oh dear, I simply don't know what's come over you, Tally," sighed Edna, finally abandoning indirect methods. "I never thought to see a daughter of mine flaunt—yes, flaunt—an...an *irregular* relationship in the face of the whole family. Right there where everyone knows just what you're doing, and then to refuse to do the decent thing, the right thing, when Bram is not only willing but *eager*—no, *desperate*—to marry you...well, I just don't understand you at all, and you'd better know that everyone, *everyone*, in the family is extremely upset. Your Uncle Alden—"

"Ma, I never have and never will run my life according to the gospel of Alden and Myra. This whole discussion is a waste of time. The problem is between Bram and me, and no one else can solve it for us. And I assure you, I'm not going to jump into marriage just to satisfy everyone else's ideas of right and wrong. I don't believe in marrying first and worrying about the problems later, not when they're such basic ones. Bram, I really wish—"

"Well, young madam, what have you to say for yourself?"

Tally bit back a remark she definitely shouldn't have made and looked up over her shoulder at her grandmother. "Good afternoon?" suggested Tally.

"Don't get sassy with me, miss. You're causing enough trouble as it is. We don't need a pert manner to go along with your unconscionable conduct. Yes, thank you, Bram, I shall sit down. Since none of you seem to be able to handle this intelligently and bring Miss Know-It-All Bishop to a sense of what she owes her family and herself, I see I must take a hand in matters."

"Grandma Amy," Bram said soothingly, "I'm not at all sure that the bulldozer technique will work in this case."

He smiled his most charming smile at the indomitable old lady, cursing the fates that had brought her to the Gazebo at this moment. She was sure to put Tally's back up even higher than it was now. The two of them, grandmother and granddaughter, struck sparks from each other just saying "Good morning." Lord only knew what would happen if they got into a serious disagreement.

"Never mind trying to turn me up sweet, young man. It isn't necessary. I don't blame you for a moment for this disgraceful business. I know you're more than willing to do right by her. I knew this day would come the minute her father agreed to let her go to that boys' school in Boston."

"If you please, Grandma Amy, MIT is *not* a boys' school. There are any number of women who go there, and it's not—"

"Not the place for a proper young lady. I said it then, and I'll say it now. You didn't need anyone filling your head with all this feminist nonsense and encouraging you to think for yourself. You do too much of that as it is. Always have. I hope you're going to keep a tight rein on her, young man, or she'll walk all over you."

"If you'll all excuse me, I'm through," said Tally, rising from her chair, angrily indifferent as to how they interpreted her comment. "I've got a busy afternoon ahead of me."

She looked pointedly at Bram. "Do you want a ride back to the house, or would you rather stay here and amuse yourself with plots and strategy sessions?"

Her smile would give a charging bull pause for reflection, thought Bram, and he opted for conciliation over plots and plans. With murmured apologies, he rose to follow Tally's rapidly receding figure.

With the sure knowledge that he was pushing her too hard too soon, Bram played a waiting game for the next couple of days. He gave her the breathing space he knew she needed so she could work, but still he managed to coax her into spontaneous bouts of lovemaking. In his arms, she was all love and laughter and tenderness, until those moments when she burned with a fierce passion that met and matched the intensity of his own.

They had so much going for them, he reflected in the dark hours, that it seemed unbelievable that they couldn't come to an accord on how to live together and satisfy both their career needs. Of course, it would help if he could make up his mind what he was going to do. Something in the film world, probably, but that didn't help matters. Tally vehemently did *not* want to live full-time, or even half the time, in London. Well, actually, she didn't want to live in England. In a way he could understand her reasons, but that didn't stop him from feeling that she didn't love him in the same way he loved her. A woman in love was willing to follow her man wherever he had to go, wasn't she?

His preoccupation gradually consumed his daytime hours as well as his nights. The latest bout of futile debate with himself arose while he was relaxing in the hot tub on the second afternoon after that disastrous luncheon. He was so lost in thought, he didn't even notice Tally's presence, until her naked body slid into the tub beside his.

"Hi. Want some company? I need a break from drawing; I think my back is permanently bowed."

"I know the feeling. Merton put me through a positively evil workout in the gym. I've discovered three new muscles, and I wish I hadn't," he said, groaning.

Tally noticed, however, that none of those muscles seemed to affect his arms, which had slid around her to lift her onto his lap. She squirmed for a moment, until she had matters arranged to her satisfaction and could feel the strength of his almost instant arousal pressed between their bellies. She linked her hands behind his neck, but leaned back just enough so that they could talk. It was her favorite conversational position.

Bram watched her exertions with considerable

amusement. There really were times when she reminded him of her crazy cat in more ways than just the color of her eyes.

"Are you settled comfortably now?" he asked finally, locking his hands beneath the enticing firmness of her bottom.

"Ahh. Oh, my, yes, that's a lovely ideaaaa. ."

"I thought you'd...like it. Where's...our pesky...swimming companion?"

"Lovely...oh, Bram? What are you...?"

"One small action says...more than...a thousand words. Where's that bloody cat? I'm not moving a finger until you tell me."

"He's...move it, do...please...oh, all right. He's napping on the pool table, and I closed the door. Now, will you...ahhhooow...please, let me...."

Bram let her have her way, but couldn't help wondering with his last intelligent thought for some time, if he was a fool for not taking advantage of her complete emersion in their passion to worm a commitment from her. No, he decided as reality grew dim in the sensuous haze enveloping them, it wouldn't be cricket. *Or baseball, I should say. When in Rome...have an...orgy. Thank you, I do believe I shall.*

UNFORTUNATELY, THE ACCORD REACHED in hot tubs under the influence of ancient Rome and strawberry bath oil often fades in the light of a new day, Bram thought morosely as he faced his recalcitrant lover across the breakfast table the next morning. He'd had a marvelous idea for compromise in the wee hours and had immediately begun explaining it, forgetting that Tally donned her "heiress watching her money" hat first thing in the morning and checked the stock market in the *Wall Street Journal*. In typical Tally fashion, she gave the market reports and various interesting new items her full attention and didn't take kindly to being distracted until she was finished.

"All right, Bram," said Tally, finally putting aside the paper, "run this by me again."

"We can compromise, I said, by agreeing to spend six months, turn and turnabout, in England and in New Hampshire. That way—"

"What are you going to be doing that you can split your time between both sides of the Atlantic?"

"I'm not sure yet. Sid and I are exploring some ideas. Maybe directing, maybe scriptwriting. I've done a bit of both and liked it."

"Fine for you. What am I going to do for six months in England while you're off on location or buried in your den?" she asked, thinking specifically of the private retreat he'd made for himself at the library end of the living room by closing one of the sliding walls. Not that she minded, she thought, since she had her tower. In all fairness, he should have his own place, too.

"What does any woman do to pass time?" snapped Bram in total frustration. No matter what he proposed, she immediately began arguing without even thinking over his ideas. "You can shop, make friends, go to cultural things—there are dozens of things that normal women—"

"Are you implying that I'm not normal?" demanded Tally in an ominous tone.

"No, damn it all, you're not!" he exploded in a rare display of temper. "You're a bloody freak, but I love you anyway, and I don't care if you've got two heads. In fact I wish you had. Then maybe you'd have learned how to discuss problems instead of being so stubborn."

Tally stared at him furiously. "You aren't making a nickel's worth of sense, but I did get the part about being a freak, you crummy chauvinist, and let me tell you, I'd rather be a freak who achieves something worthwhile and real than a bubble-brained airhead who wastes her life shopping for more clothes than she'll ever wear and exchanging meaningless chat with socially redundant people!"

In a burst of fury, she slammed her fork onto the table, leaped to her feet and raced out the back door, grabbing her shoulder bag and keys on the way.

Bram jumped to his feet with every intention of following her, but he jumped too quickly and landed off balance on his left foot, staggering and clutching at the chair back to keep from falling. By the time he regained his equilibrium, the Wagoneer was roaring down the drive.

He cursed in frustration and looked at a too-bland-faced Merton when he heard a sound suspiciously like a choke of laughter.

"It's not funny, Merton," Bram muttered. "That woman is taking years off my life."

"Oh, no, sir. I rather think she may add ten or

twenty. Gets your adrenaline flowing, she does, and that's a healthful thing.''

"Oh, damn, I wonder where she's off to. The temper she's in, she's liable to wrap herself around something that won't yield.''

"I believe she said something about Concord and then checking on a building site?''

"Right, so she did. That's the job that Cameron's so concerned about, so she'll probably be a while. I believe I'll go for a swim at the inn's beach and see if I can find someone congenial, and quiet, to lunch with.''

TALLY WAS SO OCCUPIED with furious plans for retaliation that she almost missed hearing the piercing whistle as she passed the main drive to the inn. She slowed and looked around, wondering if she'd imagined the sound, and then heard it again. It was a common signal between the younger Bishops, and she backed up to turn into the drive.

As the car came into sight, Phil Stanton trotted down the front steps and waited in the drive for her to stop. Tally pressed the button on her door to open the window nearest Phil.

"Good morning,'' she said, making an effort to tamp down her anger and speak in her normal, friendly tone. "Were you calling me?''

"That I was. Your mother said something about you going into Concord this morning. Mind if I hitch a ride? I've got to pick up a special order for a guest, and my car's in the shop.''

"Sure, no problem. Hop in. I do have one stop to make on the way back, though, so if you're in a hurry to return—''

"Anytime today is fine. Been fighting with Bram again?" he asked with amused interest as she swung the car around and headed back to the main road.

"Whatever makes you think that?"

"The red flush on your cheeks, the fire in your eyes and the fact that your braid is trying to stand straight up."

"I'll grant you the first two," she conceded, "but I'll argue the last. It's all in your vivid imagination."

"Mmm. Answering by not answering. Okay, we'll talk about something else. What do you think of the Red Sox this year? Think they'll have a shot at the pennant?"

For the rest of the drive to Concord, they discussed a variety of topics, but carefully avoided the touchy subject of Tally and Bram. Their several errands didn't take long, and after a brief stop to see Steven, only to discover that he'd gone to Snow Meadows, they turned toward home.

A few miles south of the exit for Bishops Falls, Tally swung off the Interstate on an exit leading to the road on which Rob's shopping center was being built.

"Hope you won't be bored," she said to Phil as she rapidly maneuvered around the bends in the road. "I really have to keep an eye on this job. Vester Jaketon won the contract over Rob's violent objections, and he's caught the sneak cutting corners several times. I've already had one argument with him over the specifications. They're installing the unit air conditioner this morning, and I want to be sure the client's getting what he's paying for."

"Isn't an air conditioner an air conditioner?"

"Not when it's designed for a large building. It goes on the roof, and has to be put in place by crane. The thing's very heavy, and I'm not too pleased with the strength of this wind. It could be a bit tricky getting it seated properly."

"Sounds hairy. I never realized architecture could be so exciting."

"I wish I could convince Bram of that. He seems to think I can simply drop it for half the year and be happy doing nothing." Tally hadn't meant to broach the subject, but Phil had always been easy to talk to. There was also the matter of his being a "Bishop husband." Perhaps he'd have a suggestion or two about coping with that situation that she could use with Bram.

"I would have thought he'd know you better by now."

"In a way I think he does, but he's got some chauvinist hangups about a woman following her man. In our case, though, it makes much more sense for him to base himself here. He doesn't really have close, sentimental ties to England except for Alicia. She comes here a couple or three times a year, and we can always pop over there to visit. I don't object to vacationing there; I just don't want to live there. Their architecture isn't at all where I'm at, and I doubt that I could work effectively, never mind derive any particular satisfaction. Oh, it's all such a tangle."

"Do you think it would help if I talked to him? After all, I went through something similar with Pip. She'd never have been happy in Arizona, and luckily I could live here and still do what I loved doing. It's worked out well for us, but some of that could be because I don't have a problem with her having more money than I do. Beyond a certain point, it simply ceases to matter. *I* know I could support us very comfortably, and Pip knows it, too."

"Maybe it would help if you spoke to Bram. I know I'm being stubborn about this, but I also know I'd be miserable in London and even more disgruntled without my work. I wish someone could make him see that. It would eventually destroy our whole relationship."

"Okay, favorite sister-in-law, I'll see what I can do. Is this the place?"

"Yep. Hang on. This road's atrocious."

Tally guided the Wagoneer around potholes, through ruts and puddles and past a rather insecure-looking stack of pipe. She took a closer look at the pipe and made a mental note to check the numbers against her master materials list.

She stopped beside a red pickup truck with the Jaketon logo on the door and reached into the back seat to retrieve her lavender hard hat.

"I'd offer to show you around," she said as she opened her door and slid to the ground, "but you don't have a hat. It's an insurance rule: no one in or near the building without proper head covering."

"That's all right. I'll wait out here. Is that the crane that's going to place the air conditioner?" Phil asked, gesturing toward the building.

Tally looked up, squinting against the sun, and she nodded as she saw the crane slowly rising into the air, its cable taut with strain.

"You can get out of the car and watch, if you like, but don't go any farther. Okay?"

"I'm cool. Don't hurry. We can always have a late lunch when we get back," he said, glancing at his watch. "It's only eleven-thirty."

"I won't be long," she assured him, starting toward the still-windowless front wall of the long L-shaped building. She stepped over a tangle of cables to enter the skeletal structure and immediately looked around for Vester Jaketon. She'd recognized the truck as his, and why deal with a foreman when she could fight with the head honcho himself? She spotted his stocky form on the far side of the "room" she was standing in and started moving slowly in his direction, glancing around at the work in progress and assessing how much had been accomplished in the two days since she'd been here last.

All of the steel framework was up, of course, and the exterior walls and roof were in place and secured. Ducts and wiring were being strung now, and several men were working from platforms near the ceiling. She turned around when she heard her name spoken in a gravelly, insolent voice and found that Vester had come to meet her.

"Well, missy, what're ya gonna find fault with this time?"

"Nothing, I trust, Vester. But if I do find something wrong, you may be sure you'll be the first to hear about it. When did that pipe come in?"

"What pipe?"

"That pipe," she snapped, pointing to the leaning stack beside the roadway.

"Oh, that pipe. Yesterday sometime."

"Have you checked it against the specs? It doesn't look quite right to me."

"Smart one, ain'tcher? Ya can tell the size just eyeballin' it on ya way by?"

"All I asked, Vester, was whether you had checked it with the specs."

"Don'chew git yer feathers in a uproar with me, Miss Bishop. I knew more'n you ever—"

"Tally! Get out! Run! The roof!"

Tally'd been so intent on her argument with Vester Jaketon that she'd heard nothing of the clamor around her, but Phil's terrified roar brought her whipping around to see him racing for the building, frantically swinging his arm in a get-out signal. At almost the same moment she heard the sharp snapping of overstressed rivets and the creaking and groaning of overloaded metal. One quick look up at the sagging roof and an I-beam breaking loose at one end, and she spun around and began to run for the opening into the next intended shop.

"Go back! Go back! Get out!" she screamed at Phil who had changed course to intercept her.

She screamed and dodged as one of the platforms fell beside her. From the corner of her eye she saw the sprawled body of the man who had been working on it, and, unable to help herself, she swerved to go to him.

"No! You've got to get out!" yelled Phil in her ear, grabbing her around the waist and running for the still-safe area.

Tally struggled in his tight grip. "Put me down.

I can run. Oh, God," she moaned as a section of
ductwork and a tangle of heavy electrical cables
crashed in front of them. "You don't have a hat.
Get out of here, Phil! Go ahead! I'm right behind
you."

She could hear the screams of men and rending
metal behind her, but didn't dare stop to look
around. Pieces of roof and supporting structure
were beginning to rain down around them. She
dodged and leaped obstructions, Phil stubbornly at
her heels, and felt as if she was running through
mud. Something clanged off the back of her hat
with enough force to stagger her, and she heard
Phil grunt.

"Keep going, dammit!" he yelled as she started
to turn.

Another bundle of cables tumbled down, strik-
ing Tally with a glancing blow on her left side. She
fell against Phil, going down on one knee. He
yanked her up as a horrendous groaning and loud
snapping reports came from above them. One terrified look upward, and Phil grabbed her tightly
against his tall body, her back to him and his arms
clamped around her, as he began to race in giant
leaps for safety, bending over her to shelter her
smaller frame with his larger one.

Instinctively Tally ceased to struggle and relaxed, knowing it would make it easier. She was
dazed by the appalling cacophony of screams,
groans, reports like rifle shots, crashes, and thuds
from all around them, but still she realized that Phil
wouldn't put her down. He could move faster,
but—

She felt the blow through his body an instant before something crashed onto her head and she felt them both falling, and then. . . nothing.

"I DIDN'T KNOW you were coming up today," said Bram, as he almost bumped into Steven at the entrance to the dining room. "Is this business, or can you join us for lunch?"

Steven's gaze shifted to Sidney Cater, and he smiled and shook hands with the older man. "My pleasure," he said to Bram, "if I'm not intruding on a private meeting."

"No, no. We're just having another strategy session."

"Tally still being stubborn?" asked Steven, laughing. "You may have to resort to drastic measures before you bring her around."

He spoke over his shoulder as the three men wended their way between tables to a window overlooking the lake. "Hope you don't mind the main room," he added, "but the Gazebo's full with a tour group."

"This is fine," said Sid, sitting down with his back to the room so he could enjoy the view. The other two sat on either side of him, and for a few minutes they all watched the activity along the shorefront. Between swimmers and boaters, it was a busy scene.

"Well, what's the latest twist in the romance of the year?" asked Steven after they'd given their orders to the waitress.

"Same thing. Tally is adamant about not living in England, and I—"

"Tell me something, Bram," said Steven, for once without a gleam of amusement in his gaze. "Is living in England all that important to you? Truly?"

Bram stared at him thoughtfully, holding back the quick answer he was going to give. Was it that important? He wasn't attached to his house; he'd only bought it in recent years so it didn't have the sentimental value of a family home.

"No, it's not, I guess," he said slowly, looking from Steven to Sid. "I'm not sure exactly what—"

"I'm sorry," murmured their waitress, leaning over next to Steven and speaking very softly. "Steven, Brian's on the phone and he says it's urgent. In the office."

With deceptive calm he rose and moved across the room. His pace looked casual, but he was through the entrance to the lobby in seconds. Bram and Sid exchanged puzzled looks but said nothing, waiting with forced patience for Steven to return.

Bram glanced around the dining room with assumed disinterest and found several pairs of eyes fixed on their table. He sensed there was trouble, and he knew that despite their efforts to appear calm and natural, they'd somehow tipped off several relatives and close friends who were lunching there that day. There was an air of hushed expectancy in the room as Steven, no longer pretending anything, ran across the room and grabbed Bram tightly by the arm.

"I hate to tell you like this, but there's no time. We've got to find Dare and get some of his men. That damn building of Jaketon's has collapsed, and Tally and Phil are under it."

For an instant, Bram went totally cold. He felt as frozen as the heart of an iceberg. Then Steven was pulling him out of his chair, saying rapidly to Sid, "Aunt Edna's in the Gazebo with the tour. Tell her, please."

Bram cursed his knee as he strove to keep up with Steven's long, half-running strides, and then they were in the Porsche, roaring out of the drive onto the road. Steven whipped the powerful car around corners with one hand, while his other held the mike of the two-way radio to his mouth as he called for Darius. It seemed an endless time to Bram before he heard Dare's answering call-sign.

"Dare, forget the FCC. Jaketon's building has collapsed on Tally and Phil. Fifteen minutes ago. A state policeman called me in Concord, and Brian relayed. He's getting all the able bodies he can out there. We'll need all the men you can round up and a crane. How soon can you get there?"

"I'm not fifteen minutes from there, and I've got a couple of dozen men and a crane right here. I'll get somebody on the horn to round up more men. Did they say. . . ? Are Tally and Phil. . . ?"

Bram could hear the break in his voice even over the static of the radio.

"We don't know anything yet, except that they were in the building. The cop recognized Tally's Wagoneer and asked where she was. Someone said she was inside with Jaketon when a crane dropped an air-conditioning unit on the roof, and it started to cave in. The man said that a guy leaning against Tally's car ran into the building, shouting her name. That had to be Phil. He'd gone to Concord with her. Before they could get out, the whole thing came down. They're trying to get to the people under the mess, but their crane was damaged and it's inoperable."

"I'll get this one there as fast as I can, and I think Morelli's got one on a job near here. Get off, now, and I'll call him. What about Pip?"

"I don't know where she is. Sid's telling your mother. Bram's with me. Brian's got someone calling Cyrus. Go now. We'll see you in a few minutes."

Bram and Steven didn't speak. Steven concentrated on driving as fast as he could without losing control. What else he was thinking about, Bram could only guess. He knew that Tally was special to her cousin, and he wished that he could say something to make it easier. What? He was so terrified himself of what they might find that he couldn't have spoken a coherent sentence if he'd tried. He wished he could blank his mind, but horrifying visions of his beautiful Venus lying crushed under tons of steel and God knows what else filled his mind. Perhaps even more horrible were the uncontrollable thoughts of her being broken but conscious and crying for help and—

"Easy, man. Don't fall apart yet. They may...."

Bram looked over at Steven, and it was only when he peered at the other man's blurred outline that he realized his eyes were full of tears. "Sorry. You're right, of course. I just—"

"I know. I'm trying not to think about it.

Here's the road. God, they've got everything here *but* a crane," he muttered as he squeezed the small car around and between fire trucks, ambulances, police cars and wreckers. "I guess they're going to try to drag some of the stuff off with the wreckers."

He stopped beside an officer in the familiar state police uniform who was trying to organize the incoming vehicles so they wouldn't impede rescue workers.

"Tony!" called Steven. "Darius Bishop will be here with a crew and a crane in a few minutes. Can you get that road back there cleared? And Pete Morelli will probably be bringing in another crane shortly."

"Right, Steven." The officer turned to several of his men who were waiting for orders and began snapping out directions.

"Tony! Any word yet?" asked Steven.

"Nothing yet. Sorry. Be sure you park that out of the way."

Steven waved acknowledgment and drove slowly around a cluster of rescue vehicles. Bram stared in disbelief and muttered an unrepeatable curse as he saw the scene for the first time. The outer third of the building at each end looked perfectly normal, but the center section was an enormous pile of jutting l-beams, secondary girders, black tangles of cable, huge chunks of roof and other things he couldn't identify. It looked exactly like the pictures he'd seen of bombed-out buildings in London during the blitz of the Second World War. His heart sank as he stared at the tons of debris. How could anyone possibly be alive under all that?

"Come on, Bram. Let's see if we can help. It's not hopeless," Steven said fiercely. "That stuff's all in a jumble. There'll be pockets of clear space under there where one thing is propped up by something else."

It was a scene of chaos at that moment. The fire fighters were doing the best they could, but collapsed buildings of this magnitude were beyond the experience of rural volunteers. The construction men on the job who had been outside were all laborers. The foremen and Jaketon had been inside. But the rescuers were eager, and Steven had to get Tony to back him up when he stopped the wrecker operators from just hauling away at anything they could get their hooks on.

"Clear all the loose stuff away from the perimeter," Steven finally ordered the assembled men. "You can take anything loose from the edges of the pile, but don't touch anything that's supporting something else. What we need right now is as much clear space as possible for the men Dare Bishop is bringing."

"What can I do?" asked Bram, desperate to help but knowing that he was limited in how much he could handle.

"For right now, you can move Tally's car. She keeps a spare key in the ashtray."

By the time Bram had parked the Wagoneer well out of the way and walked back to where Steven was directing the clearing project, the first of the Bishop Construction pickups, its load bed full of men, was pulling into the site, rapidly followed by three more. The men piled out and followed Darius as he walked toward his cousin, his eyes checking over the huge pile of rubble.

Tight-lipped, he merely nodded to Steven and Bram before turning to his men and beginning to rap out directions. Finally he turned to Bram and Steven, saying, "I'm taking some of the men around back. The rear wall was solid cement block, and it may have held up enough to provide some cover." He left unspoken the qualifying, "if they reached it."

The sound of an airhorn brought them around in time to see Dare's big tractor-flatbed rig pulling in with the crane. A few minutes later, several trucks with the Morelli Construction logo on their sides drove in, closely followed by another crane. Darius and Pete Morelli conferred briefly, and then divided their crews around the site and set to work slowly and carefully clearing away the jumbled pile. As they worked, they called out periodically, straining to hear any answering sounds.

Bram waited, watching and praying. He turned after what seemed like a long time, when he heard Sid speak his name.

"Anything?" asked Sid.

Bram shook his head before he looked past his friend and saw Edna and Pip standing behind him. Pip was staring in horror at the slowly lowering pile, her hands pressed over her mouth, her head moving stiffly from side to side in instinctive denial.

Edna moved next to her daughter and put a supporting arm around her, staring in equal anguish at the men trying to reach her other daughter and her beloved son-in-law.

Brian, who had arrived some time before with a dozen men, and Steven spotted the small group at the same moment and ran toward them. Steven took his cousin gently in his arms and slowly mouthed "We don't know yet," when she looked up at him in agonized questioning. He looked at Sid and murmured, "She shouldn't be here."

"We couldn't stop her," Sid replied. "She insisted on coming. As did your aunt."

A shout of discovery brought them around to search for the source. One of Dare's men saw them and called, "It's a Jaketon man."

They waited, standing close together in silent support of each other. Steven and Brian left for long periods to work with the men, but returned again and again, slowly shaking their heads.

By the time Cyrus arrived shortly after three, eight of Jaketon's crew had been found and Vester Jaketon himself. Four of the men and Jaketon were dead, the others injured to varying degrees. The waiting ambulances screamed away to the hospital in Concord that had been alerted to expect the victims from the disaster.

Dare had come to speak to Pip and his mother when Cyrus arrived in a state police cruiser that had picked him up at the airport in Concord.

"Have you found them yet?" he asked his brother as he folded his mother in his arms and held her tightly.

Dare, who was holding Pip in an equally tight

hug while she buried her face in his neck, shook his head. "We think they're on this end, but there's a main I-beam that's balanced very precariously. We've almost got it cleared enough to lift it out with the cranes. Once that's removed we'll be able to go faster. We can hear a couple of men, but neither of them's Phil."

Cyrus didn't say anything, simply shifted his mother to Sid's waiting arms and took Pip from Darius. And they waited. They watched the cranes lift away the huge I-beam. They watched as every man that it was safe to have on the rubble worked carefully but swiftly to shift the mass. They were watching when Darius gave a shout and reached down into the tumble of girders and roofing, standing up a minute later with a lavender hard hat in his hand.

Bram started forward, but Cyrus's hand on his arm stopped him, and they continued to wait. All of them stood with eyes fixed on the spot where Darius, Steven, Brian and several Bishop construction men were frantically shifting the debris. They were so totally concentrated on the tense drama in front of them that the helicopter was almost directly over their heads before they noticed it.

One of Brian's men trotted toward them, dust-streaked and sweating from his efforts. "Mr. Bishop, would you meet the doctor. Steven called him in along with the chopper just after we found Tally's hat."

Bram stepped up to take his place beside Pip as Cyrus ran toward the now silent chopper to meet the man who was descending with a black bag in his hand. Dare's yell of "We've got them!" brought everyone forward to watch with held breath as first Phil and then Tally were carefully shifted onto stretchers and brought across the remaining rubble. Pip started to run to Phil's still body, but Dare was there before her and caught her in his arms.

She looked at his face, and he said firmly, "Wait. Don't panic. Wait until the doctor can examine him."

Bram couldn't breathe as he walked woodenly to the stretcher on which Tally lay, her face white, the scratches and bruises standing out in sharp relief against the pallor, and her left wrist cocked at an unnatural angle.

"Is she...?"

The doctor looked up from his rapid but thorough examination. "No, she's not. She's out cold—probably concussion." He motioned to the lavender hard hat lying on the ground, its surface scratched and dented. "That undoubtedly saved her from a fractured skull. That and her hair. She had her braid coiled up under it, and it cushioned the blows. Broken wrist, badly sprained ankle. I don't think that's broken, but we'll see."

After a brief, hurried conference, it was decided that Bram and Steven would go to the hospital with Tally, while the others would follow with Pip.

It was six hours before Tally opened her eyes, struggled to focus on the blurred shape hovering above her, and finally saw Bram's beloved, but anguished, face.

"What...what is it? The building fell in," she

whispered through a painfully dry throat. "I remember...Phil. What happened?"

She struggled through the fog of shock and concussion, not sure what was real and what was a nightmare.

"Did it fall on us? Bram? Phil?"

"Easy, luv," Bram soothed. "You're going to be all right. Just a broken wrist and a wrenched ankle besides a mild concussion."

"And Phil?" she rasped fearfully.

"We don't know yet. He's got severe back injuries, but he's still unconscious, and they're not sure of the extent of damage."

"Poor Pip. She must be frantic," moaned Tally, beginning to cry.

Bram gathered her carefully into his arms, rocking her and whispering words of comfort and love into her ear. In a few minutes she calmed and reached for a tissue to blow her nose. She was awkward with one hand, and Bram had to help her.

"If you hadn't been wearing that crazy hat.... God! I'm going to buy you a dozen of them."

He settled her back down on the bed, belatedly remembering the doctor's instructions to keep her flat.

She caught his hand and asked urgently, "What happened? Does anyone know?"

"Dare says that the air-conditioning unit slipped, there was too much stress for the faulty rivets, and they popped. Damn that Jaketon. If he wasn't already dead, I'd break his neck."

"Bram," said Tally hesitantly. "I've just remembered something. When I knew the place was caving in on us, I had one of those last-second flashes that you hear about. I realized how ridiculous it was that two intelligent people like us hadn't been able to work out our differences.''

''I did more than that,'' said Bram, smiling at her lovingly. ''While I was waiting for them to find you in all that mess, I solved the problem. It will mean just a dash of compromising on both our parts, but I'm sure it will work out just fine.''

Tally blinked up at him sleepily as her head began to spin again. ''What...what did you... decide?''

''Don't worry about it now. You need to sleep. We'll talk about it when you wake up again. The only truly important thing for you to know right now is that I love you more than anything else in this world.''

''Me...too...love...you....''

EPILOGUE

"Is THERE ANYTHING ELSE I can do, Tally, ma'am, Mr. Bram?"

"We're fine, thanks, Merton. Better get a good night's sleep to recover from this evening's do. Tomorrow looks to be even wilder."

"Good night, Merton. Remember now, no peeking if you hear strange noises on the roof, or Santa Claus won't bring you any super surprises."

"If you'll forgive me, ma'am, I can assure you that I never bother with strange noises either on the roof or anywhere in the house," Merton murmured with a slight inclination of his head and a familiar gleam of amusement in his eye. "Good night, then, and Merry Christmas."

"Merry Christmas, Merton," chorused Tally and Bram, lifting their brandy snifters in salute as he turned from the doorway and disappeared down the hall toward his apartment in the east wing.

Bram leaned back on the deep sofa, kicked his shoes off, and propped his feet on the fossil-rock coffee table. "The party was nice, but this is very much nicer," he said with a contented sigh, snuggling Tally close to his side and wriggling his toes in the warmth of the blazing fire.

"It is, isn't it," she agreed. "A snowy Christmas Eve outside and a roaring fire, fine old brandy and thou inside."

Bram chuckled and tipped her head back against his shoulder so he could see her face. "Was that a Freudian slip or a suggestion?"

"Well. . .if you'd like to take it as a suggestion, I'm just loaded with the spirit of Christmas and love for my fellow man, so. . . ."

"Loaded with Christmas spirits is more like it. As for loving your fellow man, it's well for you that was in the singular."

She gave him a provocative look but merely said, "Mother and Jean outdid themselves with that party. I'm no end pleased that we were in England these last two weeks, and I had the perfect excuse for not getting roped into helping."

"Selfish little beast, aren't you?" Bram teased.

"Only sometimes. Have you decided about the book yet? That is what you've been mulling over these past few days, isn't it?"

"Partly. I'll probably do it. I hadn't really considered writing a book, but I think it might be an interesting challenge. I've told Sid to hold the publisher off for another month or so. I've got to get the script changes done by mid-January, and I'd like a short breather before starting a project the size of a book. Are you going to have the set designs finished by then?"

"Oh, yes, I should think so." Tally grinned at him. "You're not missing a film, are you? If they want a Bram Ramsdale script, they get Tally Bishop Ramsdale sets, or else."

"You have to admit it was a great idea for keeping us together. We don't really have to be away from here all that much, and you get a chance to do something different every so often.''

"Bram?" Tally gazed up at him with a faint hint of doubt in her tan eyes. "You are happy this way, aren't you?"

He smiled down at her and slid his hand from her shoulder to cup her breast, rubbing his fingers sensuously over the deep green velvet of her dress. "This way is just fine for the moment, but I'm sure—"

"That isn't what I meant, and you know it," she chided, returning his smile.

"Mmm, all right. Yes, I'm happy. How could I be anything else? This mountain air seems remarkably conducive to my creative bent. I can't believe how fast I finished that script. I really do think the switch to writing was a good move. Then, of course, there's this marvelous house, which is an inspiration in itself, and we mustn't forget Splendid who is, I'll admit, a far better companion than any stuffy old dog.''

Tally scowled at him in mock indignation. "I sometimes wonder if you married me for my house and my cat rather than for my—"

"I married you because you're my feisty, independent, contrary, stubborn, funny, unpredictable, talented and beautiful Pocket Venus, and I love you beyond imagining. The house and the cat were just the frosting on the pudding.''

"I'll buy that," she said, tiny gold sparks beginning to glitter in her eyes. "Do you know what I love best about you?"

"My talent for making waves in the hot tub?"

"That, too. But I was thinking about your willingness to let me be me, even when I do things that drive you up the wall or don't accord with your ideas of ultimate femininity."

"If you're referring to that Saturday you got clobbered playing touch football with Dare and your overeager cousins—"

"Let's not dwell on specifics," she said hastily. She stared pensively into the fire and murmured, "Pip used to play, too. I hope this operation is going to help Phil."

"We can only pray that it does," said Bram. "Remember, though, that all the doctors agree it's going to be a long haul. His back was almost crushed." He peered at Tally in sudden concern. "You're not still feeling guilty, are you?"

"I think I'll always feel some degree of guilt," she answered slowly. "He's such a great guy and he was such a marvelous athlete...and if he hadn't come after me and saved my life...."

"Oh, love, you can't expect me to regret that he did, but I do most deeply regret that he was so badly hurt. We all do, but no one would have expected or wanted him to just stand and watch you...."

Tally sniffed and brushed a hand quickly across her eyes. "Don't get me started. This was supposed to be our own private celebration, remember? We've been married five months, and you promised me a treat."

"All in good time, luv. Keep working on that brandy. I want you in a mellow mood."

"I don't need brandy for that; I just need you.

Do you remember how hot it was the day we were married? And everyone kept handing me glasses of Merton's special champagne punch? I think he made it twice as potent as usual in retaliation for the microwave.''

Bram laughed and gasped, ''I wish I'd been able to film that. Poor Merton, determined to get the door open, never realizing that you, my innovative darling, had turned it into a tamper-proof safe.'' He sighed and gazed up at the large painting above the fireplace that reached from the mantel to the ceiling. ''I'm more than delighted, though, that your mother remembered to have a photographer at the wedding and that Steven arranged for that portrait. You were so lovely that day.''

Tally looked at her almost life-size image, and laughed. ''I'll grant you that my hair looked great, although I did think it was a bit sacrificial virgin to leave it loose. But that topaz-and-diamond headband you gave me to match my ring really turned it into something totally pagan. An interesting contrast to Great-Grandma Letty's wedding dress. Ivory lace and so very Victorian. You know, the more I look at the contrasts there, the more I can appreciate the rakish touch of that cast.''

''I suppose we could have waited until your wrist had healed, but after almost losing you like that....''

''But you didn't,'' she said, looking up at him with love and a growing awareness. ''And you're not going to. I'm afraid you're stuck with me. Do you know what fun I've had with that standard question of 'What did you wear at your wedding,

Mrs. Ramsdale?' I give them my blandest look and reply sweetly, 'Victorian ivory lace and a contemporary cast.' "

"I didn't notice that it slowed you down any in the performance of your wifely duties," he said suggestively, insinuating one long-fingered hand into the deep V of her neckline. "And speaking of wifely duties, where's that cat?"

"Right there," said Tally, shrugging one shoulder free of the dress and nodding toward the pool table where Splendid was curled up on the padded cover.

"Let's hope he stays there until we can get the door to the greenhouse closed behind us," murmured Bram, standing and pulling Tally to her feet.

He made short work of her zipper, and the dress fell in a green velvet heap, leaving her standing before him in a lavender-silk-and-ecru-lace teddy under which he could vaguely see a matching garter belt securing her pale green patterned nylons.

The familiar ache was tightening his loins, and he reached out with one finger to tease a pale pink nipple through the lace. "Shall we? I did promise you a Christmas treat," he said huskily, urging her toward the door.

His deep green velvet dinner jacket landed on a chair back and his shirt was hung on the corner of a painting in the dining room. Her teddy was tossed over one of the dining-room chairs, and she draped his navy briefs over the dolphin.

"No, not yet," he protested in a voice hoarse

with passion as she reached for the fastening of her garter belt. "I like you like that."

He sank down on the foot of a chaise and drew her to him. She clenched her hands in his hair as he leaned forward to trace enticing patterns on her stomach with his tongue.

"Oh, Bram," she whispered as his mouth moved lower and his hands positioned her as he wanted her.

"A hot tub, a sauna, and thou. What man could ask for more?" he murmured against her.

"I'll take thou, now," she moaned. "The tub and sauna can wait for New Year's."

It was the last coherent thought either of them had until well into Christmas.

Introducing

Harlequin Intrigue

Because romance can be quite an adventure.

Available wherever paperbacks are sold.

INT-5

Dreamweaver

**THE EXCITING NEW
BESTSELLER BY THE STAR
OF TV's ANOTHER WORLD**

FELICIA
GALLANT
WITH REBECCA FLANDERS

The romance queen of
daytime drama has written a passionate
story of two people whose souls exist
beneath shimmering images, bound
together by the most elemental
of all human emotions...love.